THE CYPRIAN

The
ELEMENTAL
MASTERS

*Also by Mercedes Lackey
and available from Titan Books*

FAMILY SPIES
The Hills Have Spies
Eye Spy
Spy, Spy Again

THE HERALD SPY
Closer to Home
Closer to the Heart
Closer to the Chest

THE COLLEGIUM CHRONICLES
Foundation
Intrigues
Bastion
Changes
Redoubt

VALDEMAR OMNIBUSES
The Heralds of Valdemar
The Mage Winds
The Mage Storms
The Mage Wars
The Last Herald Mage
Vows & Honor
Exiles of Valdemar

THE ELEMENTAL MASTERS
The Serpent's Shadow
The Gates of Sleep
Phoenix and Ashes
The Wizard of London
Reserved for the Cat
Unnatural Issue
Home from the Sea
Steadfast
Blood Red
From a High Tower
A Study in Sable
A Scandal in Battersea
The Bartered Brides
The Case of the Spellbound Child
Jolene
The Silver Bullets of Annie Oakley
Miss Amelia's List

THE FOUNDING OF VALDEMAR
Beyond
Into the West
Valdemar

KELVREN'S SAGA
Gryphon in Light
Gryphon's Valor

MERCEDES LACKEY

The ELEMENTAL MASTERS

THE CYPRIAN

TITAN BOOKS

The Cyprian
Print edition ISBN: 9781835416419
E-book edition ISBN: 9781835416426

Published by Titan Books
A division of Titan Publishing Group Ltd
144 Southwark Street, London SE1 0UP
www.titanbooks.com

First edition: December 2025
10 9 8 7 6 5 4 3 2 1

This is a work of fiction. All of the characters, organizations, and events portrayed in this novel are either products of the author's imagination or are used fictitiously. Any resemblance to actual persons, living or dead (except for satirical purposes), is entirely coincidental.

Mercedes Lackey asserts the moral right to be identified as the author of this work.

Copyright © 2025 Mercedes R. Lackey.

No part of this publication may be reproduced, stored in a retrieval system, or transmitted, in any form or by any means without the prior written permission of the publisher, nor be otherwise circulated in any form of binding or cover other than that in which it is published and without a similar condition being imposed on the subsequent purchaser.

A CIP catalogue record for this title is available from the British Library.

EU RP (for authorities only)
eucomply OÜ, Pärnu mnt. 139b-14, 11317 Tallinn, Estonia
hello@eucompliancepartner.com, +3375690241

Printed and bound in the United Kingdom by
CPI Group (UK) Ltd, Croydon, CR0 4YY.

To Joshua Starr; amazing editor, total superhero

PROLOGUE

Father was absent on one of his rare visits to Bath when Benjamin Whitstone heard someone sobbing in his mother's room. He wasn't supposed to be in this part of the house; the rooms on this floor in the west wing were reserved for his father, his mother, and important overnight guests. But his tutor, Beecham, had eaten something last night that disagreed violently with him, and without Father about to shame Beecham into at least supervising the oldest children even though he was ill, Ben, Arthur, Carl, David, Emil, and Felix had been left to their own devices. Five-year-old Gustav and Elena, of course, were still under the care and control of Nanny in the nursery, so they were fully occupied with their ABCs and numbers. Carl and David had taken the opportunity to escape into the grounds to play at being highwaymen. Emil and Felix were exploring the attic—also technically forbidden territory, but as long as they didn't drag what they found up there down into the main house, no one ever bothered to chide them for the transgression. Ben's twin Arthur was alone in the schoolroom—reading, not studying, although *technically*, Ben supposed, the English translation of *The Odyssey* could count as "study." Mind, they were supposed to be reading it in Greek, but both of them found it heavy going, and often snuck in chances to read the translation they'd found in Father's library to give them a leg up on the Greek as well as to relish the sheer adventure of it all.

Ben, however, had other things in mind. He'd discovered that the little winged creatures in the house and grounds, the ones that he and the other children were not supposed to talk about in front of anyone but Mama and each other, were perfectly willing to aid and abet his curiosity and explorations.

Fairies, was what the siblings called them, though Mama called them sylphs. She was the one who had warned all the children as soon as they could talk to never let anyone but her know they could see the entrancing creatures.

It was just another thing they were never to do around Father. Always mind your manners, never be outwardly affectionate to anyone or anything. Control your temper at all times. Do not speak unless you are spoken to. Never ask for favors or presents. Master your lessons before play, and if the lessons were not mastered by bedtime, then you would have no playtime the following day. "Children should be seen and not heard, and seen as little as possible."

Were all fathers like that? It was hard to tell. Certainly Father had no interest in them except when he briefly lined up the boys (not Elena), presented them to guests, and boasted about their intelligence. He never boasted about their looks or other accomplishments, although, in Ben's limited experience, he and his siblings were quite handsome children. Maybe Father ignored how they looked because they all looked like Mama, blond and lithe, and not like him, darker haired and square faced, with an oddly high forehead and tiny eyes.

Ben often wondered why Father had had children in the first place, since he thought so little of them as to forget them for weeks and months at a time.

And Ben often wondered why Mama had ever married Father in the first place. Every time he was around it was as if the light that was inside her when she was alone or only with her children was extinguished.

At least when Father or the servants weren't about, the fairies were only too willing to amuse and be amusing. Recently, mind inflamed by recent history lessons about the Tudors that included mentions of secret passages and priest's holes and other equally entrancing things, he'd enlisted their help in ferreting out hiding places all over Whitstone Manor. So far he had not uncovered any secret passages, but now he knew where there were some concealed doors that let out into the servants' stairs and passages, and a few smaller places where things were hidden away or otherwise out of reach. So far he hadn't found anything particularly exciting—certainly no treasure—but knowing that he was privy to secrets the others weren't was reward enough to keep hunting.

His first thought when he heard the crying was that one of the servant girls had hurt herself, or had been beaten by the housekeeper. The housekeeper was not normally a cruel woman, but she was very strict, and if a servant girl was slacking, or suspected of dallying with one of the menservants, or had broken something through carelessness, Mrs. Farthingworth did not hesitate to use the birch on her. Whenever Ben found one of the girls crying—provided he wasn't in a position to be discovered and lectured, usually by the tutor—he'd do his best to comfort her. A nice comfit or sugarplum usually did the trick, along with a kind word and a loaned handkerchief. Not one of his good ones, of course; one of the ones little Elena was using to practice her sewing on. The loans always came back neatly washed and pressed, but there was no point in getting a lecture over "losing" a good handkerchief that was supposed to be in the laundry when one of Elena's gifts served the same purpose and wouldn't be missed.

He eased the door open carefully and peeked inside, only to find his mother hunched over a hassock, blue skirts spread about her, sobbing inconsolably. "Mama!" he called, startled. "Mama, what is wrong?"

His mother started like a nervous deer and looked up, blue eyes red and swollen, a curl of golden hair escaping from the careful arrangement her lady's maid would have put it into this morning. The door to her balcony was wide open, summer sunlight streaming through it, illuminating her grief unmistakably. Even so, Ben thought, she was the most beautiful lady he knew.

"Ben!" she replied, recognizing it was him rather than his twin—something she and no one else except his siblings seemed to be able to do. "What are you doing here? Shouldn't you—"

"Beecham is sick, and never mind that now," he replied, running to her and falling to his knees beside her. Her delicate perfume, something he could never identify, wafted over him. "Mama, whatever is wrong? Are you hurt? Did you lose something?"

Those simple words seemed to send her into a world of sorrow, and she buried her face in her hands. "Yes—no—*yes!*" she sobbed. "Yes, but it was taken from me before you were born, and—and—and—I cannot *bear* this anymore! I need it! I need it more than I can say! If I do not find it, I shall surely die!"

Ben knew what Father would have said to such a statement: *Don't be ridiculous, Elsa. You're not going to die.* But Father had an intense dislike for tears, and what he called "vapors" and "hysterics," to the point that even five-year-old Elena knew better than to cry around him, and the boys had learned to endure any amount of pain without expressing anything but verbal discomfort. But Ben was not Father, who could sail past a weeping housemaid without anything other than a sharp word and the instruction to "take yourself to Mrs. Farthingworth if you cannot control yourself," and so he responded by awkwardly patting his mother on the shoulder and saying, "Mama, don't cry. I'm very good at finding things that are lost. I'll help you find it, whatever it is."

She took her hands from her face and gave him a watery and insincere smile. "You're a dear boy, Ben, but you'll never find it. It is not *lost*. Your father took it from me to keep me with him, and has hidden it away from me on purpose. He knew very well what he was doing."

The words—the phrasing—were very odd. *Keep me with him,* and *He knew what he was doing.* And that was when Ben had one of those moments of inspiration and certainty that came to him without any warning—but were always right. The memory of finding something inexplicable in one of those hiding places . . . something that could only be connected with Mama, for there was no one else in the household who could have been connected with such an odd but entrancing object. "Father hid it from you? What was it?" he asked, then without waiting for an answer, continued, "Was it something like a cloak of white feathers?"

His mother sat swiftly erect, gasping. "*Yes!*" she exclaimed. "But how—"

"Because I saw it," he said. "I know where it is."

"Take me to it!" she interrupted, springing to her feet. "Take me to it *right now*!"

He, too, shot to his feet, grabbed her hand, and pulled her along behind him. It wasn't far, after all, just in Father's rooms. He pulled her to a section of the wainscoted wall in the bedroom, and carefully counted dark wooden panels from the left end where the two walls met. Two, three, and four—he pressed in the carved rose at the intersection of the fourth and fifth panel, and turned it. It had taken quite a bit of trial and error to figure out just what he should do when the little fairy had shown him where there was a hidden space, but he'd managed to figure it out. There was a *click*, and the fourth panel popped out, just a bit. He pulled it open, showing the yellowed silk lining of the storage area behind the panel, and there, pressed into the space, was what he had guessed to be a cloak made out of pure white feathers. Why anyone should want such a thing—especially Father—he'd had no idea, but there it had been when he had first found it, and there it was now.

With a faint cry, his mother buried both hands in the feathers, and lifted it out of its silk prison.

And then, paying no heed to Ben, she turned and ran—ran as if she was running away from peril.

He followed her, calling, "Mama, Mama, wait!" but he might as well have been voiceless. She swung the cloak over her shoulders as she ran, and pulled up the hood. She was entirely enveloped in it by the time she reached the door of her room, and by the time Ben reached that same spot, he saw her racing through the door to her balcony. She paused there for just a moment—and then jumped.

Too struck with horror to utter a sound, he raced to the balcony himself and looked down, expecting to see her sprawled on the pavement of the walk beneath, dead or gravely injured.

But there was nothing there.

Frantic *and* baffled now, he looked up, in time to see a pure white swan beating her wings in rapid flight away—away from the mansion and into the east.

There were no swans on the Whitstone estate. Father wouldn't allow them. He had the gamekeeper shoot at them to frighten them, or trap them and carry them off. He said it was because all swans belonged to the king, but Ben just knew that wasn't the reason. And why would a swan have been so close to the manor that it could have jumped from the balcony to take wing?

"M-mama?" he stammered.

But the swan did not answer, and did not look back. In moments, she was out of sight.

Ben had always been the quickest of the children; even in a crisis his mind remained clear, and his thoughts logical.

Mama can see the fairies and told us not to tell Father we could. Fairies are magic. Mama could be magic, too.

Nanny told us stories about the seal people who shed their skins to become human. There could be swan-people too, like them. And in the stories, men who want a seal-person wife, because they are so beautiful, steal their skins and hide them away. Is that what happened? Did Father steal a swan-girl's skin so he could have a beautiful wife? Certainly Mama was the most beautiful lady he had ever seen, and there were plenty of beautiful women who came to Father's parties with their husbands or parents. More than once, when he shouldn't have been eavesdropping, he'd heard other men congratulate Father on his "conquest." Father always preened when such compliments came his way, gloating almost.

Gloating, because he didn't win her, and it wasn't even an arranged marriage. Gloating because he stole her away from her home and people! So much came clear in that moment: why Mama had always been so subdued, why she showed Father obedience but never affection, and why Father treated her more like a treasured possession than a beloved wife. Of course she was subdued! And obedient! She had been a prisoner!

Ben had never cared much for his father, which was unfilial, but nevertheless a fact—but in that moment, he hated the man. To hold someone captive against their will like that—someone who was used to being wild and free and magical—someone as kind and sweet as his Mama—it was an abomination!

But in that moment he also understood that Mama was surely gone, gone forever. He knew from the behavior of the fairies that it wasn't wise to count on their affections; Nanny's tales of the seal-wives told the same story. When the choice was between her children and her freedom, a magical creature would always choose her freedom.

And now he was torn, torn between grief and sudden caution.

THE CYPRIAN

Father would be enraged when he found this out, and he *would* find it out, because Mama would be missing when he returned, and so would her magical cloak. So he dared not show his grief to anyone, at least not until Mama's disappearance was known to the household. Then he could cry with feigned confusion like the rest of them. He could not confide what had just happened, even to his twin. No one could know where Mama had gone, only that she was inexplicably missing. He had to give himself an alibi, so no suspicion would fall on him. And he had to close up that panel, so Father would never know how Mama had found her cloak.

It was a very good thing he had never confided his hunt for hidden spaces to his twin. He was a much better liar than Arthur; if Father burst into a rage, Arthur would give away anything he knew.

Then grief took over for a time, the loss of Mama obliterating the anger he felt at Father. He dropped to his knees beside the hassock where Mama had been crying, and allowed himself a moment of inconsolable blubbering.

When the worst of his sorrow had been purged, he washed his face in Mama's washbasin, returning to Father's room to close the panel as if it had never been opened. Then, he slipped down a servants' stair to the garden to join Carl and David in the grounds. It would be a lot easier not to cry if he was playing at highwayman. He'd even volunteer to be the victim; then, if his voice faltered or he started to tremble, they'd take it for play-acting. It would be hard not to tell the others. The servants would certainly set up a hue and cry when they couldn't find Mama anywhere by teatime, and his siblings' hearts would be broken when she couldn't be found, but Father's wrath would have nowhere to fall as long as he didn't know who to blame.

Things would probably be horrid—well, they *were* horrid, because Mama was never coming back—but as he paused on the edge of the garden to look for Carl and David, then cast his eyes to the sky for one last resigned look, he knew he could not have done anything else.

"I'd do it again, Mama," he said, though no one could hear him. "I'd do it again."

1

Elena sat on her hands on the high stool in the nursery and tried not to squirm as Nanny braided her dark blond hair so tightly it brought tears to her eyes. "Stop moving, do!" Nanny scolded. "Your hair is a state. I won't have your new mama thinking I have raised you to be a hoyden."

Elena bit her tongue to keep from saying, "I'm *not moving*," because that would be talking back, and Nanny would pinch her for being pert. She knew Nanny was anxious; anxiety always made Nanny strict, and Elena knew she had good reason to be anxious. Elena was thirteen and should have had a governess by now instead of Nanny, and Nanny was afraid she was about to be dismissed once this new stepmother cast her eye over the household and took charge of it all.

Really, Elena should have had a governess years ago, and would have, except that Father paid her little to no heed. Of all of his children, he paid the most of his scant attention to the two eldest, Arthur and Ben. She was a girl, and the youngest, so of very little interest to him except as an expense in the accounting books. She just felt that she was lucky that the boys' tutor allowed her to sit and take the same lessons as her twin, Gustav, and that Nanny was able to give her instruction in *most* of what a young lady was supposed to learn. Not dancing or music, but she couldn't imagine Father having any interest at all in her coming out, and only girls who were out needed to have accomplishments like singing or playing and dancing. She was about as likely to be invited to a ball as Arthur was to be invited to join a traveling circus. *I will probably live here for the rest of my life*, she thought with resignation. *Father won't care, as long as I am out of his sight and his mind.*

Not that Father paid a great deal of attention even to Ben and Arthur, except to quiz them now and again at dinner, to make sure their tutor was earning his keep. Once there had been parties and feasts at Whitstone Manor, when Father would line up the boys (never her) and show them off to visitors, but for a long time now, there had been nothing but quiet and occasional trips to Bath on business matters. Since Mama had disappeared when Elena was five, Father had mostly left the care of his children to the servants. It probably had not even occurred to him that his daughter had outgrown her nurse, as her twin had. It was enough that Gus was now under the purview of the tutor. In fact, he probably assumed that Nanny was giving her all the education she needed, and the housekeeper would not have challenged that assumption. Mrs. Farthingworth was happy in her place as the sole authority over females at Whitstone Manor and had had no intention of bringing in a new woman. The boys' tutor didn't matter to Mrs. Farthingworth; he was male, and under the governance of the butler. But a governess would have had her own room and a place at the table with the family and complete jurisdiction over Elena—and, most importantly, would outrank Mrs. Farthingworth. Most governesses were of good birth, but poor—often the daughters of clergymen, which made them gentlewomen—where nannies were just servants trustworthy enough to leave in charge of children. Nanny slept in her own little room off the nursery, ate in the nursery with Gus and Elena, was subject to the housekeeper's orders when it came to Elena, and was equal in rank to the chief housemaid, well below Mrs. Farthingworth. The housekeeper was the undisputed ruler over everyone female at Whitstone Manor, which was exactly how Mrs. Farthingworth liked things.

The nursery was not a very interesting room. Faded yellow wallpaper was interrupted only by pictures. Some were framed prints of botanical specimens, some were unframed pictures the siblings had made over the years that had been deemed worthy of being pinned to the wall. Heavy, plain canvas drapes framed the windows, and the floor was plain wood much scratched and stained, like the furnishings, which showed the abuse eight lively children had put it through. A pile of worn cushions had been tossed in one corner, the low bookcases were full of old school books and picture books, and there were four chests still full of battered, much-loved toys. From where Elena sat, the most interesting thing was the window, which didn't show much except an overcast October sky, without even the interruption of a crow or a starling. The nursery at least was not cold; Nanny liked a good fire, and kept them burning in the nursery, the schoolroom, Elena's room, and her own. That was one economy that Mrs. Farthingworth did not dare challenge, because the one time she had, Nanny had threatened to quit, which would have left the housekeeper in charge of Elena. Mrs. Farthingworth did not want that responsibility any more than she wanted a governess brought in.

When Elena's braids were bound off, there was more torture to be endured, for at thirteen Elena was old enough to have her hair put up for this occasion, and Nanny seemed determined to anchor the braids in place by jabbing the hairpins directly into Elena's scalp. Not a whimper escaped her lips, however, though her eyes stung with tears. She knew very well that they would *all* have to look perfect and behave beautifully today. Father's temper was an uncertain thing at the best of times, and now that he had finally done what he had threatened to do for the last eight years since Mama vanished, and married a new wife, Elena did not want to take a chance on angering him.

Besides, Nanny was normally the kindest of souls, and Elena didn't want to fray her temper any further. Nanny was under quite enough stress as it was, and it was just as well that Elena's twin brother Gus was now answerable to Beecham, the tutor, because he had gotten the devil in him this morning, and had been making a nuisance of himself since he woke. Beecham had nearly been tearing his hair out, from the sounds coming from the bedroom Gus shared with Emil and Felix.

Poor Nanny! Elena wished that there was a way she could

assure Nanny that her position was safe, but the fact was, she *was* very likely to be dismissed as soon as the new stepmother settled in. Unless—well, Stepmother *might* keep her for any children *she* would have. *If I am good and obedient, that will show Stepmother what a good job Nanny has been doing. Perhaps then she'll let Nanny stay.*

"There," said Nanny at last, giving Elena's sore scalp a pat. "Very neat and tidy. I've laid out your Sunday best for you to put on, so run along and get ready. They'll be here within the hour, according to Mrs. Farthingworth."

Elena gratefully climbed down off the high stool she had been perched on and took herself down the hall to her own room, just off the nursery. Dear Nanny, trussed into her most uncomfortable Sunday-best of gray serge, with her gray hair tucked into a lace cap and her bosom properly covered with a modest lace fichu, went on her way. All the children were on this floor of the east wing, though of course they were all treated quite differently. Gus shared a room with the next-youngest twins, Emil and Felix, a room almost as big as the nursery, and far more chaotic with all of their games and toys spread out over it. Carl and David shared a room as well, not nearly as untidy as the three young hooligans', and it would not be long before they each got their own room. At the moment, though, only Arthur and Ben had rooms to themselves as she did, because they were seventeen, almost men, and in a year or two would be going to university.

She closed the door behind her with a sigh of relief. The room was just big enough for her bed, her wardrobe, a washstand, and a blanket chest at the foot of her bed; it had a single window and was papered in faded yellow wallpaper with a design of green branches that still managed to be cheerful. She often wondered if this room had been intended for something else—the wet-nurse's room, perhaps. But at least she had it to herself, and some shred or two of privacy, though Nanny was inclined to barge in without knocking. She had mostly outgrown toys, except for her two cherished dolls, carved for her by Ben and sitting on the blanket chest, dolls that she used as little mannequins to plan out potential or imagined gowns for herself. There was a row of storybooks on the mantelpiece, and her three workbaskets next to the hearth;

she was as tidy as her twin was messy, and the housemaids had very little work when they came to "do" her room.

The thin late-autumn light coming in her window at the head of her bed fell on her dark blue "Sunday best" dress, laid out on a faded green wool counterpane that matched the green wool hangings of her four-poster bed. This gown would probably remain her best for another couple of years, as it had a deep hem and she was not tall and not growing very fast. It was not much to her taste, but then, no one had asked her what she would have liked when she outgrew the last best gown to the point where not even adding a flounce at the hem or letting out seams would make it fit. The seamstress from the village had turned up, taken her measurements, appeared two weeks later with this, fitted it to her, then returned a day later with the finished garment, never to be seen again. Apparently the handiwork of the maids—and of herself!—was not deemed good enough for Sunday best now that she was old enough to put her hair up. That had rather hurt her feelings at the time, since her current everyday gowns, spencers, and pelisse had mostly been made by her own two hands, with assistance from the head housemaid, Mary Ann, with fitting. She was very proud of her sewing; not only had she cut and sewn the everyday gowns, she had added touches of embroidery and needle-lace to brighten them, and had knitted the spencers, her shawls, most of her stockings, and her knitted gloves too. She had even made slippers to match and the slippers that she was going to be wearing, cut from the scant leftovers of this new gown. Nanny might not have given her the kind of education a governess would have, but she had given Elena excellent tutelage in plain and fine sewing, and indeed needlework of all sorts.

Elena had been sewing since she was five, knitting and crocheting since she was six, doing lacework since she was eight, and even knew how to spin, though that was scarcely an accomplishment Father would have approved of. She'd teased Nanny into teaching her, though Nanny had been reluctant. "Not what your father would like," she would tut whenever Elena brought out the drop spindle and flax. "That's not the work of a lady." But Elena liked it; it soothed her, and it suited her very well to have all the linen thread and lambswool yarn she cared to use without having to wait for someone to buy it and bring it from the village. The shepherd who tended the sheep that kept the manor lawn close-trimmed was happy to supply her with lambswool, and it was easy to get finished flax from his wife in return for butter from the dairy.

This gown was a very sober blue linen, with long, tight, buttoned sleeves, fitted very closely in the high bodice. It was unrelieved by any embroidery or touches of lace, and Nanny had not permitted her to make any additions of that sort. She decided today to make up for that lack with one of her lace kerchiefs tucked into the neckline as a fichu.

As for the rest of her outfit, since they were all supposed to be standing outside at the front door to greet Father and the new stepmother, and the wind had some bite to it today, she elected to wear lambswool stockings and a lambswool shift over her chemise and stays instead of the silk and cotton stockings and shift Nanny had put out. She reasoned no one would be able to see them anyway. *And I don't think Stepmother is going to demand that I pull up my skirt so she can inspect my underthings.* She slipped her feet into the blue slippers she had made to match the gown, tying the ribbons around her ankles while she could still move freely because her gown was not yet laced up the back.

Nanny came bustling in, as usual without knocking, just in time to lace up her gown while she used the button hook to do up the buttons on her sleeves. If Nanny noticed the change in shifts, she didn't say anything. But probably, given the obvious state of Nanny's nerves, she wasn't thinking about anything except hoping she wouldn't be dismissed on the spot.

"Take your pelisse, it's right cold out there," Nanny said, turning her around and inspecting her. "Make sure you keep your gloves on. A lady isn't without her gloves." She went to the clothes-pegs on the wall where Elena's bonnets were, selected the plain blue bonnet that matched the gown, and tied it over Elena's hair. "Go down and wait in the front hall for your brothers."

"Yes, Nanny," she said obediently, pulled the pelisse over her gown, and slipped out the door before Nanny could tell her not to run. Then she ran, down the two flights of stairs to the first floor and to the front hall. Ben was already there, though none of the others were, sitting on the hallboy's bench, hands clasped between his knees. He looked up as he heard Elena's footsteps, and his blue eyes warmed as he smiled. He was, she judged, very handsome: chiseled features, thick blond hair, and bright blue eyes. But then, again, they were all judged to be handsome children, and as alike, as Nanny liked to say, as peas in a pod.

"Come sit with us," he said, patting the bench beside him. "Beecham and Addams have had to enlist Arthur's help in forcing the barbarians into their clothing. Your twin in particular is objecting to having a cravat tied properly under his chin."

By "us," of course, Ben meant himself and the little flock of fairies that had dispersed themselves all over the hall furniture, what little there was of it—the staircase, the hallboy's bench, a landscape on the pale blue wall, a little ornamental table, and a chandelier. The fairies were mostly festooned on the chandelier and the wrought-iron handrails of the staircase.

The hall bench was not particularly comfortable—the hallboy, after all, was not supposed to get so comfortable there that he would fall into a doze—but it was better than standing on her feet. She sat down next to her brother, who made an abortive movement, as if to ruffle her hair as he was inclined to do, but he pulled back his hand. "You look very proper," he said instead. "I am certain Father will approve."

"I don't look anything like Mama, you mean," she replied shrewdly. "She never looked *proper*."

"She did when there was a party, a ball, or a dinner, but otherwise . . . no, you are right, she never looked *proper* when she was being herself," Ben agreed, with a wistful tone to his voice.

She sighed. "I miss her."

Ben patted her hand. "I do too. But she is probably much happier now that she has gone home." That was all that Father had said, when he returned after he had been summoned home when Mama had disappeared. "She's gone home to her people."

"I wish she had taken us with her." That was something she could never have said to anyone except Ben, not even Gus. But Ben would understand. Ben always understood.

"Father would never have let her," Ben reminded her. "We're *his* property, not hers. Well, according to the law, *she* was his property as well, which is probably why she slipped out of the house while he was gone. He never would have let her go, you know." He grimaced. "It would have been hard enough for her to get away; she'd never have been able to escape trailing a crowd of children, like a s—a hen trailing a flock of chicks."

"I wonder how ever she escaped," Elena said, voicing something that had occupied her thoughts many nights over the past eight years. "No one saw her go."

Ben got an odd look on his face, as if he knew something. But what he said was what he always said. "She must have been writing to her people, and perhaps had help. She must have, really, she could have slipped out of the house and run down the drive to the road without anyone noticing she was gone, but she didn't take any of the horses, and she couldn't have gone any farther without flying." He paused. "And of course, that's absurd. She didn't have wings like our fairies do."

Elena sighed. "She must have been dreadfully unhappy, to leave us without saying goodbye."

"She was." Something about the way Ben said that made her look up at him, to see certainty on his face. *Did Mama confide in him?* She might have, though he wouldn't have been all that old at the time. Nine—but then, Nanny called him an "old soul," and certainly, except when they were playing games, he always seemed much older than his years. Arthur might be the better scholar, but not by much; Ben always seemed to understand how the world worked better than anyone, even Beecham.

"What do you think Stepmother is like?" she asked.

"Well, she has to be handsome. Father won't settle for anything he can't boast about." There was a bitterness to his tone she understood completely. Father always had to have the best of anything, whether it be offspring or horses. Anything that wasn't the best was gotten rid of, or at least put somewhere out of sight.

Maybe that's why I'm put out of sight. I'm not the best because I'm not a boy.

"Will she be kind?" Elena asked, more out of forlorn hope than anything else.

"I wish I knew." Ben sighed. "I don't even know her given name. Beecham let me look at the letter Father sent him, and all it said was that he had married and he was bringing his new wife home today from Bath and that we were to be made ready to be presented and receive her."

"That sounds cold," Elena said, with a shiver.

"That sounds like Father." Again, that bitter tone, but Elena could scarcely blame him. It *did* sound like Father. If they hadn't had Mama and Nanny and Beecham—who were very kind, really, when all was said and done—none of them would have known what the word *kindness* meant.

Arthur came down at that moment, looking exactly like Ben except that his coat was gray to Ben's blue, and he joined them on the bench without needing to be invited. "This is a dead bore," he proclaimed, a little crossly. "I'd rather be doing Greek. And your twin, little sister, seems to have been possessed of the devil this morning. Beecham and I only just managed to wrestle him into his clothing, and he tore off his neckcloth three times before Beecham threatened him with being put into a gown like an infant if he didn't behave. You'd think he wasn't old enough to have been breeched!"

"I don't think he likes the idea of someone replacing Mama," Elena said cautiously. "I think . . . maybe . . . he kept hoping that as long as Father didn't replace her, she might come back some day."

Arthur made an abortive attempt to pat her head and turned it into a pat on her shoulder. Ben grimaced.

"Do you remember that wild starling that Arthur tried to tame?" Ben asked. "Mother was like that bird."

She nodded. "It was never happy. It had grown up wild and free, and it could see the world outside the window and wanted to be free again."

"That was why I let it go," Arthur confirmed. "If I wasn't going to university soon, I would try again with an orphan baby; they can be very happy pets if you raise them before they have feathers, and you can let them fly free because they'll come back to you and wish to be with you. Father should have been contented to marry a—a tame lady. One that was raised to be tame. I don't know where he found Mama, but perhaps he should have left her there."

"Well, I suppose he finally found a tame lady he likes," Ben replied. Then added, crossly, "I suppose the only reason he married anyone in the first place was so he could have more sons he could boast about."

They exchanged a look she couldn't read, but from the little she remembered of Mama, and all that she knew about Father, they were probably right.

"What I don't understand," Arthur continued, "Is how on earth Mama managed to escape without anyone seeing her or even knowing she'd escaped until long after she was gone."

Ben got that opaque look again, the one she didn't understand. "Well, she came from *somewhere*, obviously, so she must have had family. If I'd been her . . . I would have found a way to get messages to them, letting them know I was unhappy."

Arthur nodded, knowingly. "The same as we manage to do, to get things with our pocket money Father wouldn't approve of. Like using Soames." Soames was the groom.

"Father dismissed her maid immediately, so it could have been her," Ben pointed out. "Then, well, someone could have lurked in the village until she got word to them that Father was gone. Between breakfast and luncheon everyone is busy, and no one would notice if she took a walk down to the gate to meet someone. At least, that's how I would have done it."

Arthur shook his head. "I'd have made a muddle of it. Good thing she was as clever as you are."

Just then Carl and David came clattering down the stair noisily in new shoes as well as new suits—also gray and blue. Economies, Elena supposed, since all of the boys were in sets of suits from the same blue and gray cloth, with one twin in blue and the other in gray so they could be told apart. "Beecham managed to get the heathen to stay in his neckcloth," Carl announced self-importantly. "But he had to send Nanny for one of Elena's old gowns as a threat before he'd behave."

"I don't blame him much," Arthur said after a moment. "He's been running free all summer in whatever he happened to throw on in the morning, and Beecham hasn't done anything about it."

"He's never gotten on Father's wrong side," David pointed out, and shuddered. "There's something to be said for Father not paying any attention to you."

All the little fairies seemed to be listening to this conversation with great interest. Obviously they understood what was being said, but Elena had never heard any of them speak—at least, not to any of the siblings.

"I wonder if Mama could talk to the fairies, and they got word to her people that she was unhappy," she said aloud. "That makes more sense than thinking she'd have trusted any of the servants with a letter. *She* could see them and talk to them, so it stands to reason that the people she came from could as well."

Ben gave her a sideways look, but Arthur seized on this idea. "That makes perfect sense . . . and it explains how she'd be able to tell a rescuer exactly when to come, that they should stay out on the road, and how she knew when the rescuer was out there. You're very clever, little sister!"

Elena blushed, but didn't say anything, because just then Beecham and Nanny turned up with Emil, Felix, and Gustav in tow. Gustav was very red-faced and sulky, and Arthur reached out and cuffed his ear.

"Ow!" he shouted, startled. "What did you do that for?"

"Because you were about to say things you shouldn't have," Arthur said. "Now you listen to me, you little barbarian. Father is *not* going to be in a mood for any nonsense, especially not out of you. He's about to show off his property and his children to his new wife. If one of those children makes a poor showing, it will embarrass him. If he's embarrassed by you, believe me, you will be regretting every sour look and cross word for the rest of the winter. Do you want to spend the rest of the winter on bread and water and gruel?"

Gus looked startled—probably because he'd never gotten on Father's wrong side before. "N-no," he stammered.

"Then you had better be a paper saint from now on in his presence and in the presence of his new wife. In fact, you'd better be a paper saint for Beecham too." Arthur crossed his arms over his chest and looked sternly at Gus, who paled and shrank into himself. "That's better. And don't be pranking about, either.

Father will either order Beecham to birch you, or do it himself, and believe me, you don't want Father to do it."

"I d-don't think I like having a new mama," Gus stammered.

"Then you'd better keep that opinion to yourself, or birching will be the least of your worries." Arthur frowned. "You've been very lucky that you've been in the nursery as long as you have, but it's time to grow up."

Gus looked to Beecham for confirmation; the tutor nodded. Instantly, he went from "miscreant monkey" to "very subdued and alarmed little boy."

Nanny was in her best gown, of course. Beecham didn't actually *have* any suit that was what Elena would have considered "best," but his stockings were an immaculately white pair she had knitted for him, his coat and breeches had been brushed and cleaned, his shoes shined, and his fine muslin neckcloth—which she had also made for him for his birthday—was as white as his stockings. He was, at the best of times, a studious, pale, and anxious bespectacled young man, who looked every bit of what he was—the son of a respectable but penurious clergyman. Right now that anxiety was foremost on his face.

They all sat or stood in silence in the hall until Mrs. Farthingworth put in an appearance, resplendent in her very best black gown, with a snowy white fichu and apron, every graying hair in place and a little lace cap on top of her head. Her usually unreadable round face bore an expression of dignified stress. "Jackie has come up the drive to say that the carriage is in sight. Hobart is gathering the rest of the servants. Come along, do."

They went out into the biting wind, and Elena was immediately glad of her woolen chemise and stockings, her pelisse, and the shawl she had brought on impulse. Mrs. Farthingworth arranged them on the right side of the portico, all in a row, with Arthur and Ben furthest from the door and Elena and Gus nearest. Then she placed Nanny behind Elena, and Beecham behind Arthur, and went to take her place at the head of the servants on the left side of the portico, next to Hobart, the butler. Just as Hobart got the last of the servants in their row, a carriage appeared at the end of the drive.

This was *not* the carriage that Elena had expected, their old, green carriage with the four bays and the crest that needed a slight touch-up on the door. This was a brand new—and, she supposed, much more fashionable—black carriage, with Father's initials and his crest picked out in gold, pulled by six spanking matched grays. And there was a new coachman on the box, with a new groom beside him. Behind came the old coach, with all manner of boxes and cases tied on top, suggesting the passenger compartment was equally full. *Why, Stepmother must have more gowns and things than me, Nanny, Mrs. Banning, and Mrs. Farthingworth put together!* The old coachman, Grimes, a taciturn old whip of a man who didn't say more than five words in a week, drove the old bays, alone. The coaches rolled to a stop in front of the door, wheels crunching in the driveway gravel. The handsome new groom, black of eye and hair, trim of figure, with a *very* neat leg, jumped down and placed a stool that matched the carriage beneath the new coach door, and Father emerged.

Father, brown haired, brown eyed, with a narrowish face, who looked nothing like his children, was wearing a blue suit she had never seen before, with clocked silk stockings, a cravat much too fine to be called a mere neckcloth, and an expression on his face that she did not recognize. He put up his hand, and a graceful hand in a white glove emerged from the depth of the carriage, followed by the most elegant woman Elena had ever seen in her entire life.

Her immaculately coiffed chestnut hair was as smooth and shining as a polished agate, beneath a highly fashionable bonnet with three ostrich feathers; her face had the delicacy of fine marble, and was as perfect as a statue's. She was very tall, very voluptuous, and wore the most beautiful gown Elena had ever seen, all blue brocade and gold lace. Matching shoes with red heels just showed beneath her hem as she stepped down onto the stool. Over the gown she wore a cloak of black fur as shining as her own hair.

Elena immediately felt as unfinished and clumsy as a baby goat.

A smartly dressed lady's maid exited right behind her, although, of course, no one offered *her* a hand down. *Mrs. Farthingworth isn't going to like her,* Elena thought, with one look at her narrow, too-clever face. *She looks like a very knowing cat.* Her hair was pale rather than blond, and her green gown was as good as or better than Elena's.

Father led his wife up to the family and servants assembled in the portico. All the servants bowed and curtsied without being prompted by Hobart. Father did not introduce them. Instead he turned to the siblings.

"These are my children: Arthur, Benjamin, Carl, David, Emil, Felix, Gustav, and Elena. Children, this is your new mother. You will honor and obey her."

As her cool blue eyes passed over them, Elena dropped into a curtsy a hair before Nanny did, and all the boys bowed, with Beecham bowing lower than any of them.

"I am sure that they shall," she murmured, and cast a sideways glance at Father.

And that was when Elena could put a name to the expression on Father's face.

Besotted. She'd seen that expression on Beecham's face, when he caught a glimpse of a certain very pretty village girl that he fancied in church, and again on the face of Harris, one of the footmen, on the rare occasion he was able to catch sight of the prettiest of the dairymaids. It was not an expression she had ever expected to see on Father's face.

He certainly had never looked at Mama that way.

"It's perishing cold, my love," Father murmured. "Let's get you out of this bitter wind."

She offered him a hint of a smile, and her hand, and they swept grandly into the front hall. Hobart followed closely behind, followed by Mrs. Farthingworth and then the children. Nanny and Beecham trailed behind, with the servants crowding after.

"Hobart, how are the arrangements for tomorrow's dinner party?" Elena heard Father ask the butler as she and Gus cleared the door.

"Satisfactory, sir," Hobart responded immediately. "Only Lady Ashling declined, begging her health."

"Lady Ashling always begs her health; I was expecting that," Father said shortly. "Good."

"Shall I show her ladyship to her rooms, sir?" Mrs. Farthingworth said diffidently.

"Yes, do," Father said, although the look he gave his new wife suggested he could scarcely bear to be parted from her. "Hobart, bring my steward to my office. I shall need to make some arrangements with him."

"And will the children be dining with you, sir?" the housekeeper asked.

Only then did Father look back over his shoulder, where they all stood huddled together in the hall, as the servants parted and moved around them. Stepmother's maid pushed through them to get to her mistress's side. Father's eyes finally focused on children. Then he glanced at his wife.

There was the faintest of frowns on her face, a fleeting expression Elena wouldn't have caught if she hadn't been watching her new stepmother so intently.

"I think not," he said. "We're tired from the journey. I'm not in the mood for gabble."

We never gabble! Elena thought indignantly. On the contrary, dinners with Father were subdued and almost silent, with not even Gus saying anything except to accept or decline a dish. The only time anyone spoke was if they were spoken to by Father, and then with only the briefest of replies.

But it seemed as if Father had an altogether different impression of those occasions.

And with that, he headed deeper into the house, leaving Mrs. Farthingworth at the new stepmother's side. "If my lady will follow me?" the housekeeper said, diffidently.

Stepmother nodded brusquely, and Mrs. Farthingworth led the way up the stairs, with Stepmother and her maid following wordlessly behind.

At just that moment, the children were shunted aside by the arrival of what seemed like every male servant in the household, heading for the servants' stair laden with boxes, bundles, chests, and bandboxes. Beecham and Nanny dealt with the ensuing chaos by sorting the children out from the servants and sending them up the stairs to the schoolroom once Stepmother was out of sight.

"I want you all out of your best clothing," Nanny ordered them. "You may put on what you wore this morning. Leave your clothing laid out *neatly* on your bed for the maid to put away, Gustav!" she added, as Gus pulled at his neckcloth.

Elena waited for the boys to start up the stairs, because there was something . . . something not quite right that she couldn't put her finger on. Now that no one was looking at her, she raised her eyes, pushed back the brim of her bonnet, and took a look around.

And that was when it struck her.

The fairies were gone.

She was grateful to get out of her best gown and into something much more comfortable: her everyday winter woolen gown with generous sleeves ending in narrow cuffs that had been cut loosely with plenty of extra in the seams so it could be let out several times. Like most of her everyday gowns, it had been cut down from one of Mama's old gowns that were in a chest in the attic. This one was brown superfine, a fabric usually used for men's coats, but Mama hadn't cared about that, and neither did Elena. Merino wasn't as soft as lambswool, but it was soft enough, and delightfully warm. She put the linen gown back in the wardrobe with no regrets, but left on the lambswool chemise and new stockings. The next thing she did was to take her hair down, and put it back up again in a loose coil at the back of her neck.

The fairies still had not appeared when she had finished changing; she took a moment to peer out the window into the cold and overcast day to see if there were any outside, in the leafless trees or playing in the dormant garden.

There weren't. And that made her very uneasy.

Weather didn't seem to bother the fairies at all, despite the fact that all they ever wore—when they wore anything at all—were bits of ribbon and gauze. She'd seen them playing in the snow countless times, naked as Adam and Eve, so the weather had nothing to do with why they had disappeared.

They do go into hiding for a bit when Father has dinner parties. But they always come back out once their curiosity gets the better of them. But perhaps Stepmother's mere demeanor, so cold, had put them off. Or perhaps it was her maid.

We should all talk about it once the servants bring us supper and we're alone, she decided. But in the meantime, she would finish another lace-trimmed handkerchief, the one she had started when Father had sent back word he was remarrying and would be bringing Stepmother home. She had intended it for a welcome gift, but in the face of that exquisite gown, it seemed inadequate.

I'll finish this, then think of something more.

She sat on a cushion next to the fire, propped a book up on another, and glanced from one to the other as she worked. Ben had given her an English translation of *The Odyssey* to read, one that he and Arthur had used to help them with their Greek. It had come out of Father's library, but Father rarely went in the room, and she doubted he would notice it had been removed. The story was strange and violent, but she found herself drawn to it. It was not an easy read, however, full of words she had never seen before, that she often had to puzzle out from context.

She had finished the handkerchief and had lit a candle to continue reading the book when Nanny came into her room. Again, without knocking.

"Beecham and I are going down to supper. Your new mama has said you all are to take your meals in the schoolroom from now on, unless otherwise ordered," Nanny said, and frowned to see the unmistakable library binding on what was clearly not a storybook. "You should not be reading such stuff. It's not suitable for girls."

"Ben says it is," she replied, without disclosing what it was.

"Oh, well, then. It must be something improving. A book of sermons?" Nanny didn't wait for an answer. "Don't sit reading by candlelight for too long, it will give you a headache."

And with that useless admonition, Nanny left. Elena went back to the book, although she was not sure she was going to like what was coming next. She had the feeling that things were not going to go well for Odysseus.

2

Dinner was served, as it usually was when Father was away, in the schoolroom, a room that was singularly unwelcoming, being painted a stark white, with nothing on the walls but maps, and full of hard, uncompromising furniture. It was as far from the kitchen as it could possibly be. This meant that most dishes that arrived upstairs were lukewarm at best, and cold at worst, but they were used to that by now, for when Father was home, they actually took most of their meals here, saving only breakfast, because cold toast was vile and could not be saved. Many things could be reheated by putting them over the fire on a scoured ash shovel, or held directly in the flames with fire tongs, and even the soup and sauces and things not easily put on a shovel could be heated to a tolerable state by putting the tureen or plate on the hearth and eating the courses out of order. Nanny and Beecham would have remonstrated with them for this, but Nanny was eating her own dinner in the servants' hall, and Beecham was either eating with Father and Stepmother, or had found himself banished from the master's table to eat with Nanny. The servants didn't care that they did this sort of impromptu cookery—indeed, it was the servants who supplied them with the extra shovels. The make-do nature made meals seem like a picnic of sorts, and the fact that they were served on the sturdier pottery dishes from the servants' table instead of the fine china of the dining room meant they didn't have to worry about breaking anything.

Well, meals usually felt casual and even cozy up here. Stepmother's obvious coldness had cast a pall on the meal, even though the food itself was rather good in honor of her arrival, and Mrs. Banning the cook had clearly exerted herself to impress. They all ate in silence, and not even a particularly nice baked apple custard for pudding was able to raise their spirits.

"What do you suppose is going to happen to us?" Felix ventured, after the servants came to take the dishes away, and the shovels had been plunged into the heart of the fire to clean them.

"Well, Stepmother can't sack us," Arthur pointed out, garnering a weak laugh. "It might not be so bad. If they don't want to see us at meals—if they don't want to see us *at all*—that just means we can be by ourselves up here and be jolly instead of on our manners and dealing with all the proper forks and spoons."

"That's true," Felix replied hesitantly. "We'll have to be extra careful about not being seen, though, if Stepmother does not want us about. That means no more playing in the gardens."

"So we play in the woods," Gus said with more enthusiasm than his brother showed. "*I* don't mind staying out of sight."

That seemed a good opening for Elena to mention the thing that had been bothering her since she noticed it. "The fairies are gone," she said, her voice troubled. "I think they disappeared right after Stepmother got out of the carriage."

"What?" Ben said, sounding startled. He looked around quickly. "By Jove! They *are* gone! Whatever can that mean?"

"Well, they never show themselves around Father, so perhaps it means they don't like her as they don't like him." Arthur pulled at his lower lip.

"Or perhaps it means *she* has magic and they don't want her to see them," Elena offered, a notion that had come to her right after she finished the handkerchief. She shivered, because the idea that this cold, unlikable woman had *magic* and could perhaps use it to spy on them was very disturbing.

"Maybe just having a stranger about frightened them, and they'll turn up later," David offered optimistically.

"I surely hope she does not have magic," Emil murmured,

his brow furrowed with worry. "And we mustn't let her know *we do*."

"That might be the most intelligent thing you have ever said," Arthur declared. "But here is something else we absolutely must do. It's not just Gus who will have to be a paper saint, we all will. Nothing to make the servants complain about us, so no teasing the sheep, or taking out the pony cart without permission, or riding *any* of the horses either, except when *both* of them are gone."

"She seems very fashionable," Ben observed. "Perhaps she'll want to be in Bath most of the time."

That seemed to be the best they could hope for, and Elena wished very, very hard that this would prove to be true.

The whole affair cast a pall over the evening, however, and none of them even wanted to play a game. Instead, they sat as close to the fire as they could, as if the heat of the flames could somehow warm the cold from their hearts. Gus and Emil poked at the fire or added wood; David and Carl picked out old favorite books to re-read. Arthur and Ben stood to one side of the hearth and talked too quietly for Elena to hear what they were saying. Felix mended a toy boat with a snapped mast. She went to her room and got her knitting workbasket, and selected her softest lambswool yarn in fine lace-weight. Perhaps she might soften Stepmother's heart with a gift of a lambswool shawl. She seemed far too grand a person to wear any stockings but silk, and any gloves but silk or kid, but a lambswool shawl should be welcome with winter coming on.

She cast on the needed number of stitches, and began a lace pattern that she knew by heart and could knit in the dark.

Felix went off to bed first, followed by Gus. Soon after that, the other boys followed, all but Ben, who lingered as she put the knitting up in her workbasket and prepared to seek her bed too. Nanny had not put in an appearance to harry her off, but Nanny and Beecham might be talking about Stepmother with some of the servants—perhaps even Hobart and Mrs. Farthingworth would have unbent to join such a conversation.

"I don't like her," Elena said plaintively, after a glance around, although if her stepmother was using magic to spy on them, she was not sure how she would know. "I *do* think she has magic, and I think she frightened the fairies."

Instead of assuaging her fears, Ben nodded. "It seems the most likely explanation," he replied, quietly. "In the past, when Father has had strangers to the house, they *have* flitted off, but only for a little while, and they've always come back up here by the time supper arrived. I don't like her either, and I am certain she doesn't like us. But perhaps once she gets to know us—provided we can keep Gus from playing the fool—she will at least come to tolerate us."

He sat down on the hearth beside her, and she cuddled up to him for reassurance. He had always been her favorite brother, and he had always been very protective of her. "Well . . . as you said, she can't sack us. But soon you and Arthur will be at Oxford. . . ."

And then I'll be alone was what she wanted to say, but she knew he'd just tell her not to be silly, so instead she said, ". . . and the others aren't as sensible as you are."

"Beecham will keep them under control," he replied. "And if Stepmother really *is* a dragon, fear of being caned should prevent them from getting out of hand."

The darkness in the schoolroom, the whistling of the wind in the chimney, and the memory of Stepmother's cold eyes conjured up a dozen nameless fears, but there was nothing either of them could do about the situation, so what was the point in voicing them?

She looked up into Ben's face and saw the same uncertainty there that chilled her, and wanted to cry. But instead, she managed a smile. "If she has magic, perhaps she will be so busy with that, she won't even care about what we do," she offered, then changed the subject. "There seems to be quite a *lot* of magic in the book you gave me. But there don't seem to be anything like fairies."

"Well, that's because the Greeks had other kinds of magic, and most of it came from their gods," Ben told her, obviously glad to have something else to talk about. "Shall I explain some of that to you?"

"Yes, please," she replied, just as grateful, and sat pressed against his side while he spun tales of the Greeks and their heroes and strange creatures and gods until it was time for bed.

It was a maid who woke her late in the morning, much later than Nanny usually woke her, coming in to mend the fire and build it back up again. She always made the point of learning the name of every servant she came across, and their rank, so she knew immediately that this was not the maid who normally tended to the rooms the siblings lived in, but someone who usually worked cleaning the less important rooms downstairs, like the pantries, kitchen, laundry, and privies, and not a chambermaid at all. "Rosie," she said, sitting up, and startling the girl so much that she yipped and dropped the ashpan. "I'm sorry, I didn't mean—where's Nanny?"

The cold wind rattled the window at the moment, and she inadvertently clutched the bedclothes up around her.

"Miss, I heard in the kitchen that the new mistress said she and the master wanted to see her and Beecham, and that I was to come do your room. That's all I know, miss." The girl picked up the ashpan, tried to curtsy at the same time, and dropped it again. "I heard nothing else, miss. You and the young gentlemen are to have breakfast in the schoolroom, miss."

Breakfast in the schoolroom was not unusual, but Elena got a sinking feeling in her heart when she heard that her stepmother and father had ordered Nanny *and* Beecham to appear before them—and so early in the morning, too! *Nanny is being dismissed. I just know it. Poor Nanny!* It wasn't just the cold wind rattling the windowpanes that made her shiver. She waited in bed until Rosie finished her work, then slipped out of bed and out of her nightgown, putting on fresh body-linen, washing up, putting that second woolen chemise over the linen one, and putting on her woolen gown from yesterday. She braided her own hair and coiled it at the nape of her neck, binding it all up with an unobtrusive ribbon. She took the lace-trimmed fichu she had finished, tied it up with another piece of ribbon salvaged from a bonnet in a bit of paper that she had decorated with some of the same sort of drawings she used as embroidery patterns, and put it in her pocket. Then she went to breakfast.

Ben and Arthur were already well into their meal. The other four had just started, and Gus, as usual, was nowhere to be seen. Neither was Beecham. Breakfast, it seemed, was porridge and nothing else; whoever had brought it up had brought all of it in a big pot and set it down on the hearth, so at least it was warm. At least there was sugar and cream on the table, and a big pot of tea on the hearth. She filled a bowl and a cup for herself, added sugar and cream to both, and sat down with the rest. Gus appeared after that, looking disheveled, his hair quite uncombed and his shirt untucked.

This did not bode well.

They all ate in silence, not chattering as usual. Ben and Arthur looked apprehensive, Gus indifferent, the rest puzzled. When they had all eaten as much as they could, they continued to sit in silence—long past the time when Beecham should have appeared—until two of the kitchen maids came to collect all the crockery and cutlery, followed by Mrs. Farthingworth, in her usual dove-gray gown.

"Mistress and Master wish to see you all in the winter parlor," Mrs. Farthingworth said, without much expression. "Gustav, you are a fright. Tuck your shirt in and smooth down your hair at once."

Immediately cowed, Gus did as he was told. Mrs. Farthingworth *tsk*ed, pulled a comb out of one pocket, and roughly combed his hair into place. For once, he made no objections, even when it was obvious she was yanking the knots out of his hair. When she was done, she made an imperious gesture, and they followed her out into the hall and down to the winter parlor.

This room was called that because it was on the southern side of the house, leeward to the wind, and was the warmest sitting room in the winter. Father and Stepmother were already there, Father leafing idly through a newspaper, Stepmother with her hands folded in her lap, eyes half-lidded, as if she wasn't used to being up this early. Mrs. Farthingworth cleared her throat and said, "Here are the children, master," then curtsied slightly and left, leaving them standing in a group at the edge of the carpet like a huddle of ducklings.

"Come here," Stepmother said. Today she wore something a bit more practical than yesterday's brocade and gold lace, but still far more expensive than anything Elena ever recalled her mother wearing: heavy deep green silk with elaborate pintucking, and a cream silk shawl with heavy fringes. As usual when at home and intending to ride out to attend to the business of the manor and lands, Father wore white leather breeches, buttoned at the knee, top boots, his usual blue wool frock coat, a woolen waistcoat, a second waistcoat over the first, and a simple neckcloth rather than a cravat. His light brown hair had been carefully combed, but not arranged at all. His expression appeared bored except when he looked at his new wife, when it took on that besotted look.

They made their way in a group slowly across the floor, Ben and Arthur in the lead. When they had come to stand before the two chairs in front of the fire, Stepmother looked them up and down without a hint of expression on her face.

Is Father going to leave it all to her to speak to us?

"Your tutor gave a good account of you older boys, and was honest enough to say that he could not teach you anything more. For that reason, we have dismissed him with a letter of recommendation," she said. "Benjamin, you and Arthur will undertake to teach your brothers; it will be good practice for you in case you are called upon to be tutors yourselves at university. The rest of you boys will obey them. Your father will test your learning from time to time, and if he finds it faulty, whoever of you is lacking as well as Benjamin and Arthur will all be called to account. Do you understand me?"

"Yes, ma'am," Ben and Arthur said together, clearly, while the other five murmured or mumbled the same thing.

"In addition, you two eldest will be permitted to use your father's library freely to continue your education until you are ready for university," she continued. "Concentrate on those subjects that you intend to study there. Your father feels that the two next eldest should prepare themselves for careers in religion, or, perhaps, the law. It will do no harm to begin that preparation now. The library should be adequate for those purposes. There are plenty of books of sermons and other improving subjects there."

She paused, waiting for just a moment, perhaps to see if they would dare to object. This time Ben and Arthur answered alone, "Yes, ma'am."

Stepmother turned her cold gaze on Elena. "You are far too old to have a nanny, Elena, so she has been dismissed as well, with a good character. I trust you are capable of reading, writing, and arithmetic?"

"Yes, ma'am," Elena said, trying to meet those cold eyes without looking impertinent, although her heart ached for poor Nanny. "And history and geography and a little French."

"A *little* French is all a girl requires," said Stepmother. "And what of your other skills?"

She fumbled in her pocket for the wrapped package, and edged forward the couple of steps she needed to get barely close enough to the woman to hand it over. "I made this for you as a welcome gift, ma'am," she said, managing not to stammer, and backing away as soon as the woman had taken it from her hand.

Stepmother looked at it, at first with indifference, but then with a lifted brow once she had had a chance to examine the paper. "Did you do the drawings on this paper?" she asked, showing her first signs of interest.

"Yes, ma'am," she said softly, as her stepmother opened the package and took out the fichu. She held it up, examining it closely, the second brow joining the first.

"My word," she said, as if astonished. "This is rather fine."

"The girl has been making her own ordinary clothing for some time now," Father put in from behind the newspaper. "I believe she is accustomed to ornamenting her garments and making her slippers and bonnets."

Stepmother crooked her finger. Elena stepped forward again, just as reluctantly as the first time, and stood there rigidly while the woman examined the embroidery on her bodice, and even pulled the bodice away from her body to look at the hem and facings of the neckline and the neckline of her shift. "Well, then," she said, motioning Elena back into place. "There will clearly be no need of a boarding school or a governess. I doubt there is anything anyone can teach you in the way of needlecraft."

"Good," said Father, and finally put down his paper. He exchanged a look with Stepmother, and nodded. At last he turned back to his children. There was something not quite right about the way he looked at them, as if they were almost strangers to him. Elena couldn't account for it. And surely the boys should have had another tutor, and now that she had a stepmother she should have had lessons in dancing and music!

But maybe he doesn't intend for me to be anything but a nurse for him and Stepmother when they get old. You don't need dancing and music for that.

Part of her felt nothing but resignation. Part of her felt trapped.

"You may all return to the schoolroom and resume your studies where Beecham left them off," he said. "Pray do not come downstairs today. We are hosting a supper to welcome your new mother to her house, and I do not want children underfoot, interfering with the servants."

Then he put his paper back up, and Stepmother picked up a book from the table beside her. Since they had clearly been dismissed, they left, moving as quickly as they could, trying not to look as if they would rather have run.

The boys went straight to the schoolroom, but she took a detour to her own room, where she found a bit of folded paper laid on her newly made bed. Had it been left by Rosie? She picked it up and unfolded it, and her heart contracted when she recognized Nanny's imprecise handwriting.

Dear Child; They woodn't give me Leave to say Goodbye, so I arst little Rosie to leave this for you. They give me my Quarter-wages and a Letter of good report and a Ride with my Things down to my Daughter in Lacock. I reckon I can start a Dame School, cuz there ain't one there. Don't fret about Me. Listen to Ben, and stay outa your new Stepmother's way. Love, Nanny.

Tears rose in her eyes, and her throat closed, tears as much for herself as for Nanny. How much of that letter was true? Had she really been paid her wages to the end of the quarter? Had Father really ordered the horses put to the cart and arranged for her to be taken all the way to Lacock? Or had she been promised such a thing then been taken only as far as the village and left there to find her own way? It seemed all too likely.

On the other hand . . . Father had an intense dislike for

having his reputation sullied, and if he had been so shabby in his behavior as that, with so many people coming through Whitstone Village on the way to the supper party, word would get about. For that matter, even *before* people began coming to the supper party, word would get about—all this must have happened before she was awake, and a disconsolate Nanny set down with her bundles and bags in the middle of Whitstone Village would certainly make a stir, and the gossip would be all over the village before breakfast, and in the kitchens of the gentry by dinner and the ears of the master and mistress by tea.

But poor Nanny.... She had been here since Ben and Arthur were born.

She was so good to me after Mama left, even if she was cross sometimes. And now I don't have anyone except the boys.

She allowed herself a sob or two, but no more than that. Crying, as she had been told repeatedly, did not help anything. She took a long, deep breath, got one of her own shawls and the workbasket with the shawl she was working on for Stepmother in it, and went back to the schoolroom.

At least Stepmother liked the fichu I made for her. Perhaps if I keep making her pretty things, she—

Well, it was too much to hope for that Stepmother would be *nice* to her, but perhaps she would refrain from being horrid. Best of all if Stepmother would just ignore her.

The boys had built up the fire rather well, and someone had made a foray down into the kitchen and found a sympathetic servant, because there was a hessian bag of potatoes, a basket of nuts, and a peck of apples tucked discreetly out of sight of the doorway, so no one just glancing in would see them. Ben and Arthur had divided the work of tutoring between them; Ben had taken the three younger boys, and Arthur had taken the older twins. Blond heads were bent over books and workbooks all around the schoolroom table. There were new books on the shelves as well; presumably a raid had been made on the library while she was in her room so that Ben and Arthur could pursue their own courses of study.

Ben looked up as she came in and smiled at her. "Beecham left us a letter; he said he had been paid until the end of the year, that he got a good letter of recommendation, and Simon was taking him and Nanny in the farm cart as far as Lacock."

Well, at least that confirmed that poor Nanny was not being set down in the village.

"He also said he knows the rector there, and the rector will certainly put him up until he can find a new place, and perhaps the rector will exert himself and help Nanny find a place as well. So, now all we need to do is look out for each other." Ben's voice faltered a little on that last, then strengthened, as if he was straightening his shoulders to bear up under some invisible burden.

"Is there something you would like to start learning, Elena?" Arthur asked, kindly. "You have always been a good student. I don't see any reason why you can't go on the same as Gus."

She felt far too upset and unhappy to take a formal lesson right now, but it seemed shabby to say so. "What is Gus studying right now?" she asked.

"Geometry," Gus moaned, his hair already a mess from running his hands through it. Elena hesitated. She really had no interest in geometry.

"I could go on reading history," she said. "If that's all right. Or practice my penmanship and spelling."

"Well, I saw that Ben gave you that old *Odyssey* to read, so why don't you pick up with the Greeks?" he replied. "We can start with their gods and myths. Nanny never would let us teach you anything that 'heathen,' and it will help with understanding the *Odyssey*."

So she found herself tucked up next to the hearth with a book called *The Greeks, Their Gods, and Their Myths,* which had the virtue of being illustrated with sketches of statues and the paintings on vases. She could see why Nanny would never have let her see something like this; most of the people were naked. But after all, she and the boys had been seeing the little naked fairies since they were born, so none of this was a shock to her. Well, except for the naked men, but she had been in and out of the manor farmyard and stables (where there were plenty of male animals) enough that she knew what a male's nether regions looked like, mostly.

Since she could read and knit at the same time, she continued the work on the gift shawl, with her own shawl, of a much heavier weight wool and plain knit, wrapped around her shoulders and her waist. She saw immediately that this book was where Ben had gotten some of his stories from. It was heavy going, though not as bad as the *Odyssey* itself, but after a while she got so deeply into the text that she missed Arthur calling her name until he came and touched her shoulder; she started and looked up.

"Ben has gone down to the kitchen to see what the cook will give us for luncheon," Arthur said, as her stomach growled, making her cheeks redden with embarrassment. "I've put potatoes in the ashes, just in case."

"In case?" she asked doubtfully. "In case of what?"

"Well, the kitchen is preparing for the dinner. And Stepmother might not have thought to order any luncheon for us." His lips formed a thin line as he said that, and she realized with a sinking heart that Stepmother was entirely the sort of woman who *would* forget. "But he can get cheese and bread and butter, he's the eldest son and they won't deny him that, and we'll be jolly enough with apples and nuts and jacket potatoes."

She marked her place in the book with a bit of yarn and set it and the knitting aside.

Ben, when he appeared, was with one of the scullery maids, Jenny, and the hallboy Jackie. All three of them carried laundry baskets. The boy had crockery and cutlery, the scullery maid had a pair of jugs and some napkins wrapped around something, and Ben had what looked like plates, also covered with napkins. When all was disclosed, it appeared that they had been presented with the remains of breakfast. A few cold sausages and some bacon, bread that was a little stale, a few boiled eggs, half-finished pots of jam and marmalade. Ben had also gotten some wedges of cheese and a pot of butter. The jugs contained tea, and there was a pot of milk and another of sugar. As a meal, it was somewhat worse than their usual luncheon by virtue of being cold and, in the case of the bread, stale. But it wasn't terrible. They'd be able to heat things as usual, and with the hot jacket potatoes, they could make a sort of mess that would enable everyone to get a bit of everything warm, and fill up the corners with toasted bread and jam. Sadly, there were no cakes or biscuits, not even leftover ones from breakfast.

Rosie and the scullery maid came back up for the crockery and baskets, and they all went back to their studies; the day was raw and cold enough that there was no temptation to go outside. Although the games sitting on their shelves could have been a distraction, Elena knew from experience that no one would be able to agree on one that they could all play. Probably Arthur and Ben were well aware of this as well.

Arthur put her to penmanship for a while, then quizzed her on yesterday's geography and set her a new reading. Gus was doing better with history and Latin than he had been with geometry, so at least they were all spared his inarticulate moans. Then, as a treat, Ben sat down and translated something of Julius Caesar's adventures among pirates from the Latin, and by then, the supper guests started arriving and they all went to the windows to watch.

Coach after coach pulled up, disgorging people both familiar and unfamiliar. Mostly unfamiliar, at least to Elena; Father had not given a big supper party since Mama had left. It was a pity it was so cold; the ladies were all bundled up in cloaks and pelisses, and very little of their gowns and nothing of their jewelry was to be seen.

When no more coaches appeared, they turned their attention back to the schoolroom. Ben refreshed the fire, they put their books and papers away, lit candles around the room, and then . . . waited, with growling stomachs.

"Should one of us go downstairs to the kitchen?" Felix wondered aloud.

"No. Father specifically said he did not want us getting in the way of the servants," Ben declared. And sighed. "I hope they remember us—"

But just then the welcome sounds of feet in heavy shoes in the hallway heralded the arrival of at least *someone*, and a moment later, Mrs. Farthingworth herself appeared, leading Jackie, one of the grooms, and a laundry maid, all burdened with laundry baskets again.

Mrs. Farthingworth herself had jugs of tea and more milk and sugar, she set the jugs of tea down on the hearth. They all helped to set the table, and then Mrs. Farthingworth directed the placement of the dishes in the middle.

"It's not what I would like for you," she said, with unaccustomed sympathy. "But your stepmother is very— economical. And she was in the kitchen overseeing everything and directing what we were to bring up after everyone at the party was served."

She didn't have to explain that statement. What had come up was clearly the remains of the feast, and those remains were scant and inferior. The crusty ends of the roast beef, the dry fillets of fish that sauce couldn't save, chicken wings, imperfect rolls and ones with burnt bottoms, bruised fruit, little bits of side dishes thrown together into one larger dish, cheese rinds, wilted salad, overcooked vegetables. All of it cold. No soup.

"Thank you, Mrs. Farthingworth," Ben said with false cheer. "We'll manage."

"Just leave the dishes in the baskets; someone will collect them in the morning before breakfast," the housekeeper told him.

As the rest of them looked askance at the offerings, Ben took charge. "Chicken wings first," he declared, and got out an ash shovel. "You all pour yourselves tea. I think there are enough wings for everyone to have two. Let me just heat them up."

"I'll help," said his twin, and both of them began re-grilling the wings on their shovels.

Anxious to be useful, Elena looked over the remains and decided that the bits and pieces could probably be mixed together and left on the hearth as a single dish, and for good measure she added the wilted salad and the vegetables.

"I don't like salad!" Gus objected strongly as she did just that.

"Then I'll have your share. I'm hungry," said Felix.

Gus looked at Felix, decided that he was serious, and didn't object again.

They ate their chicken wings in turn as they came off the shovel, devouring skin, gristle, fat, and all and sucking the bones clean; by that time, Elena's "mess" was warm, and they all took shares. It was odd. But not unpleasant. Elena swapped her share of the crusty beef for Carl's fish, because she knew he was not all that fond of fish at the best of times, and he'd probably choke on this dry stuff. She picked out the bones, then mashed it up with some of the jacket potato, lots of butter and a touch of milk, and it was edible. They all cut up the cheese rinds as small as they could and mixed those into their jacket potatoes with a bit of butter. There was a cup of something that turned out to be sweetened cream, presumably sauce for a pudding that had been completely eaten downstairs, and they cut up the fruit—the bruises were not terribly bad—and mixed it the cream into it. It wasn't a proper pudding, but it did make a kind of finish to the meal. But this time there wasn't any jam or marmalade, and anyway, there hadn't been much bread either, so none of them felt quite full.

That called for an apple apiece, while the eldest boys set to roasting chestnuts on the fire on their shovels. They all ate every bit of their apples, leaving only the stem, seeds, and little dry "flower" at the end.

"We need to cultivate someone in the kitchen," Carl said, as they all gathered around the fire and waited for the chestnuts to burst along the lines that had been scored into them by Arthur and Ben, the only ones who had penknives.

"Well, *we* got what was left after all the servants had their go," Felix pointed out. "So we need to reckon how to persuade *someone* to bring us up a bit more."

"Brown bread and plain, ordinary cheese should do," David said thoughtfully, and tentatively picked at a chestnut to see if it was cooled enough to peel. "Plenty of pickles would help. I don't mind eating brown bread instead of white. I wouldn't be offended by more vegetables if we aren't going to get much meat."

"Then I'll talk to Mrs. Farthingworth and Cook tomorrow before anyone brings up breakfast," Elena offered. "I used to spend time in Mrs. Farthingworth's parlor with Nanny and Cook when it was really cold and I'd finished my lessons early, and I did make them all shawls last year for Christmas. I'll ask them what can be spared that Stepmother won't notice. Oh!" she exclaimed, as she thought of something. "If we trade our tea for small beer, she'll *surely* be willing to help!"

"I don't like small beer," Gus began to object.

"Mint tea? Chamomile? Rose-hip?" she suggested, and Gus licked his lips and reached for a chestnut.

"I like those," he admitted.

"I'd trade all my tea and my sugar and milk too, if it gets us a bit more sausage and bacon," put in David. Elena looked around the fire and saw nods all around.

"Then I'll wake up early and go down while they're putting together Stepmother's morning chocolate." She made a face. "I just *know* she is the kind that has chocolate and biscuits in bed."

Felix sighed. "I don't mind not eating fancy stuff," he said, voicing what they all felt. "I just don't like going hungry."

"We're not doing that tonight, not while there are apples and nuts and potatoes," Arthur reminded him firmly. "As for tomorrow, I have faith that Elena can work something out with Cook and Mrs. Farthingworth." He smiled at her, as the light from the flames in the fireplace danced across all their faces. She blushed a little.

A handful of chestnuts quelled the not-entirely-satisfied feeling in her stomach, and she settled back to keep knitting that shawl, because at the moment, it seemed to represent their best chance at appeasing their new stepmother. Ben fetched the mythology book and began reading some of the tales aloud, but Elena realized that if she was going to get up early, she would have to go to bed early, and slipped away before she'd heard more than one.

As she had half expected, no one had put the warming pan in her bed, but she'd seen it used often enough, and scooped some coals into it from her fireplace, and put it between the sheets while she undressed, took down her hair, and got into her nightgown. The bed wasn't as warm as she would have liked, but at least it wasn't damp and cold.

It was dark when she woke, but she could hear faint sounds from belowstairs, coming up the staircases. No one had come up to mend her fire or put a new pitcher of wash water on the hearth, so she gave herself a "promise" cleaning with a damp cloth, loosely braided her hair, and slipped into her clothing as quickly as she could. She padded downstairs as quietly as she could, because the last thing she wanted to do was wake Stepmother, and kept a firm grip on the handrail just in case her foot slipped.

By contrast with the rest of the cold, dark house, the kitchen was warm and bright, and while it was not as busy as it would be in the middle of the day, it certainly had some activity. Cook was taking bread out of the oven, Rosie emptying the baskets of crockery from last night into the sink to be washed, Annie, one of the scullery maids, was heating water for tea and milk for hot chocolate, and Mrs. Farthingworth was looking at a piece of paper and frowning. The stable hands and dairymen and girls were all sitting at the enormous table, eating bread and butter and bacon and drinking something that steamed. Hot ale, perhaps. There didn't seem to be any other servants about. One of the stablehands looked up from his knife and fork, squinted at her, and said with surprise, "Miss Elena! What are you a-doin' up so early?"

Mrs. Farthingworth turned and stared at her in surprise. "My days! What *are* you doing here, child?"

"I—I wanted to talk to you and Mrs. Banning about our meals," she stammered.

Cook turned away from the oven with an unreadable expression on her face, and said to Mrs. Farthingworth, "We should go to your parlor."

"Yes, yes, we should. Annie, Rosie, don't slack. We'll be right back," the housekeeper said firmly. She walked to a door on the left of the kitchen where her bedroom and parlor office were. Cook paused just long enough to slide more risen loaves into the oven and followed. Elena sheepishly ducked her head and scurried after. Once they were all in the parlor, Cook closed the door after her, so no one in the kitchen could hear.

"I did tell you there wasn't enough there for eight hungry children," Cook said in a cross tone.

"Oh, we had potatoes and nuts and apples," Elena interjected, before Mrs. Farthingworth could retort and perhaps start a quarrel with Cook.

"Yes, dear, but that's not sufficient for growing children," Mrs. Banning replied in a kindlier voice.

"That woman!" Mrs. Farthingworth exclaimed. "*You* saw how it was last night! In *your kitchen* after everyone had already eaten and before we could fix them a decent meal, and telling you that what we were about to set aside for the pigs was good enough for them! I never in all my life saw anyone so *cheese-paring*!"

"Yes, and she's started as she means to go on, I reckon," Cook said grimly. Elena let out a little sigh of relief; it was obvious both women were on the same side and against Stepmother.

"Well, we talked about it, and we think there are things we would like that she won't notice or care you are making for us. Brown bread instead of white, dripping instead of butter, common cheese of the sort that the gardeners and stablemen eat. We'll trade you our tea and milk and sugar for things like chamomile, rose-hip, and mint with honey. I don't think she'll notice you feeding us lots of vegetables, or fruit that is in season and not from the hothouse. And if you can keep the potato sack, apple peck, and nut bag full, we should do quite well, really. We all like pease porridge, and we like oatmeal porridge in the morning. It would be lovely with currants or raisins, and I don't think she'll miss those either."

Both women stared at her in astonishment. "You clever little minx!" exclaimed Cook. "I never would have thought that of you!"

You never would have thought we'd eat farmer's food and like it, you mean, Elena thought without any rancor whatsoever.

"And there's our practical solution." Mrs. Farthingworth nodded. "My days, child, I was going to discuss this with Mrs. Banning, but I am exceedingly glad you came down early and brought this plan to us directly. Did all of you agree to this?"

Elena nodded, and the skepticism faded from the housekeeper's face. "You've never lied, child. This was a very good idea. The mistress likely won't care if Cook bakes a hundred loaves of brown bread a day, but I would not be surprised if she came down here and weighed out the sugar and white flour and butter with her own two hands to make certain no one got any but herself and the master."

"Now that we *know* what she's like, I expect I can make what little meat is left over from luncheon into a nice stew for the children, Mrs. Farthingworth," Cook said, looking pleased with herself. "Beans and bacon are good and filling, even if Her Majesty would turn her fine nose up at them. And if I make jam tarts for their pudding or tea, well, I doubt she'll go into my pantry and count the jam jars."

"Especially if it's currant, apple, or plum, and not strawberry." Mrs. Farthingworth pursed her lips and patted Elena on the head like a child. "You just leave the rest to us, my clever little girl. Go on back up to your room, and go back to sleep if you can."

The housekeeper opened the door and they all left; Cook stopped her for a moment to give her a rasher of bacon off the platter on the table, folded into a slice of hot bread. She was glad for it, because last night's thin fare had already worn off.

The bed was cold, but she was too sleepy to care; she finished the last bite, got into her nightgown again, and managed to find a corner of the bed that was still warm. The next thing she knew, it was light, and Rosie was making up her fire.

When Rosie and one of the grooms and Jenny, the other scullery maid, came up with their breakfast, Rosie informed them all, as Mrs. Farthingworth had said yesterday, that Stepmother had decreed that unless their father specified their presence at meals downstairs, they were to continue to take them in the schoolroom.

They were frankly too busy serving out food to do more than nod. This was a *much* more satisfactory meal. There was bread fried in bacon fat, lots of oatmeal porridge and plenty of honey and raisins for it, stewed apples, a rasher of bacon apiece, and chamomile tea. None of them really missed butter, nor their usual tea. Well fortified, they all settled down to work, and not even the intrusion of Stepmother, who had come all the way up to the schoolroom to look them over, cast a pall on the day.

Elena did notice that Stepmother was wearing the lace fichu Elena had given her, but the sharp look she cast around the room left no doubt in Elena's mind that she had not intended this as a pleasant visit, and had probably expected to find them engaged in anything but studying.

She had to content herself with an abrupt nod as they all scrambled to their feet politely, with little bows and a small curtsy. "I will not interrupt your diligence," she said, expressionlessly. "I was just making sure you were doing as your father directed you."

And without so much as a "good morning," she turned and whisked off, as if she did not want the dirt of the schoolroom on her hem.

They all held their breaths, listening to the sound of her footsteps going down the stairs, and it was only when they were sure that she was truly gone that they exhaled again.

"Did you *see* her?" David asked. "I do swear she was sniffing for a hint of chops and eggs!"

"Well, all she got was a nose full of porridge for her pains." Arthur smirked. "And if she does go down to the kitchen, she'll be disappointed twice over." He stretched and came to look over Elena's penmanship practice. "That's quite good. Now let your fingers rest for a little bit, and look over this bit of French."

"Have you seen any of the fairies yet?" she asked him.

He shook his head. "Not a wisp of hair nor a flutter of wing," he told her, as the others all looked up from their work and shook their heads as well. "Not inside nor out. I think Stepmother frightened them all right away."

"That *does* argue for her having magic, though," Ben said slowly. "We should be careful around her, and not talk about her, in case she's listening, somehow."

"I'd as lief not talk about her at all," said Gus, with a scowl.

Cook was just as good as her word when the time came for luncheon; there was plenty of brown bread and bacon dripping to spread on it, good plain cheese, a whole dish of pickles, a plum jam tart each, and rose-hip tea—and a replenishment of the potatoes, apples, and nuts. Tea time meant chamomile, more brown bread and jam, cheese, and little apple tarts. And when supper came around, there was plenty more brown bread, a lovely stew with lots of vegetables, thick brown gravy and even some bits of meat, mashed parsnips, mint tea, and currant jam tarts. It was a good thing, too, because the smell of the meal coming up the stairs made them as ravenous as wolves, even after that good luncheon and tea.

Afterward, when everything had been cleared away, Ben and Arthur set to roasting more nuts on the fire, and Gus screwed his face up, as if he was screwing up his courage, and asked, "What do you remember about Mama? Nobody's talked about her since she went away."

The two oldest twins looked at each other, and Ben shrugged. "Father wasn't always the way he is now," Arthur said carefully. "I remember him being jolly with us. After you and Carl were born, though, David, something happened. I don't know what it was. Just that he spent less and less time with her and more time with the business of the manor and the manor farms. And when she tried to get close to him, he'd just go behind his newspaper, or tell her not to be silly, that he was busy. After Felix and Emil were born, she stopped trying to engage him at all."

"I don't remember it that way. And anyway, Father loses interest in things after he gets them," Ben said, with a touch of cruelty. "And don't look at me that way, Arthur, you know it's true. Don't you remember all his pastimes? For a while nothing would do but that he go riding out to the fox hunts every chance he got—then he sold all his hunters but three one summer and never rode to the hunt again. There were at least six different schemes he had for improving the manor farms, but he lost interest in all of them before a season was over, and that was including the scheme to raise racehorses and hunters. Once he has something, if it takes too much effort, he gives up on it; I think Mama was too much effort for him."

"But—well, he might have been impatient with Mama, but I don't remember him being indifferent," Arthur objected, with a little heat. "And I remember him actually playing with us, and prompting us to recite our lessons."

"*You,* maybe. You're the oldest and the heir. *I* was just the spare, and then there were two more spares, then two more spares, then one more spare." Ben sounded really angry. "He didn't care about me. Not as long as he had you."

"That's not true!" Arthur exclaimed.

"It is, and you know it is. How many times did he ever say one good thing to me? I can count them on one hand and have fingers left over." Ben rose to his feet and stood over his twin, fists clenched. "And he treated Mama the same way, once Elena and Gus were born."

"*Stop!*" Elena cried, on the verge of tears. "Oh, stop, do! Arthur, you are always making excuses for Father, you know you are!"

Arthur got very red in the face, but he didn't get to his feet. Ben stood over him, glaring, then after Elena tugged at his sleeve for what felt like an hour, he finally sat down. "I suppose you'll just say I was always taking Mama's side," he grumbled. "But she left *me*, when she left all of us. So there, see, I am not taking her side. You just always wanted to please Father, and because you're the oldest, you were the only one of us that could."

Arthur grumbled, but hung his head. "I guess that's fair."

Elena sighed. At least the fight was over.

"And . . . now he has something new, so I guess he'll treat me the way he treats the rest of you. Or actually, he's already doing that. Here I am in exile in the schoolroom with the rest of you." Arthur made a face. "Maybe that's not so bad. It made me tired, trying to figure out ways to please him. But he wasn't indifferent to the rest of you; Ben, even you have to admit that he was more forgetful than anything. It was only when she left us that he turned cold, the way he is now." He sighed. "All I remember is that Father went to Bath for some reason. I remember Mama coming in to kiss us all goodnight, and then some time during that next day she disappeared, and Father's steward sent for him when no one could find her. When Father came back, he told us she had 'gone home to her people.' But he never told us anything about her people, and neither did Mama. It's almost as if she was some kind of fairy-tale creature that decided to vanish because— well, maybe because he lost interest in her."

He looked to Ben, who nodded. "I've thought about that," Arthur said. "I think Elena was right; I think she had magic in her, the same magic that lets us see the fairies. Maybe Father even knew about it, and that's why he married her. Maybe he wanted magic too, and thought it could be taught, or something,

THE CYPRIAN

and found out it couldn't be. So she used the fairies to get her own family to come for her."

"Or it's just as likely that once he had enough children—lots of *spares*—he lost interest in her like he did in everything else," Ben growled.

"I just don't know why she'd abandon us like that," Felix said plaintively, too upset even to reach for one of the hot nuts. "*We* all loved her!"

"All the fairy tales Nanny told us say not to trust the fairies," Elena put in, softly and sadly. "The fairy tales say they don't have hearts and souls. That's why they leave their own babies as changelings and steal human babies."

Ben's face looked as if he was struggling inside himself. "I know she loved us," he said, finally. "But I also know that she felt trapped. And what do you think Father would do to her if he caught her again?"

It was Arthur who finally answered into the silence, speaking slowly and reluctantly. "He'd make sure she could never escape from him again."

Ben nodded, as they all listened, cooling nuts forgotten. "And if she came back for us, she *would* be caught. I—I guess she thought he'd take care of us, because we're *his*."

"She didn't count on him marrying anyone else, did she?" Felix asked, bitterly.

This time Arthur spoke up. "I don't actually know how he managed to be able to do that," he admitted. "It's almost impossible to get a divorce. Unless he . . . oh, he'd hate that."

"Say she ran away with another man?" Ben asked, so cynically that Elena was shocked. "He *would* hate that, and that's probably why he never did it until now. But did you *see* the way he looks at Stepmother?"

"Besotted," said Elena into the silence.

"So he would do anything for her, including making himself look foolish in the law courts. Which explains why he let her take over *everything*, exile us to the schoolroom, and dismiss Nanny and Beecham." Ben's lower lip quivered a little. "I'm not *entirely* sure he'll let us go to university."

Arthur shrugged. "So what if he doesn't? It's not as if he can lock us up in the schoolroom once we're of age. Too many people already know about us and will start asking about us, because they have children the same age we are. He made the mistake of showing us off too many times."

Ben got control of himself again, as Elena patted his hand for comfort. "No point in worrying about something that hasn't happened yet," he said, after a long moment. "Thanks to Elena, at least Stepmother can't starve us. And I will be d—" he looked down at Elena, and changed what he was going to say. "I will be blown if I do anything that lets her claim we're dunces who won't succeed at university."

"Neither will I," Arthur agreed firmly, and looked at the younger boys. "And neither should you. If you want to escape her, you'll crack your heads over your books. If *nothing* else, once you've learned enough, you can go be a tutor like Beecham."

"But *Elena* can't!" Gus wailed, grabbing her hand, and she almost cried, seeing this demonstration that Gus was actually thinking of her, the way he used to when they were much younger and could scarcely be separated.

"No, but *I* can study religion and get a living, and I can bring her with me as my housekeeper," David said, surprising all of them. "Father won't dare shame himself by getting me a living at some poor parish; he'll not want tongues wagging, so he'll do me handsome. I'll do it, too! And once everyone knows that she's my sister, they'll know she's gentry, and when they see everything she can do, they'll line up to court her! She'll have a lovely little cottage with maybe a handsome young doctor who won't let anyone make her unhappy!"

"Or she can start a lady's boarding school," Arthur said thoughtfully. "She don't need to know dancing and music herself, she can hire masters to teach those things."

That got all of their minds off Mama and onto ways to help Elena escape without her being able to do the kinds of things that they could do, like join the navy or the army. She let them rattle on, happy that they were getting their appetites back and tucking into the neglected nuts, even if she didn't much like most of their ideas. Being David's housekeeper wouldn't be bad, at least as long as he was unmarried, but he *would* get married eventually, and she rather doubted his wife would like a spinster underfoot. She doubted even a young doctor would want a wife without a portion of her own. But she didn't like to think of any of that, and anyway, that would be *years* away. It just made her feel a little better to know they were thinking about her and weren't going to abandon her to live alone here, under Stepmother's thumb.

Silly, you wouldn't be alone. Arthur would be here. He's Father's heir, and Father will want him close enough as long as they don't quarrel. Arthur is too sensible to quarrel with Father.

So she listened to them make all kinds of wild plans—Gus, of course, was all for running away to the colonies and sending for her once he had made a fortune. And finally, when she thought they were so engrossed in their plans—stories, really, as much building castles in the air as anything—she packed up her workbasket and went to bed.

3

The weather continued to be as miserable as anything Elena ever remembered, which meant they were all cooped up in the schoolroom and nursery. That might have brought on quarreling, except that Arthur had had a very clever idea. Since neither Father nor Stepmother had troubled themselves to come up to this part of the house, Arthur organized a general clean-out of all the toys and too-small furniture and picture books. Then he did the same with Nanny's old room as well as Beecham's. Emil and Felix got those rooms, leaving Gus in glorious sole possession of the room he had shared with them. It turned out that Beecham had had a study as well as a bedroom, so Carl got the study, and David got their old room to himself. The five younger boys were so busy fixing up the rooms to their personal liking that they had no thought for quarreling. And this meant everyone had their own room and privacy, and rather than quarreling, could retreat to their own space to cool their tempers when differences cropped up.

Once all of the discarded things were up in the attic, and during a day when Father and Stepmother were out making visits and were not there to ask about the noise, Arthur had them all bring old furniture down from the attic to refurnish the former nursery. There was nothing wrong with any of it; it was just outmoded and battered, so they were able to make themselves a kind of parlor of their very own. There was plenty of shelf space now for books, so a series of raids on the library saw some very interesting books brought up to be enjoyed.

But even more critical than that, Arthur and Ben constructed hiding places for food in that parlor. With Mrs. Farthingworth and Mrs. Banning's collusion, the potatoes, nuts, and apples were joined by pots of very common jams and honey, raisins and currants, a sack of oatmeal and another of barley, several kinds of dried beans and peas in casks, their own little "root cellar" of winter vegetables and cabbage, a battered old kettle, jars of herbs for making tea and flavoring soups, and an old stew pot for making the soup. If you didn't know where those things were, you would never have found them. The kettle didn't need cleaning between uses, just rinsing, and if they needed to use the stewpot, Rosie and Jenny would take it down after they brought up the dishes and bread and any other food the children had been allotted from the kitchen for that meal, and bring it back up after they came to fetch the dirty crockery.

If it hadn't been for this cleverness, they would have subsisted on bread and water nearly every other meal. Cook tried to keep them properly fed, but Stepmother had installed a brand new man-cook, a Frenchman named Monsieur Paul, who kept a sharp eye on everything in the kitchen. He *did* ignore everything he deemed "peasant food," but due to Stepmother's demands for much fancier meals than the children ever remembered being served outside of supper parties, Cook sometimes didn't have time to make them soups or stews or even oatmeal or stewed barley.

But Cook *did* send up Rosie and Jenny, who knew how to make all manner of simple things, and smuggled up root vegetables under the firewood regularly. Jenny in particular taught all of them how to cook these simple dishes, so although their meals were plain and monotonous more often than not, at least they weren't going hungry. They never once burned anything, either; food smells could be explained away by "a wind in the chimney," but not the smells of burning victuals.

The one thing that Stepmother didn't seem to be conspiring to short them on was firewood. Sometimes Elena wondered if that wasn't because Stepmother never really paid attention to things like fires—for her, they were just *there*; she never had to tend one herself, they were always alight when she rose and banked when she went to bed, and she never saw the building or feeding of them, nor the sweeping up of ash, nor the daily blacking of grates and firedogs.

Candles, though. . . .

The luxury of beeswax candles was no longer allotted to them. They got tallow, two for the schoolroom and two for the sitting room, plus one apiece for the bedrooms. Tallow candles needed to be carefully watched, and the wicks trimmed regularly, or they would gutter and spill hot tallow all over everything. So generally, when Arthur and Ben declared that the school day was over, they took the schoolroom candles into their parlor, and everyone took a turn at minding one. Tallow for candles wasn't fit to be eaten, but Arthur had the clever idea of saving the stubs, melting them into cracked cups, and installing wicks, so that gave them candles they could use in their rooms without the fear of setting fire to something if they fell asleep.

The first Sunday of Stepmother's residence, with only the moves to new bedrooms done, they all went down dressed in their best, unsure if they would be going to church in the village since Nanny and Beecham were not there to accompany them. The other servants usually went to the early service before breakfast before dawn, led by Mrs. Farthingworth. Hobart generally went with them, Nanny, and Beecham. The question was, would Hobart—who generally held himself aloof from the children—order the coach for them all, or just accompany the other servants? But to Elena's surprise, Father and Stepmother appeared downstairs with the butler Hobart, Stepmother's sharp-faced maid, and Stephens, Father's valet. So two coaches were required; they crammed into the old one as usual, Hobart sat up top with the old coachman Grimes, and Father, Stepmother, and their personal servants went in the new coach. The family pew at the church was very crowded, and Elena could practically feel all the villagers behind them burning holes in the backs of their heads with their eyes as they tried to make out whatever they could of the new ladyship.

Stepmother seemed bored; Father couldn't look at her without being rude to the vicar, but Elena saw him holding her hand under cover of holding the hymn book for her. She didn't sing, and neither did Father, but the rest of them made up for that. After the service Vicar Steadman fell all over himself to greet them both obsequiously. Elena was embarrassed for him. He kept going on about how delightful her ladyship's welcome supper had been, and how pleased he was that they had thought to invite him, and it was just as well that the old coach was at the end of the gravel walk almost as soon as they left the church. The children were able to pile into it and out of sight of Stepmother and Father before any of them lost countenance. Hobart seemed not averse to making a getaway with them.

As soon as the wheels were turning, Arthur bowed to Ben, his face all screwed up into an unctuous expression. "Oh! Lady Whitstone! How *good* of you to *grace* us with your *august presence* on such an *inclement morning*!"

Ben broke into laughter. "Oh, he's angling for another supper, especially with the new *chef* in the kitchen, I'll be bound."

"There's certainly no point in looking to him for anything other than sermons on how grateful we must be to have a new mother," Felix said in disgust.

"Well, I'm just glad Whitstone Village is not one of the vacant livings at Father's disposal," David put in, from where he was squashed up against Elena. "I don't think I could bear looking at Stepmother's face without preaching a sermon about the duties of a mother to her children."

"I do wish I could work magic to spy on them just now." Arthur smirked. "They're going to be trapped there for at least a quarter hour while the vicar toad-eats, tries to get Stepmother to volunteer for *something*, and tries to pry money out of Father for church improvements. They won't be able to leave without looking rude, and you know how Father feels about appearances."

They all piled out of the coach as fast as they could so Grimes could get himself and the horses out of the cold, and ran inside. There was still no sign of the new coach, and Elena wished maliciously that Stepmother could be trapped out in front of the church for at least another half hour or more.

She hurried out of her clothing, and into her more comfortable gown, then dragooned Gus and David into going down to the kitchen with her. Sunday's elaborate roast meant most of the servants would be too busy to bring anything up to the schoolroom until much later, and she was hungry *now*.

Mrs. Banning greeted her with relief, freed Jenny from her duties at the sink, and sent them all back upstairs with the usual laundry baskets of crockery, silverware, and provisions. It was a far cry from what they would have gotten if they'd sat down to table with Father as had been the case before Stepmother's arrival, but Mrs. Banning managed to slip in a bit more than usual.

They ate quickly, and Ben and Arthur took down the soiled crockery themselves, before they all retreated to their rooms. Sunday meant they were supposed to be reading the Bible or other "improving" work, not stories, and certainly not together playing games. Elena took the pillows from her bed and made up a comfortable seat on her little hearth, propped up a book of Bible stories she already knew by heart where she could "read" it, and set to work on mending her brothers' clothing. They were dreadfully hard on stockings in particular, and she had a notion for making a kind of felted sole with toes to protect the most vulnerable parts. By all rights, these things should have been done by the two laundry maids, but there was no sign that this would happen any time before they ran out of stockings and smallclothes.

She was so used to Nanny barging into her room that she didn't turn a hair when someone shoved the door open without a knock. She looked up, thinking it was Gus or Ben, and tried not to blanch when she saw it was Stepmother.

She was just very glad that they had all anticipated that Father or Stepmother was likely to send *someone* up to make sure they were all spending their Sunday appropriately.

She just hadn't thought Stepmother would have come up herself.

She scrambled to her feet, mending in one hand, and curtsied. "Good afternoon, ma'am," she said, faintly.

Stepmother said nothing, but her eyes lit on the mending, then went to the book, which had fallen over, face up. She nodded.

"I am pleased to see that you are employing yourself in a useful and improving manner," the woman said. "Go on as you have begun."

"Yes, ma'am," Elena said to the already closed door, and heaved a sigh of relief.

I don't think she'll come back up here today. If we are very lucky, she'll stay downstairs from now on as long as we're quiet. She closed the book of Bible stories and took another out from under her mattress, a much more satisfying volume Arthur had found for her in the library about Princess Elizabeth Tudor.

By the time Gus came to collect her for tea, she'd finished the mending and was able to give them all back their clothing.

By the next Sunday, they had their own parlor set up, and to everyone's pleasure, neither Father nor Stepmother was inclined to attend Sunday services. The vicar was not pleased, but at least he didn't blame the siblings for their absence, and did not keep them standing at the door of the church for any longer than to tell them that "your good parents are missed," and that he hoped whatever indisposition kept them away would soon be cured.

Ben and Arthur, however, were met with the unwelcome announcement from Hobart that Father expected them to take luncheon in the dining room.

With a sigh, they slumped their way deeper into the manor, while David, Emil, and Carl went off to the kitchen.

The two eldest did not make an appearance back upstairs until after the crockery and soup pot had been cleared away and their younger siblings were curled up under spare blankets or coverlets in their little "parlor," munching apples and amusing themselves. David was drawing next to the fire, Carl was reading, and Felix was building another, more elaborate boat for sailing on the pond when summer came again. Emil was brooding, staring into the fire and occasionally poking or feeding it. Elena, of course, was knitting. She wanted to get Stepmother's shawl out of the way quickly so that she could start on more Christmas presents. She wanted to make things for the servants who had been going out of their way to help them. Pretty bonnets for Jenny and Rosie would be the easiest. She thought perhaps a lace fichu each for Mrs. Farthingworth and Mrs. Banning, because neither of them had much of anything with lace on it. But perhaps Mrs. Farthingworth would more appreciate fingerless gloves to keep her hands warm? Gus was in the window seat, though what could be so interesting outside, Elena could not imagine.

They all looked up as soon as they heard the familiar footsteps of their elder brothers. Arthur was first through the door, followed by Ben.

"Not even two slices of roast beef and iced cakes was worth that," Arthur said, looking for an empty chair to fling himself into. "The Spanish Inquisition would have been more pleasant than Father quizzing us about our studies."

"In between making calf eyes at Stepmother," Ben added sourly. "And I don't like that Frenchified food half as much as Mrs. Banning's. Too many fancy sauces."

"Did he ask about us?" Emil asked.

"Only what we were teaching you. We gave a good account of you all." Elena handed Ben a soft woolen blanket she had been keeping warm for him, and he joined Emil and David at the fire.

"There's still no sign of the fairies," Gus announced forlornly from the window. "I wish they would come back. I was hoping we could ask them to spy for us. Or at least keep a lookout and warn us when Stepmother or that cat-faced maid of hers are coming."

"What do you want the fairies to spy for?" Ben asked, sticking his feet between David and Emil to get them warm.

"I want to know what she's doing when she's not got Father following her about like he's on leading-strings," said Gus, with a dark look. "If she's magic, and if she's *doing* magic, I want to know about it."

Ben shook his head. "If she is, she'll take great care about it. I don't think any of us would have a chance at catching her at it. Though . . ." He looked thoughtful. "Well, perhaps we can sharpen our own magic. We can see the fairies, so if we start looking for things out of the ordinary, we might be able to see more things that are magic. It can't hurt to try."

Elena got the distinct feeling that he was saying that just to keep Gus pacified. Still, it wasn't a bad idea. "What would be out of the ordinary, though?" she asked.

"I . . . don't know," Ben admitted. "The fairies have a kind of glow about them, though. Maybe that?"

"It's a place to start," Arthur said, and pulled a stool up closer to the fire. "Stepmother was not very pleasant this evening. I hope you all had a better time of it than we did. She didn't say a word but looked at us as if we were some species of vermin."

"We did hold our own with Father, however." Ben got an apple, and began methodically peeling it. "He tried to catch us out several times, and never could." He turned his attention from the apple to his younger brothers. "Just you all be certain of your lessons. I don't know that he'll interrogate you about them, but I don't know that he *won't*, either." He took the long peel, draped it over a stick, and held it in the fire until it was crisp, then ate it. Only then did he eat the rest of his apple. "I don't understand what's changed," he added fretfully. "After Mama left, he might have turned cold, but this was positively antagonistic."

"Maybe he thinks he can replace us with children he has with Stepmother," Elena said in a soft voice.

"By Jove, you may be right," Ben said, turning to her in surprise. "That never occurred to me. The estate is entailed, but that doesn't mean *we* inherit if he doesn't want us to. All he has to do is specify any new sons he has."

"Is that right?" David asked. "I'm not sure that's right."

"All the more reason to get to university and establish ourselves in professions where we can support ourselves," Arthur said firmly, ignoring his question. "The law, the clergy, honestly I wouldn't mind being a tutor like Beecham if it came to that." He laughed bitterly. "After all, it's not as if we are used to living in luxury! If it weren't for the servants, we'd be missing meals, and if it weren't for Elena and her clever fingers, we'd be in rags."

Elena felt her cheeks growing hot, but it was with pleasure.

"Do you think he'd buy me a set of colors?" Gus asked, out of nowhere.

"I suppose it depends on how much a commission would cost, and whether Stepmother would be so grateful to see the end of you that she'd encourage him to do so," David said, when neither Arthur nor Ben had an answer.

"Well, if he *won't*, I'll just join up." Gus looked more

determined than Elena had ever seen him before. "It can't be worse than staying here."

"Don't do that," David admonished. "Emigrate to Canada. Everyone says that a fellow with determination can make a lot of himself there."

"Maybe that's what we *all* ought to do," Ben said thoughtfully, and looked at Arthur. "Men of the law are needed everywhere. Between the two of us, we could support everyone while the rest of you figured out how to find employment. Or, yes, join the army; I expect as sons of a gentleman they'd be happy to see you as officers without needing to purchase a commission."

"I'm not sure that's right, either, unless . . . unless you go somewhere that officers are being killed," said David.

"And Elena can take care of all of us," said Emil, copying Ben's trick with the apple peel. "The only question is how we'd get money for passage."

That seemed insurmountable, and they fell into silence. "Well," Ben finally said. "It's a year or more before we can go, and then four years or so until we can pass our examinations. That's a lot of time. Perhaps she won't have sons, or even any children at all. Perhaps we can find someone to help us, or we can persuade Stepmother that we won't stand in the way of her ambition if she gets Father to set us all up and let us go."

The weather finally took a turn for the better the next day, which allowed Elena to take her usual walk in the garden in the afternoon, and the boys to run much farther afield once all their lessons were done for the day. She was very glad to be out of the house; there was the illusion of freedom out here in the fresh air, even if the freedom wasn't real.

She enjoyed wandering the winding paths in the shrubbery, which was—at least according to visitors—a very good, mature, and attractive part of the garden. She was short enough that even the smaller bushes tended to overtop her, which gave her the feeling that she was alone in a kind of wilderness. And even though it was the middle of October, this was a mixed shrubbery, so there were still parts of it that were green, and on some of the bushes, there were still berries that birds enjoyed, if people did not.

And this was where she found a fairy, at long last.

If she hadn't been paying attention, she would have missed it. It had gray, cobwebby clothing, gray-brown wings like a sparrow, and gray-brown hair. It perched amid a cluster of brown leaves that had not yet fallen, and watched her with wary, dark eyes.

She sidled up to the bush it was in, pretended to examine something else, and whispered, "Hello. Are you well?"

Cautiously the little thing nodded imperceptibly.

"Are you all afraid of my stepmother? The new lady?" She assumed it would know that by "you all" she meant all of the fairies who used to hang about her and her brothers.

Again, the cautious nod.

She sighed. If the fairy wouldn't speak, getting information from it would take a while. "Is she magic? My stepmother, I mean."

This time instead of nodding, the little thing shivered all over, as if terrified.

It took a good quarter of an hour, and even then, Elena didn't learn what she wanted to, because the fairy was startled into disappearing by the approach of one of the gardeners. She resumed her own walk, trying to wring every particle of knowledge out of the "yes" and "no" answers she'd gotten.

The trouble was, she didn't really know what questions to ask. *Arthur would be so much better at this than me. Or Ben.* But at least she had found out that Stepmother had some unspecified sort of magic, that her presence was the reason for the fairies' absence, that the fairies could not (or would not) help in any way. It was clear that the fairies were terrified of their stepmother, though since this one refused to speak, there was no telling why.

She emerged from the shrubbery not much wiser than she had entered it. The place where this path exited boasted a very pretty, but deep, ornamental pond. In keeping with the general illusion of wilderness here, its boundaries were irregular, and there were artificially rustic benches around it. As she skirted the edge, a bit of paper fluttered out from beneath one of them.

She followed it before the wind could carry it away and snatched it up.

It had been torn from something larger. The words, carefully printed on it in block letters, were in Latin. She knew just barely enough to recognize them as being in that language, though not enough to translate them. *"Aqua in sanguine tuo,"* the first line read. Then there was just the beginning of a second line, *"Tantum me . . ."* and nothing more.

It wasn't her father's handwriting. It wasn't Mrs. Banning or Mrs. Farthingworth. Hobart, perhaps? She didn't think it was Beecham, and it certainly wasn't one of her brothers.

She slipped the scrap into a pocket, and a sharp breeze sprang up out of nowhere, cutting right through her pelisse. She shivered and decided to go back to the house. The fire in the old nursery suddenly seemed very desirable.

". . . and you couldn't get the fairy to say anything at all?" Ben asked, when she told all of them what had happened over tea.

"She was very frightened," Elena said apologetically. "I didn't want to press her too hard." Then she remembered the scrap of paper she had found, and pulled it out of her pocket. "I found this; it blew out from under a bush at the edge of the pond."

Ben took it from her, and frowned over it. "It looks like a bit of poetry, but it's nothing Beecham ever taught us. I wonder who wrote it?"

Arthur took the scrap from him. "I wonder *why* they wrote it, unless they were trying to write a poem in Latin on their own. *The water in your blood only . . . me.* What a strange thing to write! And it doesn't say what the 'water in your blood' is doing for the writer. And why 'water in your blood'? It doesn't sound like a love poem."

"Calls only to me?" Ben hazarded. "I don't know. What are the four humors again?"

"Blood, yellow bile, black bile, and phlegm," said Carl with some authority. "Blood is supposed to be a mixture of all four elements, earth, air, fire, and water. Blood corresponds to spring, according to Galen."

"So what is water in the blood supposed to be?" Ben asked, handing him the scrap of paper.

"Well, water corresponds to winter, and it's cold, so too much water in the blood would be an imbalance that would make you slow, cold, not very emotional, and might give you a disease of the lungs or brain," Carl told them. "And if blood is spring, but water is winter, too much water in the blood is pulling you in the opposite direction of where your health should be. So maybe it's not a poem or anything to do with love. Maybe it's a kind of medical direction."

"Cold, slow, not very emotional." Arthur snorted. "That sounds like Father. Maybe it's something Doctor Fisher gave him to remind him to take some medicine or tonic."

"Well, if so, it looks like he tore it up, or at least was awfully careless with it." Ben turned the scrap over and over in his fingers, but apparently couldn't glean any more information from it. "It's definitely not Father's hand, nor Beecham's, not even printing. I confess that I am baffled. There isn't anyone else closer than the vicar who would know Latin."

"I certainly can't imagine Stepmother knowing any Latin." Emil snorted. "She strikes me as the sort of person who never bothers to learn about anything that isn't immediately useful *to her*."

Elena took a nervous look over her shoulder. "Be careful!" she whispered. "If even the fairies are afraid of her, we shouldn't be saying things like that."

"Elena is right," Ben agreed. "But that does answer one question; I cannot imagine why the fairies would be afraid of her if she doesn't know some kind of magic. So we need to take a great deal of care."

"The best thing we can do is keep to ourselves as much as possible, and be very respectful of her when we *must* be around her." Arthur was stating the obvious, Elena thought, but perhaps he needed to for the sake of the three youngest boys. "We must not give her any excuse to work against us. No matter how badly she treats us, we must be meek. I think Mrs. Farthingworth and Mrs. Banning are on our side, and I know Rosie and Jenny are. They won't let us starve." He looked around at that. "Speaking of which . . . I am starving. I wonder where Rosie is?"

"Rosie be right here, Master Arthur," Rosie said, just coming in the door with her laundry basket full of crockery. "Right sorry I am to be late, and sorrier I ain't got much for you, but the kitchen's all in a state, and Mrs. Banning sent up what she could."

Arthur jumped up and took the basket from her, and laid out the plates and cups. There was the water for the kettle, and three nice loaves of brown bread, but only cheese, butter, pickles, and raw carrots by way of food, plus a pot of mustard. "Why is the kitchen in a state?" he asked.

"Oh, sir! You would not believe the cheek!" Rosie replied, with more indignation than Elena had ever heard in her voice. "Vicar *and* his wife come over, just afore teatime, *and* his two lads, and a'course, master must ask 'em to tea, and didn't they gobble! *Then* they stayed and stayed and stayed, and finally master asked 'em to supper! Well, imagine how Mon-sewer Paul and Mrs. Banning took *that*, four more mouths to feed, and them only planning on feeding two! So every last thing that was left over from luncheon and tea got gathered up and put into a soup, or made into something else, and ham to come out of the larder, and steaks to be fried up 'cause there weren't no time for a roast, and chickens to be killed and plucked, and I'm right glad I don't know no French, cause I do think Mon-sewer was cursing to turn the air blue! And oh, they gobbled like they hadn't just had a gracious great tea! I'd be right ashamed of Vicar if I wasn't chapel and not church," she added primly. "So Mrs. Banning's 'pologies, but this is the best she could do. Mon-sewer feels so bad, he peeled the carrots with his own two hands. They got fruit and cheese for pudding, and they should be glad of it, for there weren't no time to bake nothin' for all that crowd."

"Tell Mrs. Banning that it's fine," Ben told her, patting her on the head. "Well, I suspect there is one good thing to come out of Vicar's greed. I am dead certain that Msr. Paul and Mrs. Banning are no longer enemies."

Rosie broke out in a peal of laughter. "Right you are, Master Ben! They weren't neither of them a-going to let their kitchen be thought of poorly, so they hauled alongside together like a pair in harness, and when the fruit went up, they sat down together and she fanned him with her apron, and he fanned her with his towel, and arter they put the basket together they poured each other tea and they're tradin' stories like old friends!"

"There's a mercy," Elena breathed. "Let there be concord!"

"Well, look, I don't like you to be wantin' something hot, so let me show you a trick," Rosie said. "Slice and toast some o' that bread and spread some mustard on it."

There were four sets of tongs up here now, so it didn't take long for bread to be toasted. Meanwhile Rosie took one of the ash shovels, heated it enough to melt some butter in it, and laid a generous slice of cheese in the shovel. It wasn't long before it was melted, and she slid the hot cheese right over the toasted bread on one of the plates. "It ain't a rarebit," she said apologetically, "But it ain't far off. It's what we all be eating downstairs since them visitors are gobbling everything up."

Arthur was already setting to with knife and fork, blowing on the bites first to keep from burning himself. "No need to apologize, Rosie, this is capital!" he said, as Ben set up all the shovels they had and passed them to Emil and Carl, reserving one for himself. Elena nibbled a carrot, resigned to getting her share last, but Ben served her before he made a plate for himself.

Satisfied that she had done her best, Rosie went back downstairs, leaving them to their meal.

"I wonder how Stepmother is taking all of this," Elena said aloud. "I should think she would be furious."

"I druther not find out," Gus replied, and buttered up a shovel for a second round, which he—somewhat to her surprise—generously shared with her. "I could do with never seeing her again, ever."

Elena was hard at work at her penmanship, making a careful copy of the Lord's Prayer in Spenserian script, when her stepmother's cat-faced maid came barging into the schoolroom without so much as a knock. She wasn't quiet about it, either, so all eight of the siblings raised their heads from their work and turned at nearly the same moment, while the maid surveyed them with disdain, then pointed a long and perfectly manicured finger at Elena.

"Her ladyship requires your presence," the woman said, stiffly, in a melodious and accented voice. "Now." No "If you please," and no indication that she considered Elena to be anything but an inferior creature and potentially a great deal of trouble. But from the little that Elena had observed, which included the fact that the maid wore clothing that was far superior to anything a servant of her position should, Elena had deduced that the maid was probably a close confidant of her stepmother, that the clothing was probably Stepmother's cast-offs, and that, thus, it would be unwise to disobey, much less anger her. So she carefully cleaned her pen, corked the ink bottle, and set her work aside, and got to her feet.

Once she was standing, the woman turned on her heel, showing a bit of kid boot, and strode away, not looking to see if Elena was following. She was quite tall, and Elena was quite short, so Elena had to scramble to keep up. The maid did move gracefully, though, and practically glided down the stairs.

Once they were on the first floor, Elena was fairly certain that they were going to the winter parlor, and slowed down just a little bit, so as not to arrive ruffled and out of breath. The maid paused at the entrance to the winter parlor and looked back at her, frowning and tapping her foot impatiently, before proceeding into the room before her.

That was very rude, and more than that, was extremely impertinent. No servant should precede a member of the family into a room. A servant should stand at the door, announce the person in question, and only go into the room *behind* their superior. But this neglect of protocol certainly showed Elena where *she* stood in her stepmother's eyes.

The winter parlor was not a room she had spent much time in; Father did not like the children to be seen outside their own set of rooms upstairs. It was light and airy, with high ceilings, white-painted walls, rugs on the floor, and comfortable, upholstered furniture. And it had a huge fire in the fireplace, much larger than anything they were allowed in their rooms, a fire that lent the space a comfortable warmth Elena could feel even from the doorway.

"I've brought the child, my lady," the maid said, as Elena reached the door.

"Very good, Fleurette," Stepmother replied—which told

Elena two things. The maid's name, which she had not known until that moment, and that, as her accent had suggested, she must be French.

Elena paused in the doorway, clasping her hands together nervously, her heart beating faster with anxiety. Fleurette actually came back to the doorway and shoved her into the room with a hand between her shoulder blades. She stumbled over the threshold and could not help but notice the faint smile on her stepmother's lips as she hunched her shoulders, dropped her eyes, and approached with the caution she would give a serpent.

"Don't hunch, child," Stepmother said, coldly. "You are already unattractive enough without rounding your shoulders."

That stung. Elena had no illusions about her beauty, or lack of it, but being called outright unattractive brought the suggestion of tears to her eyes and a lump to her throat. She straightened up with an effort, but kept her eyes cast down.

"Why do you think I summoned you here?" Stepmother asked, as Elena locked her gaze on the center motif of a small India carpet at Stepmother's feet.

"I don't know, ma'am," Elena replied, settling on "ma'am" as the least offensive thing she could call Stepmother. She had no intention of calling the woman "Mother," she might take offense at "Stepmother," and "my lady" seemed too servile. As silence filled the cozy parlor, she finally added, "I would not presume."

"And so you should not," Stepmother said. "Look up at me."

Reluctantly she raised her eyes; she looked, not into her stepmother's eyes, but steadfastly at her chin.

Apparently that was not good enough. Stepmother reached out, took her chin in a tight grip, and raised her head so that she looked straight into Stepmother's eyes.

Elena tried not to wince away, though those cold, cold blue eyes bored into hers, made her feel like a mouse meeting the gaze of an owl, and sent her heart into a frenzy of fear. Eventually Stepmother let go of her chin, but her icy, hard gaze commanded that Elena not drop her eyes. She wanted to; she wanted to very badly. She even tried, briefly. But she *could* not. Stepmother's eyes filled her vision until they were the only thing she could see.

"Are you as good at mending as you are with fancywork?" Stepmother asked, after a pause so long that Elena wanted to scream.

"Yes, ma'am," Elena said faintly.

Stepmother snapped her fingers, and the maid handed her a small basket. In it were what looked like folded stockings and a few pairs of gloves. On top of the basket rested balls of darning cotton and silk in the same colors as the stockings. "See what you can do with these," Stepmother ordered. By the tone of voice, it was an order, and not a request.

"Yes, ma'am," Elena replied obediently, although the idea of handling Stepmother's intimate clothing made her skin crawl—and redoubled her unhappiness at adding yet another chore to the mending she was already doing for her brothers. She took the basket awkwardly, and found that, since it did not have a handle, she would have to hold and carry it with both arms wrapped around it.

Stepmother sat back in the sofa she had selected for herself, a very comfortable piece upholstered all over in striped pale green silk, and one of two that faced each other beside the fireplace. Nothing like fully upholstered furnishings existed in the part of the house where the siblings lived—they were lucky to see thin upholstery on the seats of the chairs only. *She* did not have a workbasket beside her, as Elena did at all hours when she was not doing lessons or eating. The only things on the seat beside her were a small, very new book, most probably a novel, and a plate of candied cherries, glistening and glowing in the light as if they were giant rubies. Father did not approve of novels, and Father had forbidden food in this room, but then, what Father approved of seemed to no longer matter where Stepmother was concerned.

Stepmother picked up a cherry delicately, and bit into it, slowly, making a deliberate show out of eating it. Elena flushed a little, but with anger rather than embarrassment. This was nothing more nor less than bullying. Stepmother knew what she and her brothers were eating, and knew that they rarely got anything other than apples as a sweet, and when they did, it was nothing as indulgent as candied cherries.

She dropped her eyes to keep Stepmother from seeing the flash of anger in them, purely from instinct. Instead of looking up, she looked down into the basket she still held awkwardly. Silence chilled the air between them, a silence punctuated only by the sounds of the crackling fireplace, a silence she feared to break. She was not sure she could keep her temper if she did. Her cheeks flamed, and beneath her gown, her knees trembled. Her stomach knotted, and she clutched the basket to keep her hands from shaking. She was acutely conscious of Stepmother's perfume, something musky and cloying all at the same time, and certainly not Eau de Cologne, or the fresh, watery scent she remembered Mama wearing.

"Run along, now," Stepmother said, her tone silky, but dismissive. With her head down, Elena couldn't see her expression, but she assumed it was smug. *Why does she find it so important to humiliate me?* "I'm sure you don't need Fleurette to lead you back to your proper place. She has much more important things to do."

Elena turned and walked away, shaking with impotent rage. After all, what could she do? Father had never cared about her when Mama was still with them. She had become invisible to him when Mama left—and now? She was pretty certain that now any of the maids could put on her clothing and pass for her, so far as he was concerned.

Most of the time I think he forgets he even has a daughter.

Of all the people in this household, she was the most powerless. Even the scullery maids and hall boy had more agency than she did. She was expected, by custom and even law, to obey everything a parent told her to do—expected to do so without complaint, without argument, without hesitation. Her whereabouts had to be known every waking moment. And the person in charge of her? Stepmother. The servants had free days and afternoons off, unsupervised. The boys could go where they chose. If she disobeyed, she could be *cast off*, and then what would she do? She had no real skills except sewing. Perhaps—if she was very lucky—she could find her way to a big town and get employment in a *modiste*'s shop, but she would have to find one who would take her without an apprenticeship and without references.

And Stepmother could make that happen with no warning.

No one else had any authority over Stepmother. Only Father. And from the look of things, it was *she* who had all the authority over *him*, and not the other way around.

Behind her, she heard Stepmother and her maid laughing, and anger drove out any other emotion. Her first impulse was to turn and fling that basket back down the hall at them, but she instantly repressed it. There was no point in giving that woman a reason to make her and her siblings' lives any more uncomfortable.

We have enough to eat, even if it isn't what we used to have, we all have our own rooms, we have good fires in every room, and we're left alone. She could make things much worse for us. For me.

That didn't stop her from being furious, but she was very careful not to show her anger. Stepmother had magic and could have ways of watching her unseen. *Be wise as the serpent and harmless as the dove,* she reminded herself. Or, at least, *look* as harmless as the dove. Let Stepmother think that she and the others were cowed. *Me, most particularly.*

So she kept her head down and shoulders slumped, and walked as quickly as she could to the stairs and the relative safety of what she was now, in her mind, calling "our sanctuary." The hallway, with its strip of carpet down the center, patterned with bright streaks of sunlight from open doorways on the western side, gave way to the stairs, which gave way to the second-floor landing, then more stairs, then the third floor and the rooms reserved for any children and their nurses and nannies. Their floor. Sanctuary.

She stopped first in her own room, and put the basket down on her bed to assess what she had been charged with mending. No woolen stockings (how did that woman not suffer in the winter cold?), but fine cotton and both fine and heavy silk. Well, perhaps that woman didn't need woolen stockings, given the fact that Elena had no less than *six* pairs of silk stockings to mend, and certainly Stepmother had more than that in her possession. Silk, for all its light weight, was warm in the winter.

She examined all the stockings carefully; at least they had

been laundered before being turned over to her. Some had ladders, some had both ladders and a worn-out toe or holes. The cotton would be easier to mend by candlelight. The ladders, once all the threads were caught up, might need embroidered clocks to cover the hole that had started the ladder in the first place. Slowly, she felt her rage ebbing, and she took deep breaths, reminding herself that she could be an almost-unpaid drudge to a seamstress, working for food and a place in the shop to sleep. She reminded herself how much she loved embroidery. That this would be a pleasure if it weren't for whom the stockings belonged to.

She closed her eyes for a moment and steadied herself. *Being angry doesn't accomplish anything, except to be angry.* She felt her cheeks cool in the slight draft from her leaky window, and stood that way in the silence of her room until she could hear the faint sounds of distant voices elsewhere in the house. *Our parlor will be warm and nice. Ben might read us a story. There will be a good dinner, and even if the dinner is only toast and melted cheese and apples, it will still be more than poor beggars on the road can dream of.*

When she opened her eyes, calmer, at least for now, she reassessed her task, and was fairly certain that as far as the ladders and the holes went, she would succeed better than Stepmother could even imagine. As for the toes, she had an answer for that, because Stepmother would expect a darned toe, she was sure of it. There was nothing worse than a clumsily darned toe making a great lump in one's shoe, or the worse option, cutting the toe off to re-sew a new toe, which of course made the stocking too short. She was rather certain that Stepmother would make her pay for doing either of those. So she would re-knit the toe; tedious, and she almost hated to show off her skills, knowing it would only cause Stepmother to make her do more, and more complicated mending, but better that than bring on punitive malice.

She picked out a pair of fine white silk and another of heavier silk that were a bit shabbier, and took them with the matching thread and her workbasket to the old nursery.

The boys were still out except for Gus, otherwise they would have distributed themselves around the room. Gus's pink nose suggested he had been outside until a few moments ago, as they all usually were for at least an hour every afternoon. There was a very fine fire, and she felt the last of her anger melt away. For once, Gus noticed her arrival, and he frowned when he saw her come in. "What did that mean old cat want you to do now?" he asked, as she moved a chair to the window for the best light. Without being asked, he brought her a lap robe and tucked a second one around her shoulders to keep off the drafts. The light might be better here, but it was far from the fire.

"Shh!" she cautioned. "We don't know . . . she might be able to see or hear us!"

He shrugged. "I don't care."

"You will if she finds a way to keep Mrs. Banning from feeding us with anything but leftovers," she reminded him. "She wants me to mend her stockings."

Gus rolled his eyes, but didn't comment further, just bent down to tuck the lap robe in around her feet, which that touched her to no end.

"I suppose that fancy French miss she has as her personal maid is too good to do mending. Well, she *tried* to get rid of Butterburr today," he said instead.

"Our pony?" Elena gasped. "But—"

"Oh, don't worry. Grimes had an answer for that. He pointed out that the only dogcart we have is sized for a pony, and that if she wanted to learn to drive, she'd need to start with the dogcart before she could handle that fancy curricle she's been wanting. He said that Father told him to make room in the carriage house for a curricle or a gig, and since Father doesn't care to drive himself, I expect he's ordering her a present." Gus smirked. "Grimes is a good fellow. He tells me everything. I don't know how he knew she doesn't know how to drive, but he did. Maybe it just followed from the fact that she doesn't know how to ride, either. Grimes is too clever by half, has one ear in the stable and the other in the kitchen and somehow manages to know all the estate gossip as well."

"I hope she doesn't hurt poor Butterburr," Elena worried. Butterburr was at least fifteen years old, with a good ten more years in him; he had been the first ride for all of them, and unlike some ponies, had a steady temper and wasn't inclined to play tricks on a green rider. He saved those tricks for imposing his will on someone who thought they were a good enough rider or driver that they could make him do whatever they wanted.

"Butterburr is smarter than that. If she vexes him, he'll just step up his pace to a canter, and rattle her scrawny bones," Gus chuckled. "He's had four sets of us to learn all kinds of tricks on if he wants to teach someone a lesson."

Elena had to agree that this was true; he had outsmarted her more than once until she had learned it was best just to give him his way when it was about something that didn't matter. And if Stepmother tried a whip on him? Well, she would find out what it felt like to be helplessly clinging to reins that did nothing behind a runaway pony. Butterburr was as quick as a thought when it came to getting the bit in his teeth so he could run, and nothing made him run away faster than being mistreated. *She* never had, but Emil had once done so in a temper, and he'd learned the error of his ways by being dragged through every thicket on the estate and tumbled over Butterburr's neck into the farm pond at the end of the gallop. He'd come home wet, muddy, with his clothing torn and hair full of twigs, and Grimes had laughed at him. Butterburr had, of course, returned to the stable a half an hour earlier.

She picked out her smallest crochet hook, an expensive piece of equipment that she kept on a chain at all times to avoid losing it. Father hadn't even bought it for her; she had found it with most of the contents of her workbasket up in the attic. There had been a beautiful pair of shears and another of snips, a set of crochet hooks made of the finest steel wire, a larger set made of ivory, papers and papers of pins and needles, and ever so many more useful things of the best quality. She was shocked they had somehow escaped finding their way into the hands of one or more of the maids, or of Mrs. Farthingworth or even Nanny. All of these tools had been carefully laid away in one of the trunks that had held gowns that predated Mama's arrival as Father's wife. She thought perhaps they had all belonged to her Grandmamma, who had died before Father married. When she discovered them, it had felt like a beneficent gift from an unknown hand.

She could still remember with some embarrassment how she had squealed when she'd found the items, carefully wrapped in oiled paper and then in waxed canvas.

She bent her head to her task, carefully catching up the last stitch at the bottom of the ladder, then taking up the runner-threads one at a time, essentially re-knitting the stocking until she reached the top. This took great patience and a high degree of skill; she knew this, because she had once heard a lady-visitor complaining to another about the "scandalous" cost of such a service. Eavesdropping shamelessly, she had learned that there were actually women in the bigger towns and cities that performed such a service, often sitting in the display window of a haberdashery to show off their skill. The lady had claimed that their work was so fine that instead of a silk thread, they would use a human hair! Elena was not altogether certain if that was true or just a fable—but in this moment it occurred to her that if something terrible happened, perhaps she was not entirely without resources. This was a skill she could *prove* she had in the course of a quarter-hour, without relying on references she didn't have. Provided, of course, that she could get to a town.

When the ladder had been knitted up, she secured the top and bottom with an almost-invisible stitch, then examined every thread of the stocking for holes that had not yet begun to ladder, made certain that the toe and heel were in good order, and turned the stocking right side out again, stretching and massaging it until the last traces of the ladder and holes had been worked back into the fabric. Then she picked out a pretty pattern of clocks in a thicker white thread up the instep and the outside of the foot and leg, so that the embroidery showed white-on-white. In her opinion, this was far superior to colored or black clocks on white stockings, although the next pair was going to need colored thread to make the mending less visible by contrast, because they were in worse shape than the first pair she had chosen.

Gus flung himself into a chair by the fire and took up a piece of kindling to poke at the embers and form them into patterns to his liking as the rest of her brothers slowly came in. Stepmother's arrival had brought an end to servants waiting for them to take their outer coats away when they came in from outdoors, so they all tended to come up still dressed for the weather, and would hang their coats and neckscarves and caps up on pegs that had once held aprons, caps, and shawls for Nanny and the nursery maids.

From their chatter she gathered that they had all been in the stables, listening to Grimes dispense gossip from the kitchen. Grimes was proving to be a shrewd and observant informant. Mrs. Banning in particular liked him, and was inclined to share afternoon tea with him in her little "parlor" (which was really just a part of her room partitioned off from the rest by an old screen). From her, Grimes got all the gossip of the household, which he was not at all averse to sharing with the boys.

She, alas, was not allowed in the stable. It wasn't seemly. She might be exposed to "rough talk," although that consideration didn't seem to matter when it came to her brothers.

She worked on the second stocking while the boys shared what they'd learned today.

She soon learned why Fleurette was in the boys' bad graces, even though they'd had nothing to do with Stepmother's maid. Fleurette, it seemed, was in the habit of flirting in private with one after another of the male staff, then giving the poor lad a cruel and humiliating set-down in public. She had already worked her way through the house staff, and had launched her first sally into the stables. One of the two very handsome and brand-new grooms, Dick Jenson, had fallen for her trick, and although under normal circumstances this would have been the occasion for jeers—for he was very proud of his looks and the inroads he had made amongst the maids, atop of being new to the household—on this one occasion the stable denizens had taken this as an offense against one of their own.

That was when Felix unburdened himself of intelligence that none of the others had been privileged to hear. "—well, they're laying a trap for her," Felix confirmed. "Not but they wouldn't have told any of you, but young Sam owes me a favor or two, and let it slip. They all reckon Phillip will be her next flirt, but it'll be *him* leading *her* this time, pretending to be shy, so she'll try and see him alone. That's when they'll all show themselves, and shame the devil."

"Truly?" She finished the second white-on-white stocking, and moved to the shabbier pair. "I would have thought they would have preferred to see both of those fellows to perdition."

The two new grooms had come with the new coachman and the new carriage, and the rumor in the stables had been that Stepmother had picked them out herself. Elena wasn't supposed to be aware that such things went on, but—rumor ran both ways, from the stable to the kitchen, and as she had sat with Mrs. Banning, she had overheard Rosie, Jenny, and Simon speculating that Stepmother was probably readying a flirtation herself, with eyes on one or both.

"Well, Phillip's not so bad, and Dick was proper hurt, they say. And you know how it is, the best way to bring everyone over to your side is for an outsider to give you a set-down," Ben said wisely. "She's got *all* the airs *and* she's a Frenchy, so there you are."

Elena knew that none of the other maids liked Fleurette at all, because she did carry herself as if she was superior to all of them, and demanded special treatment, such as eating alone on a tray in her room rather than with everyone else in the staff dining room just off the kitchen. She claimed she could not abide the kitchen smells, which had put Mrs. Banning's back up immediately. Even Msr. Paul didn't like her.

I wonder if he knows something about her the rest of us don't. They were both French, after all. Msr. Paul always pretended not to hear her when she said something to him, or so Rosie claimed.

Fleurette always found fault with how the laundress treated Stepmother's clothing, yet she didn't lift a finger to do anything about it—other than the most usual things she couldn't avoid doing, like brushing out the hems of skirts after a walk, or giving a more vigorous brushing to a cloak or outer garment after a stint outside. She didn't do any of what should have been shared work, such as bringing up Stepmother's water for washing, or bringing up her trays if Stepmother fancied something to eat or drink; in fact, the opposite, it was *Fleurette* who rang for the household maids, not Stepmother, and she made sure they knew it, too, standing beside the bellpull and smirking.

Needless to say, it was just as well for her that she had held herself aloof from the rest of the staff, because after a mere month she was decidedly unwelcome.

"Well, it will be a good Christmas for them, then, and New Year's, and possible several more days besides," said Ben, just a *bit* smugly, as Elena decided that the light had gotten too bad to do any further work on silk stockings, carefully folded the mended ones in paper to protect them, and put everything neatly away in her basket.

"What?" exclaimed Arthur. "You dog! What have you learned?"

Ben smirked. "Father called me into his office just as he came in from making rounds with his steward. He and Stepmother are going to *several* balls between now and Twelfth Night, and two of them are far enough away—all the way to Glastonbury—that they will be staying a few days at their hosts—one Christmas Eve and one New Year's Eve. They might even go to Bath for some of the Christmas concerts and plays. They'll take his valet and Fleurette, and he admonished me that I am to see that the servants don't get into mischief."

"As if they would!" David said indignantly. "That's all *her* talking."

"Father hasn't gone to a ball . . . why, not since Mama left us!" Elena said wonderingly. "And even then, most of the parties were ones *we* held!"

"Mark my words, that's *her* doing again," snorted David. "Not enough excitement here, I'll be bound. And no one nearer Glastonbury that she feels is high enough in the instep that she'll set foot in their guestroom."

"Oh, I think it's simpler than that." Felix chuckled. "I think she wants as few occasions as possible when the entire vicarage can make free of our pantry. And I *know* she don't want to sit through Vicar's Christmas and New Year services. They'll have to give a ball, or at least a party with dancing, for the gentry, and that includes Vicar and his family and Doctor Fisher, but they don't have to keep town hours for it. They can start it early and end it early, especially if the weather looks chancy—or Stepmother pretends she thinks it does."

"Do you—think they'll let us come to that party?" Elena asked wistfully. "I should like to see the gowns."

"*I* should like to see something of ham besides the knuckle," moaned Carl. "Or goose! Or game!"

Ben blew out his cheeks. "I don't want to promise anything, but I should think we will at least be allowed to table, if not to the dancing afterward—unless the ladies will be short of partners. Then Arthur and I will probably be told to stay. It would look strange if we weren't. We're not in the nursery anymore, after all."

"It wouldn't surprise me if Stepmother said we were," growled Emil.

"People can count," Arthur said dryly.

"Can they?" Emil asked, the firelight dancing over his frown. "I doubt they care enough to."

Elena shivered, for that was what she wondered too.

4

When Mr. Hobart, the butler, appeared silently at the door of the schoolroom one afternoon in mid-November, it was so unexpectedly that only Elena noticed him, and only because she was facing the door at the time. Her brothers all had their heads down over their lessons. Arthur and Ben were both deeply immersed in translating something by someone named Ovid, a writer who was new to them, and the rest were maths lessons that had fortunately been thriftily saved by their former tutor so he could use the same lessons over and over. The butler's appearance surprised her so much that she froze and could not speak, and it wasn't until he cleared his throat ostentatiously that the rest looked up, wearing expressions ranging from shock to suspicion.

"Children," Hobart said, as usual without any hint of what he was feeling. If anything. Elena was not entirely certain he actually had feelings. A craggy man, very erect in his black jacket, vest, and knee breeches, he was younger than he looked, and had been hired after Mama had fled and Father had retired the (very) old butler on the grounds that a younger man would have prevented (or at least noticed) her absence. "Your father requires your presence in his study." He took a deliberate look about the room, eyes resting on each of them in turn. "I see you are presentable. You may follow me." He turned to go down the hallway.

As if we would not be presentable! As if we are incapable of washing and dressing ourselves! Elena thought indignantly. *And as if we didn't know the way to Father's study without any help, and couldn't be relied on to go there when ordered!* She could tell from her brothers' expressions, quickly hidden, that they felt the same resentment.

But Hobart undoubtedly reported everything he saw to Father, so they all quickly hid what they were feeling. By the time they were halfway down the upper hall and Hobart had looked over his shoulder to see if they had obeyed him, they were all as blank-faced as statues. Apparently that was satisfactory, for he continued on his way without looking back a second time. They followed him all the way down to the ground floor, to the rooms reserved for the business of running the estate. Father had the largest and most prominent (and the one with the view out into the garden and the best fireplace), but there was a set of smaller offices here for people Elena almost never saw: his secretary, his estate manager, and his steward. This part of the house had a separate entrance, completely apart from the servants' entrance itself, so they could come and go without disturbing the rest of the household or requiring the services of the doorman or hallboy. Father often came and went using this entrance as well when he intended to go straight to the stables without changing.

Their father's study was an exceedingly masculine room, crafted entirely of dark wood (which might have been stained that color by all the smoke over the years). It was lined with bookshelves, although the only books on those shelves were ledgers going back at least a hundred years, *Burke's Peerage,* railway timetables, coaching timetables, *Cary's New Itinerary,* books of maps, and other similar and similarly dull volumes. The rest of the space was taken up by small items of great value, none of which he had collected himself, and none of which were what Elena would have called beautiful, except for a very small marble bust of a Roman goddess, perfect in every way, that was turned so that the viewer saw her in profile rather than face-forward. There was a withered pair of bejeweled gloves with "E*R" picked out in seed pearls on the beaded cuffs, a decidedly ugly pottery dog said to have belonged to Charles II, and an

English Bible that was allegedly one of the first printed by King James. A yellowed elephant's tusk took up all of one shelf, and a spiral tusk of a sea creature called a "narwhale" on another. Furniture consisted of a couple of comfortable chairs in front of the fireplace, with a chessboard between them, ivory and ebony pieces and board. Over the fireplace was a large painting, a landscape. There was one window in the room, which was behind the desk, so that the occupant of the desk was silhouetted against the light and was quite hard to see unless the day was overcast. That window had a lovely view of the garden in summer, but right now, everything on the other side of it was uniformly bleak, gray, charcoal, and brown. Even the sky was a lowering gray. Although Father didn't smoke, his father and grandfather had, so the predominant scent in the room was of woodsmoke from the fire and old tobacco. There was no other light in the room except that which came from the window. When the light faded too much to work, Father left his study and did not return until the next day. He often breakfasted here, while Stepmother breakfasted in her bedroom.

They all filed into the room, while Hobart remained outside, and stood in two rows in front of the desk. The logical way to have arranged themselves would have been with the youngest and smallest in front, but well aware of where they all ranked in Father's regard, it was Ben, Arthur, Carl, and David in front, and Emil, Felix, Gustav, and Elena in back. This suited Elena very well; she could peep at Father from between Ben and Arthur without being easily seen herself. Of all things she dreaded, it was coming under Father's eye, for she could only recall him giving her three compliments since Mama had fled, but many criticisms.

Father was writing something; he waited until they were standing quietly before he spoke. "You may go, Hobart," he said, without really looking up. Hobart vanished silently.

"Children," Father said, finally looking up, but only at Ben and Arthur, "Your mother and I are hosting a small party for our local gentry on the last Saturday in November."

Elena winced at "your mother," and she was sure the others were wincing inwardly as well. But she knew that was how

Stepmother was going to be called by Father, so there was nothing to be done but endure it and concentrate on what else he had said.

There was one thing that stood out. *Oh, clever, calculated so that the vicar cannot stay too late and overstay his welcome, or he will not be able to conduct the earliest service.* Stepmother, of course, never attended the early service; half the time she never attended any service at all. Elena had heard via kitchen gossip that there were tongues clacking in the manor village about that, but Stepmother seemed indifferent to it all, and from the same kitchen gossip, Elena knew Father hadn't said anything to his new wife about it. Then again, he didn't attend services often either. He left it to his children to stand in for the entire family, and Mrs. Farthingworth made certain they did.

"There will be an early evening festive meal, at six o'clock, which you will attend," he continued. "After the meal, and after the ladies withdraw for coffee and the gentlemen have their port in the dining room, there will be casual dancing until ten. At this dancing, you four eldest, Benjamin, Arthur, Carl, and David, will be expected to dance with whatever ladies wish to dance but do not have partners. You will dance with any of them. I do not accept excuses. I do not care if they are twelve or a hundred and twelve; if they came with their party and wish to dance, you will dance with them. Do I make myself clear?"

"Yes, sir," they all murmured.

"The rest of you may, if you are good and quiet, observe the dancing from the gallery above the ballroom. Otherwise you may go to your rooms or gather together for quiet games until bedtime. I am not inviting any other children—" here he sighed and looked pained, "—but there is no telling whether some fool will decide to bring his. If this occurs, you will entertain and look after them. Do not concern yourself about infants. Should anyone have the poor taste to bring an infant, the maidservants will care for very young children who shall be put to bed in a guest room and supervised. I sincerely hope, however, that nothing of the sort shall trouble our festivities."

Elena could only reflect that, as usual, her father's idea of what was "festive" did not seem to include anyone actually enjoying themselves. The local gentry would be there to gawk at the new wife and old children, eat his lordship's fine food, and be seen. Father was clearly making a pretty setting for Stepmother to queen over.

But Father was continuing. "The dancing will end at exactly ten. There will be no supper following. You elder four will then go to the hall and supervise the servants as they assist ladies with coats or cloaks, as your mother and I bid our guests goodnight. You younger four, if you are not already in your rooms, will go there and go to bed. I expect you all to be in your beds by eleven. Attendance at late church service rather than early will be allowed. Do any of you require updates to your wardrobes?"

This was the only time he looked interested. Ben cleared his throat. "We all need dress shoes, Father, except for Elena, because she can make slippers to match her gown," he said diffidently. "And we all need new white silk stockings. We only have woolen."

Father nodded, and reached for his ledger to write that down, then frowned. "Take tracings of your feet, all of you boys. I suppose none of you have dress shoes that might be resoled and handed down. . . ."

"No, Father," said Ben. "We've never needed them."

"And your Bluchers won't do for dancing, of course," Father grumbled. "Very well. Give the tracings to Hobart in the morning, and he'll take them to the cobbler in the village. Elena will not need anything new, which is a mercy."

Father's frugality. Except where Stepmother is concerned. More kitchen gossip said that he never questioned her purchases and never hesitated to supply more pin money whenever she asked for it. Had he been like that with Mama? Elena couldn't remember, except that she'd scarcely noticed anything except to be happy when a beloved toy had been mended, or weep when, despite her care, one had been broken past repairing.

He hesitated a moment, and peered between Ben and Arthur to give her a glance. "Well . . ." he said grudgingly, "I suppose you are old enough to have a small, modest piece of jewelry or two from . . . whatever your mother did not want when I showed her jewels to choose from. I'll send something up with Mrs. Farthingworth. Take care that you put it by safely and do not lose or break it."

"Yes, Father," she said, between gritted teeth. It was easy to tell what he was not saying. That she was getting a piece or two of Mama's jewelry that was too cheap for Stepmother to want and had been discarded. Probably a string of beads or seed pearls. Father had no idea what her good dress looked like, of course; she was only a girl, why should he care, even though he had seen it the day he and Stepmother arrived. So if what he pulled out of the discards turned out to be beads, they would probably not match. She ducked her head so he wouldn't see her expression of resignation and said, politely, "Thank you, Father."

Perhaps I will be fortunate, and it will be seed pearls. She could not imagine Stepmother wanting anything so inexpensive, except to take apart to be used in embroidery on a gown.

She did not say anything more; she felt that anything more would attract unwelcome attention.

"That will do, children," he said, turning his attention back to his correspondence. "You may go."

They filed out—Hobart was not there to escort them again, of course; his presence had been to ensure they arrived promptly, and once that duty had been fulfilled, he had more pressing household matters to complete or oversee. The butler was in charge of the wine cellar, the silver, and all the menservants inside the house, and Hobart was positively fanatic about seeing all his duties done.

Once safely up to the first floor, they paused, and Arthur let out his breath in a whoosh, as they stopped in the entry hall, tenanted only by the hallboy, who was asleep on his bench. It had been very windy last night and the poor little fellow must have been awakened over and over by the front door rattling. He slept on a pull-out bed in the hallway connecting the servants' hall with the main house, and he'd have startled awake every time the door rattled, and run up to be certain it wasn't someone beating on the door.

"Well, at least we will be getting a fine meal," Ben said, and rubbed the back of his neck. "And everyone will be coming, of course, because everyone will want a taste of what the vicar has, without a doubt, waxed more eloquently about than about God's mercy."

That made them all laugh, but quietly, so as to avoid waking the hallboy.

"Mama quite enjoyed giving dinners," Ben said wistfully. "You wouldn't have thought so, because she was so shy, but she did. She liked seeing other people enjoy themselves. She generally left everything to Hobart, Mrs. Banning, and Mrs. Farthingworth, though, and there was never dancing, so I don't imagine the vicar had anything to say except 'Very good dinner, m'lord, very good dinner.' This is going to be a much more important event for everyone 'round about here. With Msr. Paul in the kitchen, and dancing and cards after, this will likely be the event of the year, if not the event of the last decade." He looked over his siblings. "Be very careful what you say the entire time. There is no telling what will turn into salacious gossip that spreads across the village like wildfire, and be bound Father will find out whose tongue was too loose."

Although Elena was not all that fond of dancing—except for the very simplest of dances, she tended to get her steps all mixed up—Beecham had made sure they all knew how to dance, with all of them changing partners at least once per lesson. Dancing, as he reminded them constantly, was an expected skill of someone of their class—although as far as she could tell, it was an expected skill of almost anyone, since dancing was a welcome feature of every village fete, and there was a subscription ball once a month in the Wool Hall in the manor village. The manor servants would roll up any rugs and push the furniture against the wall to have a dance in the servants' hall any chance they got (which was not often enough, as far as they were concerned). But Elena found it more of a chore than a delight. *I will be very much happier up in the gallery.*

A gust of wind rattled the front door as it must have last night, and sent a cold draft through the entrance hall. Elena, who had not brought a shawl with her in her haste to obey Father's summons, shivered. Ben glanced down at her. "Let's get upstairs where it's more comfortable. It should be time for luncheon soon anyway."

*

They learned more over the course of the next few days. This would be a large party; everyone who could be termed gentry for ten miles around had been invited. There would be paid musicians, which had not graced the ballroom since Mama had left! And none of your paltry village bands made up of amateurs, oh no. These would be professionals, perhaps from as far away as Glastonbury. There would be at least sixty people at the ball itself; more, if extra family members came besides the invited couples or singles.

There would be so many dishes at dinner that the sideboards in the dining room would be required, as well the entire table. The sliding partitions at either end of the dining room would be opened, all the silver and all the dishes used, and all the leaves put into the dining room table. The ballroom would be similarly opened, card tables set out in one of the side rooms for the benefit of those who did not dance, and even though Father was not providing a late supper, there would still be light refreshments in another side room, in the form of drinks, delicate sweet bread-and-butter sandwiches, biscuits, and cakes. Possibly cut fruit from the conservatories and oranges from the orangery as well; Mrs. Banning and Msr. Paul were both still agonizing over whether it was worth the risk of staining someone's gloves with fruit juice in the interest of providing more variety. *Everything* had to be cleaned, and many dishes had to be prepared in advance. So many, that extra help in the form of girls from the manor farms was brought in every day for basic preparation and cleaning of items that normally were in storage. The biggest farm cart made the rounds of the farms every morning, picking up yawning girls who snuggled down into a bed of hay for the ride, and brought them home every night.

Before long, Elena was grateful for their stores of extra food up in their "parlor." And the boys took it on themselves in turn to run down at mealtime and see what was available to be snatched up and brought up in baskets and trays. The option for the poor servants was mostly cheese, cured sliced meat, bread, and soup. A kettle of soup was a constant on the hearth, so that anyone who could take a moment could have a bowl, and porridge set to cook overnight so a hot part of breakfast was readily available. But except for pease porridge, soup was somewhat thin stuff to sustain one in this cold weather. The siblings might be getting some rather odd meals, but at least they were eating something solid.

And at least we aren't so overworked we are falling asleep over our plates as they are in servants' hall. It had been a very long time since there had been a party of this size here; not within Elena's memory, for certain. The largest party she could recall had been when Father had hosted some relatives for a summer dinner. There had only been four couples and an aged pensioner aunt, there had only been a dinner and a late supper, and the entertainment had consisted of cards while the aunt had inexpertly picked out tunes on the piano. The staff clearly had fallen out of practice.

In the middle of all this, Father somehow remembered his promise, and Mrs. Farthingworth appeared at Elena's room with a blue velvet–covered box, much larger than Elena had expected. She bustled off before Elena could do more than thank her, leaving Elena to take her prize to the bed to open it. She was not going to take the chance—all too likely!—that whatever was in this box had a broken string and was now nothing but loose beads. This was scarcely an insurmountable problem given that she had needles, silk thread, and time, but since she had no other jewels in her possession, she was loath to lose a single bead. Even if they didn't match her gown.

The lid of this box proved to be hinged; she lifted it to find herself presented with a piece of fine white lawn fabric, lying over several lumps. Lifting that finally revealed her gift.

To her delight, it was not a random set of stone or glass beads; it was, in fact, all that she could have desired and had not dared to hope for: a complete set, or *parure*, of modest seed-pearl jewelry. She found herself the happy owner of a seed-pearl necklet with a small cameo pendant, a dainty pearl ring that she could easily wear under a glove, two slender bracelets of woven bands of seed pearls, a pair of modest seed-pearl earrings, and a few pearl-topped hairpins. All were of the same design, so it was obvious that they had been constructed as a set rather than put together from individual pieces. A gentle tug proved the stringing was sound and the clasps easy to manipulate. Clearly this set was far too modest for Stepmother's taste—she wore far more elaborate jewels to supper commonly—but it exactly suited Elena.

She brought the little cameo closer to her eyes; the workmanship was superb, and she doubted that if Stepmother had seen it closely, she would have relinquished it so easily. The tiny carving was not, as she had thought, of a three-petaled flower. It was of three impossibly detailed swans, necks and heads intertwined in the center, executed in pearl shell. She had never seen anything like it!

When her fingers touched the necklace for the first time, she experienced an odd little tingling, surprising enough that she inadvertently snatched her fingers back. But when she touched it again, she did not sense anything, so she shrugged, counted herself as extraordinarily lucky to have had such a prize out of Mama's treasures freely granted to her, and put it away in her glove drawer until the great day. It could not have been said that she thought no more about it—she peeped inside the box at least twice a day, just to assure herself that it really *was* just as nice as memory painted it—but she was contented to leave it in the drawer until it was needed.

The boys were left to conduct their days normally, though they fretted to be out of the schoolroom even if being out would mean they were working rather than playing—but *she* was not. There was a never-ending stream of "requests" accompanied by articles of clothing coming up from Stepmother for Elena to tend to. There were no more silk stockings (yet), though Elena was certain that there would be, once Father and Stepmother started on their round of parties away from the manor. There were, however, other things for her talented fingers to deal with. A petticoat that urgently required the application of tiny ribbon rosettes just above the flounce. Necklines of two different gowns that needed embellishment with embroidery. A net over-dress that needed mending. Lace fichus that needed mending. Gloves that required both mending with tiny, invisible stitches, and shortening, to remove stains that inexplicably appeared only above the elbow. She found herself doing these tasks during most of her waking hours, although by rights it should have been Fleurette that had been so employed.

The indignity of doing this work was softened by the nature of the work itself, for she loved working with these rich, luxurious materials. And there was a certain perverse pleasure in knowing that the rest of the household staff were well aware of the goings-on, and were without a doubt gossiping about how incompetent Fleurette must be that these little wardrobe chores had built up and now had to be amended by Elena.

The day itself fell in the midst of not-terrible weather; very bright and clear, cold, but not bone-chilling. Carriages began arriving shortly after noon, and the siblings hastily gulped down a luncheon of pickles, bread, meat trimmings, and cheese before changing into their proper day-garments (their best, of course) and descending to the parlor to entertain, as best they could, the newcomers.

Not everyone who had been invited to the dancing had been invited to the dinner beforehand. Only those with titles, or some pretension to titles. Stepmother was clearly behind this, although Father's penury may have played a role. This was not a "dinner and ball," according to Stepmother; Stepmother wasn't going to designate a gathering that was "merely" to entertain the neighbors as a ball. But everyone else was calling it a ball, as far as Elena could tell from the bits of servant gossip she overheard.

But not being officially a "ball" meant that the reception lines before the dinner and then before the dancing would feature only Father and Stepmother and Arthur and Ben, not the entire family. The next eldest went off to the billiard room to see to the male guests, Elena was "in charge" of seeing to the ladies' comfort in the large parlor, and the rest of the boys oversaw the putting away of cloaks and coats, and whatever else was too important to be left to the servants alone.

Firmly established in the larger of the two parlors, Elena didn't have much to do, after all, except listen to a few elderly biddies who surrounded her and gossiped interminably about people she didn't know. Since they had all complained about the cold, she made certain the group was ensconced nearest to the fire, which kept her from the draftiest part of the room. Married ladies and spinsters formed a second group who were intently examining every single object in the room, probably with the goal of being able to discuss it in detail at later dates. There were a few girls about her age and older, but they did not join this group; instead, they either remained demurely with their mamas, walked about the room in pairs and trios, or ventured into awkward conversations with the boys and young men exiled from the billiard room under their Mama's watchful eye. It was hard to call these interactions "flirtations," as none of the parties were able to accomplish much with the parental eyes firmly upon them. It was also hard to call these things "flirtations" when the girls in question clearly didn't know anything more about courting than she did.

Since there was very little for Elena to actually do except to nod when appropriate, she was able to feast her eyes on gowns to her heart's content. She was more than happy about that, and frankly the old ladies were more entertaining than she had expected, with their low-voiced gossip about everyone who came in the door. Except Stepmother, after Stepmother put in a (very) brief appearance with a bright smile to "make sure everyone was enjoying themselves." They didn't seem to quite know what to think about her, except to be suspicious. "Seems sharpish, that one," said one of them. "Hmm," remarked another. And "Looks aren't everything," judged a third.

Elena felt that these ladies were far wiser than the younger ones who were fawning over Stepmother and admiring her gown and jewels. *I would give a very great deal to hear what is said in the carriages going home.* She suspected there would not be nearly as much fawning admiration then.

The footmen were the only servants present at this part of the entertainment; they looked quite smart in their livery. Stepmother had ordered new livery for all the menservants as soon as she had arrived, and given presents of brown and white fabric to the women to make new, uniform clothing from. This was a first for Whitstone Manor; heretofore, maidservants had been expected to wear their own clothing, with only matching aprons provided for them. There was only enough white fabric for aprons, collars, and cuffs; female servants were *not* supposed to "ape their betters" by having white dresses!

It was not long after the last person arrived for the dinner that the bell rang, signaling that they were all to process into the dining room. It was, indeed, a procession, with Father taking in the highest-ranking lady, Stepmother taking the highest-ranking gentleman, Arthur and Ben taking the next-highest-ranking ladies, and the rest of them following in order of precedence. One of the older, unaccompanied gentlemen took her in. That put her quite far down on the table, since she was the youngest female present. Stepmother had not stinted on anything; despite the fact that it was still daylight, there were candles in the chandeliers and the candelabra on the table, and hothouse flowers about the room in abundance. Because the number of male and female guests was unequal, Elena found her card between one of the other young ladies and some gentleman somehow associated with Father, who greeted her nicely enough, but obviously felt that the two of them could have nothing to converse about except the weather. The girl ignored her entirely, being preoccupied by the boy on her left and the admonishing looks of her mother across the table. That left Elena studiously reading—with some dismay—the menu card placed between her and the girl.

The First Course: Green Pea Soup, Hare Soup, Soup a la Reine, Pheasant Soup.

The Second Course: Pigeon Pie, Braised Ham, Cold Pheasant Pie, Saddle of Mutton.

Entrees: Quails, Braised Beef, Roast Duck, Roast Goose, Scallops of Chicken.

The Third Course: Charlotte Russe, Compote of Cherries, Custards, Tartlets, Apples, Filberts, Neapolitan Cakes.

Dismay, not because she had not had plenty of practice in eating with all the correct cutlery—Beecham had taken great care in training them, sitting them all down at this same table after luncheon and drilling them until they could perform flawlessly—but because she had never in her entire life been presented with that much food at once. That was something Beecham had neglected to tell them. She had always assumed that a "course" consisted of a single main dish and a few side dishes, like bread and butter, jellies, starches like rice or potatoes, or vegetables. Not this!

And before she could even properly react, the first course came in. The dishes were placed on the table in all their profusion, great tureens of soup, baskets of rolls, entire loaves of bread, and she was at a complete loss.

Fortunately the footman behind her was more quick-witted than she was. She heard a soft voice in her ear: "May I suggest the green pea soup for the young miss?"

She looked up, and it was one of the footmen she actually knew, Thomas Spencer.

"Yes, thank you, Thomas," she replied gratefully. Thomas ladled a very modest portion into her soup bowl, acquired a small roll and butter for her bread plate, and moved on to care for the guests on either side of her.

So the dinner went; the girl beside her ate very little and ignored her *and* her mother, the gentleman ignored everyone in favor of the food in front of him, and Thomas managed to secure small portions of things she *liked* from each course, making suggestions when she hesitated. He met her looks of gratitude with a small, kind smile, then proceeded to his other charges. The girl was rather obnoxious, in Elena's opinion, changing her mind several times in rapid succession, then leaving most of the food on her plate.

When the dessert was brought in, Thomas got her some of the cherries and custard before all of the servants left. Father began serving wine and other drinks from decanters on a little cart, before the butler took it over and brought it down Elena's side of the table. When he reached her, he filled her glass generously with water before adding a little wine. She tasted it cautiously; decided it was drinkable, and ate and drank quietly until Stepmother got up.

This was, as she knew, the signal for all the ladies to leave and go to the parlor again. And although she wished she could go to her room, she would not be allowed, not yet. She was there to represent the family—particularly with the ladies that Stepmother would ignore. That was her job.

But at least I can sit with the old ladies, she reminded herself, as she trailed at the end of the procession of skirts back to the parlor.

By this time the candles in the parlor had been lit, making it easier to efface herself when she got there. The chairs and sofas were all fully occupied now, but she found a stool to sit on, not so near the fire that the heat was stifling, and not so far that she was cold.

Stepmother was in fine form, taking up most of the attention in the room, talking about living in London with a coterie sitting as near her as possible, although several of the younger ladies were taking a turn about the room together. Most of them seemed to know each other very well, and Elena felt a strange pang of loneliness. *I've never had a female friend,* she thought, suddenly overwhelmed with a sadness she had not expected. No female friends, no sisters . . . her brothers had each other, but did they miss having friends that were not their brothers? *Probably not.* They'd always been remarkably close, although when they were all younger and Beecham had permitted, they *had* sometimes included some of the farm boys in their games.

Now she looked at these women filling the parlor, listened to them chatter comfortably with each other, watched them as the little ways in which they moved and interacted with each other betrayed their feelings—friends, mere acquaintances, "friendly" enemies, and rarest of all, very good friends indeed.

Stepmother alone had none of those connections; she was an unknown quantity to most of the room, and unless Elena was very much mistaken, she liked it that way. So presumably she didn't feel the need for a female friend. Unless, of course, Fleurette filled that need.

Beecham and Nanny had made it very clear that they were not to "make friends" of the servants, but did that hold true with one's valet or personal maid? It was all a bit of a muddle to Elena.

The loneliness deepened into melancholy, until Elena shook it off with a surge of will, grateful that Stepmother had not noticed her woolgathering. This would not be forever. The boys would end this situation one way or another, and had already made it clear that when they did, she would be going away from this bleak house. Whether she ended up as housekeeper to a brother who was now a vicar or following a brother who was now an army officer into a strange new land, every one of her brothers had insisted that she would be welcome at his side. *India, Canada, or just another part of England. Anything will be better than here, and more fun, I am certain of it.*

So she waited a decent interval until it appeared that even Stepmother had forgotten she was there, and slipped out, heading for her room to change. Oh, she could have asked for permission, perhaps should have, but Stepmother was clearly enjoying being the center of attention and conversation, and any interruption would spoil that.

Stepmother had made it clear that she was not old enough for the dancing, despite the fact that there were girls here who were certainly no older than she by more than two or three years. But she had been given permission to watch the dancing. That meant she could change into her ordinary day-gown, get her sketching materials, and make herself a comfortable little nest in the gallery above the ballroom and watch and listen. The gallery was where musicians would have been performing if there had been more room up there for them. She was fairly certain she would have the spot to herself; none of the younger boys were in the least interested in watching the dancing, and she thought it unlikely any of the older ladies would climb the stairs for a better view.

She raided their private "parlor" as well as her own room. Some cushions, a shawl, and a lap robe later and she had a fine view of the servants making the ballroom and the two rooms just off of it ready for the dancing, refreshments, and card-playing that would continue until ten. At the moment, the musicians were just setting up, and it looked to be a fine band of ten. The piano and harp from the music room had been brought into the ballroom and tuned. The lady at the harp had a smaller harp at her side. Besides the harpist and pianist, there were two violinists, a cellist, a flautist, a clarinet player, a drummer, a horn player, and a fellow with a lute. The fellow with the lute seemed to be in charge, and kept turning away one of the servants who was trying to bring them wine. Finally, with exasperation, he said loudly enough to be heard up in the gallery, "*Thank* you, my good man, but no matter how hilarious you may find it to hear a drunken musician, your master certainly will *not* be of the same mind."

Butler Hobart, who at this point was presiding over the arrangement of the ballroom, actually allowed a flash of fury to appear on his face. He did not bustle over, but the other servants parted before him as he crossed from the farther part of the room. He entered into low-voiced, but clearly angry, one-sided conversation with the servant—Elena finally recognized the man as one of the new grooms Stepmother had hired, the one called Phillip—and the man scuttled off, to return with pitchers of lemonade and glasses, which were left on a couple of small tables on either side of the musicians.

A tiny titter, just barely loud enough to be heard, came from the curtains at Elena's side of the gallery. The sound made her heart leap, and she carefully looked out of the corner of her eye, hoping against hope, to see if the sound had been out of her imagination, or if it was—

It *was*! Hiding in the folds of the draperies was one of the fairies! Wings folded tightly against her back, she was tucked into the cloth so that only her head and shoulder showed.

"Hello," Elena whispered.

The fairy nodded a wary greeting.

"I don't think Stepmother will be able to see you from down there," she continued. "And I think she will be too busy leading the dances to bother to look up."

The fairy relaxed, just the tiniest bit.

Down in the ballroom, servants set bouquets of flowers on stands around the room, stood on ladders to light the candles in wall sconces, and brought the chandeliers down so that candles could be installed and lit. "Don't get near those candles," Elena warned the fairy, who seemed to be warming to her. She couldn't tell if this was a fairy she had seen before; they seemed to like Ben the best of all of the siblings. The fairy made a scornful face at her, clearly showing that she was well aware that she shouldn't emulate a moth.

Then footsteps on the stairs made the little thing pull the curtain around her so that only her eyes were showing. Elena turned to see that Thomas had come up the stairs, laden with a glass carafe of lemonade, a glass, and a plate of sweet and savory biscuits and hothouse grapes on a tray. "Your brother

Ben sent me to bring you some refreshments," the footman said, with another of his kind smiles. "Don't trouble yourself about cleaning up. I'll send one of the maids up here to collect things once the ball is over."

She colored. "This is very kind of you Thomas," she managed shyly.

The footman laughed. "It is very kind of your brother," he corrected her. "Ben sent me up. I hope you enjoy the dancing."

And before she could respond, he placed the tray beside her, and turned to go back down to his work.

5

"Well," Stephen, Lord Endicott said to his mother, as they proceeded into the ballroom of Whitstone Manor. "You were right, Mama. This is not *completely* boring."

His mother's lips twitched. "Now, my dear, please set your mind to enduring the tedium; it will only be until ten. I have it on good authority that Lord Whitstone will bustle us out on the stroke of ten like a housewife chasing her hens into the coop for the night. Meanwhile, my sister will get a rare chance to gossip in person to her heart's content, and look at gowns in person instead of in a ladies' magazine."

Her son softened at that. "You know I cannot deny anything to Aunt Carrie."

"Of course I do. And you know that your aunt will never divulge that you have both a title and a fortune. So far as all the marrying mamas here are concerned, you are plain Stephen Endicott, taking a year or so between finishing Eton and going to Cambridge." She patted the hand that rested on her arm. "If you had rather not dance, there appears to be a gallery above the ballroom; the musicians seem tolerable and you can enjoy the music without anyone glaring at you because you are not dancing with her daughter."

Anyone looking at the two of them would have been forgiven for thinking that Stephen and his mother were younger brother and elder sister; he had inherited all of his looks from her, which was, as his late father had often said ruefully, a very good thing. Hair as black as a rook's wing and just as shining, graced with natural curls; startlingly blue eyes; truly heart-shaped faces with prominent cheekbones. The one thing that distinguished them from each other was his rather stubborn chin. Stephen and his mother had been visiting his aunt Caroline, who had married happily beneath herself to a mere country squire—with her parents' blessing. No one could have been happier than a pair of Elemental mages to discover that their Earth magician daughter had fallen head over heels with another.

In fact, the Skylen sisters had been equally blessed in falling in actual love with suitable partners, though Marianne had married as high above her station as Caroline had married beneath it: to Andrew, Lord Endicott, much older than she, and possessed of a grand property, fine income-producing farms, a title, and everything that the heart of an anxious mama could ask for. And—an Air mage to match Marianne's power. The one thing he did not have, sadly, was as much time on the earth that his wife and son wanted for him. He had passed peacefully and suddenly in his sleep two years ago, and Marianne had mourned him desperately—in fact, it was only on this visit to her sister that she had left off half-mourning, which, to Caroline, meant this was an excellent time for her to attend Lord Whitstone's ball, to which Caroline and her husband had been invited.

"And you know Gregory will go straight to the card room, leaving me all alone with every unpleasant cat in the neighborhood," she had urged. "Come, do! We can sit together and gossip about all of them."

Stephen had known that his mother could not, would not attempt to resist her sister. And if someone took pity on her and asked her to dance, all the better! She hadn't danced since Papa had died, and surely by now she had earned some gaiety. So while he had teased both of them about how grim and tedious it was all likely to be, if it had made Marianne Endicott smile, he'd have gone to a hymn-sing or an amateur poetry reading and pretended to like it.

His aunt had said that there were *eight* children in this family, though only two, the eldest sons, were present to greet the guests. It was not those lads—good-looking, lean blonds who were surely twins—who had aroused his suspicion and his covert interest.

It was Lord Whitstone's new wife, for whom this ball was being held.

Firstly, there was something about her, despite being impeccably gowned, coiffed, bejeweled, that was subtly *wrong*. He couldn't put his finger on it. It was as if something was telling him that she did not belong here, despite having every sign that she did.

Secondly, he would bet every particle of his own power that she, too, was an Elemental mage, and was hiding it.

Still, there was nothing much he could do at the moment except observe at a distance. It was made very clear in the first few moments of entering this house that the only people who would get near Lady Whitstone were those who were willing to fawn over her slavishly, or who were of sufficient rank to do her good in the local social network. Because they had only been introduced as his uncle's guests, he, his mother and aunt and uncle had gotten only the most cursory of nods in greeting, and that had displeased the four of them not at all. Uncle and Aunt regarded this as a good opening to the holiday round of parties and balls, his mother had already brightened at the sight of the ballroom, and he—he had spotted what was probably the opening to the stairway up to the gallery, and with a nod to his elders, he began to make his way toward it.

For reasons he could not articulate, but which, nevertheless, he paid heed to, he made his way obliquely toward that unlit stair, and slipped inside only when he was certain no one was watching. For the same reasons, he kept his footsteps as light as possible—easier than usual, because he was wearing dancing pumps. Nevertheless, as he emerged from the darkness and entered into a space indirectly lit by the chandeliers of the ballroom, the sole occupant of the gallery heard him and spoke before he actually spotted her.

"I'm fine, thank you, Thomas," whispered a girlish voice. "Please don't get yourself into trouble on my account by neglecting your duties."

He only realized *where* she was—huddled up on the floor against the balustrade—when she turned and said "Oh!" in a startled tone.

"Has my lady reserved this box for herself?" he asked, quietly, keeping his own voice light. "Or may one join her?"

He judged by the sound of her voice that she was probably younger than he, and was not permitted to dance yet because she was not out. She certainly was not a servant, because they would all be occupied with cleanup from the dinner and waiting on guests.

"I'm allowed to be here," she said defensively, cementing his impression.

"I wouldn't dream of assuming otherwise," he assured her, and made his way to the balustrade. He looked down at her, and her little flower-face looked up at his. The golden hair told him she was, without a doubt, one of Lord Whitstone's eight children. The thin, solemn face belonged, he thought, to someone about three or four years his junior—thirteen, perhaps. Certainly not much older than that. Her gown was not suited to a ball; a golden-brown wool, it would have been plain if not for the elaborate embroidery at the neckline and hems of the skirt and sleeves. "May I?" he asked, gesturing at the floor beside her.

"Oh!" she said again, and shifted to free a cushion for him. "Please sit down before you are seen!"

He took the invitation and arranged himself beside her, glad that his moleskin breeches were not so fashionably tight as to make the exercise perilous. "Why?"

"Because you would not be up here if you wanted to dance, and if you are seen, anyone in this household will know you are not one of my brothers and will come to fetch you back downstairs," she replied artlessly. "Would you like a biscuit? Or some lemonade?"

"I would, thank you." He helped himself to both after first making sure that there was more than one glass. In fact, there were four, so whoever had brought her food and drink must have assumed one or more of her brothers would join her. "My name is Stephen Endicott. You must call me Stephen."

"I am Elena Whitstone. Please call me Elena. 'Miss Whitstone' doesn't sound like me," she replied, and picked up the drawing board and papers she had set aside to give him the cushion he was sitting on. Curious, he craned his neck to see that she had sketched out two gowns—neither of which seemed to be ones on display beneath them.

Just the gowns, with nothing more than ovals for heads and a mere suggestion of arms and hands.

"I cannot draw properly," she said, when she saw what he was looking at. "Beecham didn't know how, except for botanical specimens. Beecham was our tutor."

"Ah," he replied noncommittally. "Well, the gowns are quite good."

"I'm taking bits I like from the gowns in the ballroom and combining them. I can draw gowns, but I do not have many opportunities to see new ones." She paused. "Stepmother might want one of my designs, and it won't do for her to be seen in some other woman's gown, would it?"

"Definitely not." That was when he heard a faint titter at the side of the gallery. Carefully, without turning his head, he cast his gaze to that side, to see a sylph, an Air Elemental, hiding in the curtains on the right side of the gallery. The little thing put her finger to her lips, and tucked herself more securely out of sight among the curtains.

Well, that's curious.

He decided that although he did not know the reason for the sylph's desire for stealth, discretion was the better part of valor. "Is that the only reason why you are up here?" he asked.

"Well, I wanted to hear the music and see the dancing. The only music I've ever heard was from the village musicians at fetes and the fiddler who plays with the choir on Sundays." Her candor was quite charming and refreshing. Although the girls from the close-connected households of Elemental magicians were not as hidebound and stuffy as those from most of the elevated households the Endicotts socialized with, they still tended to be a trifle artificial, and, thus far, seemed as intent on single-mindedly pursuing marriage as any of their non-magical contemporaries.

"I confess I have been extraordinarily lucky in that way,"

he told her, just as candidly. "Although Mama has been in mourning, she is extremely fond of music, and has had musicians to the house often. Talented amateurs, as many as six or seven at a time. Papa indulged her in this as often as possible, and even in deep mourning there are no strictures forbidding a widow from having some music and a few friends to cheer her."

It was surprisingly pleasant up here, above the ballroom. The chatter wasn't as overwhelming, there was no crush, and it was a distinct relief to be sitting down without having mamas glaring at him because he was not dancing. The only aspect he could possibly object to was the mingled scents of varying perfumes, which was a bit more than he liked. But he glanced over at the sylph—or at least at her eyes, which were all he could see at this point. So while the child was intent on her drawing, he waved his hand in front of his nose, wrinkled it, and winked at the little Elemental. He heard another faint giggle, and the air somehow cleared. Then, to his surprise, the girl looked in that direction and mouthed the words "Thank you." So she knew the sylph was there!

"Which lady is your mama?" she asked, still in a voice so low as to barely be heard above the music.

"Down on the right-hand side of the room, speaking with animation to the lady in the grass-green silk," he told her. "The black-haired lady in lavender half-mourning."

The child peered between banisters. "She looks very pleasant. Do you think she would like one of my designs? Stepmother won't need as many as I've drawn."

He laughed softly. "I think you fail to understand how very many gowns a lady as fashionable as your stepmother 'needs,'" he countered. "But I am sure she would like one. I think she is ready to re-enter society fully, and much of her wardrobe was re-dyed black when she went into full mourning."

Elena took a sheet of paper from beneath the one she was working on and handed it to him. He examined it. He was no judge of gowns, but he thought it looked like something Mama would appreciate, especially the modesty of the bodice, which had a kind of pleated business rising into a tiny ruff at the neck. He'd never seen her wearing anything quite like it, but it had the *sense* of her. "This is quite clever," he said with admiration, folding the paper and tucking it inside his coat for safekeeping. "Exceptionally pretty, I would say."

"Stepmother wouldn't like it," Elena replied, tapping her pencil against her lips as she stared down at her current drawing, then through the banisters to look at the dancers. "I don't think she likes high necklines. At least, I have never seen her wear anything of the sort, even in this bitter weather."

He had to laugh at that. "Well, your stepmother strikes me as an extremely *modish* lady. My mama would never describe herself as modish. Practical, yes, although she does love a pretty gown. But not modish."

"Am I boring you, speaking of gowns?" Elena asked, looking up at him with her big eyes, which, now that his eyes had adjusted to the light, he could see were a limpid blue.

He laughed again. "Not at all. Obviously I have no *personal* interest in them, but Mama and her friends sometimes press me for an opinion."

She smiled. He got the feeling she did not smile often. "Then perhaps you can explain something to me?"

"I will certainly try!" he said, finding himself far more entertained than he had any expectation of being when he sat down. He took another sip of lemonade, refilled both their glasses, and waited.

"Those two ladies—the older ones, sitting near to the musicians beneath the plinth with the vase of lilies. *Why* does it look as if they have . . . *shelves* under their arms?"

He almost choked on his lemonade, because it certainly *did* look as if the ladies in question had long shelves under each arm, covered by their gowns. But he managed not to choke, or even make a sound.

"Well," he said, seriously. "Certainly a young lady like you, who is knowledgeable about dress, knows what a pannier is?"

She looked up at him expectantly. "But why are they wearing panniers at their bosom height instead of properly at their waists?"

"Because, Elena, these are ladies who are torn between the mode of the present day and the mode of the past. They do not wish to give up their panniers, but at the same time, they fear having a natural waist to their gowns will make them look as if they cannot *afford* the current mode."

Her sweet mouth made a silent "O."

"It is only at court that the queen insists on the mode of the past. I have never been," he added, "but Mama has told me that no lady or gentleman is allowed to enter unless they appear in the full resplendence of the years when poor King George was young and in his prime."

"Perhaps the queen wants this because as long as she is surrounded by the images of those days, she will not feel the passing of the years," the child said, softly, startling him with her maturity.

"I think that is very likely," he agreed. "No one wants to grow old."

"Oh! *I* do!" she said passionately. "I want it very much! If I were old, or at least older, I would be with one of my brothers, taking care of their household!"

"And what if your brother was married?" he teased.

"Pfft!" she responded, to his delight. "I have *seven* brothers. They can't all be married! Six of them will have nothing except what my brother Arthur gives them, and as Beecham told them many times, they will have to either make a living on their own, or live as a dependent in his household. And when *he* marries, his wife may not be best pleased with six idle men hanging about."

He blinked. "My goodness. You are rather ruthless!"

"Not me. Beecham. Our tutor." She offered him the plate. "I *do* love my brothers, but Arthur's eventual wife may *not*."

"Will she love you?" he asked without thinking.

"Perhaps not. That is why I will probably keep house for one of the others," she said with indifference.

He was startled by how casually she seemed to accept what to him was a bleak outlook. And so young! He changed the subject immediately.

"Well, tell me about things you like. Besides inventing gowns, that is."

Her eyes finally lit up, and she began waxing eloquent about her newly discovered passion for the ancient world and mythology. He only listened with half an ear—the subject was an open book for him, after all—and examined her more closely while she was engrossed in her enthusiasm. There was something about her that struck him as decidedly odd. He rarely saw Elementals hanging about anyone who was not a magician—but the father certainly was as ordinary as a boot, and although Stephen was not yet come into his own full powers, he was usually able to tell when someone had magic, and generally which Element it was. But although there were glimmerings about her, they did not correspond to those of a magician.

Perhaps she has not come into her powers at all yet. That was the only thing that made sense.

And yet, that didn't seem quite right either.

It was as if she was something he simply did not have the experience to identify. Like—oh—a pineapple. If you had never seen one, never seen a picture of one, never even heard a description of one, what would you think? That it was some sort of cactus, probably.

He found himself oddly charmed by her. And it was a pity that she did not seem to be valued at all by her father.

It is a great pity, but I suspect that he has no plans to see her married. That would explain why she does not seem to have had a conventional education. He probably has no intention of parting with a marriage portion. Most likely his intentions are for her to become his nurse and caregiver in his dotage. Certainly that glittering ornament he has married will be utterly useless in that capacity.

Well, serve him right, then, that she had plans of her own to escape. This was not the first time he had heard of a father who made no plans for a daughter to do anything other than be his caretaker and nurse in his old age. Even worse, such a father might not make any provisions for her after his death! He recalled his mother being incensed that one of the London Elemental Masters had been so crass as to do exactly that to his daughter. He'd been privy to only part of that conversation and had never learned the outcome, since his parents had discovered him listening with all the intensity of any nine-year-old overhearing something he shouldn't, and had banished him from the room.

He did manage to answer some of Elena's more esoteric questions about mythology without having to think about it too much, but then she threw one at him that *did* force him to think.

"Why are all the gods so...." She waved her hands helplessly as she searched for a word. "I don't know. *Ordinary?* Zeus pursues women, Hera is horribly jealous, Aphrodite is terribly vain and thoughtless, Ares is *stupid*, and *why*? They're gods; shouldn't they be, well, above such things?"

He did her the service of treating her question seriously. "Perhaps because the people long ago created the gods in their own images. They imagined what they themselves would be like if they had such immense powers, I suspect." He hoped that she would not ask him any uncomfortable questions about Christian theology, but fortunately, before any occurred to her, there were footsteps on the stair, and they both turned to see who it was.

He had expected a servant, but it was a boy who *had* to be Elena's twin; he was the right age, and they could not have looked more alike.

Just then, the musicians stopped playing, and he clapped his hands over his mouth. "Elena," he whispered, taking his hands away as the dancers began chattering below them. "Msr. Paul and Mrs. Banning sent up a tray. Have you seen enough dresses?"

"Gus," the girl said, "this is Mr. Stephen Endicott. Mr. Endicott, this is my twin brother Gus."

Suddenly recalled to realization of his terrible manners, Gus flushed. "I beg your pardon, Mr. Endicott," he said politely (at last!). "I think I was overcome by thoughts of the sweet tray."

Stephen didn't laugh, which probably would have mortified the poor lad. "Quite all right," he said gravely. "I am quite certain I have been overcome by thoughts of a sweet tray more than once. But *you* have reminded me that I have been derelict in my dancing duties, and my mama will have every reason to chide me if I don't go down now."

He stood up, and bowed slightly to Elena. "It was a great pleasure to meet you and speak with you, Miss Whitstone," he told her. "I am certain my mama will view your design for her with great pleasure." Then he bowed to Gus. "And it was a pleasure to meet you as well, Master Gus."

He sidled past Gus and made his way down the dark stairs. Behind him he heard the lad exclaiming, "Did you hear that? He called me *Master* Gus!"

It made him smile.

It appeared that the musicians were pausing for a brief rest, so he made his way to where his mother and aunt were sitting, fanning themselves. It had been pleasant up in the loft, but it was quite warm down in the ballroom, and they were not the only ones fanning themselves. He detoured to the refreshment room long enough to procure two glasses of lemonade; he knew his mother's tastes well enough to know that she would not care for wine, ratafia, or negus, and he did not think his aunt would turn up her nose at a nice glass of lemonade. And he was certain that anything produced by the kitchen of this household would be very nice indeed.

"And here he is at last," said Aunt Carrie, as he eased his way through the press and presented his glasses to them with a flourish. "Ah, just what is needed! Where have you been, you naughty lad? You weren't dancing."

"I was entertaining a young lady," he said archly. "A *very* young lady. The only daughter of the house, in fact. Her name is Elena, she is perhaps thirteen and not yet out, and she has a gift for you, Mama." He took the paper out of his coat, unfolded it, and handed it to her. The two ladies bent over it immediately. "She is up in the gallery, designing gowns, based on what she has observed in the ballroom."

"She has *quite* the talent!" his mother exclaimed, to his satisfaction. "This is delightful, and exactly to my taste! I will see if I can get it made up in time for New Year's Eve!"

"You like it, then?" he asked, smiling in spite of himself.

"It is just the thing!" With a satisfied smile of her own, she folded the paper carefully and put it in her reticule. "As soon as we return to Endicott Manor, I shall get that blue velvet and the light blue sarsenet that Andrew gave me before he died and pay a visit to my modiste in Glastonbury. Your young lady must, I think, be observant as well as talented."

Stephen raised an eyebrow. His mother must like the design very much indeed, if she was taking the last gift his father ever gave her out of storage in order to have a gown made of it.

She patted her reticule with every evidence of deep satisfaction. "The musicians are returning, my dear, and you have many young ladies who need dancing partners—"

"Yes, Mama," he said obediently, and went in search of one.

It was in the carriage on the way home that the subject of Elena came up again. It was exceedingly cold, but their coachman knew his job, and there were footwarmers full of fresh coals waiting for them, as well as fur lap robes. The coachman had also lit the little oil lamps on their pivots, which added a tiny bit more heat along with soft, dim light. His aunt and mother sat side by side in the forward-facing seat, while he sat across from them, as a gentleman should.

Stephen could not stop thinking about the girl, and how she was treated. As the evening had gone on, it was clear that her stepmother had no use for her, and her father did not value her enough to speak up for her. Then again. . . .

He only noticed that his mother and aunt were speaking quietly together because their speech intersected with his thoughts. ". . . utterly besotted, our host," said his aunt in tones that suggested she found this unseemly at best, and possibly worse than that.

"I heard a suggestion," said his mother, in a near whisper, barely audible over the rolling of the carriage wheels and the sound of their horses' hooves, "that she may have been a Cyprian."

"What's a Cyprian, Mother?" he asked, attention captured.

"You weren't to have heard that!" she exclaimed with chagrin.

"Oh, tell him," his aunt said, with a smile in her voice. "Better for him to be warned now, than find out later when he's in the toils of one, and it's not as if his father is here to tell him."

But Stephen was more than intelligent enough to intuit what was meant. "Oh! It is a kind of scarlet woman, then?"

"Yes, dear," his mother said, fanning her cheeks a little with her gloved hand, despite the cold. "A very expensive one."

"Ah! Then like the *hetaerae*, then!" he exclaimed, glad to have a category to put the lady in. He knew about them from his extensive reading in Greek, since neither his father nor his tutor had ever put any restrictions on his reading.

"Less erudite," his mother replied, obviously relieved that she did not have to go into any detail. "Or so I am . . . given to believe. Obviously I do not have any personal experience. And it is only a rumor. Someone who knows someone else who spends a great deal of time in London swears that her ladyship could be the twin of a Cyprian who has since vanished from the muslin ranks. They saw her in Bath as she was leaving that new town house Lord Whitstone bought when he married her."

"Gossip! Three-quarters of it false and the rest exaggerated!" His aunt laughed. "And how, indeed, was this person supposed to recognize a woman that our sort pretends doesn't exist? Don't trouble your head about it."

Stephen fidgeted, but managed to cover it by bracing himself against the sudden motion of the carriage as it encountered another bit of rough road. He really could not account for his own interest in the child. She was only thirteen, after all, and not even out. And yet, the thought of her living as she was, an afterthought in her own home, her fine mind neglected, not to mention her magical talents—well, it made him want to do something about it all. Perhaps it was because she was female. Her brothers could very well look after themselves, after all. If they had the makings of mages about them, as soon as they were out in the world, *someone* amongst the Elemental Masters would notice and take them under a wing. But Elena was female, and from the looks of things, her father and stepmother had no intentions of ever allowing her to leave their manor. "Well, I just hope . . . it's clear as the nose on my face that his lordship has not got a hint of magic about him. But Elena *does*. She had a sylph hanging about her, and she could see it. And . . . there is something unsettling about her ladyship."

"And you're worried the stepmother might be unkind . . . or worse . . . to the child." His mother pursed her lips, and peered across the carriage at him. "Stephen, what do you expect me to do about this?"

He realized at that moment that he actually had expected her to do something . . . though what, he had no idea. Obviously she couldn't make any inquiries of the father—

"I don't know," he said, suddenly unhappy. "But surely—"

"We are not closely enough connected for me to pursue closer acquaintance," she said, sympathetically, but with finality. "If he were an Elemental mage, which he is not, I could speak to him as one mage to another, with concern for his untutored daughter, but that road is closed to me. The best I can do is bring the situation up to the White Lodge, and perhaps a means can be found to keep an eye on her."

There were a great many "if"s and "perhaps"es in that statement, and it certainly did not satisfy him.

"Surely—" he began.

"Stephen, are you *attracted* to this child?" his mother asked. And before he could blurt out that *no, but I don't like to see a child so neglected,* she continued. "Because if you are, it is not unheard of for mages to find themselves—I will not say *enamored*, but there is a calling of like to like—with other mages, in otherwise extremely unlikely circumstances. And if that is the case, I *could* pursue the possibility of a betrothal. *Obviously* a marriage would have to wait until she was older, but—"

"Piffle," said his aunt merrily. "Thirteen can be wedded with parental approval."

"No, please—that is out of the question, I am not—" He felt his face flaming, and he certainly did not need the warmth of the lap robe, only of his own embarrassment.

His mother smiled. His aunt laughed, which only embarrassed him further. "I didn't think so. But, if you are adamant that this child needs to be nurtured and protected, that is the only way I can think of to assure that—a betrothal to you."

He shook his head, unhappy, but, well, he really did not want to find himself leg-shackled to a child he scarcely knew.

"I am sorry, my love, but it is a sad truth that we cannot help everyone we may wish to." His mother leaned across the space between them and patted his hand, her breath a visible cloud in the dim light. "And I *will* put this before the White Lodge. This child—children! Her brothers might also have the gift!—must at least be watched over from a distance. She clearly has no one training her, and that must be addressed at some point."

He sat back in his seat, wishing there was a better answer.

Wishing that this was something he could somehow *fix*—somehow persuade the girl's father to send her to a proper school for young ladies, where one of the young ladies his age or older among the mages could get herself a place among the teachers, and make sure that Elena got tutelage in magic along with piano or drawing, or whatever other folderol females got schooled in at such places. And he was about to suggest to his mother just that, when he realized that such a plan would violate half the strictures of the White Lodge—the *first* of which was, *do and say nothing to outsiders that would even suggest there is such a thing as magic.*

Mind, there *was* quite a plethora of non-mages that knew about the Elemental mages, but generally they were servants and tenants who had ties to the families in question going back centuries. But to approach someone like Lord Whitstone out of the blue and begin insinuating one's self into the intimate matter of how he raised his children would certainly be taken as highly suspicious, if not insulting . . . unless one used magic to make his mind malleable. And *that* would violate several more strictures.

On the other hand, though, there was a somewhat guilty feeling of relief. He'd done his duty. It was out of his hands, and his mother and the other members of the White Lodge—which he was not yet old enough to join—were the appropriate hands for the situation.

"I must say that I am just as pleased that you did not find any of the eligible young ladies as interesting as little Elena," his aunt said, a little tartly. "That would create quite a tangle."

He had to laugh at that, and did. "Oh some of them were interested in me, but their mamas nearly slew me with the daggers from their eyes. I think they all had other plans for their daughters, and those plans certainly did not include me!"

That set the conversation on a more comfortable track, and by the time they reached his aunt's home, Elena's plight had been comfortably consigned to the back of his mind.

6

Without Stephen to keep her company, and with all of the really interesting gowns consigned to her sketchbook, at least half a dozen new ideas all sketched out, Elena grew bored with watching the dancers, and Gus, of course, was bored with the dancing the moment he arrived. They both tried getting the little fairy to talk to them, but that had never worked before, and it didn't now.

Finally they looked at each other, and Elena shrugged. "We might as well go," she said, and they took the remains of the feast with them upstairs to wait in the nursery for Ben and Arthur to discharge their duties and join them.

When they got there, they found a fine, roaring fire, plenty of wood to feed it, and more of Mrs. Banning's largesse, which included a pitcher of lemonade and another of negus. The other boys were not at all interested in the details of the party; to their minds, it was all rather a lot of nonsense. "I don't know why people make all this fuss about balls," said Emil, helping himself to apple slices and cheese. "They just don't seem important to me."

"It's not unimportant to Stepmother, though," Gus said, carefully selecting a biscuit and nibbling on it. "She was certainly queening it down there."

"I think she enjoys being in the company of people who are her social inferiors," Carl observed, speaking slowly. "Father didn't invite *anyone* above his own rank, or even really equal to it. I think she likes that above all things. I haven't seen her as happy, ever, as she was sitting at the head of the table with Father."

"I am going to be *very* happy when she and Father move to the town house in Bath for the holidays," David declared. "Just think! We'll have the whole house to ourselves! They're taking the new carriage, the new coachman, the new footmen, Msr. Paul, and that cat, Fleurette, so it will be comfortable again!"

"We should tell Mrs. Banning that we would like to take our meals downstairs with the staff," Elena declared. "It will be less work for her and the maids, and we'll get our food hot!"

"You're already Mrs. Banning's pet, you don't need to curry favor with her," Gus teased. "That *is* a good idea, though. I'm tired of heating things up on the shovels. What do you want to do first when they're gone?"

"Sleep!" declared Emil. "Sleep late in the morning and not get up until the fires have properly warmed all the rooms. Do you think we can convince Arthur and Ben that we don't need to do any lessons while they're gone? After all, if we'd been sent out to school, we'd be at home with no lessons to do until the middle of January." He yawned hugely, and his twin poked him in the side.

"You old bear!" teased Felix, as the firelight illuminated all their faces. "You would hibernate if you could!"

"I'd sooner be a bird and fly south for the winter, so I could sleep in the nice warm sun," Emil replied good-naturedly. "Wouldn't you?"

"Winter is beastly," Gus agreed. "Everything is cold and dead and gray, it's too cold for games, the woods are ugly, and it's worse if it rains. The only place nice is right by the fire, and we can't do lessons *and* sit by the fire. The only time winter is nice is when it snows."

Elena did not point out that in their trousers and boots and nice warm coats, being outside in the snow was a great deal more fun than it was in thin shoes, thinner stockings, dresses that got soaked at the hem, and either a spencer that did nothing to protect the stomach and legs, or an enveloping cloak or pelisse that dragged and got wet just like the skirts of her dresses did. "We can read. Chess? Perhaps we should have card games, or play at lottery," she offered.

"That's a capital idea!" exclaimed Emil—but then his face sank. "But we don't have any fish for lottery."

"I can make some from ribbon scraps," she promised. "I've almost finished all the sewing Stepmother asked me to do. She certainly isn't going to leave me anything to do while she is not here to supervise, and it would feel strange not to be working on something."

As the others began making happy plans for what they would do in their parents' absence, she became aware of something—a sensation familiar, but long missed. The feeling that there were eyes on her.

Reacting on instinct, she looked up to the tops of the framed pictures above and to either side of the fireplace—and there, to her delight, were the fairies, all sitting with legs dangling on the tops of the frames.

"Look up!" she whispered into a gap in the conversation.

They all did. "You're back!" Emil crowed. "Fairies! We missed you!"

But David shook his head. "They are probably not back for long; they'll probably wait until Father and Stepmother leave. I wager they are only here now because there is no chance Stepmother is thinking about anything but her party."

"It's all right," Felix said to the fairies. "We'll be happy to see you when it's safe for you to come."

The fairies were half-hidden in the shadows, with only their eyes glittering down at the siblings, but it *felt* to Elena as if the fairies were pleased with that response.

Arthur and Ben finally came up, undoing their cravats as they entered the nursery. "Is there anything to drink?" Ben asked, as he flung himself down among them, heedless of his fine suit. Elena snatched the cravats from him and Arthur before they could ruin the fabric by using them as handkerchiefs. "It's hot as midsummer down there, and my mouth is like the Sahara. I fetched drink for everyone but *me*, or at least it seemed that way."

"Just the negus," said David, lifting both pitchers. "None of us liked it."

Ben made a face, but reached for it, as Gus offered a glass. "I would drink ditch-water right now," he admitted, and to prove it, downed a full glass before pouring himself another, then offering the pitcher to his twin.

"Did you dance with many young ladies?" Emil asked.

Both of the eldest boys and Elena—who had been keeping an eye on them when she wasn't drawing—laughed. "One dance *only* with each of the four young ladies of an age to be eligible as marriage material for us," chuckled Ben. "We had very strict instructions from Father, as he did not want anyone daring to *presume* that his sons were on the marriage market, and he certainly did not want either of us to lose our heads over a pretty girl with no prospects."

"Then he muttered something about *unlicked cubs* and added out loud that it was our duty to see that every female that was in attendance got to dance at least once," Arthur added. As he said that, two of the fairies lifted off a map frame, twirled together in the air, then flew back up to their former places. "Like that," he said, pointing to them. "We even danced with the mothers of those girls, so they couldn't delude themselves that our attentions were *particular*."

"What did Stepmother say?" Elena asked.

Ben shrugged. "Not much. She was fidgeting the entire time Father spoke to us, as if she was impatient to get to the ballroom."

Before either of them could say more, the fairies suddenly flew up in a state of agitation and vanished. Elena touched Ben's sleeve, and pointed up at the now-empty picture frames. The others noticed, and within a mere moment, all of them had come to the same conclusion, and an air of caution replaced the mood in the room. Emil tossed another couple of logs on the fire, Gus and Carl began picking up the empty dishes and stacking them to one side of the hearth, and David said, in a voice that was just a little louder than usual, "When Father and Stepmother go to Bath, I think we should investigate the library thoroughly for books that will help Ben and Arthur when they go off to university. We haven't really done that ourselves; we relied on Beecham to pick things out he thought were suitable."

"Well, we ought to think about you and Carl as well, David," Arthur replied in a similar voice. "And you all ought to think about what course of study you intend to take, and look through the library for books to sharpen those skills, or at least, give you a good beginning."

"I don't believe we'll find more mathematics than we already have up here in the schoolroom, but we might find some law, and we'll certainly find plenty of books of sermons. Possibly even some religious studies," Ben agreed, and yawned hugely. "Let's get a nice bed of coals going. We can all get our bedwarmers and bring them here, so we won't have to climb into cold beds to sleep. I imagine the staff are still busy cleaning up, and I don't want to wait for them to come do it."

Elena yawned too. "I would show you all the gown designs I made for Stepmother, but there is not enough light, and you don't care anyway."

They all laughed—even if it was just a trifle forced—and Emil built up the fire while the rest of them got up and went to their rooms for their bedwarmers. *I wonder why Stepmother hasn't told the maids to stop warming our beds,* she thought, as she took the awkward, long-handled metal pan from its spot behind the door. *Perhaps she just didn't think of it.* And she grimaced, realizing that if her stepmother had kept listening through that boring discussion of books, they had just given her the notion to do so.

It won't be that bad if she does, she consoled herself. *Just one little thing to do before bed.*

But she didn't say anything to the boys when she joined them to get her share of the coals, with Arthur shoveling and Ben latching the top closed. Why give them something to fret over?

The dinner and ball had been rather enjoyable, after all. And she'd even met and had a pleasant conversation with a very nice young man. She was glad she had given him the best of her designs to give to his mother. It had looked from the balcony that she liked it very much.

It will be delightful to think something I made will adorn the form of someone nice. I am certain that as amiable as Stephen is, his mother must be the same, for she would have guided him.

She quickly undressed, taking extra care for her best gown, and slipped, shivering, into her nightdress. Chilled as she was, the warmed sheets felt heavenly, and the next thing she knew, it was morning.

The summons they had all been expecting since they woke came after they had gone to church as they were all bending studiously over their various books. The schoolroom was warm, and breakfast had consisted of very acceptable leftovers from the refreshment tables at the ball, but Elena knew they were all only half tasting what they ate. The fact that the summons did not come while they ate only meant that Father and Stepmother were sleeping in late.

So once the last crumbs had been devoured, they went back to their studies, as if yesterday had been an ordinary day. It was unlikely that Father would come in person, but not unheard of, and if they were *not* heads-down in schoolwork, he would be Displeased.

It was impossible to concentrate perfectly, of course. And when the summons finally came, it was a relief.

Jackie, the hallboy, clattered up in his boots to the open schoolroom door. He didn't even knock, he just blurted, "Begging your pardon, masters, miss, but Lord Whitstone and her ladyship want you all in the parlor."

He didn't wait for any kind of answer, just clattered away again, possibly concerned that his absence from his accustomed place and the various chores that occupied him when he was not answering the front door would be noticed and noted. It wouldn't matter to Hobart that the master had sent him on an errand; Hobart was a stern taskmaster to Jackie, who, to be fair, was easily distracted.

They all exchanged looks, and put their books away. In silence, they made their way as a group down to the winter parlor, the room that got full sun for all of the morning hours in winter. The hallways were cold, the staircases colder, and all of the house seemed echoingly empty. It was hard to believe at this moment how full of sound and light and people it had been last night.

They presented themselves at the door to the winter parlor, slowly and quietly approaching the hearth and the chairs on either side of it. Father, who would never acknowledge that he had spent any time waiting for someone, was reading a freshly ironed paper from London. Stepmother was holding a book, but probably had not been reading it. Elena had never seen her reading anything at all. Her hands were never occupied, as Elena's always were, with needlework; she left that to Fleurette, and, increasingly, to Elena.

Father made them stand there in a double line for several minutes before he folded the paper and acknowledged their presence. But rather than speaking, he looked them all up and down, critically, as if looking for something in their appearance to find fault with.

But they had all known this was coming—the critique following their performances at the dinner party and the ball afterward. So without needing to coordinate their actions, they had all dressed with great care this morning; in Elena's estimation, they had all done pretty well, although Gus looked as if he had combed his hair with a rake. They were all wearing their everyday clothing, and they all stood with their hands clasped in front of them, looking attentive.

Father graced them with a thin smile, and Elena relaxed inside. So this was not to be an occasion for being shamed.

As thin sunlight poured over furnishings that had probably not been new in Grandfather's time, he addressed them. His expression was pleased, but he kept glancing over at Stepmother as he spoke, as if gauging her reaction to what he was telling his children.

His children. We will never be hers, she has made that very clear.

"You all accounted very well for yourselves last night," he said, folding the newspaper and setting it aside. "I received compliments about all of you, and no complaints—" the smile warmed just a bit, "—well, not *precisely* no complaints. Two ladies who were faintly displeased that Ben and Arthur followed my orders and made certain that every lady had a dance, rather than showering your attentions solely on their daughters. That would have been unwise. There are far too many idle minds and busy tongues among our acquaintances, and the ladies in question would have been among the first to suggest romantic inclinations where there were none—" He paused, and arched a brow at Ben. "—*were* there?"

"Absolutely not, Father," Ben replied immediately. "To tell the truth, I found their conversation rather insipid. I got much more amusement from the older ladies; indeed, the older, the better. Several of them were quick-witted indeed. I remained grave and polite, as was proper, of course."

Father actually chuckled. "Well, you comported yourselves so very well that your mother and I are of the opinion that—"

Oh please, please, *dear God, I pray you do not let him say he is taking us with him!* There was *no* doubt in her mind that being confined together with Father and Stepmother in the much closer proximity of a relatively small town house would be a nightmare. She knew, from reading newspapers when Father and Ben were done with them, just how very much larger the manor was than a Bath town house. And although there would certainly be amusements aplenty in the city, they would *never* be allowed to leave the house except—well, there would be no "except." She did not have Nanny, and the boys did not have Beecham, to act as proper chaperones. There was no use even thinking Father or Stepmother would take them anywhere. So instead of comfort and privacy and at least *some* amusements, there would be crush, no privacy at all, and nothing to do that they had not brought with them—

"—you will be fine with Mrs. Farthingworth and Hobart overseeing you for an extended period of time. We intend to leave for Bath now as soon as the packing is complete, and not return until well after Twelfth Night."

She could have cried with relief. But she took care not to show anything but careful gratitude, as did her brothers. It was an enormous piece of news, though; in the past Beecham and Nanny had been there to supervise when Father took a rare trip to Bath or even London. They had all wondered if he would seek out some somber, distant relative to keep them under tight rein.

Evidently not!

"Thank you for your trust in us, Father," Arthur said, quite as if he was not jumping with glee inside.

"We expect you to fill the days with studies, of course,"

Stepmother said coolly, as Father gazed at her with an adoration that the simple statement in no way warranted. "To that end, you may make free of any book you might find, including using the ladder to reach the upper bookshelves of the library."

I knew it! I knew she was listening, somehow!

"Nothing would suit us better, Father," said Arthur, quite as if he meant it.

"You and Ben may also ride my hunters, Arthur," Father said graciously—as if this was a rare treat, and not a sort of punishment. The remaining hunters in the stable had been ridden so seldom, and then only by the grooms, that they were half wild and inclined to any number of bad habits, including murderous attempts to scrape their riders off on any wall, tree, or fence that was available.

Still! Being able to ride the hunters implied being able to use the old carriage, and *that* implied a trip or even two down to the village! There were only four shops, the butcher, the baker, the seamstress and hatmaker (she did not reach so high as to call herself a *modiste*), and the general goods store, but that was four more than were on the estate. They all got pocket money at their birthdays and Christmas, and didn't often have a chance to spend it. *And then we could pay a call on the vicar and his wife, and I will have the pleasure of watching his concealed anguish as we eat all the nicer biscuits.* That would be ample revenge for his stodgy sermons.

"Thank you, Father," Ben answered, as if he looked forward to the experience.

"You lads may go back to your studies," said Stepmother. "However, Elena, I wish to speak with you."

The boys managed to leave without breaking into a run, although Gus did look back over his shoulder at her with great sympathy, as Elena stood there, feeling very much like a mouse looking up at a cat.

"A little bird tells me that you made some very pretty sketches last night, Elena," Stepmother said, with false sweetness, her eyes betraying cold calculation.

She didn't speak once to Stephen's mother after I sent down that drawing. And they left early, so I know she didn't speak to Stephen's mother or aunt when they departed. Now I know she was listening and watching, because I was looking over the sketches while we were talking about what we would do when they were gone. She was extremely glad now that she had cautioned the boys to be careful what they said when the fairies vanished. *I wonder how she is doing it?* Elena's notions of magic were rather vague, and drawn mostly from what she could observe of the fairies (not much) and what was in Greek and Roman myth. *Doesn't Circe use a mirror? Well, there are certainly enough mirrors in the house.*

"I never had any instruction except from Beecham," she demurred. "But I *did* want to see the gowns, and draw some of my own invention; seeing a gown in person is so much better than an engraving in a newspaper. I'm probably not much good, though."

"Why don't you run up and bring them down, and let me be the judge of that," Stepmother said smoothly. This was clearly *not* a suggestion.

She obeyed, turning and not-quite-running off. This was going far too well!

When she'd had this idea, it had been sparked by the deep fear that she of all of the siblings was the most vulnerable to Stepmother's whims. The boys were immune to her whims to a great extent; Elena was not. And it had occurred to her, after several sleepless hours, that the best way to attain the same level of immunity was to supply Stepmother not only with hands skilled at needlework, but with something she could not get anywhere else.

Gus intercepted her at the door to the schoolroom. "Are you all right?" he asked breathlessly. "What did *she* want?"

"To see my drawings," she replied, getting the pasteboard portfolio off the shelf where she had stored the drawings she most particularly wanted Stepmother to see last night while they were all talking. She could scarcely believe her luck; she'd drawn those gowns with Stepmother in mind after seeing her current wardrobe. She had *hoped* that there could be some time when she could offer to show Stepmother those pictures as a means of currying a little favor with her, that extra *something she cannot get anywhere else.* And now Stepmother had actually *asked* to see them!

Now if only she will like them....

She did not run back down; the last thing she wanted to do was fall and tear the paper, or drop the precious sketches and tread on them. They were, thank goodness, done in pencil rather than charcoal, but they would not be improved by footprints.

She found herself clutching the drawings to her chest and taking short breaths of anxiety as she approached Stepmother, who kept her fixed with an unblinking stare. "H-here, ma'am," she stammered, holding out the papers in their portfolio in a hand that trembled and felt as cold as the garden outside. "I beg your pardon, but they really are nothing special."

"I will be the judge of that," Stepmother purred, clearly enjoying Elena's subservience. *Be as gentle as the dove and as wise as the serpent. The Bible says that. If she thinks I am compliant, even a little stupid, she won't trouble to watch me. Let me amount to nothing more in her mind than a pair of clever hands and a fine eye for a gown, and she won't think of ways to torment me out of boredom.*

She wasn't sure *why* she was so certain that Stepmother would do that sort of thing, but nothing could be more certain in her mind.

Stepmother began her perusal of the drawings with a cynical little smile on her face. That smile faded almost immediately, and was replaced by a look of incredulity. She held the first drawing to her face a little closer, as if to be certain of what she was seeing. She placed the first drawing on the table at her side carefully, as Elena's heart gave a little leap, and picked up the second.

When she had finished examining the drawings so closely that she could have been memorizing the lines, she gathered them respectfully together into neat stack and replaced them in the portfolio. But rather than address Elena, she turned to Father.

"Darling, why didn't you tell me your daughter was a budding *modiste?*" she asked, kittenishly.

Father reacted immediately to the sentence, which had been presented in such a sickeningly sweet manner that Elena felt faintly ill. "My darling!" he said, leaning toward her in such a way that Elena feared he was going to fall on his knees before her and take her free hand in his. Which would be terribly embarrassing for her and *should* have been embarrassing for him. "I had no idea! The child has always made fripperies for her doll. Don't all little girls? I didn't think such nonsense would be of any interest to you!"

This was utterly unlike the Father she knew, who was so undemonstrative, except when he was angry, that he might have been an effigy filled with straw.

And suddenly, she remembered that scrap of paper they had found, with the inexplicable Latin on it.

They had not been able to recognize the handwriting. But what if it *had* been Stepmother's? What if it *had* been a spell? What if it had been a *love* spell, the kind she had read about in the myths? Was Stepmother a kind of Circe?

"It is when she's somehow not only drawn a beautiful gown, she's drawn *six* of them, all *quite* unique!" Stepmother's eyes glittered with an emotion Elena could not name. "*And,* since we are leaving early, I will be able to have at least three of them made up in Bath in time for all the dinners and balls!"

"Is that important, my dearest?" he asked, languishingly. "If it is important to you, it is important to me."

Only magic could explain this sudden change in Father. *And he's only like this when he's around her. When there are other people—obviously I am not thought of as being important—he acts normally, just a little bit besotted with his beautiful new wife.*

"It is. Very important to me," she stated flatly.

"Then I shall move heaven and earth to see that it happens," he replied, adoration in every word. Elena wished that the floor would open up beneath her in that moment. Fortunately, Stepmother recalled she was still standing there.

"You've surprised and delighted me, child," she said, her eyes glittering again, cold and hard, exactly like ice. "You may go— oh!" she exclaimed, as Elena turned to leave. "Wait! What do you need to keep making drawings like this?"

"Drawing paper, drawing pencils, rubber," Elena replied, surprised that this wasn't obvious. Had Stepmother never learned to draw? She would have added that now that Beecham was no longer here to ask Hobart to order such things, she wasn't sure how long her current supplies were going to last—

But Stepmother turned back to her husband with that treacle-sweet smile again. "See to it that the child gets all of those she can use, won't you, my love? And get subscriptions to *Lady's Magazine*, *Gallery of Fashion*, and *Le Beau Monde* for her, there's a dear. If she's to keep making magnificent creations for me, she will need to know the current mode."

Father all but leapt to his feet. "I'll tell Hobart to see to it immediately," he said, and positively rushed from the room. Stepmother made a little shooing motion with her hand—the one that wasn't clutched to the portfolio as if one would have to sever that hand at the wrist to get her to release it.

"You can go, child," she said, and she actually sounded happy. "You should have everything you need by the new year. Possibly before that, one never knows."

Elena curtsied and—well, she did not quite *flee*, but she did leave as quickly as she could, and broke into a run as soon as she was out of hearing of the winter parlor. Fortunately her soft slippers made almost no sound as she ran.

One thing was certain, she was not going to tell her brothers about this until Father and Stepmother were gone and she was safe to do so. Safe.

Were any of them safe if Stepmother could do this kind of magic?

Elena and her brothers all stood with Hobart and Mrs. Farthingworth on the steps in front of the manor to bid Father and Stepmother farewell, just as they had when they had gathered to welcome Stepmother when Father brought her here. There were many differences between then and now; only the butler and housekeeper, of all the servants, were here to bid the master and mistress a safe journey. This time they were not all dressed in their best; they were dressed in their warmest, for it was even more bitterly cold now than it had been then, and even Stepmother had chosen comfort over fashion for her journey. She had opted for a fur cloak over her woolen pelisse, with woolen stockings instead of silk, a muffler wound about her throat and head. And she had hurried out the door and down the steps without a word or a sign to any of them, immediately muffling herself in the carriage robe, feet on the iron foot warmer.

The new coach was laden with trunks and boxes strapped to the top and the back. Stepmother was clearly impatient to be gone. Father emerged at last, inside his many-caped greatcoat, and turned to inspect them all. "Satisfactory," he said, and reached into the right-hand pocket of his greatcoat, and came out with a handful of little envelopes. "Since we will not be here for Christmas, you might as well have this early," he said matter-of-factly, as he passed an envelope to each of them. This would be their Christmas pocket money, and Elena had not expected him to be so generous as to allot it to them early. But there was a difference in one of them; it had been sealed with a blob of wax. That was the one he gave Elena.

"There is a little more in yours, child," he said, and his eyes took on just a hint of that strange softness they had during the unsettling scene in the winter parlor. "Your dearest mother said you were to have it and take the carriage down to the village and buy whatever drawing materials you require. She wants you to have enough until what I have ordered arrives, in case there is a delay."

Elena was so astonished that it was as if her mind blanked out for a moment, and she could not think of what to say or do.

Somehow, habit and training took over. "Thank you and thank Stepmother for me," she said, and curtsied, envelope clutched in her hand. As far as she could tell, there was a single coin inside, much bigger than a shilling.

Satisfied with that, Father turned and hurried down the stairs to the waiting coach. With a shake of the reins, the coachman, Trevor was off, with the grooms, Phillip and Dick, clinging to the seat on either side of him as Elena and her brothers dutifully waved goodbye. None of them dared to head to the door until the coach was the size of a ladybird beetle in the distance. They were taking no chances on the possibility that the coach might have to turn back for something that had been forgotten, and any signs that they were not appropriately dutiful would add to Father's irritation at having to return.

Then they all scurried into the warmth of the house, followed by Hobart and Mrs. Farthingworth. Hobart immediately lengthened his stride to head for the butler's pantry, his domain, and Mrs. Farthingworth's brisk steps took her in the direction of the master and mistress's rooms, presumably to oversee the maids who were taking the rooms apart to do a thorough cleaning in their absence.

"Wait!" cried Gus, before they could all make for the stairs. "I want to find out what Elena got in her envelope!"

Since she was eager to find out too, she stopped, and the others gathered around her. She broke the seal and pulled out a coin—

And nearly dropped it.

"Cor!" Gus exclaimed, as she held it up for all of them to see. "That's a sovereign!"

What they got in their envelopes depended on their ages. When they had been small, it was a couple of pennies. Of late, Arthur and Ben had gotten four shillings, Carl and David three, and so on down to Gus and Elena, who got one apiece.

She was not sure how much paper and so on that she could get down in the village, because the single store that carried such things was very limited in stock, but she was pretty sure buying everything on hand would cost substantially less than a sovereign.

The heady thought crossed her mind of all the things she could buy with the remainder—

And then came anxiety. Would her brothers be jealous? Or would they remember how Elena had always been an afterthought in Father's mind, how Nanny had taught her how to sew because although Arthur and Ben always got new clothing when they outgrew the old and passed it down to their younger brothers, Father never seemed to notice she needed new things until she was going about in garments so patched and perilously short that it bordered on indecency. Or how Father had gotten *them* a proper tutor, but had relied on Nanny for what scant education she got, rather than getting her a governess?

It's a good thing Beecham never minded teaching me with Gus, or I never would have learnt anything but sewing and a little reading and writing.

"I don't think Stepmother knows what paper and things costs," she mused aloud.

"Or she doesn't care," Arthur pointed out. And chuckled. "I was going to say 'be careful how you spend that,' but we all know you will be."

Her anxiety vanished as all of them beamed at her, as if she had finally won a prize she had been striving for.

"I think it's both those things, and perhaps that she thinks she will make me so grateful that I won't think about how much I am doing for her. Don't anyone tell her that I enjoy needlework! I would rather she didn't know that, or she'll heap me with Fleurette's mending as well as her own," she said, and dropped the coin back in the envelope, folded the envelope to secure it, and put the packet in her pocket. "If you like, I will go talk to Mrs. Farthingworth and Mrs. Banning about taking our meals in the kitchen while you go upstairs and see if there are any games in the attic."

"Capital," said Ben. "Come on, lads!"

They stormed up the staircase, while Elena ventured deep into the house to make their case. She knew Mrs. Farthingworth would be horrified at the mere notion of the "master's children" eating with the staff, but Mrs. Banning, who had come from a farm where everyone, servants and masters alike, ate the same food at the same table, would think it was practical. But she was pretty certain that pointing out that it was going to make *less* work for everyone would carry the day.

She was right; between them, she and Mrs. Banning wore down the housekeeper's scruples, and even Hobart, when consulted, gave the plan his blessing. Then there was the slight difficulty of fitting everyone around the staff table—there *were* eight of them, after all—but Hobart had a solution for that.

"The children," he pronounced, as if it was an edict, "can take their meals after the staff has eaten. There will be no hardship for them if they come down for a nuncheon at ten and again at four, since their tea will also be late. I leave it to you, Mrs. Banning, to determine what that nuncheon shall be. I will make an allowance in the household budget."

Thus, Mrs. Farthingworth found herself overruled, but she

took it well. "Well, if there is no unseemly *mixing* of staff and the master's children, I can see nothing to object to."

"And it will all be so much easier for everyone," Elena reminded them. "No need to send someone up with meals, and again to collect dishes! And no need to make anything special for us. Mrs. Banning is such a good cook that surely no one of any sense could turn up their nose at anything she would prepare!"

Mrs. Banning actually blushed, as Hobart nodded gravely. "I do not wish to malign Msr. Paul in his absence, but I find a good wholesome roast or stew much more palatable than all his Frenchy sauces and messes."

With that settled, Elena ran back up to the schoolroom to deliver the good news that not only had Mrs. Farthingworth capitulated, but that they were to get *two* nuncheons a day in addition to their meals!

This already had the makings of the best holiday season of their lives, and it wasn't even the first day!

7

Elena had hoped that Bath would be far enough away—or that Stepmother would be so occupied with gowns and bonnets and amusements—that Stepmother would not have an opportunity to use her spying magic. But Elena was also certain that Stepmother could somehow induce Father to not notice if she employed her arcane arts in the carriage on the way. So she really had not expected to see the fairies before a couple of days had passed.

But as they all lazed about the schoolroom, doing whatever they wanted, even if, as in Emil's case, that was nothing at all, a bit of movement at the mantelpiece caught her eye, and to her delight, it was a fairy! This one looked like a ghost of a moth, for her folded, moth wings were white, her hair was white, her scant draperies were white, and she was so pale as to be only the faintest shade of pink.

"The fairies are back!" she cried happily. "Look! That means Stepmother can't spy on us!"

They all looked where she pointed. Carl gave a whoop, and Ben exclaimed, "So you discovered that she really *is* spying on us?"

She quickly told them all about what had happened in the winter parlor after they had left her alone there. "I think we ought to look for more papers hidden about," she said when she had finished. "Didn't the Romans write down spells and hide the papers or lead tablets somewhere that they would affect whatever or whoever the spell was meant for?"

Ben nodded. "You're right, and that is a very good idea. We would have noticed her if she'd come up here, but there might be something hidden elsewhere. Oh! Since the maids are turning out their rooms, we should look in the dustbin!"

"Or among the draperies or pasted under the bed," said Arthur. "Anyplace that the maids would skip or Mrs. Farthingworth wouldn't think worthwhile to clean. I cannot see them taking the rugs out to beat, for instance; it's too cold."

"I'll look in the dustbin," Felix volunteered. Elena wasn't surprised. Felix had an astonishing tolerance for dirt.

"I think we ought to find out what the fairies are willing to do for us, and what they want in exchange," declared David, with a glance at the fairy on the mantelpiece.

He would have said more, but just at that moment the gong that usually announced luncheon and dinner service for the master and mistress and their guests rang up from belowstairs. That was the signal for their first nuncheon, and they all threw decorum and manners to the wind and ran down to the servants' hall, which was delightfully warmed by its proximity to the kitchen.

A quite satisfactory meal of leftover cake and buns from the staff's breakfast, together with some odds and ends of toast and jam, occupied them for about three-quarters of an hour, when they returned to the schoolroom to find an entire row of fairies now on the mantelpiece. Emil, who was always hungry, had carried away in a napkin what they had not eaten, and now took out a bun to munch on, as Ben undertook to interrogate the little creatures. There was quite an array of them, some with butterfly or moth wings, some with dragonfly or beetle, and some with bird wings. They all seemed very much at ease and quite curious. This was far more fairies than Elena had seen in one place before, and it occurred to her that they probably wanted to communicate with the siblings quite as much as everyone wanted to communicate with them.

They looked rather like fantastic ornaments created by someone with no sense of modesty whatsoever. Their little swaths and drapes of what appeared to be silk did not leave anything to the imagination.

But then, why should fairies be modest? It's not as if they were Christian creatures.

They all dragged chairs and cushions to the fireplace, and squeezed in around it.

"Manners," cautioned Elena. "They can just disappear again if they don't like what is said. Be polite. They're not toys you can order about."

By unspoken agreement, they left Ben to do the talking. "We are very glad that you are back, and would like to know if you can help us, please," Ben said, politely. "And if you are willing to."

There was a sort of silent colloquy among the fairies for a moment, and then it seemed they managed to choose one as their spokesperson. They were all pretty—this one had pale blue butterfly wings, dark blue hair tied in a tail at the nape of her neck, and solemn blue eyes. And was wearing just a scrap of ribbon covering her breasts, and a silky skirt so short it was almost an afterthought. She flew down from the mantelpiece, then hovered at Ben's eye level. By way of an answer to his question, she nodded.

"Why doesn't she speak?" Carl asked.

"Perhaps she can't," Ben said after a moment. "Or won't. It doesn't signify, I can just ask yes or no questions."

The fairy waited patiently through this, until Ben turned his attention back to her. "Is Stepmother spying on us?" he asked.

The fairy shuddered visibly, and nodded.

"Is she a witch?" Emil blurted, his hands twisted together in his lap. One of Nanny's more gruesome stories had impressed him so much that witches haunted his nightmares.

The fairy shook her head.

"But she *is* using magic, isn't she?" Elena asked anxiously. "To spy on us, I mean. And probably for other things?"

The fairy nodded.

"Can you tell if she starts spying on us again with magic?" Ben persisted. Once again the fairy nodded, and made little fluttering motions with her hands. "Does that mean you'll tell us by flying away and vanishing if you sense she is doing that?" he guessed, and she nodded, lips pursed.

"Can you help us in other ways?" asked Arthur. Much more pleased with this question, she nodded vigorously. "Then how can we pay you for your help?"

She pointed at Emil, who paused, nonplussed, bun halfway to his mouth. "What? How am *I* supposed to repay them? I'm not giving them my pocket money!"

Ben laughed. "I think she means that bun you're eating."

The fairy nodded so hard Elena feared she would give herself a headache.

"Why don't you just help yourself from the kitchen?" Emil asked, blinking in confusion.

"Nanny always said that fairies and other creatures can't *take* anything from people, it has to be freely given," Elena said, thinking aloud, and recalling those nursery tales she never would have thought would have practical application. *Now we're going to have to put our heads together to remember all of them. There is probably more in them about magic that we can use.*

The fairy nodded.

"Well, here," Emil said, getting the last bun out of the napkin and holding it out. "I'm sure we can manage that. Have this by way of advance payment and thanks for coming to talk to us."

Ben took the bun from him and placed it on the mantelpiece, where the fairies descended on it like a flock of hens on a particularly tasty bug. There was nothing but a scrum of wings, legs, and tiny behinds, and it was all Elena could do to keep from laughing. A glance at her brothers showed they were all muffling laughter behind their hands, or contorting their faces trying to keep it in.

When the fairies moved back to their places again, there wasn't a single crumb to be seen.

They all settled in for a question session that was going to last for at least two hours, by Elena's estimate. When it was over, they had a fairly good idea of what the fairies could and could not—or, perhaps, would and would not—do for them. Crucially, they now knew (thanks to careful questioning) that Stepmother had left hidden pieces of paper with writing on them in three places in the house.

And most importantly, the fairies had agreed that they would lead Emil to these papers, which Elena reckoned were probably spells. Why they had chosen Emil, well, perhaps because it was he who had given them his bun.

By then, it was time for their second nuncheon. Although they were all seething with the need to see what the fairies had uncovered, their rumbling stomachs urged otherwise, and when the gong sounded, they headed down again.

They came back up again with a couple of honey cakes, which the fairies devoured. Then it was a matter of waiting until the fairy that had been sent to watch the maids cleaning the room where the papers were hidden appeared in a little burst of golden light. Emil followed her back down the stairs, and the rest of them waited breathlessly until he returned.

It felt like forever to Elena, but they'd only had to replenish the schoolroom fire once before he was back, with a piece of letter paper in his hand. "I found all three, and they were pretty small. One was in a book that had so much dust on it Father couldn't have bothered to look inside it in a very long time, one was pasted to the bottom of the bed, and a third was pasted to the wall behind the bed-hangings. The fairy was upset when I tried to touch them, so I guess maybe Stepmother could tell if they were moved? Anyway, they were all alike, so I just got some paper from the study and copied everything down. She didn't seem to mind that."

He held out a slightly grimy piece of letter paper, much smudged, with mistakes crossed out, and Ben took it from him.

"It begins like the piece we found," he said, and read the words aloud. "Aqua in sanguine tuo tantum me spectat. Aqua in sanguine tuo desiderat tantum mihi. Aqua in sanguine tuo tantum me amat." And before any of the younger ones could complain that they did not know as much Latin as he did, he translated. "The water in your blood looks only for me. The water in your blood longs only for me. The water in your blood loves only me."

"That's a *love* spell!" exclaimed Arthur before anyone else could speak, in tones of anger and resentment. "That's how she got Father to marry her! She *trapped* him! Like Circe, she made him fall in love with her!" His fists were balled with rage, and his face reddened.

"And there is nothing we can do about it," Ben countered, then looked at the fairies. "Is there?"

As if their heads were on a string, they shook their heads in unison.

Arthur looked as if he was about to explode. Ben placed his hand on the shoulder of his twin, and stared into his furious eyes. Finally Arthur let out his breath and his shoulders sagged.

"Father has never been warm to us, but he's never been unkind either," Arthur said, around gritted teeth. "And now that I know that *she* is the one behind sacking Beecham and Nanny—"

"Not to mention banishing us up here, and if we weren't in Mrs. Banning's good books, we'd be starving!" said Emil, just as resentfully.

Elena's emotions were very much mixed, but fear predominated. This was like one of Nanny's tales that didn't end well. What if Stepmother's ambitions didn't end with marriage to a wealthy aristocrat? What if she hadn't known he had children? What if—she wanted everything?

Elena cut that thought short, and anger rose to the surface. She could not in all truth say that she loved Father, but she respected him, and to make him into that . . . besotted fool . . . was outrageous. How *dared* she!

Following the anger came determination. So what if she wanted everything? She wasn't going to get it. The estate was entailed, and unless she found a way to murder them all, one of Elena's brothers was going to be the heir. As for the rest, well, the plans they had already made would get them out of her clutches long before Father died. Six of the boys *would* escape this place and this woman, and at least one of them would take her with them. "As long as we are careful, and don't irritate her, or give her any hints that we know what she is, I think that she won't do anything terrible to us," she said, though that was more of a wish than a certainty. *I'm already valuable to her. She won't do anything to me.* Though that was a double-edged sword, when it came to the future. Stepmother wouldn't let her go, not easily. But that was something to deal with in the future when they had a better idea of how much magic she could do.

"I hate it, but you're right," growled David.

"Look at what she's done so far," his twin added. "Not much. She *could* have sent us to some horrid, useless boarding school in the north, some place where we'd know more than the teachers."

Or sent each of you to a different school, where you'd be alone as well as miserable. Children sometimes die at those schools, pneumonia or cholera or consumption, like in that song that Nanny sang, where the mother sends her three children to the North Country and their spirits come back to tell her they've died. She wouldn't have to lift a finger, she could be rid of the boys that way!

Carl wasn't finished, although it appeared that the idea they could all be separated, scattered to the winds to face their fates alone, had not occurred to him yet. "And she could have sent Elena off to one even worse." The way his face darkened suggested that "worse" did not mean ignorant teachers and insufficient food, cold, drafty rooms and damp beds, but something he was unlikely to elaborate on. "Instead she exiled us up here and did what?" He let out a pent-up breath. "Nothing much. She didn't hurt us, not really. Well, she sent Nanny and Beecham away, and that was *bad*, but we're all clever enough to teach ourselves out of books. What she did was *small*. Just the pettiness of putting us on scant rations, and we outfoxed her there. And Elena was very clever, and protected herself so we don't have to worry about her. All we lads have to do is stay out of her mind until it's time to go to university."

Arthur nodded. "Father might be besotted, but he is still minding the business of the estate. If we were in London or Bath, certainly, she could throw his fortune away on jewels and gambling, but there's nothing to spend money on here. And even if they go to Bath, he won't allow her out of his sight, and her opportunities to waste his ready will be fewer."

"But what if she tells Father sending us to university is an extravagance?" David asked anxiously. "What if she tries to prevent him?"

But Ben seemed confident in his answer. "I can see no way she can avoid Father sending us; she wants to be in his social circle, and be the most important lady in the area, and she cannot do that if Father doesn't send us to university, keep Arthur as his heir, and send the rest of us off to our respectable places in society. It wouldn't look *normal*. People would start asking questions about why we're lingering about the place, useless, doing nothing."

"No, that sort of thing is just not done," Arthur agreed. "And it's not as if she can make us disappear out of the minds of everyone who knows us. We'll have to swallow our anger and be pleasant to her. She's vain enough to think that her beauty and charm have won us over."

"I am *not* calling her 'Mother,'" Felix seethed.

"But what do we do if Father orders us to?" David fretted.

Elena had a sudden idea that made her laugh. The others turned to stare at her.

"Father won't do that unless she's there too, because she will want to watch our reactions," she explained, and laughed again. "And if that happens, Arthur, you just look innocent and say, 'But would she really want people to think she's old enough to have a son my age?'"

They all stared at her blankly for a moment. Then, one by one, as they worked out what she had meant, they all began to laugh, the sort of laugh that releases tensions that have nothing to do with the cause of the laughter.

"How did you think of that?" Ben asked, when their laughter had finally subsided.

"I don't know," she confessed. "It just came to me. But we need to work out the limits of what she can do, and, well, how indolent she is. We don't want her to decide to exert herself. Ben, when we've performed plays, you are a good actor. Do you think you can be a good enough actor to convince her that you're a bit besotted yourself?"

"Oh lud, must I?" He ran both his hands through his hair as all the fairies seemed to convulse with laughter. "Well, she clearly craves attention. I'll try, and you should, too, Elena. Only you should make it more worshipful than besotted. As if she is everything you admire and want to be."

She sighed, and turned to the fairies. "Do you think I can convince her that I admire her and would like to be like her?"

The fairies looked at one another, and back to her. One or two nodded, the rest shrugged.

"You know, it shouldn't be that hard," Arthur told her coaxingly. "Just tell her that you think she's beautiful a great deal, and then be very shy. You can do that, I know you can, Elena. You're extremely clever."

She blushed. It wasn't often that the boys praised her, and to be told she was *clever* was much better than being told she was pretty. Pretty could get you into trouble, like having some horrid old man decide he wanted her for his new wife, and persuading Father. *I'm safe from that, though, as long as Stepmother finds me useful.* Suddenly flattering Stepmother didn't seem quite so difficult.

"I think we have accomplished quite a bit," Ben said with satisfaction. "We've found out, thanks to the fairies, quite a bit about Stepmother. We have the outlines of a plan. And we have *more than a month* and the manor to ourselves. It's time to truly enjoy ourselves! We can do anything we like!"

The faces of her brothers lit up with pleasure as they all realized that they had the run of the manor and lands, and no one to answer to except themselves. It was a pity this hadn't been in summer, but at least they were all old enough that they could depend on each other to think of amusements.

"As long as we don't incur the wrath of Hobart, Mrs. Farthingworth, or Simon," Arthur cautioned. "Which means no enormous messes, no tracking mud about, no trying to ride the rams, no larks of that sort."

Gus blushed, since the part about riding the rams was aimed at him.

"But we *do* have the run of the stables, and the old coach horses are sedate enough I expect they'll let us ride them," Ben said soothingly. "The pony is used to being ridden, and I'm sure Simon can find riding tack for the coach horses. And there's the pony cart Elena and Gus can drive. With work, Father's three hunters can probably be tamed, too."

"*You* can try that," said David. "I had rather not have to choose between having my leg scraped between a horse and a wall, and trying to dismount from a horse that is dancing about and won't answer to the rein." He looked just a bit cross, though not at Ben. Probably his misadventure with one of the hunters was still vivid in his memory.

"Simon will have some ideas, I know," Ben retorted confidently. "Actually, Simon will know how to take them right back to their first training, and we can do that. It won't be as jolly as riding across the countryside, but I rather like the idea of properly schooling them by way of getting our own back."

As the rest of them discussed riding, Elena got her workbasket. She had gotten Hobart to order her some fine muslin and she was making cravats for Father and her brothers and Hobart himself for Christmas. Of course, only Arthur and Ben were likely to appreciate such a thing, and it was almost a certainty that her present to Father would languish in a drawer or wherever he put the slippers she usually made for him at his birthday, but one couldn't outgrow a cravat, and eventually the boys would be grateful for an extra. It was meticulous work and needed daylight, for only the smallest, most invisible hems would do. One of the fairies came to see what she was doing, and then sat on the back of her chair, eventually drowsing a little. Elena longed to sketch her, but the possibility of Stepmother seeing such a sketch made it far too risky. Stepmother had proven that whatever she was using to spy on the siblings made it possible for her to see Elena's sketches as well as what they were all doing—and presumably hearing what they were talking about. The best way to keep the fairies a secret was to make certain there were no drawings, no writing, and no verbal mention of them.

She glanced at the dozy fairy at her shoulder. "I wish you could speak," she sighed. "You could tell us all about magic, and perhaps we could learn some."

The fairy woke up and gave her a wide-eyed look Elena could not interpret. Was she surprised that Elena would want such a thing? Incredulous to think such an ordinary girl had the idea that *she* could *learn* magic? There was no way to tell. Elena went back to her hemming. Her brothers were already making plans for Christmas, which would be the first one without Father. That meant Christmas games of the sort they had not often gotten the chance to play.

"Do you think Mrs. Banning will let us play at snapdragon?" Emil asked eagerly.

Elena shuddered. The one time she had participated in that

perilous game, she had gotten burnt fingers, and the idea of a flaming bowl of brandy and raisins surrounded and jostled by her rowdy brothers was terrifying. Nanny had been *full* of cautionary tales about skirts getting too near a fire, or ribbons near a candle, or burning liquor spilling and setting the house afire. Those tales always ended in the reckless party being burnt to cinders, which did not appeal.

"I don't think Hobart will permit it," Arthur replied, squashing Emil's dreams of winning the game by stuffing himself full of the most raisins. "He's not likely to let us do anything that could burn the house down."

"Old stick," muttered Emil, and sulked. But just for a moment, because Arthur reminded them all that this year *they* would dictate everything about the holiday, rather than Father, whose preferences were austere to say the least. "We can have garlands, and a Yule log, and all manner of merry things. And when gleemen and carol singers come by, we can invite them in and *enjoy* their music, instead of sending them away immediately without even a groat like Father ordered Hobart to do."

The room grew dark, and since no one else seemed to be willing to leave the fire, Elena went around lighting the candles and the four lanterns Hobart had somehow arranged to have mounted on the wall. For the first time since Stepmother arrived, the schoolroom felt like a sanctuary instead of a prison. *Why, I can go use the winter parlor myself if I want to sew alone. And I can sprawl on the sofa or the fainting couch if I please without anyone coming to scold and correct my posture.*

It was too dark for fine sewing, so she joined the others in their planning, until the gong summoned them for supper.

Aside from rising as late as they pleased, and reading for pleasure rather than study, their days did not seem to change a great deal. But there was great relief in knowing that Stepmother was not going appear to persuade Father into doing something that they would not like, and great relief in knowing that Father's looming presence was looming elsewhere. The vicar turned up three days into their holiday "to make sure they were getting on all right," but since they were in no way obliged to offer him more than a glass of cordial, and he had *not* arrived at the belated hour of *their* teatime, he had to content himself with awkwardly trying to be jolly and failing utterly, and sipping at a tiny glass of liquor which, although it was undoubtedly of fine quality, in no way made up for the generous tea he had been anticipating. They saw him out as soon as he had finished his glass, and he had not asked for a second. And when he was safely down the drive in his creaky little chaise, they spent the next hour or so in the pleasant pursuit of mocking nearly everything he had said.

The weather was bleak and cold, with gray skies most days, but there was no snow, so there was little reason to go outside except for daily walks. The boys did that; Elena preferred to get her walking done indoors, where she could poke curiously at things she had never dared touch, because Father had forbidden his offspring to venture outside of a handful of rooms without his express permission. The conservatories were the most pleasant to idle through, even though Father would not waste an inch of space on flowers. She was able to purloin an occasional grape or fig, although she dared not touch the precious oranges, since she was certain Mrs. Banning knew the location and degree of ripeness of every single one of them. Most of the conservatories were devoted to herbs and vegetables, and, as such, about as attractive to walk through as a kitchen garden, but the orangery was delightful. There was a little pond with goldfish, big, slow, old ones. When they bred, Father had the small ones netted and sold off. She liked to sit on the edge of the pond and feed them. There were clusters of chairs here and there under the branches of the fruit trees as well. Some of the trees were in bloom, and the scent of orange and lemon blossoms vied with faint scent of smoke from the stoves keeping the conservatories warm. Unlike the fireplaces in the manor, these stoves were fueled with coal, which didn't need replenishing as often. She never got to walk in the conservatories when Father was home, but that might have been due to her age, and Father's notion that a child could not be trusted to leave the fruit alone.

Then again, remembering those stolen grapes and figs . . . perhaps he was right.

About a week into their adventure, the weather broke, and Arthur, Ben, Carl, David, and Elena commandeered the carriage to go down to the village and the shops to spend their pocket money. The other three had already taken the pony cart down. Well . . . it was two shops to patronize, in Elena's case. Mrs. Banning had sent Arthur to the butcher for some cuts from a prize cow that had been specially promised, and Ben was in charge of putting in the weekly order of beer at the tavern. Elena got the impression that the servants were indulging themselves in superior foodstuffs ever so slightly on the grounds that they were sharing their meals with their master's children, which certainly seemed reasonable to *her*. Certainly Hobart, who was in charge of procuring and paying for everything that was not produced on the estate, would have put an abrupt end to the festivities if he thought they had gone too far.

The shops were all in a row in the center of the village. Butcher, baker, general goods, seamstress, all of them doubling as homes for their owners. There was no greengrocer, since everyone in the village had their own "bit of garden" and anything they could not raise themselves they bought at the weekly open market. For anything else, one had to wait on an itinerant peddler or go to the town five miles away, which had a superior collection of many shops. Elena would have liked to do just that, but Father's instruction had been "to the village," and she was fairly certain that Grimes would have refused to take them that far. Unlike most of the buildings in the village, these were true two-stories; the front half was the public part, and Elena wasn't sure how the back half and upper stories were arranged. Unlike the cottages and houses of the village, the front of each shop had one or two large, many-paned windows, in which particularly desirable items were displayed. In better weather, the front was often enhanced with tables displaying more common goods.

Arthur and Ben went off on their errands, and the Elena and the younger boys went to the general goods shop to spend their money.

Inside, they were greeted by a counter, behind which the daughter of the shopkeeper currently reigned in a dress of good wool, a cap, and a spotless apron. The air in the shop was scented with a mélange of spice from the spice cabinet, leather, a hint of the six oranges that gleamed like golden orbs from their precious box well out of reach of children, and things not quite identifiable. The only items in front of the counter were too large and heavy to be snatched and carried away—today they were greeted by a wooden chair, a barrel, a stack of metal coal-buckets, and a mechanical object she did not recognize. The first thing she did was to strictly obey Stepmother's stricture and purchase every bit of drawing supplies that she could use. The watercolor paper and colors, high up in the section where paper goods were kept, although she gazed at them enviously, were of no use to her, as she didn't have the least idea of what to do with them. The girl in charge of the shop brought down all of the drawing supplies, then looked at her with her mouth open as she tapped the stack of drawing paper, the box of pencils, and the one of rubbers and said "all of this," while David and Carl put their heads together, debating about how to spend their three shillings each.

When the girl totaled it all up for her, as she had expected, she had the satisfaction of knowing she had the lion's share of her sovereign left. She sent the girl for felt for penwipers that she would make for the boys to go with the cravats at Christmas, and seven packets of the sorts of sweets Mrs. Banning could not or would not make, each packet tailored to a particular brother. For Arthur, licorice, though no one else liked it. For everyone else, boiled and sanded sweets in the flavors they liked best—lemon for Ben, ginger for Carl, clove for David, currant for Emil, orange for Felix, and cinnamon for Gus. This was the first time she'd had money for boiled sweets as a Christmas gift and she was ridiculously happy about being able to buy them. She got a packet of peppermint for herself, and told herself she would save it for Christmas—but she knew she wouldn't make it that long.

She also bought a few more odds and ends, because she always needed needles, pins, and pen nibs, then presented the girl with her sovereign. The girl gaped again, then brought out her father to make change, since there was not enough in the till.

The boys had been joined by Arthur and Ben as she left with her parcels to secure them in the coach. Then she walked into the place she had longed to be the entire time she had been in the general-goods shop. The seamstress, whose window was full of bonnets, laces, ribbons, and a dummy with a nicely made woolen spencer and muslin gown.

And there in the shop window was something that actually made her fire up with the desire to have it—a beautifully warm winter bonnet. She did not possess such a thing; until now she had made do with straw bonnets that she lined with wool and embellished on the outside with remnants of whatever she had left when she made over a gown from the attic. This was a beaver bonnet, a lovely shade of brown, adorned with woolen flowers, and instead of a simple ribbon to secure it, it boasted a kind of scarf or muffler one could wrap warmly about one's neck. And with it was a matching beaver muff—something else she did not possess. She was suddenly aware of how cold her hands were, even in her gloves, and longed for that muff as Moses must have longed for the Promised Land.

She'd had vague ideas about what she would buy—but one look decided her. She must have these!

She emerged from the shop with the bonnet triumphantly secured on her head, and both hands tucked warmly in the muff, which had room in it for the little packet of lace trim she had bought with the last of her gift. Her old bonnet was now in the hatbox that the seamstress's little boy carried to the carriage for her.

Ben was waiting for the others in the carriage, several intriguing packages at his feet. "That's an uncommonly pretty hat," he said admiringly as she got inside and accepted the hatbox from the seamstress's boy. "And warm too! I think even Father would approve of its practicality."

She beamed at him as the other three emerged at last from the general-goods shop and climbed into the carriage.

I think this might be the first Christmas, ever, that we'll all be happy.

The carriage rolled away in the thin winter sunlight, and she relaxed into the cushions, experiencing a rare moment of utter content.

"I wish Father and Stepmother would *stay* away," said Carl, saying out loud what they were probably all thinking. "I don't suppose Stepmother is likely to persuade him of that...."

Ben shook his head, as the carriage bounced and jounced over frozen ruts. "I've never known Father to enjoy being away from home, and I don't think Stepmother's spell is going to change that. Once all the balls and routs of the season are over, she won't be able to distract him, and he'll want to return."

"There's another thing," Arthur put in. "When she is *here*, she can queen it over all the ladies in the neighborhood. But in Bath, she won't have the highest rank at *any* of the festivities she attends, and eventually she'll want to come back, where she will be deferred to in all things. And if she wants a ball or a rout or a card party, she need only persuade Father that she will be unhappy unless they hold such a thing."

"I wouldn't be unhappy if she did so," David observed dispassionately. "It will keep her mind on something else, and we'll get the benefit of leftovers."

Ben laughed. "Well, we'll see what she manages to persuade Father into. Right now, anything past Twelfth Night is all speculation. Let's enjoy our freedom while we have it."

8

The first issues of the promised ladies' magazines arrived a few days later, the promised drawing supplies the day after that, and Elena found her days enjoyably full once those two events occurred. In fact, she could not remember a time when her life was so pleasant!

In the morning, when the light was best in the winter parlor, she worked on fine sewing—not just cravats for the boys and for long-suffering Hobart, but fichus decorated with lace she had cut and frugally saved from remade garments out of the attic. So many of those dresses were overloaded with lace and flounces that she had an abundance of material left over when she remade one into a modern gown. Those fichus were for Mrs. Banning and Mrs. Farthingworth. She also worked on silk handkerchiefs cut from silk shirts taken from another trunk in the attic, full of menswear, which had the fronts too stained to be worth remaking. Since the stains were very often wine, it appeared that the Whitstone men were given to drinking to excess, and maybe that explained why Father was so straitlaced. These handkerchiefs were for Stepmother and Father. She made the handkerchiefs as elaborate as possible and still be fit for their use. Faggoting at the hems, French convent-made lace from ancient chemises so delicate that they were literally crumbling for Stepmother, and their initials embroidered in white silk at the corners. Greek key embroidery above the faggoting for Father, and entwined flowers for Stepmother. As long as she didn't think too much about who the handkerchiefs were for, Elena very much enjoyed the work. The way the silk slipped sensuously through her fingers, the pleasure in doing the fine work and seeing the result, even the triumph as she finished yet another minuscule, invisibly stitched hem on a fine muslin cravat—it was all delicious. The fairies seemed to find her work of great interest, and there were always a few hovering about her or sitting on the back or arm of her chair. She did venture to ask one of them if they wanted her to make *them* something, but they laughed at her. Apparently they did not feel the cold! Or modesty!

In the afternoon, after a walk in the conservatory, she would sit and read for a little under the orange trees, where it was warm and delightfully fragrant. If she closed her eyes, she could imagine herself in some exotic place far, far away from the bleak winter, someplace wild and free. There were a lot more fairies out in the conservatory, as if this was where they lived in winter; all she had to do was look up and she'd see them flitting among the branches or playing tag in the beds of herbs. The brush of their wings against herb leaves released all manner of lovely scents, and made the lack of flowers irrelevant.

After tea, she would cluster candles—real candles, which Hobart allowed them—on the table in the warmest part of the schoolroom and study the engravings in the magazines as closely as she could, then try her hand at sketching some similar gowns herself. She wanted to have a good stock of drawings for Stepmother to pick through when she returned. There was no one in this village, or in the nearest town, who was likely to have the skills—or, more importantly, the apprentices and assistants—of a *modiste*, but that did not mean gowns based on her drawings could not be made up without resorting to the uncertain skills of the *modiste* in Charton-town so many miles away. The local seamstress could be relied on to make the untrimmed gown, and Elena was confident she could make or buy the embellishments, or use some of the attic treasures. She knew she could apply them; it was just a matter of bringing her fine-sewing skills to bear.

She was also confident in her ability to make a small version for one of her dolls, so that Stepmother would be able to see what the finished gown should look like, if Stepmother was uncertain about a design.

The fairies did not hover about while she did this, or if they did, they were out of her sight. Maybe they found it boring; she wasn't doing much except staring at a page and then trying to draw something similar on a page of her own. They did seem to get bored easily—or maybe the reason was simpler than that: since they didn't wear much, they didn't really understand why anyone would swath themselves in yards of fabric. Perhaps that was why that fairy had laughed at her for the suggestion that she might clothe them. Her stack of drawing paper was so thick now that it made her giddy to think about it. Perhaps Stepmother—or Father—thought that one threw away a failed attempt rather than using the rubber to painstakingly erase the offending drawing. Or perhaps the abundance was due to Hobart, who had probably done the actual ordering. For all his gravitas and aloof manner, Hobart was proving himself quite sympathetic to the situation the siblings found themselves in, and he just might have thought that Elena should get some benefit from the torrent of money that Father was spending on his new wife.

Her brothers left her alone except for meals, once they understood how much she was enjoying herself. She had thought she might be lonely without being with them every hour of the day, but to her mild surprise, she discovered it was something of a relief to sit in quiet solitude with nothing but the crackling fire in her ears, or the very distant sounds of the staff at work. Sometimes, when she was in the orangery or when she was working in the schoolroom, Ben would come and read to her, which was lovely. Sometimes Gus would come and keep her company while he was working on some little project of his own; when he did that, provided he didn't fall asleep in the warmth of the winter parlor or the orangery, they'd build castles in the air together about what they would do when they could leave here. It was Gus who came up with a plan of escape for her when one or all of them came to take her away.

"We'll tell you in a code or invisible writing when we're coming to get you," he said with confidence, and reminded her of the trick Beecham had taught them, of writing invisibly in lemon juice, which could only be seen when you held the page above a candle flame for a little while. "When we get here, we'll hide down by the front gate, and send a fairy to warn you that we're here."

"But will the fairies do that, if they are afraid of Stepmother?" she objected.

"Ask them," he replied.

So she did, turning to one who was sitting on the arm of her chair, a dusk-haired creature with wings as blue as the sapphires in one of Stepmother's necklaces. "Would you do that?" she asked the fairy, who made a face of distaste, but nodded.

"Well, there we are, then," he said in triumph. "The kitchen door is always left unlocked. All you'll have to do is throw what you want to take with you into a bundle, slip out the door, and come to the end of the driveway. From there, we will carry you away."

He was very blithe about her ability to get out without anyone waking and seeing her, and then getting down the drive in the dark. But then—if it meant getting away from here, and from *her*, perhaps she could manage it better than she thought. "I don't care if I end up sitting in the bed of a farm cart with bits of straw," she told him, "as long as it means I will be gone from here."

"And then we'll all go to Canada together!" he would always end, triumphantly, because he had made up his mind that he was going to go to Canada and have adventures, rather than buying a pair of colors and going into the army, and she was going to go with him. "We can become fur traders! Won't that be grand, living in tents, traveling in canoes, out in the wilderness where there would be no one to tell us what to do? Perhaps we can even live with a band of Red Indians!"

That didn't sound all that "grand" to her, and she certainly did not want to live in a tent, but she let him go on about all the things they would see and do. "I wonder if there are any such things as fairies on that side of the ocean, or if they have their own sorts of fairies there," he said at last, finally running out of things his limited imagination could come up with—though to be fair, all either of them knew about Canada was the occasional story in one of Father's newspapers, and a few paragraphs in one of the geography or history books the boys had been studying.

She looked at the little blue fairy beside her. "Are there any of your kind across the ocean?" she asked.

The fairy shrugged, which she took to mean that the little thing did not know. Or that there *were* members of her kind over there, but she didn't much care about them. The fairies, she had come to understand, were supremely indifferent to anything that did not immediately affect them.

They sat in silence for a moment, while the fire crackled, Elena sewed, and somewhere in the house, distant voices told that the staff was hard at work. The rooms that the siblings were not using had had the furniture shrouded in sheets, and the fires extinguished to save the servants from having to clean rooms no one was using, but that just meant that Mrs. Farthingworth was taking the occasion to give the rooms that *were* in use a more thorough cleaning.

None of them really cared that so many rooms had been closed up. The younger boys still enjoyed sliding about the floors in their stockings, but there was nothing much in those rooms that interested them anymore. Father's previous, much shorter journeys to Bath or beyond had allowed them to discover all that there was to discover in the manor. Ben had taken them on a kind of tour of all of the concealed passages and hidden cupboards several years ago, but as there really wasn't anything in the rest of the rooms that was interesting, there was no real incentive to ask the staff to uncover things and start warming fires in these disused rooms. She had been as indifferent to the servants' work as the fairies were when she was younger, but now she understood how much work *just the fireplaces* took—ash removal, blacking the firedogs, cleaning off the soot, sweeping the hearth, and laying a new fire and starting it—that it seemed extremely unfair of her to expect them to have fires in every room when Father was gone.

Now, sliding on the highly polished floors of the hallways was harmless and made no extra work for the staff, so that was all right. Once in a while, Gus would tease her into putting a pair of old stockings on over her good stockings and going sliding, which was great fun, and those empty rooms, especially the ballroom, made for great sliding, but other than that, she found the rooms uninteresting. Even a bit unnerving, what with all the portraits on the walls of people who were long dead, but whose eyes seemed to be watching and judging her.

Worse than the rooms full of portraits were the rooms full of dead animals. Even if Father was an indifferent game hunter, preferring to rely on the gamekeeper to supply them with pheasant, duck, quail, and the occasional deer, previous masculine Whitstones had been a great deal more enthusiastic about slaughtering wildlife and displaying the trophies. Vicar never said anything about animals having souls, but if they did, Elena was certain that they surely would want to visit pain on the people whose relatives had murdered and beheaded them, stuffed them and posed them, or took off their skins and made hearthrugs out of them.

Gus was unaffected by such things, or said he was.

She was recalled to the present by Gus getting restless and standing up. "I'm going to go play with the stable cat," he said. "Do you want to come?"

But not even the pleasure of cuddling the soft creature and listening to her purr (Father was adamant about having no pets in the house, not even a cat) was enough to get her to move from the scented warmth of the orangery, so she shook her head. Released, Gus ran off. She concentrated on her knitting; for once, she was making something for herself, a pair of warm gloves out of lambswool. Let Stepmother suffer (if that woman *ever* suffered!) in thin kid. Lambswool might not be fashionable, but who was going to see her, anyway? The staff here at the manor, the villagers (who themselves wore practical woolen gloves), and the vicar and his wife and family, none of whom would care. Lambswool gloves for when she needed to keep her hands unburdened, that glorious beaver muff for when she did not, and she knew that this winter at least she would not suffer from hands that ached in the cold.

He thinks he wants to be a trapper and fur trader, but I don't think Gus has it in him to go about killing and skinning things, she thought, as she mentally counted stitches, reveling in how soft the yarn was. *Perhaps I can think of something else he'd like to do to make a living. We could have a little house together, and I could be his housekeeper.*

But perhaps it would not be Gus she stayed with, once all of them were gone from the manor. Perhaps it would be Ben, who was perfectly content with his destined profession in the clergy. She rather thought that Ben would make a good vicar; he had the wit to write sermons that would be interesting to listen to, the interest and empathy in his fellow man that often took him down into the village to make certain that matters were all well there (which should have been the vicar's, Father's, or Stepmother's job), and a grasp of Biblical scholarship that would only be improved by a university education. And she would be happy to be *his* housekeeper and companion until such time as he found a wife, and possibly beyond that, since she did not think that any lady he might choose would also fail to be *her* friend, and it would be grand to share household duties with another female.

I should very much like to have a female friend, she thought wistfully. There were so many things she didn't feel comfortable sharing with her brothers, not even Gus. A female friend would be as close as she ever got to having a sister, and she had always wanted a sister. The boys were grand, but they were often baffled by her interests and discomfited by displays of emotion. They were helpless if she cried, and sometimes embarrassed by displays of affection, things that a female friend would understand and even share.

Finally, her hands began to feel tired and cramped after making so many fine stitches. She put the knitting aside and rested her hands in her lap, and looked up at the fairies playing in the orange branches. Seeing that she had noticed them, a half dozen flew down to hover in front of her face, looking interested. And that was when a thought occurred to her.

"Can you teach me magic?" she asked. *Stepmother learned, somehow. I wonder if there is a way for me to learn?* Their own efforts had come to nothing, and the boys had tired of trying.

The fairies looked to each other, then back to her. Finally one of them, a green-haired beauty with dragonfly wings, moved closer to her, and mimed putting a hand to her ear.

"You want me to listen?" she asked, feeling baffled. "But you never speak!"

At that last word, the fairy flew right to her face and placed a hand on her lips, then mimed listening again.

"I don't understand!" she cried.

Again the fairy, exhibiting more patience than she had ever seen them demonstrate before, put her hand on Elena's lips. But then, she hovered a little higher, and put a hand on Elena's forehead.

Elena struggled to understand. Once again the fairy mimed listening, then put her hand, with the lightest of feather-touches, on Elena's forehead. That hand felt lighter than a gnat! But it took her many moments to work out what the fairy wanted her to understand.

Finally, in a burst of intuition, it came to her. *So she wants me to listen . . . in my mind?* That actually made a kind of sense, because she was used to Arthur using all sorts of Biblical allusions, and one of them was about the "still, small voice" in the soul. Or was it the heart? Well, it didn't really matter which; she understood that she was meant to make her mind very quiet and just *listen*.

The truth was, she did that often enough when things were tense around Father. As long as she wasn't the center of his attention, she would often shrink inside herself and *not think*, on the grounds that then he might not notice her. She didn't do that with Stepmother, because Stepmother seemed to be a great deal more observant than Father, and being still didn't mean she'd forget about you.

So she took a deep breath, and just *listened*.

For what seemed like an eternity there was nothing. Then—
There. That's better. I knew you were a clever girl.

She felt her eyes widen, as the fairy backed up in the air a little and nodded at her, smiling.

"So you *can* teach me about magic!" she whispered, and made her mind all still again.

Yes, I can. Air magic, at least. We are the smallest of the Air

Elementals, the sylphs. And all of you can see us because you were born with the ability to use the magic of Air.

"Sylphs? Oh! There are little bits about you in Greek stories!" she breathed.

So there are. Now, make your mind still again, and look at me very, very closely. Don't expect anything. Just look.

Well, that was much harder to do, but she got the notion that what she was *expecting* to see was interfering with what was actually in front of her.

I'll help, said the sylph, and buzzed over to the side of her head and put her hand on Elena's temple.

Elena directed her gaze to the other sylphs, still playing among the branches, and let her eyes relax, the way she had let her mind relax . . . and after a moment, she realized that all of the sylphs were surrounded by a gentle, blue glow, not unlike the "holy" glow that surrounded Jesus and Mary and the prophets in pictures in the big family Bible, represented by a halo.

The sylph took her hand off Elena's temple and came back to her position in front of Elena's face. The glow remained.

That is magic. Air magic. And you can see it because you were born an Air Master, even if you are an uncommon kind from your mother's blood, and even if you don't know how to use the magic yet. But you must not let your stepmother know you can do this, ever.

Elena nodded; she had already come to that conclusion herself.

Now I will show you a little, a very little. This will be very like learning to ride. It will be difficult at first, and you will be very sore and very tired very quickly!

The sylph had not been wrong; before too long, her head throbbed and her eyes burned, and she felt as fatigued as if she had walked all the way to the village and back. The sylph called the others, who flocked around her and laid their tiny hands all over her head, and gradually the pain ebbed, although it did not entirely go away.

No more for today, the sylph decreed. *Go and tell the kitchen witch that your head aches. She has something for that.*

Kitchen witch? *Oh! Mrs. Banning. Does she have magic too?*

A little, of the Earth, and she does not know it, but she uses it all the time and wisely. Not enough to see us, but enough to make things that heal. Now go!

Elena was not going to disobey her, but there was one thing more she wanted to ask. Well, three things. *What is your name?* she asked. *Can I tell my brothers about this? Are they born Masters too?*

The sylph hesitated. *You may call me . . . Ivy. You may tell your brothers. They are not Masters, though they have a little magic, and can learn to use it. You are the only one to have this Gift in its fullest.*

That actually made her smile. For once, *she* was special! Certainly in Father's eyes, she was distinctly inferior to her brothers, and she was used to feeling this way.

Go, said the sylph, kindly. Obediently, she carefully packed up her knitting and her balls of wool in her bag, and left the conservatories for the kitchen.

Unlike the boys, who were always hungry, and had a habit of sneaking into the kitchen to help themselves to things like apples and a bit of bread and butter, she rarely came here. The kitchen was always a busy place before meals, though with Father and Stepmother gone and only one set of meals to prepare—and no Msr. Paul fussing about with knives and pans and sauces and shouting at the poor kitchen girls, it was not as busy and certainly not as loud. She stood in the doorway, quietly, waiting for Mrs. Banning to notice her—which she *would*, eventually. Mrs. Banning was very efficient, particularly when there wasn't a stranger lording it over what had once been her own little kingdom, and she got things done with a quiet word here, a touch, there, a moment of taking over a task from a girl who was struggling, then turning to tasks of her own. It was not very long before she noticed Elena—mostly, Elena suspected, as a foreign presence.

"My dear child, how long have you been standing there?" she asked, without moving from the place where she was rolling out pastry. As usual, she was dressed in her dark brown work dress, with a snowy apron over it.

"Not long. I have a headache, please, do you have anything

that will help?" Elena replied, pitching her voice to just carry over the sounds of pots and implements and idle, low-voiced talk among the girls.

"Of course I do, just give me a moment." She turned to a girl who was just bringing a pie dish to her. "Now, Sally, you know what to do. Line the dish with the pastry, fill it with dried peas, and pop it in the oven until it's golden. There will be no soggy bottoms in *my* kitchen!"

Sally giggled, and took over the task, while Mrs. Banning cleaned her hands on a towel tucked into the band of her apron, and came around the table to Elena. "You are old enough to come down here and get what you need for a headache from now on, child," she said kindly. Then her eyes sharpened a little. "Not a headache with a cramp here, is it?" She placed her hand on her belly. "I told you all about that before your stepmother came, because the dear Lord in Heaven knows there was no one else to. Your dear Nanny was too embarrassed to do so, and asked me."

Elena blushed, and shook her head. Mrs. Banning had, indeed, told her all about what might happen when "she became a woman," which was disconcerting and not a little embarrassing, and something she most profoundly wished would *not* happen to her. But she was very grateful, because it would have been horrid to have all that . . . mess and pain happen without warning. And she certainly would have thought she was about to die!

"No, Mrs. Banning," she replied. "Just a headache, and my eyes burn a little."

"Perhaps from all that reading you children do," said the cook, as if reading was something to be avoided. "Well, then, let me show you where the headache cordial is, and how to measure it out."

She went to a cupboard that was out of the way of the bustle of the kitchen, and took out a bottle made of red crockery from the top shelf. "This is for headache," she said, and pointed to blue, green, yellow, plain glazed, and black in turn. "Bellyache, cough, sick stomach, pain in the joints such as your father's father had, and a liniment for pain from wounds or bruising. I make them all so that you use the same measure. Here is the measure."

From the end of the same shelf she took down something that looked like a small eggcup. "One measure for a child, two for a woman, three for a man. You are small enough still you only need a child's measure. This is by weight and height, so a very small woman would take a child's measure."

She took down an old teacup from the shelf below, which had several teacups with chips in the rim, or fine cracks, or lacking handles, and poured out enough brownish liquid to just fill the measure, then emptied the measure into the teacup. "Jenny, leave off chopping vegetables and bring me the kettle," she ordered, and another of the girls put down her knife, wiped her hands on her apron, and fetched the kettle from the hearth. The cook poured the hot water into the teacup and gave it a swirl rather than using a spoon to stir it with. "Here, dear, now drink it all down. It's nasty, so best to get it all over with at once."

Elena blew on the liquid to cool it, and did as she was told. It *was* nasty, bitter and astringent, but having been warned, she didn't gag or choke on it. Mrs. Banning took the cup from her and gave it to Jenny, who in turn took it to the sink where the potboy, the only male in the kitchen, was valiantly laboring away at cleaning whatever was given to him. Mrs. Banning wiped out the inside of the measure with her towel, corked the bottle, and put both away. "There, that should make you right in no time," she said heartily. "Now off with you. There will be chicken pie for tea, and a nice English rabbit for supper."

"Thank you, Mrs. Banning," Elena said gratefully, and left the busy kitchen. English rabbit had no actual rabbit in it, but was Welsh rabbit, a lovely sort of toasted cheese like the siblings improvised in the schoolroom, but with a glass of red wine in it, along with some mustard, an egg, and a little butter. She had noticed a faint golden glow on the bottles, like the blue glow that had been on the sylphs, and that Mrs. Banning's hands had glowed a bit when she poured out the cordial and swirled the teacup. She wasn't sure what that meant—other than that Mrs. Banning had what the sylph had called "Earth magic," but she had felt oddly comforted by it.

I don't think I should look at Stepmother in this way, though, she thought, as she went up the stairs to her room to lie down with a damp cloth on her eyes until the cordial should take effect. *She might somehow know that I was doing it.*

". . . so that's what the sylph taught me," she concluded, as her brothers gathered around her beside the schoolroom fire, staring at her. "And she is going to teach me more tomorrow."

"And we can't learn any of this?" Ben asked, sounding disappointed. He looked up at the row of sylphs on the mantelpiece, and they all shook their heads. "Well . . ."

"That's not *fair*!" Gus burst out, full of indignation. "Why not?"

"For the same reason I'm a girl and you're a boy, I think," she replied. "We were just born that way."

She looked to the sylphs for affirmation, and they all nodded.

Gus sulked. He didn't quite pout, but he was not far from putting out his lip. "It's still not fair."

"I confess it's disappointing," Arthur told him, "But think of all the things that Elena is not allowed to do because she is a girl! Having *one* thing that the rest of us can't do doesn't seem so unfair."

Gus did not look convinced, but sighed. "We *are* twins," he grumbled. "At least you could share."

"If it were up to me, I would, but it's not up to me," she replied, trying to sound comforting. "And at any rate, right now all I can do is see who has magic, and pool a little bit of the stuff in my hand. I can't actually do anything with it."

"And Stepmother has *the magic of the Dark Water*," Felix quoted. "That . . . follows the spell we found. I wonder what that means, exactly."

"Nothing good," Carl replied, brooding.

"Let's put it out of our minds," said Arthur. "There's nothing we can do about it. We've been warned about her, so we know to be wary, and I cannot think what she could possibly gain by putting spells on *us*. So far, other than banishing us all to the schoolroom, she hasn't done anything to harm us."

"She could have *starved* us!" David objected.

"Well, she didn't succeed," Arthur countered, and laughed.

"And perhaps she accounted for the staff keeping us fed anyway. Let's enjoy ourselves while they are gone, and when they return, we will stay out of her sight, and hopefully she will forget about us."

"I wish *I* could stay out of her sight," sighed Elena, pulling her shawl more closely about herself. "But now she knows I can do things that she wants, so there is little chance of that."

"But she knows you can do things that she wants, which makes you valuable to her," Ben reminded her. "She's already arranged for the treat of a whole sovereign for your Christmas money. Perhaps there will be other nice things. Now! What shall we play tonight? Faro or lotteries?"

"Lotteries," Gus said instantly, for he was very enamored of the little fish that Elena had woven out of ribbon scraps too small to do anything with.

Lottery was a very simple game, in which there was no skill involved, only luck. At the beginning, the fish were divided among the six players, with Arthur and Ben being the dealers. Arthur, who was the first dealer, would shuffle the cards and draw one from the pack, placing it pips side up in the center of the table. Ben, who always played the second dealer, would take the rest of the pack, and deal out a card to each of them. If one of them matched the value of the card in the center, everyone else gave the winner a fish. If no one did, another round of cards was dealt. The game ended when one person had all the fish. Gus loved lottery, because not only did he love the little woven ribbon fish, it was a very fast game, which played to his impatient nature, and he was quite lucky at it. Elena didn't care; she just enjoyed playing. Arthur and Ben looked on benignly; they were perfectly pleased to play whatever game the others wanted.

When they ended the last game, Gus had won half of the rounds, and his pique at not having the same magic as Elena had been quite forgotten.

9

In the two weeks leading up to Christmas, the siblings saw very little of each other, as the boys were all off in various corners of the manor making their presents for each other. The siblings had always made presents rather than purchasing them, since Father felt the Christmas pocket money was sufficient in the way of a gift, and it seemed a bit shabby to them that he apparently expected gifts for the others to come out of what had been given to *them*.

Not that Father ever gave a groat about the presents we made and gave him. I know he always re-gifted some of mine to Hobart, because I saw Hobart wearing stockings I made for Father. But then, until Stepmother found interest in me, I've never mattered to Father at all, except as the disappointing child who was not another boy.

Elena, who had been working for months on her gifts to her brothers, felt this rather acutely, and no few peppermints had gone to assuage her feelings. Especially since Father was showering Stepmother with gifts both material and immaterial—gowns and probably jewelry, and plays and concerts and balls. The ladies' magazines had opened up an entirely unfamiliar world to her, a world of card parties and fetes, balls and concerts, operas and plays, and excursions to Vauxhall Gardens (which sounded like a kind of paradise); the equivalent of Vauxhall Gardens in Bath seemed to be the Pump Room, at least from what she could tell, so presumably he was paying for her entrance to that as often as she cared to go. Of course, Elena was not old enough to enjoy any of these things, but she resented that Father was spending a great deal of money so that Stepmother could.

She also resented that Father had *always* made it clear that the various troops of mummers, musicians, and so forth that traveled about the countryside at this season were to be turned away empty-handed when they came to the manor. To be sure, it was all very amateur entertainment, but since she and her brothers got *no* entertainment that they did not make for themselves, they were bound to enjoy it! It seemed doubly shabby that he denied poorer folks much-needed pennies at a time of the year when money and food were hard come by.

She did, however, worry that Father had forgotten other obligations of the season, and finally approached Hobart about it, about a week before Christmas Day. She found him, as usual, in the butler's pantry, which was his particular kingdom within the household, as the kitchen was Mrs. Banning's, and her office was for Mrs. Farthingworth. There was no food in the butler's pantry, but this was where all the bottles of liquor and all the silverware were kept, locked away to avoid temptation. She paused at the entrance, confronted with his very straight back, as he stood polishing the silver, and coughed.

"Mary Ann," he said without turning to look. "I have told you already that—"

"It's not Mary Ann, Hobart," she interrupted. "It's Elena."

He whirled, his look of astonishment at her having penetrated this far into Servants' Territory almost making her giggle. "I beg your pardon, Miss Elena," he said, recovering his dignity. "How may I help you?" Hobart was a very tall, very dignified man with a thick head of gray-black hair, who was certainly much older than Father (though not as old as he looked), and had probably served as a senior footman, if not a butler, to Grandfather.

Elena knew from Nanny's utter inability to hide anything from her that Father gave the staff—the *entire* staff, from the potboy to Mrs. Farthingworth—a gift of fabric every year at Boxing Day, enough for an entire new suit of clothing. And she wasn't certain just what she could do about it if he'd forgotten to arrange it this year—perhaps allow them all a rummage through the trunks in the attic?—but she was determined that they would not be disappointed on Boxing Day.

"I wondered if Father had made the usual arrangement for Boxing Day," she said, hesitantly, clasping her hands together in front of her. "I thought perhaps if he had not . . ."

But whatever remedy she might have come up with evaporated at his unexpected smile and answer. "That is very good and kind of you, Miss Elena, but indeed, he left it up to me as he always has. No one shall be empty-handed on Boxing Day. And I am sure your consideration speaks well of you."

She sighed with relief. "Oh, good! Thank you!" she replied, and turned to go.

"And that reminds me, Miss Elena," he continued, and she turned back to face him. "We—the staff and I—would enjoy the company of you and your brothers at our own festivities. If you feel this would amuse you, that is."

Every Christmas that she could remember, she and her brothers had come home from late services to sit down to a very formal and mostly silent Christmas dinner with Father, a dinner at which they could hear the sounds of merriment, dim and far, from the servants' hall. Beecham and Nanny had been permitted to eat at the same table on this once-a-year occasion, and Beecham's stilted conversation with Father about the sermon they had just heard had only increased the contrast between what was, for Elena, a very uncomfortable meal, and the obviously jolly one the servants were enjoying. Then they would all go back to their respective parts of the manor; it was a mystery what Father did, but Beecham went to his room, and Nanny retired to hers to write letters to those of her family that were still living, and the siblings all were expected to go to the schoolroom. That was when they would exchange gifts, but sooner or later someone would say, "I wish we could—you know—go down." And they would all look wistful and resigned.

So her response of "Oh! We would enjoy that above all things!" was both immediate and enthusiastic. And at that, to her surprise, a little smile appeared on Hobart's face.

"You have been very pleasant guests at our table, miss," he said. "Very considerate and polite, if I may take the liberty of saying so.

It was Mrs. Banning who made the suggestion just last night, and we agreed, one and all. We shall be coming and going, of course, since cows and chickens do not recognize Christmas Day, granny-tales notwithstanding, but we manage to have games, and some dancing, and to amuse ourselves and each other."

"I think it will be *lovely*," she said fervently. "Thank you again!"

"Then Mrs. Farthingworth shall extend the invitation formally at luncheon," he promised. "Now, I shall not keep you any longer."

She took that as it was meant—that he had duties to take care of, polishing the silver every day being one of them—and nodded and took herself off to winter parlor, where she was reading the ladies' magazines rather than poring over the pictures. All of *her* Christmas presents were done now, and neatly wrapped up in frugally saved paper. They took up quite a bit of space in her room, but she didn't mind. She'd attached little pasteboard tags with the proper name to each one, not that there was any difference in what each of the boys got. Cravats, stockings and gloves that she had been knitting all year, and their packets of sweets. They did appreciate the stockings and gloves, since by this time of the winter their gloves from the previous year were in sad shape indeed, and were more darning than knitting. What they would each give her was something of a mystery, and not often very practical. Arthur and Ben were better at it than the others; one year Emil had given her a boat (he had given everyone boats, even Arthur and Ben, who had been a little too old to go playing at boats on the pond). More often than not the presents were things they had found rummaging about in the attic. One year, to her horror, Felix had given her a wreath of wax orange blossoms that had *clearly* been part of a wedding ensemble. She had managed to keep him from seeing how horrified she was, thanked him, and gone up to the attic to find the trunk with a disturbed wedding veil in it and put the ornament back. When on earth he thought she would have had occasion to wear such a thing, she had no idea, but she did not want to find herself haunted by the previous owner, who must have had veil and wreath stored carefully away to grace the head of a daughter of her own. Sometimes they found very nice things up there, and indeed, except for taking out clothing to remake it, she never touched anything in those trunks, so that they should have the fun of finding things to give her. There had been a pretty string of blue glass beads once, and a mother-of-pearl bracelet, and even when something had been utterly falling apart, like beaded bags, they'd actually take the effort to take it apart and give her the beads to make up into something of her own choosing.

She had always known that Father lived frugally, but until these magazines had come into her hands, she had had no idea just *how* frugal he was. Now, given all the things she was gleaning from their pages, and the discreet advertisements, she was aware just how frugal—even miserly!—he was to his children. By now, she should have had instruction in singing, playing some sort of instrument like harp or piano, drawing (she had only had lessons from Beecham), watercolor painting, how to press dried flowers and make them into tasteful objects, and above all, much more instruction in dancing than she had received from Beecham. She should never have had to make her own gowns, much less make them from antique gowns found in the attic. She should have learned French or Italian fluently. The bits of commonplace jewelry—one could not call them "jewels"—that her brothers had given her, although she liked them very much, were not something that a girl of her rank would wear. She should have had a maid of her own to care for her wardrobe and tend to her hair, as Fleurette did for Stepmother.

And now she wondered what the villagers thought of her appearance. The boys were unexceptional; Father at least went to the trouble of making sure they were properly clothed. But—did they look at her and know immediately just how shabbily she was treated? Or had her skills with needle and thread managed to deceive them?

She had thought of balls and routs very seldom, but when she did, she had wished she was old enough to attend. Now she was glad that she had never been afforded the opportunity. She would have been a laughingstock, a joke to the other ladies. And, of course, she would have had to sit almost everything out, because she did not know how to dance all the dances that were written of in these magazines; a further humiliation.

Why is he treating me like this? she asked, not so much in despair as in bewilderment.

You remind him too much of your mother, said a familiar voice in her head. She looked up to find the fairy Ivy sitting on the arm of the sofa, looking at her with sympathy. *Partly, it is because he is angry with her for leaving him. She was his possession, and she never should have dared, he thinks. So he is keeping you simple and ignorant as a sort of revenge.*

"But—" Well, there was no use in saying that *she* had never done anything to him. This was not something that would respond to logic. She put down the magazine and sighed.

Your mother was something . . . very special. Your father caught her and held her, but did not know how to treat her so that she did not mind being held.

And then she remembered something Nanny had told them, long before Stepmother came into their lives. *Nanny told us stories about the seal folk, and how if a man wanted a seal maiden for his wife, because they were very beautiful, he would steal her sealskin. What if Mama was one of them? What if she found her skin and ran away?*

She looked the little fairy right in the eyes, and asked, "Was my mother a seal person?"

And the fairy said, *No.* But she *hesitated* a very long time before she said it.

So she asked again, "Was my mother something *like* a seal person? And did Father steal her skin to keep her with him because she was very beautiful? And did she run away because she found her skin and he couldn't hold her anymore?"

And the fairy said, *Yes.* Immediately, but with great reluctance. Elena could see it in her eyes, and by how uncomfortable she was.

And everything she didn't understand fell into place. The seal people were a kind of fairy, and fairies hated one thing above all else: to be held, imprisoned, kept against their will. They would do anything to escape. Once they had escaped, they would do anything to keep their liberty. Even abandon their children.

And hadn't she been feeling some of the same despair at the idea that Father was going to keep her here, under his thumb, forever? Hadn't she and her brothers been plotting, planning, doing everything they could to figure out a way to escape?

Some of the anger, the grief, about her mother leaving them

without a word melted away. Not all of it—she was still angry, because it wasn't fair and it wasn't right . . . but now she could understand, a little. And forgive, a little. But she wanted, she needed, to talk to someone, one of her brothers, about this. But who? Not Gus; he'd fly into a rage, he wouldn't understand, and he'd probably do something stupid.

But before she could ponder which of the others, she heard footsteps in the hall leading to the winter parlor; she knew the footsteps of her brothers well enough to be a pretty good judge of who it was, and his appearance in the doorway confirmed it. It was Ben—the very one!

"Still enjoying your new reading?" he asked, with a slight smile on his face. "It seems odd to see you without needlework in your hands." He noticed the fairy, then, and his smile widened. "But I see you are not alone. Shall I—"

"No!" she exclaimed, and cast the magazine aside. "Ben! I most particularly want to talk to you!"

He blinked. "This sounds serious. Is something wrong?" He slid into the chair across from her and leaned toward her. "If it is in my power—"

She interrupted him. "Ben, the fairy said that Mama was like a seal person, from Nanny's tales."

She did not expect the reaction she got. He sat straight up, and blanched.

Her mind began to race, as more little things fell into place. And she said, slowly, "You knew . . ." Before he could speak further, she added, "You were always the one who knew her best, weren't you?"

He put his head in his hands. "Yes—no—I don't know!" he replied, his words shaded with emotion. "I thought I did, but then she flew away—"

She interrupted him. "She *flew away*? How—" She stared at him, utterly unsure what to think or say.

He took a deep breath, as if he was trying to gain control of himself. Then he looked up, and she had never seen such sadness in his eyes before. It made her want to reach out and hold *him*, comfort *him*, as he had so often held and comforted her when she was small. "I should simply tell you everything. It is a very short tale . . . and I shall be glad, I think, to finally tell *someone*. You remember the day that she disappeared?"

She nodded. She very much remembered it, all the fuss when no one could find Mama anywhere in the house or on the grounds, the panic of the servants when no one had taken her out in the carriage or even the dog-cart, the terror when they realized how angry their master would be when he found out. But by that time, Hobart and the steward had taken matters into their own hands and sent for him.

And as for her own children, when they knew she was gone— well, Elena and Gus had been inconsolable, and the others were just as grief-stricken and showed it, each in their own way and according to their ages.

"That morning I found her crying in her room. By then the fairies had been showing me all the secret places and hidden cupboards all over the manor, and in one of them, in Father's room, there had been a giant bundle of white feathers. I thought it looked like a cloak, and put it back, and didn't think anything more about it. When I asked Mama what was wrong, she said that Father had taken something from her, and was keeping it from her, and without it she was going to die."

"A cloak of feathers?" Elena blinked. "She was a *bird* person?" Another piece fell into place, that Father hated swans, and ordered the gamekeeper to shoot them on sight, though he never would, just drove them away. "She was a *swan* person?"

He gave her a watery smile. "You always were the cleverest of us. Yes, but I didn't know that then. I only knew that Father had this peculiar thing hidden in a secret cupboard in his room, and I told her I knew where it was. She demanded that I take her to it. I opened the cupboard as the fairy showed me, and she took it out. She threw it over her shoulders and began running for her room again. I did my best to catch her, but she moved like the wind, and all I saw was her back, enveloped in feathers, as she leapt off her balcony. I thought she had gone mad and tried to kill herself, but when I got to the balcony and looked down, there was nothing there. But there *was* a great swan flying away, as fast as it could fly. I somehow knew that it was her. And I remembered those tales from Nanny about the seal people, and . . . it came to me that she must have been a swan person, like them, and father had stolen her skin to capture her and keep her because she was so beautiful."

Selkie, said the fairy, silent until now. *The seal people are called selkies. And your mother was a swanmay.*

"The fairy says that Mama was a swanmay, and that the seal people are called selkies," she repeated, a little numbly. "But Ben, why didn't you tell us?"

"Would any of you have been able to keep the secret from Father?" he asked, bluntly. "You and Gus would not have understood. Arthur is as transparent as glass, and Father would have pressed him until he told. And . . . I do not know *what* Father would have done to me when he discovered I was the means by which she escaped him."

"But it would not have been good," she said softly.

He rubbed his eyes. "No," he agreed. "It would not have been."

"But why didn't she come back for us?" she whimpered, a little.

"I have thought about that a great deal," he confessed, sighing. "At first I was terribly angry with her because she did not. But then—how could she have?"

The swan folk do not accept half-breeds, the fairy said, bluntly.

"The fairy says that her people would not have accepted us." It was hard to speak around the growing lump in her throat.

"Well, then." Ben spread his hands. "There is the reason. She had to choose between us and them. She knew that Father wanted us; he certainly paraded us in front of company on every possible occasion, boasting about his beautiful wife and eight handsome children. She probably never thought that when she left, Father would treat us as he did. And she was desperate for her own home and family."

Elena wanted to object to this, but the anger at her mother for abandoning them was fading rapidly, mostly because she had been angry at her mother for leaving for so long that it was hard to hold onto that anger anymore. There were a hundred questions she wanted to ask Ben, or the fairy, but she suspected that neither of them had the answers. So she said the next thing that was uppermost in her mind. "How did you keep this secret for so long? It *must* have eaten at you!"

"Like the Spartan boy's fox," he sighed, and she said nothing, although she had no idea what he meant. "But, again, I will admit that I was protecting myself. And I beg that you will not tell the others, for that same reason. Arthur will be furious with me. Carl will want to tell Father immediately. David will probably try to come to blows with me. Emil will have a hundred questions I cannot answer, Felix will never forgive me, and Gus—Gus will blurt it out to the first person he crosses paths with."

She wanted to tell him he was wrong, but she knew he was right. Especially about Gus.

"I will not tell a soul," she promised, and both Ben and the fairy sighed. "At least now . . . I know. And I shan't daydream about her coming back to rescue us anymore, so I suppose that is a good thing."

"It is . . . the sort of thing that a sensible person would do," Ben replied. "Would you like me to leave now?"

She thought about it for a moment. Her insides were a turmoil. Her emotions distinctly unsettled. But Ben looked as if he felt the same and, oddly, at that moment, looked no older than Gus.

Or, perhaps, close to the little boy who had just seen his beloved mama fly off, abandoning him. That little boy needed to not be alone.

"No," she said. "Stay."

It was easier than she had thought to keep Ben's secret, perhaps because Father thought so little of her. And perhaps because, if Stepmother knew what they really were, she would find some way to use all of them.

And at any rate, Christmas was almost upon them, and she didn't want to spoil it for anyone.

There were certainly plenty of distractions. The kitchen was a hive of activity, one in which they all got caught up. Not surprising, really, since they all knew that the more help Mrs. Banning had, the more delicious treats she would be able to make. There was a great deal of nut-shelling and nut-chopping, batter-stirring and biscuit-cutting, tasks without end that pairs of unskilled hands could easily be put to. And Ben had gotten the pleasing idea that anyone who was not immediately involved in the cookery could sit off to the side in the warm and fragrant kitchen and read aloud to those who were. There was no lack of reading material that interested even the relatively unlettered kitchen servants, since Father's London papers kept arriving, and they could be read from front to back to the delectation of everyone, even if some stories might leave those who had never traveled farther than Charton-town scratching their heads in confusion. Emil had discovered a couple of dusty novels hidden away in the library among the drier books, and these were read with great gusto and enjoyed with same.

At last the great day came. The Yule log had been brought in and put in the only fireplace large enough to hold it, in the great hall. Garlands of green boughs and evergreen ivy festooned the servants' hall and their dining room. The Yule log was kindled with grave ceremony by Hobart, who, with the steward, gave them all permission to enjoy it, so long as there was no drinking, eating, or unseemly behavior in the room. On the day, there were no less than four services at the village church, though the vicar presided over only the fourth, leaving his rector to take care of the other three. The staff divided themselves equitably among the four, although Elena discovered with great amusement that *none* of them wanted to go to the vicar's service. Well, except for the few servants who were chapel, not church; they walked rather than going in the carriage, dog-cart, or farm carts. The siblings, Hobart, and Mrs. Farthingworth attended the last service, of course, and all of them paid close attention to the vicar's interminable droning, the better to make fun of it later.

A kind of free-form breakfast had been laid out in the staff dining room, so that anyone could come and help themselves to whatever they liked, whenever they were free. That was cleared away just before luncheon, which was light, and featured a bit of pantry-clearing. No one minded, however, because the great feast was to come at just about teatime. Four trestle tables were set up in the servants' hall in addition to the table in the dining hall, and a grand procession of food greeted the eager eyes of everyone.

Mrs. Banning and Mrs. Farthingworth insisted that the siblings were not to be "bothered" with helping, so they all sat along one side of a trestle table and watched as platters and basins, odd objects cleaned and pressed into service as containers, and baskets and bowls filled the space that was not taken up by dishes and cutlery. None of it, save for bread and buns and rolls, would have graced the dining table in the manor dining room, had Father been home. And Elena considered that was all to the good. Pride of place was held by four geese, but there was also ham, a roast of mutton, and a boar's head provided by the gamekeeper, something Father would never have allowed on his table. Every sort of vegetable available in winter made an appearance, and great snowy mounds of boiled and mashed potatoes. Sausages split their skins to show their pink insides, rabbits appeared quartered and stewed, and there was gravy in abundance.

Elena felt almost as if she was at that formal dinner again, there was so much to choose from. She made it a point to try things she had not had before: rabbit, a bit of the boar's head, stewed cabbage—though Mrs. Banning tried to warn her away from the last as "It will give you wind," much to Mrs. Farthingworth's chagrin. The rabbit was very nice, the boar's head disappointingly just like a good bit of roast pork. There was no wine, but plenty of tea, beer, small beer, and ginger beer. She decided that she liked the last very much indeed. People came and went as their duties required, for even on Christmas Day the business of the manor and manor farm required a certain amount of tending.

When the time came for pudding, in came the plum puddings, four of them, which had been made weeks ago and had been soaking in brandy this entire time. They were borne in like heroes, blazing with blue flame and accompanied by containers of luscious golden custard. There were other sweets too, of course, but pride of place went to the plum puddings. At the family Christmas dinners, there had been a plum pudding too, even though Father didn't eat much of it, but it had been presented on a silver salver, with a silver sauce boat full of custard, rather than whatever platter happened to be clean, and whatever container would hold a decent amount of custard to be poured over each slice. The puddings tasted the same. Elena didn't eat much; the heavy taste of the brandy didn't agree with her, although the generous amount of custard being poured and ladled out at this dinner sufficiently masked the brandy that she rather enjoyed it. There were no ice creams here, nor jellies, but she didn't miss them.

When everyone had eaten their fill, volunteers carried the remains off to the kitchen, where, by tradition, Mrs. Banning and her handpicked helpers packed them all up to be taken down to the village by Grimes and distributed to the poorest of the villagers, so that everyone could share in the bounty. That was when the siblings were shooed off to the great hall to bask in the flames of the Yule Log while the servants' hall and dining room were cleared for Christmas games and dancing.

"That was the best Christmas dinner I have ever eaten!" Gus said happily, as fairies festooned themselves in the garlands of evergreen and ivy.

"Well, for one thing, it was a lot jollier than ours have ever been," Arthur agreed. "Laughter is a fine sauce."

"Everything hot from the kitchen, instead of barely warm, laughter instead of silence? Having to choke down your food while Father stares instead of making jokes with your seatmates? Being desperately careful of which fork to use? There's no comparison," agreed Emil.

"'Better a dinner of herbs where love is,'" Arthur quoted. "I've never seen a better example of the Proverb. Though I must say, I was glad to get goose instead of herbs."

"I wonder if we'll play snapdragon?" Gus speculated.

"With Hobart there? I think not." Ben gave Gus the *look* that said Gus had better not bring up the subject again. "I should think you would have got quite enough of flaming brandy, seeing as you burnt your mouth on your pudding trying to show off for Jackie."

Gus flushed; he had tried a trick he was usually moderately successful at, putting a spoon full of flaming pudding in his mouth and extinguishing the flames immediately. This time he had failed because the pudding was hotter than he had expected, and had suffered for his bravado. He hadn't been *much* hurt—thanks to a fairy who had swooped in to his rescue and blown out the fire for him—but his dignity had suffered a killing blow as everyone at the table laughed at him.

Even having that fairy sit on his shoulder for the rest of the meal hadn't been much compensation.

They were all very cozy and drowsy from the food, and it seemed almost a pity to leave the blazing fire and join their hosts back in servants' hall. But once they got there, they discovered it was well worth coming back. The entertainment had been divided between the hall, where an impromptu band was tucked into the corner, and the dining room, where the dining table had been set up for games and gossip. To Gus's unbounded joy, there was a deck of cards out, and a big box of miscellaneous fish. There were one or two mother-of-pearl, which had been handled so much most of the nacre had worn off, some brass ones, some wooden, some tin, some bits of paper cut into the form of fish, and fish-like objects of stone. He immediately claimed a seat.

Elena, quite certain that all the dances would be the simple country ones she knew, happily joined the dancers.

The band consisted of Jackie sitting on a wooden box with a couple of drum beaters that he was apparently going to use on his seat, one of the dairymaids with a pennywhistle, and Thomas Spencer with a fiddle.

As soon as the siblings arrived and everyone had sorted themselves into dancing and not dancing, Hobart nodded his head at Thomas, who gave his fiddle a scrape and tapped his foot to give Jackie the pace, and they were off.

Soon Elena was flying around the circle, skipping her way to a tune she didn't recognize, and enjoying herself so thoroughly that she smiled until her cheeks ached. Only when she was completely exhausted did she sit out a dance or two, and once she had caught her breath, she was once again in the thick of it. Finally, the circle began to lose dancers as, one by one, people who had work to do in the morning remembered that salient fact, and slipped away. That was when she decided that she, too, had had enough.

Candle ends in old saucers had been left at the door for people to take to light themselves to bed. With one of those in her hand, she left the warmth and light and music behind her, made her journey back to her room with limbs feeling suddenly heavy with fatigue, and barely got herself undressed and between the sheets before falling asleep.

10

Ben surely must have left the rout earlier than she had, because he was tending the fire and the kettle of tea when she peeked into the schoolroom. She turned back to her bedroom, got all of the presents for the boys, made a kind of carrying basket out of the front of her skirt, and returned with her skirt full. "Did you put out the name cards?" she asked, pausing in the doorway.

"Of course. Did you think I would have forgotten?" he asked, smiling.

"Well, then, here is your reward," she said pertly, gripping her skirt with one hand, and handed him his packages with the other. Then she made her way around the table to place her gifts at the proper name. She noticed that identical parcels were placed below each name except hers. Her card was on nothing but empty tabletop, and for a moment she felt a pang. Surely he had not forgotten her! Not Ben!

She took a seat on a stool by the fireside opposite him, feeling a little anxious. "We're to come down at the gong, as usual," Ben said, handing her a cup. It was chamomile, which meant he'd made the tea instead of the kitchen.

"I wonder how anyone has any strength to cook after last night," she said. "Thank you." There was a big package at his side, wrapped in yellowed muslin instead of paper.

"Here, here is your present," he said, instead of directly answering her. The shape inside an old pillowcase was unmistakable; he'd given her a workbox. But when she pulled it out, she gasped. The entire surface of the box had been covered in ornate chip carvings, and from Ben's grin, the hand that had created this beauty had been his.

"I took a leaf from your book and started all the presents early this year," he told her, as the rest began filing in, their own hands full of parcels. This was how they always spent the morning after Christmas Day, since the day itself was so fraught. Formal breakfast with Father, church, formal luncheon with Father, then the entire afternoon spent in the winter parlor reading something improving while Father read a newspaper from London. Which seemed unfair, since a newspaper didn't seem to her to be all that improving. Formal tea under Father's eye, more reading, this time taking turns to read aloud, usually from a history book, while Father and Ben or Arthur played chess. Formal Christmas dinner, the presentation of gifts to Father, and then, with relief, they were allowed to return to the schoolroom. There they each gave their gifts to Beecham and Nanny, where at last they got some of the much-vaunted Christmas spirit, because no matter how inexpertly made the gifts had been in the past, they were examined and exclaimed over. Beecham and Nanny always truly appreciated anything they got, and she had even seen both of them wear her inexpertly made and sometimes oddly shaped stockings until they wore out. And that recollection made her thoughts turn to them.

"I hope Beecham and Nanny had a good Christmas," she said, with a little grimace, because there was every chance that this was not likely.

"Oh, I am sure they had better Christmases than they ever had here," Ben replied wryly. "I am very glad that you like your workbox. It took me ages."

In her musings over Nanny and Beecham, she had quite forgotten the box, which she now did him the favor of examining in great detail. The chip carving was so precise she could scarcely believe it had been done by human hands, the geometric, radiating patterns pleasing to both the eye and hand.

"I didn't make the box itself," he admitted. "I had young Jem, the fellow who does everything that needs making in wood, do it for me. But I carved everything."

"It's magnificent!" she cried, tears coming to her eyes at the thought that he would have—must have—given up many of his leisure hours to please her. Impulsively, she set the box aside, threw her arms around his neck and hugged him, while he chuckled self-consciously. She released him, and he pulled her over to the table.

"Well now," he said in a truly cheerful voice, a vast contrast to the false cheer they'd all been forced to display in previous years. "Shall we all see what rubbish we've given each other?"

They all laughed at that, even though in the rest of the boys' cases, Elena was not convinced it would *not* be rubbish out of the attic.

She waited until her brothers had opened their gifts before opening her own. "What's this?" David said, puzzled, holding up the long piece of fine muslin. "Oh! A cravat! This is a new thing from you, Elena! And I suspect we're all going to need spares if Stepmother keeps having dinner parties and routs. I am certain I shall ruin the only one I have before six months are out." He examined the tiny hems. "This one is far superior, too."

Ben cast a glance at her and smiled at her surprise that David had welcomed such a gift. But then, David was fifteen now, and it appeared that he and his twin were old enough to appreciate such a thing, for Carl seemed equally appreciative. She made them stockings every year, and those were always welcome, as were the knitted gloves. But Gus peeked in the paper packet that was also new, and crowed with joy, as she had known he would. "Boiled sweets! By Jove, Elena, I think you are the best sister in the world to have spent some of your sovereign on these!"

Felix and Emil were just as excited over the packets of sweets as Gus was, and in their appreciation, they almost ignored the prominent, oblong, box-like packets beside each card until David opened his, and his mouth fell open. "*Ice skates!* Ben! How did you *ever*—?"

Even Arthur seemed impressed, as they all tore open the matching parcels. "That is a very good question, twin. How *did* you?"

Ben shrugged, but flushed a little with pleasure. "I made an arrangement with the blacksmith. I carved the foot beds, he made the blades, and he and I together set them into the foot beds. I got the leather straps from Grimes, and Grimes showed me how to rivet them onto the foot beds."

"But how did you know how to make them?" Arthur persisted. Ben just laughed.

"I shall go to my grave holding that secret," he taunted.

Well . . . I know that he is very good at holding secrets.

For a change, instead of boats, Emil had made everyone holders for a pen and inkwell; it appeared that he had taken a note from Ben and learned to carve. Arthur had made her a much better drawing board than she currently had, which was literally just a board she had found in the woodshed. This one had leather straps riveted to each corner, which she could slip her paper under to secure it. For the rest, he gifted them with simple bootjacks. "You'll be glad of those," he told them.

"I already am," Ben told him. "Without Beecham about to help, it sometimes gets cursed hard to get my boots off when I'm tired."

To her surprise, Gus had given her a cornucopia of well-made papier-mâché cherries, beautifully painted and glazed for trimming bonnets, and blushed when she cast him an astonished look. "I like making them," he mumbled. "I thought you might as well have them."

The rest of the boys had, as expected, presented her with their attic-gleanings, although this time they showed a great deal more sensibility than the time she'd gotten that wedding wreath. In fact, they'd shown more care, as well. They must have penetrated into the part of the attic where the stored clothing was nearly disintegrating, because they gave her a nice assortment of mother-of-pearl, genuine silver, and glass buttons, all carefully cleaned and polished. Buttons were *always* useful. The attic-gleanings they had gotten for each other were less practical—what in heaven's name Arthur was going to do with a hunting dagger, of all things, she did not know!—but boys, she had come to decide, were a great deal like magpies. They were always looking for something shiny, and no matter how impractical the thing was, once they saw it, they wanted it. Certainly Arthur spent far more time than was needful admiring his prize, even surreptitiously trying it against his side as if to try and figure out a way to wear it without a belt.

But while they were all gloating over their piles of gifts, she caught Ben's eye. "Why didn't you give me skates too?" she asked. Because while she dearly loved her new workbox—which, she had discovered, had a false bottom, beneath which she could hide things if she chose—she felt a little hurt that he had excluded her from what would surely be a great deal of fun when there was a hard enough freeze to create a skating surface on the pond.

"Because girls don't skate," he said, matter-of-factly. "Only think, Elena! You would be certain to fall, at least at first, and then your skirts would fly up and you would be mortified! Not to mention what Stepmother would probably say about it!"

The gong sounded, saving her from having to say anything in response, and they all filed down for breakfast, Elena taking with her the presents for Mrs. Banning, Mrs. Farthingworth, and Hobart.

She managed to intercept Hobart just as he was leaving the servants' hall. He had the grace to carefully unwrap his present then and there, and with astonishment marveled out loud at her tiny hem stitches. "My word, Miss Elena," he said with unaccustomed warmth. "This is just the thing! And it is better than the ones I obtain from the village seamstress! I cannot thank you enough!" Then he smiled a little, and added dryly, "I shall finally pass muster with her ladyship. She has had several things to say about my cravat."

She felt her ears and cheeks growing warm. "I am very glad you like it. Merry Christmas!" she told him, and followed her brothers into the servants' dining room, where she presented Mrs. Banning and Mrs. Farthingworth with their gifts. They loved the lace-trimmed fichus, with matching caps trimmed with the same lace.

Arthur proposed over breakfast that they spend the day giving the library a thorough going-through, something none of them had done before this. "I mean, look at *every* book, and even leaf through them if they look at all interesting. All the way up to the top shelves, as Stepmother proposed, which is probably the only useful thing she will ever say to us."

"She is probably hoping we will fall and break something," Ben muttered.

Arthur laughed. "Then it will be a pleasure to disappoint her. We can probably amuse ourselves very well if we find some volumes that are more entertaining than enlightening, and Stepmother clearly does not care to inquire into what we are reading."

"That's a capital idea," his twin agreed, and David and Felix seconded him. So Elena left them to it, while she retired to the winter parlor; she had no wish to scour over all those old books this morning. Now that Christmas was over and she needn't spend her time bent over sewing, she wanted to see if the fairy that had first taught her about magic, Ivy, was about, and was willing to teach her a little bit more.

The winter parlor was exceedingly pleasant this morning; one of the maids had taken some sprigs of holly from the garlands that had been taken down, and left them in vases here and there. They brightened the room up no end. But Ivy was not there.

Perhaps she is in the orangery. Since it is so nice here, it will probably be even nicer there. It was a long walk, but worth it, when the fragrance of the conservatories, composed of damp earth, freshly cut herbs, and the scents of the fruits on the fruit trees wafted toward her.

As if Ivy recognized that Elena had thought of her, she was perched on the back of one of the wrought-iron orangery chairs.

I felt it when you wished for me, Ivy said. *That is evidence that you are beginning to use your powers. If you do not actually want one of us for something, be careful about thinking about us, or at least, try to do so without invoking any magic, because* thinking *becomes* wanting *and* wanting *becomes a summons. A summons from a Master is something we do not ignore unless we are summoned frivolously. If that happens, often we ignore the summons, and then when you truly want and need us, we do not come.*

She sat down in the chair opposite and nodded her understanding. Mrs. Banning had taken most of the ripe fruit for Christmas cooking, but there were still some green oranges slowly ripening, which, if Stepmother did not demand something that required fresh oranges or their juice, would probably be candied. Candied orange peel was excellent in many baked goods—providing Stepmother didn't eat it herself. And the candied fruit was divine, if tooth-achingly sweet. *Stepmother will probably eat all of that too.*

It was unlikely Mrs. Banning would make marmalade. There were already enough jars of marmalade, prominent among the darker jars of berry and currant jams and jellies in the pantry, to last quite a while. Especially since they were reserved for the family, and the staff were not allowed any of it.

After Stepmother and Father returned from Bath, Elena had very little faith that they would see any of that marmalade in the schoolroom. Mrs. Banning was allowing them some on their toast now on the grounds that she was using up the jar so it didn't spoil. They had to ask for it specifically, however, and Elena did not care enough about it to do so, though several of her brothers usually did.

While she was woolgathering about the marmalade, the fairy waited patiently. "I did want to see you," she admitted. "Although I would call it more of a wish than a summons. I wondered if you would be willing to teach me more about my magic."

I thought you might, Ivy replied. *So I brought a friend.* The sylph pointed behind Elena, who turned to look.

Floating into view from the furthest part of the orangery was . . . well, Elena was not quite sure what it was, aside from strange and beautiful. It was a delicate blue, the same color as a periwinkle flower. It had six filmy wings—at least, she thought they were wings, though they were neither feathered like a bird's nor shaped like butterfly, moth, or dragonfly wings. It was not using them at the moment, even though it did not touch the ground. It was translucent, and it shimmered a little in the weak sunlight. It seemed to have four limbs, a long, trailing, scarf-like tail, a *very* long neck, and a head like a bird's. Its body was neither scaled nor feathered, but was shiny, like an insect's. Its eyes were enormous, and it transfixed her with its unwinking gaze.

This is a zephyr, said Ivy. *Her kind are a little more powerful than sylphs. She can teach you more than I can.*

Elena got up from her chair and made a little curtsy. "Thank you for coming to teach me," she said, and hesitated. Ivy had seemed reticent about giving a name for herself, so this creature probably would be even more so. "Would you object to me calling you 'Azure'?" she continued, diffidently.

The creature laughed, softly; the sound held a little of the same sound that icicles made when they fell off as a group and tinkled as they broke. Not quite like glass breaking; softer than that. *Not at all,* she said. *It is a good name. You should have had a mortal Master to teach you, someone who would have led you down the same path that every other young Master has followed for time out of mind. I shall not do that. I shall show you what you need, so that your Stepmother does not know of your magic. For if she did, she would use you, and neither you nor I would care for that result.*

Elena shivered, and nodded. She recalled Stepmother's glittering eyes, and the greed that had been in them when she realized that Elena could create beautiful gowns that no one else had ever worn before. How much worse would it be when Stepmother realized she had magic too?

So, said Azure, floating toward her. *Show me what you can do now.*

Obediently, Elena held out her hand, palm up, and concentrated until there was a ball of glowing energy resting in the cup of her hand, a ball as blue as Azure was. It had seemed very difficult the first time she had done this, and it had given her a headache. Under Ivy's tutelage and encouragement, she had persisted, practicing as often as she had a moment of free time. Now, while not effortless, it was nowhere near as difficult.

She looked up. Instead of saying anything, Azure merely stared at the ball, tilting her head on her long neck, the frills running down her spine moving slowly, as did her wings. Both her forelimbs were clasped before her, and her legs hung motionless in midair.

Nicely, cleanly done, she said, finally. *Now, imagine that this ball is a soap bubble, and you are carefully blowing air into it to make it expand. Go slowly; you do not want it to burst.*

"What if it does?" she asked, concerned.

Then you will have to begin again, replied the zephyr, unperturbed.

Relieved that nothing catastrophic would occur if she failed, Elena imagined herself with a hollow straw, carefully breathing air into this delicate thing, as she and her brothers had often done with soapy water on a summer's day. It took several moments before it responded, but eventually it began to expand, multiple streaks of slightly different shades of blue chasing themselves across the surface of the ball, just as rainbows chased across the surface of a soap bubble.

Like a soap bubble it was weightless, although she could sense a sort of tension in it as it got bigger, and she understood instinctively that she had to be very careful now, or it certainly would emulate a soap bubble and burst.

Perhaps if I add a little more power . . . With the greatest of care, she added more energy to the sphere, taking it gingerly from something Ivy called a ley line. Ivy had showed it to her, running right underneath the manor, and had showed her how to use it, teasing magic out of it like teasing a single strand out of a piece of silk thread. It seemed to work; the walls seemed a bit less delicate once she had done that, and she continued to inflate it, pushing the walls farther and farther outward. Finally, when it was about the size of a sheep's head, she paused again and looked at Azure, questions in her eyes.

Keep going, the zephyr encouraged.

"But if I make it any larger, parts of me are going to be inside it!" she objected.

That is what I intend. I want you to be completely inside it, said the zephyr.

Inside it! Why would Azure want that? But she had to trust the zephyr if she wanted protection from Stepmother. It did occur to her to *not* trust the zephyr, but that would mean not trusting Ivy, and the sylphs had given no indication whatsoever that they could not be trusted. *Well, I definitely cannot trust Stepmother; if she was a good person, she would not have ensnared Father with a spell, or banished us from meals and told Mrs. Banning to feed us on the leftovers that should have gone to the pigs.* That decided her. She would trust the zephyr.

She repeated what she had done before: gently inflating the sphere, pausing to add more magic, then inflating it again. Even though it still weighed nothing, when it got to the size of a bushel basket, she carefully set it on the gravel at her feet. At this point it had gone from translucent to transparent, but she felt that the walls were still as strong as ever, if not stronger.

She continued to make it grow, sensing the Zephyr's approval as she did. She did not sense any sort of impatience from Azure. When the bubble reached her calves, she sensed the faintest of touches on her leg, and the merest hint of resistance, but pressed on, and stepped forward so that she was more centered in the growing sphere.

Once she was inside it, it immediately became easier to enlarge it. At this point she looked up at Azure and tilted her head to the side. The zephyr hung quietly in the air, swaying a little.

You are very patient with me, she said.

Again came that tinkling laugh. *Unless something malicious destroys me, I am immortal,* Azure replied. *It is easy to be patient when you have all of time before you. You are doing well; you are careful, cautious, but persistent. These are admirable traits in an Air Master, and not ones I see, usually.*

Elena now desperately wanted to ask just what traits were usual in an Air Master, but she had the idea that Azure might get a little annoyed with her if she stopped what she was doing and started asking more questions. So she went back to her task, which was now going a good bit faster. The bubble grew to her bosom, then her neck, and then finally to her head. And for just one moment, she had a flash of panic. What if she couldn't breathe in there!

But she subdued her own panic immediately before Azure could intervene. This was *Air* magic! Of *course* she would be able to breathe!

She gave a last little push—and the bubble smoothly grew until she was completely inside of it.

Not only could she breathe—she felt completely at ease and at home.

Is this right? she asked Azure.

Perfect. Now it is my turn. Close your eyes and pay very close attention to what I do, because if your protection ever drops, you will have to put it back up yourself.

How do I do that? she asked.

Keep your eyes closed, and See the same way you See the sphere enclosing you. You will See what I do, and it is very easy to copy. I will talk to you as I work, so that you understand perfectly.

She closed her eyes and waited. To her delight, she actually *could* see the sphere around her. In fact, she could see Azure and Ivy . . . and quite a bit more. But again, she kept her questions for later, because she did not want to irritate the zephyr while it was helping her so much.

Now, said the zephyr, *I am just changing the surface of the sphere so that it becomes hard.*

She watched as a thread of magic extended from Azure to the sphere, saw how Azure gave the thread a little *twist,* understood immediately how she could do that, and watched as the surface on the outside of the bubble became reflective. *How* she knew that (because the inside did not change), she was not certain, but she knew that it had.

Now hold very still and concentrate, because I am going to collapse this around you. The zephyr moved toward her, wrapped its wings around the bubble, and ever-so-gently pushed inward. But she instinctively understood that *she* could do the same thing, by pulling on the bubble—

Can I help? Can I do this myself?

She felt a burst of pleasure from the zephyr. *Please do.*

Azure backed up, and she took over, collapsing the sphere slowly so that it didn't wrinkle, but instead thickened. After spending time in the kitchen with Mrs. Banning, she had an analogy for that—it was like a bubble on the surface of cooking jelly, which would collapse smoothly back into the whole. And when the transformed magical power touched her skin . . . it stopped. Where it rested on her skin, there was a very faint tingle for a moment, and then . . . nothing.

Now that is the work of a budding Master, Azure said, with admiration. *Where did you learn such control and patience?*

She knew the answer to that. *Sewing. Embroidery. Beadwork. Spinning, too, perhaps. You must be precise. You must work with your materials and not try to force them into the shape you want. If you do not want to unpick and start again, risking that you might weaken the materials, you must take care and take exactly the right steps.*

Azure laughed. *I shall have to recommend needlework to any other new magician I teach. Now, this is only one kind of shield. It will keep your stepmother from seeing the power in you. There are other shields that can protect you, but I will not teach them to you now. They will be visible to her, and she will know, seeing them, what you are.*

She shivered and opened her eyes. Azure was practically nose to nose with her, and that beak was very long and sharp—but she was not afraid. In fact, she wanted rather badly to stroke that long, sleek neck.

How can I know how you feel? she asked, instead of reaching out. *Because I* think *that I do.*

We are attuned, Air to Air—it is needful for a Master to understand how an Elemental feels, so that she does not harm or frighten that which she wishes to have the help of . . . Then Azure's color darkened, and so did the tone of her voice in Elena's head. *And it is needful for a Dark Master to know this as well, because the Dark Master works by compulsion, and it is just possible for some Elementals, when pushed too far, to break free. The Dark Master does not want to utterly crush his victims—unless he has called them purely to extract their power—and he does not want them to break free and warn others to keep clear.*

Elena shivered, and *did* reach out to stroke Azure's neck in a gesture of comfort. Her neck felt like the finest of silk-satin. *I am so sorry,* she said, moved by an impulse she did not understand.

Azure dipped her head. *Your Stepmother is a Dark mage. Not as strong as a Master, but very strong. You need not fear her power, now. Not only are you invisible to her, but she was taught in a very different way, and rather than using Sight and instinct as you do, she uses written or spoken spells, and, sometimes, ancient diagrams. You have only to destroy any of these you find about you, and any mischief she is trying to make will be disrupted.*

Well, that answered many of the questions she had about

Stepmother. She remembered another she had, though. *What are the usual traits of an Air Master?* she asked.

Azure's eyes finally blinked, a long, slow blink. *Speed. Impatience. Sometimes forgetfulness. But they make up for it in being able to leap straight to the answer to a problem without needing to think it completely through. Intuitive. And they do not anger easily, but when they do, their wrath is swift and terrible.*

A moment of dizziness overcame her, and she decided she had better sit down.

You have been working very hard, and expending energy, Azure told her. *You should rest.*

"I will," she said aloud. "It feels as if I walked all the way to Whitstone Village and back." *Do I dare? I want to . . .* "Do you know anything about my mother?"

She is a swan maiden, and came from the place you call Wales. Your Father saw her bathing in a pool and stole her featherskin. I do not know why he was in Wales, but all the Elementals of the Air know this story.

This simple and direct response, after the sylphs' evasion, startled her so much that if she had not been sitting down, she likely would have lost her balance, for her knees went weak with excitement. At last! After all these years! To have not only confirmation of Ben's story, but to hear the "why" of it all! She felt a tightness in her chest, and she could scarcely breathe. "Oh, Azure!" she exclaimed. "Do you know anything else?"

The zephyr nodded, all the delicate membranes on its spine moving. *She begged him to return her skin, but she was very young, only a year or two older than you, and he persuaded her that he was madly in love with her, and that if she did not consent to wed him, he would take his own life. We do not believe he was serious about harming himself, but she did, and being tender-hearted and unwilling to be the cause of a mortal taking his own life, consented. The marriage*—the zephyr paused for a very long time. *The marriage was in a small church, with a drunken vicar, so that if he tired quickly of her, he could abandon her.*

She felt nearly faint at this revelation. She felt a little sick as well as faint. And then a slow-burning anger rose in her, that he had been such a cad as to take advantage of a naïve, young magical creature and exploit her in such a way. It had been, for all intents and purposes, slavery. He had her feathercloak, and she could not leave him.

He was very good at pretending, and sympathy turned to love on her part. He kept her besotted—almost bespelled, in a way. It is very fitting that he, now, in his turn has been bespelled and enthralled. There was distant anger in the zephyr's words, probably because the zephyr was angry that any magical creature should be in thrall to a human. Well, she was just as angry, and the anger was not in the least distant.

What else do you know? she asked.

He made much of her for three years, at the end of each one, she gave birth to a set of twins. Then, his interest began to wane. She was still beautiful, of course, and he was still the envy of his peers, but she did not have the skills of a wife of a man of his stature. He began to regard her not so much as a prize, but as a burden, and was not slow about letting her see this. She gave birth to a fourth set of twins—you and your brother—but when even that did not turn him back to her, she began to despair and long for her freedom. The sky and the family she had abandoned for the sake of a love that had turned out to be false called to her, and she could not help but answer when your brother found her featherskin.

Elena wanted to ask, "But what about us? We loved her!" But it occurred to her, given what Azure had said about Elementals being coerced, that the plea might fall on indifferent ears. Azure's sympathy would be entirely with Mama, and after all, she and her brothers might have been neglected, but they were neither abused nor exploited.

Perhaps if Father had betrothed her to some hideous old man, the zephyr might have been more sympathetic, but as matters stood, life was not exactly terrible for any of them, so why waste sympathy on them?

Azure was silent for a very long time, perhaps waiting for Elena's response. Finally, she said, "It's all right. I understand." Even though she did not understand at all.

"May I tell my brothers this?" she asked instead. Azure nodded.

They should know. They should know the kind of man that your father is. You are right to wish to escape him, as your mother did.

Something else occurred to her. "Can—can we turn into swans, too?" she asked hesitantly.

Azure's tail swirled, and she thought this might be an indication that the zephyr was uncertain. *I do not know,* Azure admitted. *But if none of you did so when you turned thirteen, which is a year of changes and portents, it is probably not possible for you to do so on your own.*

She sighed, and her eyes stung a little, because that would have been the answer to everything. If they could have become swans, they could have flown off to Wales and found their mother. Even though Ivy had stated that the children would not be welcomed by her people, she had the hope that, with time, they could have been persuaded. And certainly it would be easier for Mama to make a flock of swans out of them than to support and feed, clothe and house eight young humans.

"Azure," she said, instead, with every fiber of her being, "I cannot thank you enough. I cannot think of a way to repay you properly."

But Azure just laughed. *I am a teacher, as Ivy knows. It pleases me very much to find an apt pupil. And such a pupil! It is like a teacher of music finding a child who sings like a bird, a biddable, willing child who needs the merest touch of instruction to sing the stars out of the skies. I will leave you now. Follow your instincts. But do not do too much magic while you are under the same roof as your Stepmother, for if she Sees it, she will swiftly know it was you.*

"Thank you!" she cried . . . but the zephyr faded, and was gone.

11

That night, after getting Ben's reluctant agreement, she told her brothers everything that the zephyr had told her. After the reaction they had had to what Ivy had disclosed, she expected them to be all abuzz with questions, but instead her information left them silent.

They had gathered about the hearth in the schoolroom, after each of them had carried up a small pile of books from the library and put them in the bookcases that lined each wall. Thin gray light from the windows made the room look cold and shabby, and they had instinctively gathered as close to the good fire on the hearth as they could. They sat on the usual motley assortment of stools, chairs, and cushions that had migrated up here from places in the manor where they were no longer wanted.

The servants' hall is warmer and more welcoming. It is not as shabby, either.

When Elena was done, they each showed their feelings, but without speaking a word. Ben seethed openly. Arthur stared into the fire, scowling. Carl looked blank, and David looked resigned. Felix sighed, then blinked back tears. Emil, to her shock, met her gaze with indifference, as if none of this surprised him, and none of it moved him. Gus, as she had suspected he would, sank into despair.

And what about herself? She had only vague memories of Mama, and she was obscurely grateful for that. She was angry on Mama's part, but anger was directed toward Father. What he had done merited no forgiveness, no matter what the Bible might have to say.

The fire before them crackled merrily, and there were chestnuts to roast, but none of her brothers looked as if they were particularly interested in this pastime.

Finally Arthur spoke aloud. "Well," he said cynically. "I suppose we should be grateful that he did not have us all declared bastards. Then again, he does need his heirs, since the estate is entailed and it would make him furious to think that some distant cousin would claim it for his own."

Elena was frankly surprised that of all of them, *he* was the one who had had that particular reaction, for he was generally inclined to give Father the benefit of the doubt, and try to persuade the rest of them that there must be some excuse for Father's behavior.

But with a sense of pain, she realized that this must have broken even *his* faith in Father. It must have been devastating to finally have to admit that Father not only had feet of clay, but probably ankles and calves as well. She wanted to go to him and put her arms about him, but she didn't know what to say, and he might reject her attempt to comfort him. That would sting.

"He wanted to have his cake and eat it," said Emil, just as cynically. "Keep his heirs and be released from a marriage that no longer suited him. Once his wife deserted him, he could do as he pleased. And now that he has found a . . . better, more well-bred replacement . . . he managed to get the authorities and the Church to agree he should be granted an easy release, a divorce with no one contesting it, but more importantly, no scandal in the newspapers, no *crim con*."

Ben finally took an enormous breath, and released it in a sigh that seemed to release a great deal of pent-up emotion. "Stepmother probably had a hand in that as well." He finally looked at Elena. "She would certainly have insinuated that Mother was well beneath him in rank and consequence and had treacherously wormed her way into his regard, but he, being an honorable man, rather than merely making her his mistress, was intent on making an honorable union, even if it was a union that was—as irregular as a Gretna Green elopement. But now that Mother had proven her lowly birth by deserting us all, it was only right and fair that he be given the opportunity to give his children a *suitable* mother."

Anger swelled in her again, for this had the ring of truth about it.

Elena nodded thoughtfully, keeping a hold on her temper. "I believe you must be right. That would have been a persuasive argument, I think. And cast him in a flattering light as well, rather than as the fool who was deserted."

Gus sniffled, but nodded.

"I think," said David, "that I will *never* forgive him for gulling and entrapping her. Think, all of you! Think how *young* she was! Think that she was *kind* enough to consent to be his because she did not wish him to harm himself! Think how easily he made her feel love for him! And think how easy it was for him to betray that love once his interest faded! As if she was nothing more than a fancy that held him for a while, but was readily dismissed!"

I think you are all much wiser than your years, said Ivy from the mantelpiece, startling her. She looked up at the sylph, who regarded her solemnly.

"Ivy says we are all wiser than our years," Elena told them all, and was greeted by something like smiles from all of them.

Ben looked up at the sylph. "And what else do you think, my little Oracle of Delphi?"

I do not know what that is, Ivy replied. *But I think that you all must not let this fester and make you bitter and cynical. Your stepmother has enough of both to fill this dwelling, and spill out the doors.* She flipped her wings, pertly dismissing Stepmother as inconsequential. *Now, remember that you are the children of something rare and wonderful, that your Stepmother's opinion is of no consequence. And if your mother has not come back to you, perhaps it is because* she *is afraid!*

Elena repeated the sylph word for word.

"Afraid?" asked David, his brows creased. "Afraid of what, exactly?"

Three things. That your father might recapture her somehow, part her from her featherskin, and burn it, so that she could never fly again. She would truly be a slave to his whims, for mortal law holds that a wife has no rights and no protections, and he could do as he pleased with her. She would certainly be punished in some manner for escaping him. Second, and worse, she could rightly harbor the fear that your father might kill her in her swan form, so that he might have revenge on her with everyone around her—including you!—none the wiser. Swan maidens remain swans if they are killed in that form. No one would ever guess what he had done.

Elena's throat tightened, and she felt some of that fear herself. Father *was* ruthless, and *was* perfectly capable of such an act. He might not hunt much now, but it was only because he didn't care for hunting, not because he did not like blood sports, but because hunting took too much time and energy he would rather spend in pursuit of things more pleasurable. *Third and last, I believe she feared that even if she managed somehow to get you away, because her people would not accept you, you would have to wander like beggars or common workers because she had no way to support you. We are more aware of the difficulty of mortal life without money than you realize.*

All of their eyes widened when they heard that. And Elena had to admit that this certainly cast things in an entirely different light for her brothers. She was not old enough to take on the duties of the mistress of the household and make regular visits to Whitstone Village, but the two oldest pairs went there often enough that they must have seen the difficulty of life for the poor, for Arthur at least often remarked on it, and once or twice had spoken about the improvements he intended to make there when he was Lord Whitstone.

She knew your father put value on you, even if he no longer cared for her. You would be safe, well cared for, and the inheritors of a vast estate. You would never know want. She probably reasoned that it was kinder to leave you where you are.

The boys took this in. Elena could tell, knowing them as well as she did, that everything Ivy said had the ring of truth about it, and it softened their anger at Mother quite a lot . . . and assuaged

Gus and Felix's grief. It did nothing for Arthur's anger, but then, he had just lost the last bit of faith he had in Father.

As for her? *I hate him. I hate what he did to her. And if Stepmother were not so odious, I would be glad that she has enthralled him, making him a captive of her will. If he had his own mind, he would be writhing under the bindings she has placed on him. Well, I think that, underneath his smooth surface, he might be. And if that is so, I am glad, glad, glad!*

But it was Arthur who grimaced, but looked back up at Ivy and said, "Thank you, Ivy."

Why didn't you say all this before? Elena asked the sylph silently. *Why didn't the zephyr tell me this today?*

The zephyr did not think of these things, Ivy replied. *She did not know your mother. I did. And I have been thinking about this a great deal since you began speaking to me and asking me questions. I need silence to think deeply, and my kin are boisterous. Some of this only came to me today.*

Well, that made sense. Elena scooped up a handful of chestnuts, placed them on a shovel, and set the shovel on the coals. And when the chestnuts began to pop, sending their fragrance into the air, David licked his lips and then pressed them together before he spoke.

"It might be base of me," he said, "but . . . I am quite hungry."

Ben, who was sitting next to him, patted him on the shoulder. "Nothing changes if we refuse to enjoy what we have," he said. "And really, that's why Mother left us here. So we could enjoy what is *our birthright.* Am I right?"

"Really, when you think about it, enjoying our birthright is to spite Father," Arthur said, slowly. "Send that shovel my way, would you?"

Their holiday came to an end a week after Twelfth Night when Hobart informed them over breakfast that "The master has sent a letter ahead. He and her ladyship intend to arrive in two days."

That rather turned the delicious breakfast cakes to ashes in their mouths, but they all feigned pleasure at the announcement. Mrs. Banning, however, was not fooled. As soon as the rest of the staff had cleared the table and the room, but while they were still sitting at the ample table and sipping their hot tea, she leaned over to say, softly, "I am very sorry, my dears. But you did have a longer holiday than you expected."

Ben nodded, and the rest finally joined him. It was true. Father and Stepmother had left early, and were returning late, a good *week* after Twelfth Night. Almost an entire month of freedom!

And Father is certainly fretting to be home and seeing to the business of the estate. Not even being besotted will change that. Stepmother has just learned that she will always take second place to Whitstone Manor. Perhaps she has also learned that he will never bankrupt his estate just to please her. He may not be loyal to much, but he is loyal to that. I hope that makes her furious.

"I think we should start taking our meals in the schoolroom again, Mrs. Banning," Arthur mused aloud. Then he looked directly at the cook and elaborated. "I do not like to give you and the girls the extra work again, but I think that we must. We wouldn't want to be down here if somehow the weather was ideal, the horses all fresh, and he came home early."

"True," Ben agreed. "That would get you all in trouble, and we don't want that."

Mrs. Banning nodded. "And it's good of you to think of that. Don't worry, my dears, we'll see that you don't go wanting now that *she* is back."

Elena sighed with regret. Meals with the staff had been nice, almost like being in an enormous family. Once they got over their stiffness, and once they understood the siblings were indifferent to their rank, they had taken the Whitstone children to their hearts. Christmas had been the best they had ever had. It was going to be hard to give all that up. And just a little hard to go back to the plainer fare that was all Mrs. Banning could provide for them while Stepmother was back in charge.

But we have lovely memories. Those will have to do. Regret turned to sadness, but she was determined not to show it. That would make Mrs. Banning sad, and Mrs. Banning did not deserve that after her kindness.

So they left the servants' hall with heavier hearts than they had arrived with this morning.

"Remember," Ben cautioned them all. "Not a word of this holiday once *she* is back. Remember that Ivy told us *she* can spy on us with her magic. We will have to watch our tongues at all times. We want her to believe we went on as she left us: confined to the schoolroom except when going out to walk, ride, or play, spending a miserable Christmas with no cheer at all."

Elena made a sour face, remembering what the zephyr had said. She would not dare practice any magic now that Stepmother was back. She resented that far more than she would have thought! Now that she had begun, she found that learning magic had ignited a hunger in her that was greater than her desire to create beautiful gowns or fashion intricate needlework. She felt the power inside her right now, in fact, teasing her, like a kitten that wants to play. She could tell it *not now* over and over again, but it didn't understand, and still wanted to be used.

That would be folly, and she knew it. But knowing is not the same as *feeling*.

But as the zephyr had noted, she had cultivated self-discipline almost as long as she had been alive. The desire to use her magic would not get the best of her.

They all trudged back upstairs, resigned to being confined, once again, to that small portion of the manor that had been allotted to them. Once they all arrived at the schoolroom, Ben looked about them with scorn, as if seeing it with new eyes.

In fact, Elena was doing the same. She had been spending most of her time in the luxury of the winter parlor, and this sadly neglected room, with its random assortment of cast-offs, was, definitely, inferior to the servants' hall.

Even the sleeping arrangements were, because she had had a glimpse or two of those. Other than not having to share a room with other girls, and having a fireplace, she had no more comforts than they did. And they had little things to brighten their rooms that she did not.

"Well!" she said. "There is one thing that we can do. We can stop living in rooms that look utterly shabby. Having *nice* rooms will certainly raise our spirits. We can start with the nursery, since we barely use it. Then we can move to the schoolroom, and then our own rooms, if we decide we need them livened up."

"That seems like a deal of work," Gus said, dubiously.

"I am certain that with Father and Stepmother still away, Mrs. Farthingworth will loan us a girl or a lad or two," Arthur pointed out. "Ben, why don't you go and ask her, and we'll have a look at the nursery."

Ben nodded, and trotted back downstairs while the rest of them went next door to the nursery.

Since Nanny and Beecham had been dismissed, the nursery had not been used for much except as a sort of workroom where handicrafts could be done without disturbing anyone in the schoolroom. And although they had *mostly* tidied up after themselves, and now and again Mrs. Farthingworth had sent one of the girls up to clean, there was no doubt it needed more than a bit of sweeping and dusting.

"Do we want to undertake painting or papering?" Emil asked Arthur, dubiously.

"Let's have a closer look at the walls, first," he advised. They spread out, examining the yellow paper that was already there in detail.

On closer inspection, at least on Elena's wall, there wasn't much wrong except a layer of grime and the fact that the wallpaper had faded. And the unframed pictures still pinned to it, which looked . . . juvenile. "My wall doesn't look anything but dirty," she said, regarding the unframed pictures with distaste— mostly her early sketches that she could not look upon without a blush. She began unpinning them, taking care that she did not make a larger hole in the wallpaper than was already there, and threw them in the fire.

"It is the same here," decreed Arthur, and the others agreed. "What should we do with these drawings, Elena? They are not improving the room."

"In the fire with them," she said with scorn. "They are mostly mine."

"Not this one," Gus said slowly. "I think it is Ben's."

They all gathered around him to see, and indeed, it did bear Ben's signature. They looked at the picture solemnly, and finally Elena said what they were all thinking. "I believe that is meant to be Mama."

The hands were too large, the pose awkward, the hair looked as if she was sitting in a gale. Yet there was something about the face . . . something familiar, warm, and weary.

"Perhaps we should keep it for him," David said.

"But—what if Stepmother can use it for magic?" Elena asked, speaking slowly.

"Whyever for?" Emil retorted. "She has no reason—"

"Hasn't she?" Arthur replied, with challenge in his voice. "We know now she is a creature of magic. What if Stepmother could lure her here with this picture to murder her for her power?"

The room seemed to grow very cold indeed, and Elena shivered. "I think . . . that is just the sort of thing she *would* do," Elena replied. "If only to hurt us. I think she is the sort of person to hurt someone just because she can."

Silence, as those words chilled the air for a very long time.

"I think I am very glad we have no pets," Felix said quietly. "I would not like a living thing I cared for to be hostage to her whims."

"What's that about pets?" Ben said from the doorway, with housemaids Annie and Jenny in tow, laden with brooms, mops, brushes, sponges, and buckets of water. "You know Father won't permit any such thing. He would never even allow us the toads we caught in the garden." He glanced at the sketch in Arthur's hands. "That's rubbish. Throw it on the fire."

Elena wanted to stop him, because the image in her mind she called "Mama" was all she had to remind her, but she knew that Ben was right. She took the sketch from Arthur's unresisting hands and tossed it on the fire.

Under the tutelage of the two housemaids—who must have been highly amused that they were allowed to order the master's children about—the room was cleared, and anything deemed too battered or too tattered to keep was sent up to the attic. Then they washed the walls with sponges, warm water, and a little soap. The maids took care of areas that were too high to reach, and had extendable tools to help. Already things looked better, although the prints had to be put back because there had been rectangles of brighter yellow where they had been.

Then it was time for nuncheon. They retired to the

schoolroom, while Annie and Jenny scrubbed the floor. When the two housemaids went down for their own luncheon, they all returned to the nursery to contemplate what use they should make of it.

Things looked more encouraging than they had before, just because they were clean. Several forays into the attic and woodshed (where other old furniture was kept) later, by suppertime the room looked, not completely different, but very much more suited to purpose. And much more cheerful. A series of large maps had been found, rolled up in a leather tube and apparently never used for anything, with matching frames propped on the wall behind them. Those were on the wall now, and vastly improved the place. New curtains graced the windows. Well, new to *them*, anyway. Whoever had put them away had cleaned them first and tucked them in a chest. They only needed to hang for a while to remove the creases, and as they were a fine, strong daffodil instead of plain, uncolored fabric. They even made the light from the windows seem warmer. Also from the attic were a slightly worn rug for the center of the room to cover the worst of the scratches and scuffs. Elena swiftly stitched new covers for the cushions using long basting stitches and very stout buttonhole thread. More attic finds in the form of eight mismatched chairs and two small tables came down, were given a good dusting by the maids, and set into place. In the end, they had a snug little parlor. The large cushions went into a pile in the corner, and Gus found flat cushions with ties at each corner to soften the wooden chairs. These were not ideal, but Elena was certain she could sew replacements in no time.

The next day a similar transformation occurred in the schoolroom, although here the walls, since they were limewashed, only needed another coating of lime to cover inexplicable stains and naughty scribblings that had been put there when Beecham had been out of the room. The footman who had been kind to Elena at the formal dinner, Thomas Spencer, had taken off his coat, rolled up his sleeves, and applied the brush with a will. The schoolroom table and chairs had to remain, for they had depleted the attic of practical items, but strips of carpeting framed the table, and what appeared to be a brand-new hearthrug was laid down in front of the fire. An ancient embroidered firescreen provided a nice touch of color. A couch placed beneath one of the windows made a reading area that would be very comfortable when better weather came and drafts were not blowing down one's neck. A globe that had once been in Father's study provided another spot of brightness. Draperies that, by their length, had once graced one of the parlors now hung at the windows, the table had been decently covered with a green baize cloth, and inferior busts of white-glazed terracotta—busts that Elena vaguely recalled had been supplanted downstairs by statues of marble—adorned the mantelpiece. Dented brass oil lamps joined them, dents turned to face the wall. Stools with broken legs became nice low seats with a few strokes of a saw wielded manfully by Thomas, and by candle-lighting time the room presented a much more cheerful aspect. In fact, the siblings sat down to their supper with weary satisfaction, their spirits raised by hard work and much less shabby surroundings.

"I wonder who those people are," Elena mused over her shovel-toasted cheese as she regarded the busts with a curious air. "They don't seem to be Greek nor Roman."

"I think they are not supposed to be anything, or anyone," Ben replied after a moment of thought.

But Arthur laughed. "That is where you are wrong! They are supposed to be representations of the continents! There was once an entire set, but the most interesting ones were broken. Now there is just poor, lonely Europa and Asia."

"Asia does not look very Asian," Gus observed dubiously.

"The artist was, I believe, local, and made them during the Restoration. I remember Father telling me that the man just made up what he thought would suit, and glazed everything in white to obscure his ignorance. Although I very much doubt that the then–Lord Whitstone cared, since he had been restored to his estate by King Charles, and had used some haste in bringing in comfort and what passed at first blush for luxury." Arthur cocked his head as he looked at them. "Yes, the one on the right is Europa and the one on the left is Asia; you can tell from their hair ornaments."

"He was not a bad artist," Ben observed. "They are quite lifelike."

"I like them," said Elena decidedly. "I am glad you found them."

The sylphs definitely approved of the changes; they were everywhere in the room, sliding down the curtains, playing on the mantelpiece, hiding and jumping out at each other among the books, jumping from stool to stool.

Gus watched them, and finally smiled for the first time since the zephyr's revelations about their mother. "We don't need pets," he said. "The fairies are better than monkeys!"

They had a mere half day before the sylphs suddenly vanished while they were all absorbed in the new books the boys had brought up from Father's library. To her utter amazement, there had actually been real *novels* among them! She judged that Grandfather must have bought them, since neither Father nor Mama would have had any interest in fiction.

Could Mama even read, I wonder?

The first one she attempted was *Amelia*, by a man called Henry Fielding. To tell the truth, she was enjoying it excessively, and was taking pains to read it slowly, savoring each paragraph.

And then the sylphs disappeared. As before, one moment they were there, mostly lazing about the room. The next moment, they were gone.

David noticed this at the same time she did, and sighed. "They are almost back, so watch your tongues," he said with resignation. He did not need to say who "they" were.

"I don't think that we need to worry about Stepmother coming up to examine and interrogate us again," Arthur replied, after a moment. "It is quite some distance, and she is indolent. But we had best gather our coats and be ready to put them on to go down to greet them. Mrs. Farthingworth will be certain to send for us when they are at the end of the drive, if she does not come up herself, and it would be better if we were all in place to greet them when they arrive."

"Even if Stepmother *does* come up to snoop about, she must

see that what we have done is unexceptional." Ben looked as if he would like to hit something, but smoothed his expression almost immediately. "This is no more luxurious than the servants' hall. It is just not as shabby as it was. And we have spent no money, nor have we taken anything from the public rooms."

He continued on in that vein, sounding more and more aggrieved, but Elena did not hear him past those first sentences. She had gone to her room to collect her pelisse and bonnet.

She had no more returned to the schoolroom when Mrs. Farthingworth herself appeared at the door, a little out of breath. She looked surprised to see them all ready, but said nothing about it, merely waving them all down the stairs.

Elena was exceedingly glad of her bonnet; the wind blew sharply and it was perishingly cold. Cold enough, if this weather held, to freeze the pond solid and give the boys their much-longed-for skating. By the time they were all out of the door, the carriage was almost to the steps, so it was just as well that they had been ready to come down when Mrs. Farthingworth fetched them. The grooms Dick and Phillip sprang down from the back of the carriage, and Elena pitied them; their faces were pinched and noses quite red with the cold. It must have been horrible, riding out in the weather like that. Dick set down the footstep in front of the carriage door, and Phillip opened it, while Dick offered his hand to help Stepmother alight.

She had not changed in the least. She ignored poor Dick as soon as her feet touched the ground, exclaiming loudly, "Lud! How the wind blows! I feared the carriage would turn over; the ruts in the road were frozen solid!" She was swathed in what appeared to be a brand-new fur cape, also lined in fur—perhaps reversible, since the outside seemed to be sable and the inside mink.

"We were never in any danger of turning over, my love," Father said caressingly as he alighted from the carriage, also dressed in a new suit of blue superfine, with his many-caped drab driving coat over it. "Trevor is very skilled. But pray, we must get you inside before you get a chill."

They both hurried past the siblings as if they were not there, without even so much as a nod of greeting, and Hobart looked at the eight of them, gave a faint shrug, and then directed the footmen to swarm the carriage to take down all the baggage. "Not you two," he corrected, as Dick and Phillip made as if to help. "Get yourselves inside, where there is a fire. Trevor, Grimes has been directed to see to the horses. Once the carriage is in his hands, join them." He gave Father's valet Stephens an austere greeting, ignored Fleurette altogether, and with a gesture to the siblings that they should go back inside, left the footmen to do their job.

Fleurette looked as if she would have liked to stalk inside in high dudgeon, but since she was not swathed in furs as Stepmother was, she was too cold. But she did manage to cut in front of the siblings, although she had to perform an undignified scramble to do so. Dick and Phillip very properly waited for all eight of them to pass before they hurried within, heading straight for the servants' hall.

"Back upstairs, I suppose," sighed Ben as they headed for the stairs. "We might as well not have been there. At least we weren't left standing about in the cold for long."

They all went back up to the schoolroom, stopping at their rooms to shed their outer garments. Elena brought a thick woolen shawl with her; the wind was not *howling*, precisely, but it was certainly rattling the windows.

They were left to themselves until after supper, when Ben, Arthur, and Elena were sent for. Gus mouthed a "good luck" at his twin as she followed her older brothers downstairs. They found Father and Stepmother in the winter parlor next to an exceedingly good fire; Father was standing at the fire, his back to them, and Stepmother sat in a chair to the right, a glass of cordial that glowed in the light like a ruby in her hand.

Father turned to face them as they entered. "Well," he said. "All seems well here. I trust you can give a good account of yourselves."

"Of course, Father," said Ben, taking the lead. "We did take advantage of your kind offer to investigate the library. Arthur found several volumes of sermons and Bible commentary, I uncovered some volumes of history I was not previously acquainted with, and the others found suitably improving books."

Elena smiled to herself, thinking of her novels. "Suitably improving books" indeed!

"And Elena," Father continued. "I trust that the magazines and drawing materials arrived, and are satisfactory."

"They did, Father. Everything is exactly as one could wish," Elena replied softly. "Thank you, Father. And thank you for your Christmas gift."

"I hope you spent it wisely," he replied, in tones that were not *quite* admonishing. "And I hope that you have something that will please your mother."

"I do!" she said earnestly, and Stepmother's eyes glittered in a way that had nothing to do with the candlelight. "I have been very diligent."

In the morning, because she did not want to test the limits of the protection that the zephyr had helped her make, she sent the first batch of drawings to Stepmother's room by one of the maids, hoping to forestall or eliminate another interview.

She forestalled it, but did not eliminate it. Just after luncheon, the summons came.

Once again she found herself in the winter parlor, facing Stepmother across the carpet, but this time, the woman had her drawings in her hand. "I do not like to praise," said Stepmother, "because I do not like to give girls an inflated opinion of themselves. They become pert and contrary, and eventually one has to administer a decided set-down, or even a punishment."

She paused, obviously expecting an answer to this non-question. "Yes, Stepmother," Elena said in as neutral a tone as possible.

"But these drawings and designs are quite the thing." Stepmother studied them again. "I suspect they will require the services of a genuine *modiste*, and we will not return to Bath until spring."

"Oh, no, Stepmother!" Elena said quickly. "I planned for that. You will see that each of the gowns themselves are quite simple, and can be readily made up by Mrs. Beadle in the village. It is the trimming and ornaments that make the gown special, and I have the skills to do all of that. Those will have to be sent for, and it will take me more time than it would a *modiste*, with all her apprentices and helpers, but since you are not returning to Bath for many months, that will not signify. I wish to see you gowned as befits your rank and beauty," she added, trying to look adoring. She must have succeeded, because Stepmother laughed indulgently, and basked in the flattery.

"I shall have to arrange a treat for you, then," Stepmother replied, turning her attention back to the sketches. "I confess that of all of you children, I did not anticipate that you would be the most useful to me."

Dear Lord in Heaven, what does she mean by that? I shudder to discover. And I shall have to repeat this to the boys. She restrained a shudder.

"So what would you like as a treat?" Stepmother continued, turning the drawings over on the table beside her.

Elena thought quickly. "Cakes at breakfast and tea?" she asked, timidly.

This time Stepmother laughed even harder. "Trust a child to ask for sweets. Very well, I shall order the cook to include them from now on." Then she nodded. "You may go. Fleurette will send up a basket of my stockings to mend. It is shocking how one goes through them thanks to balls and entertainments!"

Gratefully, Elena turned and fled. But those ominous words kept ringing in her ears.

"Of all of you children, I did not anticipate that you would be the most useful to me...."

12

The weather continued to be fearfully cold, though the wind died completely and, at last, the pond was completely frozen over, and the ice was hard enough to hold several full-grown men. Since there had been no snow, the surface did not need clearing, and the lack of wind made it smooth and glassy. The icy weather had kept them all confined to the schoolroom, and the boys, even Arthur and Ben, were wild to get outside and try out their skates.

Since they had never actually *skated* before, only indulged in sliding, at the suggestion of the blacksmith, each skate had two iron blades affixed to it for stability, instead of one. In order to go watch them, Elena wrapped up in her warmest gown, a pelisse, a shawl, and an old woolen cape from the attic over all that, gloves, her new hat and muff, and two pairs of stockings. She was certain that she looked more like a woolen cylinder than a human being, but she did not care as long as she did not freeze.

The weather that had made the freeze possible was also painfully bleak, and she was reminded again of why she took her daily walks in the conservatories rather than outside. The predominant color of the entire landscape was brownish gray. The trees were brown and gray, the grass was brown, the bushes were brown, the overcast sky was gray. This part of the manor gardens was as flat as a board, with nothing much to see, because it held the flowering (and fruiting) bushes and trees, and the pond itself, that were meant to be the beauties on display. The sun shone down dimly through a kind of thin haze, the air was perfectly still, and there was no sign of snow, which would have at least made the scene brilliant and sparkling.

The boys soon had their skates strapped on over their boots and ventured cautiously out onto the ice while she watched.

And thus began a comedy of interminable errors.

Elena found herself laughing so hard that her sides hurt, watching them attempt to balance on two thin blades instead of the entire soles of their shoes. Poor Gus spent more time on his bottom than his skates, and trying to get back up to his feet again was a test of his resolve solved only by crawling to the edge, grasping the trunk of a young tree, and pulling himself up. They were just as bundled up as she was, in a motley assortment of old garments, the outermost ones mostly loose woolen shirts not unlike smocks, also salvaged from the attic, and showing more than a touch of the moth's tooth. The drab, dingy colors had saved them from Elena's scissors.

Fortunately they found their own lack of balance and stability as funny as she did, and part of the difficulty of staying erect was that they were laughing so hard they found themselves unbalancing again.

All of their breaths formed clouds in the air, clouds that swirled around them before they dissipated, as flailing arms and hands passed through them.

Now Elena was very glad that Ben had not made her a pair of skates too. She would surely have found herself with her skirts flying up, and not only would that have been painfully embarrassing, it would have been hideously cold. As it was, by standing perfectly still, she was able to trap some warm air inside her skirts and petticoats. She surely looked nothing like the modish ladies in her magazines, dressed in the very pinnacle of style, who seemed to believe that a muff and a pelisse over a muslin gown were enough to keep the wearer warm.

The sylphs had appeared as soon as the boys arrived out on the pond, and flew and fluttered around them. It seemed that the pond was far enough distant from the manor that they were not afraid of Stepmother seeing them. Frequently they circled a fallen skater as if to taunt him, laughing the entire time. The exertion was enough to keep them warm, at least, and all their extra garments gave them enough padding not to bruise too badly. The antics went on for nearly an hour; then, gradually, with Arthur first, the skaters began to *skate* instead of falling. Once they got the knack of keeping their feet under them, they were flying around the pond, swooping and darting like birds, and Elena envied them instead of laughing at them.

Then the sylphs vanished.

Oh no . . . That could only mean one thing.

But she did not look back at the manor. She did not want to betray the fact that she could see the sylphs. And perhaps Stepmother would only watch from a distance, just to see what they were up to—or perhaps to make sure the group on the ice was not the menservants up to illicit larks. She concentrated hard on watching the boys instead, trusting to the protection that she still felt like a vague tingling on the surface of her skin.

She started as a hand came down on her shoulders, and looked up to see that Stepmother had ventured all the way to the pond to watch the fun, enveloped in her new sable cape, with a separate sable hood to match.

Why? What can she want? Is she trying to spoil our enjoyment with her mere presence? Does she think she'll find something to bring to Father so he can chastise us? Whatever brings her out here, into the freezing cold, cannot be for our benefit.

Her skin crawled, and she wanted desperately to free herself from that clutching hand, but she knew that if she did, Stepmother would make her pay for the gesture. So she stood statue-still, fastened her gaze on her brothers, and tried to enjoy the display.

It was not so easy to ignore the fact that after a few moments of watching, Stepmother began—muttering.

It was under her breath, and Elena could not make out what she was saying, but it all set her nerves afire.

Eventually the boys all realized that Stepmother was standing beside Elena well away from the edge of the pond—but their skating just got more dexterous when they did, as if they were daring her to do something about it, taunting her with how graceful they were. She wanted to cry out, "Don't antagonize her!" but the words stuck in her throat, and all she could do was whimper impotently, as icy dread enveloped her, and she literally shook with fear.

Then Stepmother's left arm and hand emerged from a slit in the cloak, rose, and came down as if she was striking something.

And with a terrible *explosion* from below, like a dozen lightning bolts striking as one, the ice beneath her brothers shattered, and they plunged into the water.

Elena tried to scream, tried to run for help, but she stood as frozen as an ice statue, unable to move or even make a sound, helpless to do *anything* as all seven of her brothers fought for their lives.

Their struggles were terrible: limbs flailing as they tried to get to the edge of the break, trying to heave themselves and their waterlogged clothing up onto the ice again. Trying, and failing, and falling back into the water. There was no sound except the splashing. Horribly, they did not cry out, desperately trying to keep their breath for the fight to stay alive. Each time they tried to save themselves, the attempt was feebler and feebler, their gasping breaths harsher and harsher, until, at last, one by one, they sank into the black water and did not come up again. Gus was the first to disappear, as Elena's mouth opened in a scream that would not come. Arthur was the last.

And then the water erupted in thrashing and foam, and out of the depths of the pond emerged a swan. Then another, and another, until there were seven. Seven swans, with flailing wings and splashing legs, who struggled to the edge of the ice and over it, and lay, exhausted and panting, on what was left of the broken surface.

That was when Stepmother took three steps toward them, dragging Elena with her, and made a casting motion with her left hand. Something like a glowing net made of green magic that made Elena gag with nausea just to look at it flew from her open hand, growing larger with every moment.

Sylphs appeared at that moment and frantically tried to stop the net from flying any further, but to no avail. It sailed right past their hands until it reached the swans, settled over them all, and melted into their bodies.

The sylphs fled, wailing.

Stepmother paced to where the swans lay, wings splayed out, panting. The swans (were they *really* her brothers?) tried to rise up, got their heads up on their long necks, and hissed at her, but she laughed at them.

She looked down at them with amusement and chuckled, the sound freezing Elena's breath in her lungs. "Well. Theodore was not making phantasies," she said, amusement in her voice. "It is just as well I came prepared. We—I, at least—would not want you learning how to change back, now would we?"

The swans lurched to their feet and hissed at her defiantly, stretching their necks out toward her. She made a shooing gesture. "Fly away, little boys, and go find your mother, much good may it do you," she said in a hate-filled voice that nearly made Elena faint. "Fly away and do not return, or I shall have the gamekeeper shoot you. I fancy a swansdown-trimmed pelisse."

"Swan maidens that die in that form do not become human again." The sylph Ivy's words rang through Elena's mind, and doubtlessly those of her brothers.

"Fly!" snarled Stepmother, and with calls of alarm, one by one the swans lurched into the sky, wings beating against the icy air, a thunder of wingbeats that Elena felt as much as heard. They gained height, slowly at first, then faster and higher, forming a white vee against the gray sky, until they vanished into the distance.

Stepmother turned and came back to Elena, and gripped her shoulder again. "You will say *nothing* of this, girl," she snarled, staring into Elena's eyes as tears sprang up in them and froze on her cheeks. "*Nothing.* No one will believe you. Not even your father. He is *mine*, and nothing you can do or say will change that."

And then Stepmother turned and ran toward the manor, shouting at the top of her lungs. "Help! *Help! The boys have fallen through the ice! HELP!*"

Freed from that strange paralysis, Elena dropped to her knees, sobbing.

Servants came running. Jenny and Annie from the kitchen each took one of her arms and pulled her to her feet as men with rakes and poles plunged their implements into the cold, dark water to try to find the boys, or at least their bodies. Someone pulled out a coat as Jenny and Annie forced her to come with them to the kitchen, where a weeping Mrs. Banning extracted her from her pelisse, wrapped a blanket around her, and thrust a cup of hot tea into her hands. Elena sobbed inconsolably, knowing that no one would ever find bodies, because her brothers had, impossibly, been made into swans.

And she feared that she would never see them again.

Grief enveloped Elena, smothered every other feeling, every other sensation. Grief became her whole world, her entire being. Every day was the same. Every morning, she woke weeping, from nightmares in which her brothers were shot out of the sky to fall to earth, bright red blood spotting their white feathers. Sore-eyed, she would dress in any old thing, go to the kitchen, and sit in a corner, out of the way, until someone gave her a cake and a cup of tea. She would do her best to choke both down, then bundle up and go out to the pond. The cold snap ended, and the pond water melted, the black water echoing the void in her heart. With tears streaming down her face, she searched the pond and the air above it for swans. But though there were ducks and geese aplenty, there were no swans. But at least there were no dead swans beside the pond, nor swans hanging in the larder to be—horrid thought!—plucked and cooked. Her brothers had heeded Stepmother's warning, but she felt their loss as keenly as if they actually *had* drowned. She would stand there beside the pond and weep until her cheeks and eyes were raw, and someone came to fetch her, bring her to the kitchen, and try to coax her to eat and drink something.

She would either sit in the kitchen until someone guided her up to the old nursery or the schoolroom, or until she found the kitchen too full and too busy to remain. Then she would listlessly climb the stairs and sit in the old nursery—the schoolroom was too empty and too painful—and knit, crochet, or mend. Because if she did not at least do something with her hands, she would sink into black despair. Dimly she understood that if that despair enveloped her, she would stop eating and drinking, crawl into her room, and never leave her bed again. She would not emerge from the nursery unless someone came up to look in on her, bring her something more to eat, or urge her into her own room again. More often than not, that person was Mrs. Farthingworth, who would wrap an arm and her shawl around Elena's shoulders and guide her, step by step, into her room, always saying the same thing. "Come, child, your brothers will never leave you."

Except, of course, that was precisely what they had done.

She wept as she worked, until her eyes were permanently red and sore, and she cried herself to sleep every night, only to be engulfed again in nightmares. Sometimes those nightmares played the terrible scene at the pond over again, except that Stepmother would stand there laughing, taunting her and saying she would never see them again. Sometimes they were the nightmares where the swans were shot in mid-flight. Sometimes she would be forced to sew swansdown trim on Stepmother's sable cape. Sometimes she found herself at the table as Mrs. Banning—horrors!—tried to serve her a slice of roast swan.

She did not see Father at all, and Stepmother only in passing.

From gossip in the kitchen, she learned that Father had taken the deaths of all of his sons very hard, and was as sunk in grief as she was, losing all interest in anything that had once occupied him.

She could not bring herself to care. She could not even hate him for bringing Stepmother here to ruin their lives. She could not bring herself to think of him at all.

As days stretched into weeks, weeks into months, and months into spring, her tears dried, and her despair turned into a heavy cloak that weighed her down and made every step a struggle. The nightmares continued unabated, so sleep brought little rest, and she became enveloped in a kind of fog that nothing could penetrate. She even lost interest in handiwork, and sat listlessly with needles in her hands, unable to take a single stitch.

But from the staff chatter, it was worse for her father. He had taken to his bed, dosed by the doctor over in Charton-town, nursed by Stepmother, but growing weaker every day, and had been utterly without speech from the moment he learned of the boys' "deaths." Learning that, some feeling finally penetrated the fog. A dull, sour feeling she could not put a name to. *Good,* she thought, many times, bitterly. *Let him suffer. If he had not driven Mama off, we would all be happy. If he had not brought Stepmother here, he would still have his sons.*

Stepmother seemed to be genuinely trying to help him, nurse him back to life, and the staff let slip that Fleurette had intimated that she had thought herself with child around the time of the accident, and had either been mistaken or lost it early. And now she was trying to revive him so that she could give him a new heir. That much, at least, was absolutely certain, because several of the maids had heard her attempting to coax him into eating with the promise that once he was well, she'd give him as many children as he wanted.

She could not feel anything *for* him, not even hatred. Her own pain was too great. There was just an aching void in her heart and soul where her brothers had once been.

As for Stepmother—

Well, that was where another sensation cut through the miasma, and what she felt was fear. How had the woman done that? The *why* was obvious. She had hoped all along to be rid of the boys so that her own offspring would inherit. She replayed the woman's words to herself in her mind, and it came to her through the fog of grief that Stepmother had somehow pried what Mama had been out of Father, but she had only half believed that trying to murder them would make them transform. Nevertheless, she had come prepared to lock them permanently into swan form. That net of magic—that was what had done it. She *knew* that, somehow, just as she knew her own name.

I wish I had been skating with them. We could have flown off together. It wouldn't matter if we were never human again, because we would all be together. Maybe we could have found Mama after all; perhaps not, but it wouldn't matter, because we would be together and far from her.

That was her one hope, that they would find Mama, and they would all be happy together, free from Father, escaped from Stepmother's plans.

Whatever those were.

So she passed each day, sunk in grief too profound for tears, hands sometimes working, usually idle, limping through each day until she could finally find forgetfulness in sleep.

The nightmares eased, then ceased, leaving her an escape into nothing for a little while.

And then spring came. Easter came.

And Father died.

They told her they were going to bury him beside the (empty) graves of his sons. She nodded, and said nothing until they went away and left her alone. They took away her old clothing, then gave her new, black clothing to put on, and she did. A distant part of her mind registered it as expensive, so it was unlikely that Stepmother had ordered it. It hung on her; she didn't even care to tighten the ribbons at the waist and neckline to make it fit better. What was the point? Who cared how she looked? Her hair remained uncombed, in a braid down her back, unless Mrs. Farthingworth or one of the maids made her sit while they combed it out and rebraided it.

She only knew that the day of the funeral had come when Mary Ann put her hair up for the first time since Nanny had been sacked, and coaxed her into another new gown. Black, of course, and made to fit her a little better. "Her ladyship says it is time for you to come down," the maid told her, firmly. "You must attend his lordship's funeral."

She looked at Mary Ann with dull eyes, and said a single word with a voice rusty and harsh with unuse. "Why?"

Mary Ann looked shocked, but had no answer. Nevertheless, she pulled Elena downstairs by the hand, and Elena did not resist.

But she refused to travel in the same carriage as Stepmother, registering her refusal by simply not moving until Grimes brought up the old carriage for her; she shared it with Hobart, Mrs. Banning, and Mrs. Farthingworth, the four of them pools of unrelenting black in the dim interior. She sat silently through a service where the vicar lied about her father, and droned about what a good and kind man he was. She stopped listening after a while, and finally, after so long that people were starting to fall asleep in the pews, he finished. Stepmother was escorted by one of the ushers to the coffin in the center aisle, wept over it prettily, bent to kiss the cheek of her husband, pretended to faint, and was taken to a pew.

Then it was Elena's turn. She was led to the coffin by Hobart, stared down at the gaunt, starved face of a man who she did not know anymore, and really had not known when he was alive.

Finally a tiny flare of emotion stirred in the embers of her heart, and she hated him with a tired, worn-out hatred that was a single burning spark in her void.

She stood there, doing nothing, until Hobart judged she had stood there long enough, and took her back to the pew. The vicar closed the coffin lid, then the glossy black box was lifted onto the shoulders of six of the footmen, identically clothed in black livery, and they all went into the churchyard in double file, Stepmother with the usher, then Mrs. Banning and Mrs. Farthingworth, then herself with Hobart, who kept her moving with tiny tugs at her arm. There, beneath the gray sky (though not as gray as the sky her brothers had flown into), the box was lowered into its hole, dirt was shoveled in, people came and talked in low voices to Stepmother, and everyone but Hobart ignored her. If it had not been that she was too tired to walk that far, she would have left and gone back to the manor alone and on foot.

But she went alone to the carriage and waited until Hobart and the cook and housekeeper joined her. Then they had to wait further while Stepmother was escorted to the new carriage by the vicar and was handed in, and they all went back to the manor. The carriages traveled at a walk, so that all the manor servants, who had come to the funeral, could follow on foot behind. The church bell tolled mournfully, and a flock of rooks flew by overhead, calling raucously.

She could hardly wait to get back into her bed and pull the covers over her head.

There was supposed to be some sort of funeral dinner, but since no one seemed to expect anything of her, she went back to her room and stared out the window at nothing until darkness fell, and she undressed and went to bed. And finally went to sleep, after staring into the dark, waiting for the nightmares to start again.

Nothing lasts forever, not even grief. Something of the shell of despair she had enclosed herself in seemed to crack when Father died and was buried. The next day, she woke, and noticed that there was birdsong outside her window, and for just a few moments, she listened to it without thinking how Gus would have complained about it waking him up. She dressed in black again. That was how it was; she was finally in official mourning, which meant she would dress in black for the next year. All her clothing had been redyed, so it was familiar and unfamiliar at the same time. She went down to the kitchen, and felt hungry for the first time since that terrible day. She spent the morning in the kitchen, but after luncheon, instead of sitting listlessly in her room or the nursery, she took one of the novels that Arthur had found for her outside, and read in the garden until teatime. Then she stayed in the kitchen again until Mrs. Banning sent her off to bed.

But she was thinking and feeling again. The world had gone on, and she must go with it, but there was birdsong, and there were flowers, and rabbits in the garden, and once Grimes brought her a kitten from the stable cat's newest litter to play with. He didn't leave it with her, nor did she ask, but it is very hard to be flattened by despair in the presence of a kitten.

That was her schedule for the next day, and the next, and the next. She never even glimpsed Stepmother for the next week, but since she spent so much time in the kitchen, and she had begun to listen closely to it, she knew very well what was going on. Though most of the staff gossip was concerned with what was going to happen to them when the inevitable occured and the new heir arrived to take over the estate, some concerned her. According to the gossip, Stepmother was wasting no time in trying to find a way to be rid of her. All in the name of "helping her," of course.

First, she was to be sent to Nanny. Then she was to be sent to a school to learn all the things she *should* have learned from a good governess—not that Elena believed *that* lie; she would be sent to some place where no one knew her, some wretched hovel where girls were sent to get them out of the way, probably in the hope that she would go into decline again and die. Stepmother must have decided that she was too dangerous to have about, for she might say something to suggest that the "accident" was no accident at all, and had become a burden to be rid of as quickly as possible. The destination changed almost daily, but the one constant was that she was to be sent away to some place where no one would believe her if she tried to tell them what had really happened.

She still had no energy and very little interest in any of it. *Anything would be better than here.* Besides . . . if Stepmother sent her away, the sylphs would find her again, and perhaps Azure, and she could begin to explore her magic again, safe from Stepmother finding out that she had it. For although there was a void within her, and a deep and abiding exhaustion, that spark of magic had somehow persisted, and kept nudging at her to use it.

Which, of course, she dared not do.

But every day was a little bit easier. Every day she awakened to discover that some minute part of her that had been numb was alive. Every day she tried to think of somewhere she could realistically go that would be permitted, but far enough away from Stepmother that the sylphs might come to her.

And then the bottom dropped out, not of her world, but of Stepmother's.

Three carriages rolled up to the front of the manor as Elena brooded, chin on her forearm, looking out of the open window. It was one of those May days that could not quite make up its mind whether it would rain or not, so she was in her room instead of the garden. Three men got out and were met at the door, and that was all that Elena knew, until she heard angry shrieking from within the manor.

Well, less like literal shrieking, and more like Stepmother—it had to be Stepmother—was screaming every single word, and she had *quite* a lot to say.

The noise absolutely delighted her, and she could not help herself; she found herself on the stairs and following the sound until she was outside the door of the summer parlor, where she found two maids and a footman crouched out of sight of the partly open door. She joined them, just in time to hear the *crack* of someone being slapped, and the incoherent shrieking stopped.

"You *will* control yourself, Lady Whitstone," said an authoritarian male voice, sternly. "If you do not, I will be forced to send to the carriage for our doctor, who will determine whether or not you are a danger to yourself and act accordingly. He will," the man added, "almost certainly decide you are to be sent to an institution."

"How dare you lay a hand on me, you bloody bastard?" That was certainly Stepmother, and she set off on a profane tirade that Elena did not understand, but which made the footman's face flame.

"Did you take all that down, Jenson?" asked the first voice, calmly, when Stepmother ran out of breath.

"Yes, sir, I did." That was a second male voice.

"Thank you very much, Lady Whitstone," the first voice said, coolly, though Elena could not imagine what he was thanking her for. "Now, I suggest you hold your tongue, if you do not wish to find yourself in a madhouse, and listen closely to what I have to say. The estate is entailed. Your husband very generously made over a very great deal of property to you in the event of his death, and you should be grateful, not screaming like a virago because he did not tell you that the estate was entailed. Our client is the nearest male heir. We sent you several letters, to which you did not reply. These letters informed you that your late husband's solicitors had contacted our client to let him know he was to inherit Whitstone Manor, the manor estate and lands, and Whitstone Village, and to ask you when you expected to vacate the premises. Since you did not respond to those letters, my client was forced to send us. As a precaution, he also asked us to bring the doctor, in case you were so overcome with grief that you had been unable to respond. I am saddened, but not surprised, to discover that you are not overcome with grief."

"I would suggest that you refrain from speaking, Mum," said a deeper voice, with a rougher accent.

"What you wish and what you think are of no consequence," continued the first voice. "The estate is entailed, and that is that. That the estate goes to the *next male heir*, and there is nothing that you can do about it. This is the law. If you will not vacate, we are authorized to make certain that you and the female child are evicted by force. These are facts. There is no evading them. We are here to serve notice that if you have not vacated by the twelfth of June, taking the female child with you, we shall indeed return with the magistrate and as many of his men as I deem needful to carry out that eviction. If you leave peacefully, you will be able to gather your belongings with dignity and find a home for yourself elsewhere. Do you understand what I have said?"

"*You—*"

"Yes or no, Lady Whitstone?" The implacable tone made it very clear that another slap was forthcoming if Stepmother began another screaming outburst.

"Yes." The seething rage in Stepmother's voice made the hair stand up on the back of Elena's neck.

"Very good. I am glad that you are now enough in possession of your senses to do so, and there will be no more outbursts."

"You will be hearing from *my* solicitors!" Stepmother snarled.

"I look forward to it. I hope for your sake that what I hear is that you are prepared to vacate earlier than the twelfth of June."

Elena judged that this was a good time to scuttle away from the door, and perhaps seek shelter in the kitchen where she might hear more. The maids and the footman were already edging away, the maids to the next room, where they might legitimately claim they were cleaning, and the footman making for another part of the house. Elena managed to duck out of sight around a corner, where she saw a trio of dark-suited men exit the drawing room—one of them so large and bulky that his shoulders strained at the seams of his coat.

The sound of something being smashed, possibly with a poker, came from the drawing room. Elena made haste to get into the safety of the kitchen, for she had no doubt that Stepmother would not hesitate to use a poker on anyone she suspected of overhearing the conversation. *I wonder if there will be any ornaments left in that room when her temper cools.*

She held her breath until she reached the safety of her haven, where tongues were already clattering. And there was the footman, one of the two that Stepmother had gotten Father to hire for her, unloading his budget of news.

"... and he slapped her. Slapped her! Or I think she'd be screaming even now!" he was saying, as every person in the kitchen, Msr. Paul included, listened with eyes wide. "Is it true?"

"That the estate's entailed?" Mrs. Farthingworth shrugged. "Everyone here knows that. His lordship only inherited it in the first place because his uncle died, and his own father was already dead, so the estate passed to him."

Elena tucked herself out of the way near the sink, where the potboy had given up all pretense of working, and just gawked, wide-eyed and open-mouthed. The footman continued his description of the rest, though it was a bit garbled, and ended with, "What is she going to do?"

Then one of the two maids that had been listening came flying into the room, saw the footman, and said, "Oh! Dick will have told you, then! She's sent for Master Cleveman."

Master Cleveman, Elena knew, was Father's estate manager, who handled all the business of the estate that it was not appropriate for a titled gentleman to deal with. Elena had not seen him often, for he went to his own office in the manor by a separate entrance, but that Stepmother had sent for him suggested that either she had regained control of herself enough to consult him on arrangements for leaving, or that she did not intend to leave at all and was prepared to fight the eviction.

"Well, she won't like what he has to say," said Mrs. Farthingworth, grimly. "I expect we had best be prepared for storms."

Elena remained in the kitchen, unnoticed, as people came and left with more word on what Stepmother was doing. She had not, indeed, liked what the estate manager had to say, and had ordered him to engage solicitors on her behalf.

"Much good will it do her," said Hobart, unbending enough to join the gaggle of staff in the kitchen. "Those gentlemen came prepared with a Bedlam doctor who has probably dealt with a situation like this before. The secretary who was taking notes was not doing so for his own amusement. Those outbursts will be used as evidence against her to the magistrate in Chartontown, and the magistrate can and likely *will* ask for the doctor's opinion on what is to be done with her. She might find herself in a madhouse based on that alone, if she doesn't yield to the law quietly."

The more they talked, the more frightened Elena became. It became clear to her that the "female child" they had been talking about was *her*. And that for some reason, they expected Stepmother to take Elena with her when she left the manor.

Finally, in a moment of silence as the staff ran out of speculations, she spoke up in a creaky voice that trembled with fear. "What's to become of *me*?"

All eyes turned to her, with startled looks that told her they had completely forgotten she was there. "Lawks, child!" exclaimed Mrs. Banning, fanning herself with a towel. "Whatever are you doing back there?"

"Listening," she replied, trying very hard not to cry. "What is to become of me?"

The women hesitated. Msr. Paul did not. "You are to go with her; she is responsible for you. She became your guardian the moment your papa died."

Mrs. Banning hit him with a towel. He winced and rubbed his arm. "Don't you think the girl deserves to know the truth?" he demanded. He turned back to Elena. "His late lordship's cousin has no obligations to care for you, and she *does*, for the will appoints her as your guardian, under the law. Like or not, she will be leaving here, and when she does, you are going with her."

"Unless she is taken to Bedlam," said Father's valet, Stephens, who was probably now out of a job, and must leave himself to seek another position elsewhere. "I don't suppose they would take you there too, but one never knows."

"I've *heard*," said Mrs. Banning, with sympathy, "that the new heir flatly said he will not take you himself. I'm sorry, child," she added, "but the will left you nothing. Not even a marriage portion. Your best option is to go with your stepmother."

Elena felt as if she had been given a blow to the head. Her thoughts all froze, her heart seemed to stop, and she did something she had never in her entire life done.

She fainted dead away.

13

Solicitors came and went. Stepmother raged. Elena kept well out of her way, unable to completely comprehend what was about to happen to her. She spent most of her waking hours in the kitchen, listening to the servants, her thoughts dashing around in her mind like a wild bird caught in a cage, frantic to escape. But there was no escape.

On that first evening, she had approached Mrs. Farthingworth timidly, tugging at her sleeve to get her attention, then drawing her into her office, where she asked—begged, really—tearfully, "Mrs. Farthingworth, can't you—"

But the housekeeper stopped her before she could ask the rest of the question.

"No, child," the woman said, her face showing both pity and rejection. "No, it is not possible. The law will not permit you to stay, and we are only servants. We are not permitted to take you. The only way you can escape going with her ladyship is if she sends you to a proper school, and even then, once you have completed your schooling, she will be obliged to take you back into her household."

With that door slammed in her face, Elena crept miserably back up to her room. *What if Stepmother doesn't have a household? What if she's like Mama, and has nothing?* The prospect seemed all too likely, after that explosion of profanity (she assumed it had been profanity) that Stepmother had produced before her— cousin's?—agents. What lady would know words like that?

Which now begged the question, exactly what *was* Stepmother? Some kind of adventuress? And what would an adventuress do with *her*?

Can I run away? Would the modiste in Charton-town take me as an apprentice and a stocking-mender? If I ran away, would someone come after me and bring me back to her?

For a week, Master Cleveman sent new gentlemen every day. And every day, Stepmother sent them scurrying away when they could not give her the answers she wanted.

But then, on Friday, something different happened.

Elena saw the new man arrive, in a very smart curricle, with only a single groom. She watched him take the steps to the door two at a time, and something about this brisk man made her think that he was cut from a very different sort of cloth than the previous lot. This time she slipped downstairs to join Mary Ann at the door to the summer parlor, both their ears pressed to the cracks where the hinges were.

"... certainly sympathize with your situation, Mum," the new man was saying. "You are not the first woman to find yourself cast on the world when some upstart inherits an entailed estate, and you will not be the last. But!" he added. "All is not lost. This is what I do. I discover how much you can carry away that is not entailed. I do my best to see that you are provided with an income on which you may live—reasonably well, if not as well as in this house. Some of this I have already done, and I did not come here empty-handed. With the help of Cleveman, I have investigated the entirety of his late lordship's possessions and his will. I believe I have some news that you will welcome."

"If you do, indeed," said Stepmother, cautiously, "Then I shall not show you the door as I have your predecessors."

There was the sound of rustling papers. "First of all, his lordship allotted you maintenance money, to the amount of five hundred a year, to be paid out of investments which are not part of the estate."

"Forgive me if I am not—" Stepmother began.

"Ah, but there is more. Quite a bit more. The law states that the estate comprises all the land-property, the manor, and Whitstone Village, and associated goods. Those associated goods do *not* include your personal property, any valuable gifts that his lordship may have given you, and any household furnishings that were not part of the household before your marriage, nor does it include the investments that will pay your income."

"So I have—"

"The estate does *not* include the town house in Bath which his lordship purchased after your marriage, for the express purpose of maintaining a second home for both of you." There was a smile in the man's voice.

"Tell me more." Stepmother sounded pleased—and impressed.

"The new carriage and the grooms and coachman he purchased specifically for you—are yours. Anything that you can claim was purchased for you—yours. I advise you to keep the investments, rather than selling them for immediate cash money, as they will provide you that income I mentioned. And I will be happy to go through all of Lord Whitstone's receipts to uncover the smallest object that you can claim is yours, and not part of the estate."

There was a long pause. "And what about that wretched child?"

"Unfortunately, my lady," the man said apologetically, "you are obliged by the law to take possession of her. This is an obligation that you acquired when you married his lordship. You were obliged to take on the guardianship of all his children by his previous marriage according to his will. Perhaps you should simply be pleased that there is only one and not eight."

"By God—" the seething rage in Stepmother's voice made Elena shrink into herself. "I will not—"

"I fear you must," the solicitor said calmly. "The new heir has officially refused to take responsibility for the girl. The chancery court is very keen that she not be thrown on the parish, and they can and will make things difficult for you if you do not take her. And I must remind you that if anything other than natural illness or accident should happen to the child, that same law will hold you to account. And not only the law is to be reckoned with, but there are many in this neighborhood who will not hesitate to use this as an excuse to pull you down. They smiled at you when you had the protection of his lordship, but they despised you behind your back, and know you are a pretender with nothing but your beauty—and so, thanks to your outbursts with Lord Whitstone's agents, does the new Lord Whitstone. Should they learn that the child has come to grief, they will not hesitate to disgrace you, and if they cannot put you in jail, they will be happy to send you to a cell in Bedlam."

There was a very long pause indeed.

"Very well, then," Stepmother said, in tones as icy as the pond had been. "Then find me every scrap and screw that I can claim as mine. The more you can find, the higher your fee will be."

"I take it I am to be engaged, then?" There was a satisfied smile in the solicitor's voice.

"Yes, yes," Stepmother said impatiently. "You are the only man I have interviewed who is not an utter fool."

"Excellent. I shall not require your signature of retainer for now. Now, as I said, I have gone through his lordship's receipts. I shall need to acquire the household inventory from the moment when his late lordship took possession of the estate, but I believe I can say with confidence that I have identified an extensive list. The new carriage is only the beginning of that list. If you would care to go over it with me?"

Elena had heard enough. There was to be no reprieve. Stepmother would certainly not be willing to part with the fees for schooling. And when she calmed down, she would recall all the ways Elena had been useful to her before she had so stupidly tried to murder the boys.

Why did she do that? Did she think that she would somehow profit from the act? Did she know Father was going to die?

Perhaps not. The gossip in the kitchen had indicated that her efforts to nurse him back to health had been genuine, if heartless. And with the boys out of the way, Father would not have been burdened with payments to university, nor for purchasing a pair of colors, nor furnishing out a move to Canada.

She slipped away from the door and ran all the way back to her room, choking on sobs. *How stupid I was to think that things could not get worse!* she thought, as she flung herself down on her bed to cry. *They not only could . . . they did.*

*

Elena huddled in the corner of Stepmother's opulent carriage, wedged in by a motley assortment of bandboxes, bags, jewelry cases, and other assorted goods. All of Stepmother's most precious things had been crammed in here, leaving space only for Stepmother and Fleurette to ride in comfort. Lesser luggage, such as Elena's slender belongings, rode atop the carriage, or was following in a hired cart. Elena counted as part of the baggage, and so her comfort need not be taken into account. Fleurette smirked at her in a smug, self-satisfied fashion, and daintily crossed her ankles.

The roads, at least, were in good condition, and the carriage well sprung, for with every bounce and sway, a half-dozen sharp corners jabbed into Elena's torso and limbs.

Behind them was a procession of carts containing everything that could have been legitimately stripped from the manor—and quite a few things, Elena suspected, that had been taken under more dubious provenance. Stepmother had not, as Elena had expected, carried away any furniture from the manor, probably because she realized that there would be no room for it in the carriage, and she didn't want the bother of trying to sell it in Bath.

Elena was completely numb now, left unable to think at all clearly. Mrs. Banning and Mrs. Farthingworth had sent her off with tears in their eyes. Hobart had sent her off with an encouraging smile, and with a far more practical basket of provisions—things that, she discovered when Stepmother insisted on examining the contents, were all items Stepmother turned up her nose at: a loaf of brown bread and a large wedge of cheese, carrots, some early stone fruits, radishes, and a jar of currant jam.

On seeing that basket, however, Stepmother had insisted on a hamper twice as big with provisions that were much more to her taste. Mrs. Banning had provided it with a stony expression. There was no doubt that Stepmother did not intend to share a single crumb with Elena. *But at least I won't starve on the journey.*

That hamper sat on the floor between Fleurette and her mistress, where a footwarmer would have been in colder weather. Elena's basket was on her lap, on top of the workbox Ben had made for her, further penning her in. Stepmother sat on the door-side of the coach, facing forward. Fleurette sat opposite of her. It had been made very clear to Elena by Fleurette that if she needed to relieve herself, she had better do so during those coaching stops when the maid and her mistress would be alighting, and that she had better get herself unpacked, take care of the needful, and get packed up again before they returned from refreshing themselves.

Stepmother grew bored right after the first of such stops, and fixed Elena with a dagger-like stare. "You stupid child," she said, scornfully. "You have no idea what I am, do you?"

Elena did not answer, but it wouldn't have mattered if she had.

"I am a magician. An Elemental Master of Water. You are not and never will be the equal of me, for the magic you inherited from your mother is small and weak, and unless you exert yourself to the uttermost to please me, I have a hundred ways of removing you from this earth that will look like the merest accidents. Do you understand?"

"Yes, Stepmo—" she began.

"And you will stop calling me that. You will call me 'Mistress' or 'Mistress Serafina' from this moment on," Stepmother told her coldly.

"Yes, mistress," she said, shrinking back.

"You have seen my power. You have not seen my servants. They are terrible, and they are anywhere there is water. You would do well to fear them." Stepmother smirked. "Your little sylphs are no match for them. And yes, I know that, thanks to your mother, you could see them, and you have some scraps and scrapings of power. You were not very good at hiding these things from me." She tucked an errant strand of hair behind her ear. "And I *only* gave in to those stupid, stupid men because if they had found out about me, I would have lost the little I have managed to claw from this disaster."

And already she seems to have forgotten this was a disaster of her own making.

Stepmother seemed to be waiting for a response, so Elena gave her one. "How could they find out you are a magician when no one believes in magic?" she asked.

"This is why you are a stupid child," Stepmother scowled. "It is not that I am a magician that I needed to conceal, it is that I am a Cyprian, and one of the finest and fairest of them in all of London." She leaned toward Elena, eyes glittering, "And you are so stupid you do not know what a Cyprian is!"

Oh, I can guess....

"I go into men's beds, and I make them pay dearly for the privilege," she said, waiting to see Elena's reaction to that statement. "And I can do that because I cast spells to not only make them desire me, but to make them desire to be rid of me when I tire of them, and I can make sure that they dismiss me with handsome presents of money," she continued crudely.

"You are the nonesuch of courtesans," murmured Fleurette with admiration.

Elena burned with embarrassment at such a crude revelation, although it did not surprise her.

Stepmother braced herself as the carriage rocked. "When I encountered your father, I was looking for a wealthy, titled husband, because I was tired of attracting men, then dismissing them again. Quite by chance I learned of the wealthy Lord Whitstone, so sadly abandoned by his first wife. I arranged to attend a gaming party he was at, and cast my spell over him, and of course we were married within the week. And," she added angrily, "if I had known his wretched property was entailed, and what that meant, I'd have chosen someone else." She scowled. "And that is my own stupid fault. It was taking so much of my time and attention to keep Theodore enthralled that I never asked about the estate, nor how, exactly, he had amended his will."

Elena wished fiercely that her stepmother had chosen someone else. *Father deserved his fate. But surely we did not!*

"Now what will you do?" she asked fearfully.

"Go back to Bath. Reestablish myself there. There will be less competition there, and not all my magic can keep me from growing older. Find a better patron, or at the least some wealthy old man with an estate that is *not* entailed." She yawned. "And one without any awkward children."

Since Stepmother seemed to have gotten over her anger at being burdened with her, Elena dared to ask, "And me?"

"Hmm," she said. "You're useless as a maid, except for mending my things. But you are small and slight. You'd make a tolerable boy, even a pretty one. I shall make you a footman and my tiger; those duties are easy for even an idiot to perform and require very little training. So I shall have a pretty little tiger to perch behind me and hold my horses, at least for now, and you will cost me nothing in wages and require very little in the way of food and livery. You can go on mending my things and designing my gowns when you are not playing those roles."

Elena had no idea what those things were. But she had no doubt that she was about to find out.

Bath: Three Years Later

Elena perched on the little platform behind her mistress on Serafina Valdestine's cabriolet. Had anyone from the Whitstone estate seen her, they would never have recognized her, with her hair cut short in little curls, and clothed in boy's clothing—specifically, in her mistress's colors, the scarlet and yellow livery she favored for her servants. Serafina was not a good driver, so this vehicle was not the more showy phaeton, much less a high-perch phaeton of the sort the more dashing of the gentlemen and daring of the muslin set favored. As they rolled at a sedate pace down the streets of Bath on the way to Serafina's town house—the same one that she had wrested away from Lord Whitstone's estate—Serafina made certain that she was seen. She gave flirtatious little nods to single men, and even, to the horror of their wives or daughters, to the occasional handsome married ones. If they were wise, those married gentlemen averted their eyes. If they were not, it generally meant that they already knew her from her card parties and routs, or from her visits with her "protector" to gaming halls, and there was nothing that their scandalized spouses could do about it.

As for the single men, if they were high enough in the instep, they already knew *about* her if they did not actually know her, and they knew that there was no chance those flirtatious glances would ever come to anything. It was merely that her protector,

Duke Alberton, enjoyed having his possession seen, admired, and lusted over.

Duke Alberton enjoyed having men want what he had, and as an Elemental mage, when he cared to, he could derive a certain amount—small, but not insignificant—of power from their desire. Like Serafina, he was a Water mage. Unlike her, he was not very powerful, nor was he a Dark mage.

He was also a cheat at cards, using magic to win; with Serafina at his side, doing so was a thousand times easier. He needed an income separate from the household money, which came from his wife—money for all the luxuries and pleasures that legitimate money could not buy, like Serafina. She needed an income much greater than the mere five hundred a year that she got from her inheritance.

Together, they both got what they wanted.

Elena's function on these trips into the city was to hold the horses if Serafina cared to enter a shop herself, run in and collect or make purchases for her if she did not, and supply ballast between the springs of the carriage, because otherwise too much of the weight of the front of the cabriolet would be taken by the horses. Serafina had disposed of the coach she had arrived in Bath with, because it was impractical for driving about the city streets and offered no opportunity for her to be seen.

It had been three years since they had arrived in Bath, and Elena's blank-faced demeanor gave no indication of how miserable her existence had become. She shared an attic room with one of Serafina's long-suffering kitchen maids, a room that was cold in winter, hot in summer, had no fireplace and no privacy. She rose at dawn with the "boots" and the kitchen staff, her first job of the day to make certain that whatever her mistress had worn the night before was cleaned, brushed, and if necessary, mended, in case Serafina wanted to wear it again that day. Then she got a bowl of porridge—not too much, since Serafina required her to remain as thin as she had been when they had left Whitstone Manor to keep up the ruse that she was a boy—and a cup of weak tea. After that, when Serafina rang for her breakfast of biscuits and chocolate, she was to bring it up, then go stand or sit in an alcove in the bedroom in case Serafina might want her, doing mending or other needlework. If she was lucky, she might get a bite or two between tasks, which generally consisted of playing the tiger and running errands. Eventually the duke would put in an appearance, at which point she was able to run down to the kitchen and, while they were served luxurious and lavish meals, get the only real meal of the day. Msr. Paul, who had made the journey from Whitstone Manor with them, was stealthily sympathetic to her plight, and would make sure that Elena got not just a good meal, but a share of some of what he cooked for their mistress.

Then, while the duke and Serafina went out for their usual rounds of entertainments, parties, and gambling dens, Elena finally got a chance for some rest. When they returned, Elena waited on them, as they often demanded little suppers, and the duke preferred her to a footman.

And then she was sent, not to her bed, but to that nook, where she became a deeply reluctant witness to their love-making.

Although there was very little "love" involved, she suspected.

Both of them found this amusing, though the duke enjoyed it more than Serafina did.

As she thought about these things, perched behind her tormentor, a spring breeze wafted around her, marred only by the faint scent of horse manure. The sylphs no longer appeared to her, not even when the duke and his paramour went out for the evening. But at least she was able to renew her protections when they did. She was no longer the frightened child of thirteen. She had learned many things as a tiger, and now she had a plan.

Many times these past three years, men had given her money, usually a few pence, to take notes of entreaty to her mistress. And she got more if she returned with an answer. The duke did not demand that Serafina remain faithful to him. On the contrary, he enjoyed it when she took other men into her bed, and he'd even had a special, comfortable, faux wardrobe made and placed in her bedroom that he could conceal himself inside so that he could watch when she did so.

Although on *those* occasions, Elena was sent out of the room. What the duke liked and what other male members of the *ton* would accept were two very different things. And other men would generally not allow even a servant like Elena to be in the same room as their trysts.

Either Serafina did not know about that money, or she knew and assumed that Elena spent it on trifles and food from street vendors.

But Elena had saved every groat beneath the secret compartment in the workbox that Ben had made for her.

I am going to escape, before very much longer.

She needed to obtain boy's clothing, because the boy in The Incomparable Serafina's livery purchasing coach tickets would be remembered and reported when word got about that he had run away from service. And no girl as young as she looked would be permitted to take a coach alone.

She had learned a very great deal about Seraphina and the duke, and nothing of what she had learned suggested that her future would be a good one with them.

Serafina turned the horses into the drive at the side of her narrow, cream-colored, four-story town house, and into the tiny space between the back of the town house and the small carriage house behind it. Her groom appeared as if conjured, and took the reins of the horses so that Serafina could exit the cabriolet. That meant it was Elena's turn to spring from the platform in the rear and move with all haste to help Serafina down from her seat, with the aid of an iron step affixed to either side of the vehicle. Once the mistress was out of the vehicle, the groom would be putting the horses in their stalls, and wheeling the cabriolet into the carriage house by hand. Elena had no knowledge of how he performed these duties; hers was to immediately follow Serafina into the house.

The large carriage-and-four that had brought them here had immediately been sold on their arrival, and the cabriolet and matched pair bought to take its place. The unwieldy coach was ill suited to the crowded streets of Bath, and Serafina had kept it for no longer than it had taken to sell it. The coachman Trevor had been dismissed as no longer needed; the grooms Phillip and Dick Jenson had flipped a coin to determine which of them would remain in Serafina's service and which would be let go. Elena hoped that Phillip was not unhappy with his new situation—Serafina was indifferent to those servants who did not serve her directly, but surely there was a taint associated with those who served a Cyprian.

As for the rest of the servants, the kitchen staff was safe enough, but the maids and footmen were not. The housemaids, as Elena well knew, were subject to the abuse of the duke. And as for the footmen, who had all been chosen for their looks and elegant legs, would *they* consider being lured into the mistress's bed abuse, or a benefit? Elena had not said more than commonplaces to any of them, nor to the maids either, in all the time they had lived here.

The kitchen maid who shared Elena's room could well have betrayed the fact that Elena was not a boy, but she was literally mute, and presumably the reason there were no clacking tongues about that was that Elena looked too young to be interfering with her. The only other person besides Fleurette who knew was Msr. Paul, and he was paid well enough that he had no reason to refer to that fact in kitchen gossip.

But as Elena followed Serafina into the house and up the stairs to her opulent bedroom suite, she felt again a pang of fear, wondering for the hundredth time if this would be the day when Serafina looked at her tiger and decided it was time for Elena's role to change.

Fleurette was already waiting to help her mistress change from her street clothing into a day gown. "What shall I lay out for you for this evening, mistress?" she asked, as Elena went to her cubicle and immediately began repairing a laddered stocking. There was a never-ending supply of laddered stockings. Sometimes she suspected that Serafina laddered them on purpose.

"The scarlet," Serafina said, stepping out of the carriage gown that now lay in a pool at her feet, and raising her arms so that the maid could slip the day gown over her head. "We are attending the Theater Royal, and as my reputation precedes me, I might just as well dress as the scarlet woman." Her head emerged from the gown, and her lips were curled in a smirk.

"That should set tongues clacking," Fleurette said, matching her mistress's smirk. "Ornaments?"

"The full ruby parure that Alberton gave me of late. Not

only do I want the tongues to clack, I want it known to any who wish my favors that they do not come cheaply." She sat down at the dressing table to massage some cream into her face while Fleurette took down her hair. "And three scarlet plumes. Alberton has purchased a box, and Lord Peverly and Viscount Ramton will be there with their inamoratas. They will certainly be wearing two plumes, and four would be vulgar."

"Very well, mistress." Fleurette picked up the discarded gown and set it aside to be looked at to see if it needed freshening, or even cleaning. "Would you prefer your tea in the parlor or the dining room?"

"The dining room. Tell Msr. Paul that we will need a light collation for two before we leave for the theater, and a light supper with champagne for six when we return." She closed the jar with a cork lid made to fit and began to brush her hair, which was thick and abundant, but not long, reaching to just below her breasts. She glanced over at Elena, who had just finished mending the ladder. "You may go get tea with the staff, Len," she said, using the name she had decided upon for Elena when this masquerade began.

Elena folded the stocking and placed it aside for Fleurette, and left. Being sent for tea was rare, and it signaled that Serafina had something she wished to impart to her maid, who was also an Elemental mage. All discussions of magic in this household took place out of Elena's hearing; Serafina was taking no chance that Elena might overhear clues to the control of her own magic.

Not that I would get a chance to use it, she thought, as she took the servants' stair down to the kitchen, where the staff was enjoying their tea. She had learned minuscule bits and pieces, and one of those bits and pieces was that any magic undertaking of any size required the assistance of Elementals, coerced or cajoled. The number of times she had been able to speak to a sylph could be counted on one hand over the course of three years. She would have to summon sylphs to do *anything* major, even assuming she knew how to do the thing, and no sylph would come within a block of Serafina.

*

The duke and his paramour had celebrated their triumphant appearance at the theater with great vigor, and Elena had faced the wall, concentrated on mending a flounce, and tried to ignore the moans, grunts, the eventual screams, and the *smell*. The first time Serafina had entertained a man in her presence—it had been Phillip the groom, for extra embarrassment—she had expected the noises, for she had heard all these things when she had been in her bedroom above Serafina's and the mistress had not demanded she occupy the alcove. But the *smell*, musky, animalistic, and not to be mistaken for anything else, had taken her completely by surprise.

There was quite a lot of that *smell* tonight. Afterward, they spoke in low voices for a few moments, then the duke snapped his fingers and called her name. "Len!" he ordered. "Come here."

Reluctantly, Elena did as he ordered, and stood where he pointed, which was right at the bedside. She felt as if she was going to faint. *Is this the night?* she thought in terror. The duke particularly enjoyed raping virgins, and there was not a housemaid in this establishment that had not been left in tears and bloodied by him.

"Take off your clothing," he ordered, as Serafina watched, brows furrowed.

"I don't want you ruining my tiger," she protested. "I need her tomorrow."

He waved off her objections as Elena did as she had been ordered, shaking like a birch in the wind. He swung his legs over the side of the bed and pulled her closer, running his hands over her body, tweaking her nipples, and trying to insert a finger in her nethers. Tried; he didn't get past the first knuckle and stopped when she whimpered.

"Skinny bitch," he said.

"I couldn't pass her off as a boy otherwise," Serafina pointed out, pulling the upper sheet around herself and sitting up. "And I *have* been doing the spellwork to delay the onset of her monthly flux and maturation."

"True. Still. Fatten her up like a milkmaid and she'll do." He chuckled, and Elena held back tears. "She'll do."

"You will *not* spoil my tiger," Serafina said, dangerously, her mouth angry and her eyes glittering with menace. "I don't care what you do with the housemaids, but you will not spoil my tiger or abuse Fleurette."

"Fleurette! Lud, no! I'd wake up with a blade between my shoulders. No, I have an idea."

Everything was in terrible clarity as Elena waited for the duke's next order and shook with cold and fear. Serafina was clenching her jaw, and looked as if *she* might be the one to plant a knife in the duke's back. "What did you have in mind?" she said, the words loaded with menace.

"You'll like it," he said, and chuckled, throwing himself back down on the bed, in full display. "Had this in mind for a while. How would you like to be the procuress of the best brothel in Bath?"

Serafina lost a little of that dangerous look. "Go on."

"It's getting dangerous, using magic to win at games of chance, especially in the parlors that have the kinds of stakes and ennobled idiots I like. One of these days we're going to cheat a cloaked Elemental Master, and there will be hell to pay," he said. "We'll both be up against one of those cursed White Lodge inquiries. No. Time to change. We both need an income above what we have, and I particularly want one the wife don't know about, just like she don't know about my gaming." He put his hands behind his head. "I shudder to think what you'd do to my ghost if I were to die and leave you without a patron. There's two ways to do that, a brothel or a gaming house—you can't run a gambling den, and I don't want the notoriety that comes from running one. That leaves a brothel. You can run one of those, it's expected. I'll supply the house; I already have just the place, not some shabby town house in the stews, but a nice manor with a good address I bought a while ago to rent out. Current tenant quit the lease; this will be easier than trying to find another good long-term tenant. Nobody wants to be long-term in Bath, and I haven't the patience for dealing with people who only want to rent for the season. I'll have half the income when I need it; all of the income will be yours when I don't. I'll leave you the place in my will; you'll enjoy seeing what the wife has to say when she discovers it. We'll do it proper: plenty of private bedrooms, the loveliest girls, musicians, gambling rooms, good suppers every night with that Frenchy chef of yours. The kind of place where the elite of the *ton* come. Maybe even the Prince of Wales!"

Serafina's suppressed anger had died with every word, and her eyes began shining.

"The wife don't know about this place I've been renting out. It's already furnished, and if there's anything you don't like, you can see it done your way."

"What about the girls?" Serafina asked.

"I'll recruit them myself. You can train them in doing more than just laying back and letting it happen, in how to act like a lady if that's what they're supposed to be, and if not . . ." He shrugged. "We can hire some starving actor to teach 'em the rest. And when we have everything in place, we'll have a very special opening party, an exclusive one, with a prime draw." He grinned. "A *virgin auction*!"

Serafina actually crowed with delight.

"Look at her!" he said, waving a hand at Elena, who was going white and red by turns, her knees shaking. "Young, fit, pretty—and she'll be a beauty when she fattens up and your Fleurette gets a chance at grooming her—golden hair like a Greek goddess. Plump up that bum and those breasts, and—" his grin broadened. "Every buck of the *ton* will want to bid on her!"

Serafina finally looked at Elena, who felt as if she was about to faint. "Oh, put your clothing on and go to bed, you silly goose. And stop looking as if we just proposed cooking and eating you. When we are done, you'll have everything you could want, the finest food, the prettiest gowns, plenty of time to do what you want, and all that education you were whimpering about never getting—music, literature, dancing. There are plenty of people who won't turn up their noses at teaching a potential Cyprian if the money is good. You'll need to charm the men in the parlor as well as in the bed. This isn't going to be a penny a pop against the wall! Play your hand right, and you could be the star of my establishment. You might even be bedded by the Prince of Wales, and how many girls can say *that*?"

"Well . . ." temporized the duke, as Elena gathered up her clothing and fled for her room. "From all I hear, quite a few."

She huddled her breeches and shirt on, clutched the rest of her clothing against her chest, and ran, barefooted, out of the room, up the stairs, to the ephemeral protection of her room. She wanted to throw up, but there was nothing in her stomach. Her secret part burned where the duke had tried to insert his finger into it. But worst of all was the terror, the knowing that no matter what Serafina had *said*, she would be reduced to the lowest and most disposable of her "girls." The duke did not know what Serafina had done to her family. The duke did not know, because if he *had* known, his sympathies would have been with the titled, landed man that Serafina had controlled, the titled heirs that had been turned into birds, and not with his paramour. That was ever the case, as Elena had come to know over the past three years. Those with titles sided with others with titles, and not with the common folk. And Serafina was as common as dust, except for her status as an Elemental magician. Perhaps she was from a titled family reduced to less-than-genteel poverty, but more likely she had once been a servant, was a very quick learner, and had decided to prey on the titled instead of serving them.

Elena might have pitied, even admired her, if she had not been so cruel. That she made her fortune using what she had at her disposal—beauty, grace, wit, charm, intelligence, and her body—Elena could not fault her for that. But to use cruelty as a part of that, and for her own amusement, was unforgivable.

And then there was the matter of using her magic against those who had no defenses against it . . . that went beyond unforgivable.

The duke had no compunction about using his underlings and the underlings of others as he saw fit. In that, he was a match for Serafina in his cruelty. He might believe her blood was as blue as his, he might not. He probably still thought that he was using Serafina, and not the other way around. He was mistaken.

He would be very displeased to know that Serafina had enchanted seven titled boys and driven their father into the grave. He would probably still have become her patron, but he would never have trusted her as a business partner, and he would always have been watching his back with her. He certainly would not have told her he intended to leave his brothel to her in his will. He almost certainly was lying, but he did not know Serafina was lying as much as he was.

In fact, he probably would insist on installing some person of his own choosing as a kind of manager over her, and when he was sick and old, sell it out from under her. But when it came to the day-to-day workings of the brothel, he would assume she was honest, and believe what she told him.

So he would take Serafina's word that Elena had turned out to be unfit to grace the parlor of the new brothel. Instead of a sought-for Cyprian, Elena would become a sort of pretty toy to be passed around for quick amusement at a bargain price. She knew what became of women like that: inevitably diseased, inevitably discarded into the streets, where they died the most miserable of deaths. No one from the Whitstone family had made any attempt to discover where Serafina had taken her, or what had been done with her in the three years since she had been moved to Bath. The threat that the lawyer had made had been a hollow one. After all, she was only a girl, and like all females, important only in producing heirs.

The kitchen maid was asleep, and as usual, so exhausted that it would take a cannon shot in her ear to wake her. With shaking hands, Elena undressed again, laid out her clothing on the bench at the end of her bed, poured water into the washbasin, wetted the cloth she shared with the maid, and scrubbed her secret parts until they were almost raw. And still she felt unclean.

She pulled her nightshirt over her head and crawled into bed, her throat tight, tears of shame, humiliation, and fear running down her cheeks.

But after staring sleeplessly up at the ceiling, she slowly stopped shaking. Her thoughts stopped frantically swirling around in her head. *Breathe,* she reminded herself, calling up the discipline that she had learned over the course of three years under Serafina's thumb. *Breathe. Nothing has happened yet. Nothing will happen tomorrow, or the next day, or the next. This manor and everything in it will require cleaning, repainting, repairing. Serafina will want the best of furnishings, ornaments, linens and drapery—and so will the duke. None of the other*

Cyprians of Bath will be willing to come under another woman's roof, not when they are young enough to have wealthy patrons of their own. The duke will have to search all the brothels to find women and girls beautiful and not yet pox-ridden, to bargain for their purchase with their current procuresses, for Serafina to train them. He might have to take to the streets, find girls from the country looking for work, find whores with a single keeper, or none. All this will take time. I will have that time. Her resolve hardened. *And I will make good use of that time. She has no idea what I am capable of now. What she* made me *capable of.* The death grip Elena had on her bedclothes eased, and she felt the tightness in her chest and throat ease as well. *She thinks I am still little, ignorant, naïve Elena, who was too terrified and too grief-stricken to do anything except what she told me to. She thinks that because I still look that way, and I have never given her any reason to think otherwise. I have always been obedient, caring for her wardrobe, designing new gowns, holding her horses in the rain, anything she asks of me, bowing my head to insults, resigning myself to deprivation.* She had not known that Serafina had tampered with her growth until now, but it made sense, and explained why she was still small and physically immature. And Serafina had helped her, without realizing it, by making it possible to *continue* the ruse of being a boy, once she escaped.

I have time, time to get everything I need to escape. Time to plan. Time, once I have what I need, to watch for exactly the right moment.

Ironically, this plot of the duke's would keep her safe from him; he wouldn't spoil the thing he needed to gain the attention of the *ton* and launch his brothel with favorable winds. So the one thing she had feared for most of three years, that the duke would rape her as he had raped all the house maids, was never going to happen.

With that thought, her mind settled, and she began working out the initial stages of her plan.

14

The next day, the duke turned up in his high-perch phaeton and matched bays with *his* groom up behind, to carry Serafina off to the property to inspect it. "You may sit in my room and mend, Len," the mistress said with an airy wave of her hand, as she prepared to leave the town house. "I have given Fleurette the half-day off; you shall be quite peaceful. Surely as good as a half-day off, since you have nowhere to go!" She laughed, cruelly. "Do take care not to leave the house; I shall know if you do."

And with that, she sailed out the front door in her driving dress. Elena went obediently back up the stairs to Serafina's suite, and industriously mended stockings until she heard Fleurette bid the doorman goodbye.

She waited perhaps a quarter hour more, to be sure that neither Fleurette nor the mistress was likely to return. Then she put her work aside, slipped off her shoes with their gilded buckles, and padded stealthily to the servants' stair, up it to the garret where she and the rest of the servants (except the housekeeper, Msr. Paul, and Fleurette) slept, and then up one more story to the attic proper.

Serafina had stripped Whitstone Manor of everything she could reasonably carry away in a coach and hired cart. That included everything in her siblings' rooms that was portable. Elena thought she had seen the boys' trunks in that cart; they had been only half full of clothing, maybe less, and the clothing had been used as padding for more fragile objects. She was counting on the fact that Serafina was a magpie and never let anything out of her hands once it was in them, and that *should* include that clothing. It was not good enough to sell, but it *was* made of sound materials, and she would have kept it with an eye to using it as gifts to her male servants.

Sure enough, once she was up the ladder and her eyes had gotten used to the dim light, there were eight familiar-looking trunks lined up beneath the window. One was hers, full of her female clothing, all still dyed black. Seven had belonged to her brothers.

As she had hoped, their clothing was still there—all except the clothing they had "drowned" in. That was at the bottom of the Whitstone Manor pond.

The first sight of a shirt she remembered mending nearly brought her to her knees with a sudden, overwhelming grief. She clutched the lid with both hands, restrained a sob, holding it deep in her chest, and shook for a moment with the intensity of it. *Oh, Ben! Where are you? Did you find Mama? Are you safe? Or did some cruel hunter shoot you down, never knowing he was extinguishing the life of a fellow man?*

Then she fought herself free of her pain, and began pulling out garments, measuring them against herself.

She was larger than Gus had been, slimmer and smaller than Ben and Arthur. Eventually she had a shirt from David and a pair of woolen breeches only a little shabby (thanks to moths) that had belonged to Emil. Emil's wool stockings were the least damaged among all of them; she took those, too.

Their coats, of course, were gone. The summer had been cold, cold enough to need a coat. She might have to touch her savings for that.

She closed the chests and paused for a moment, then went back and opened her own. There was the black twilled silk gown she remembered being given so that her old clothing could be dyed. It was worth quite a bit, and barely used. She took that and slipped downstairs.

She went straight to her room, since Jane would not be

in it, but rather than stowing the clothing in her own chest, she pulled up the beech-leaf-stuffed mattress and placed the garments between the mattress and the hessian pad that kept the slats of the bed from cutting into the mattress. That dress would prove useful. She could almost certainly trade it or sell it for a common coat.

Then she went downstairs to see if there was any breakfast left.

She was back in her alcove, having had not only breakfast but luncheon, when the two returned about teatime. Fleurette had returned after luncheon, but had demanded, and gotten, an early tea, and now lounged indolently on her bed in her own room, just off Serafina's.

Elena had the window open so she could hear what was going on in the stableyard, since Serafina's bedroom was on that side, away from the noise and the smell of the street. There was no mistaking the sound of horses, or the steel tires on the phaeton as they rolled over the cobbles, nor the voices of the mistress and the duke.

". . . are you going to do with this house?" asked the duke, as the phaeton stopped.

"Keep it, of course," Serafina replied. Elena sighed with relief; she sounded pleased. As long as the mistress was pleased, she would not be looking for someone to abuse. "I'm not so nice about seasonal tenants as you." Elena was not surprised to hear that she intended to keep the town house. The duke was not precisely *trusting* and he was, by common standards, very sharp. But Serafina was even less trusting and much sharper. She would not take the chance that the duke would change his mind and sell off the brothel on his deathbed. *Actually, she probably did not believe he would leave it to her in the first place. She'll be holding back some of the money the brothel earns, somehow, I'll be bound. They deserve each other.*

"Fleurette!" she called softly. "The mistress is back."

The maid emerged from her room, smoothing her skirts down and patting her hair into place, and did not bother to thank Elena, who was just finishing the last of the stockings. The duke and his paramour came up the stairs, still talking about their plans. Elena ignored the conversation, moving on to a petticoat and some torn lace.

The pair did not go out to their usual haunts that night, preferring to huddle over a table in the dining room and make lists. Elena was spared this, and so was Fleurette. The maid was not welcome in servants' hall because of the airs she put on, and spent the unexpected time off in refurbishing her own wardrobe, since Serafina had once chided her for expecting Elena to do it. Not out of any consideration for Elena, of course, but so that Elena's time would be exclusively employed in her own service. Elena *was* welcome there, since from the beginning she had been quiet, quarreled with no one, been polite and deferent to everyone, even the scullery maid Jane and the tweenie May. Nor had Serafina showed any favoritism toward her, as was rather unusual for a tiger employed by a woman. In general, such boys were pampered and not expected to do much, which generally led to a sad fall indeed, when they grew too large to stand on the back of the lady's equipage, and were demoted from favorite to ordinary footman or groom. Tigers who served gentlemen generally did not have so great a downfall, since they were generally taken on because of their skill with horses, and could be promoted from tiger to just below the head groom.

But this had earned her a place in servants' hall, and Msr. Paul had, shockingly, taken her under his wing. Not enough to cause jealousy, but enough that when she could come down here, the otherwise aloof chef made certain she was fed to his standards.

Usually no one spoke to her, or if they did, it was all commonplace things. But evidently the groom had caught part of the duke and the mistress's conversation on the way out and in, and the kitchen and dining room were abuzz with speculation. They all pounced on her as soon as she appeared, peppering her with questions until Msr. Paul intervened, a moment before Housekeeper Linnet could.

"Hush, cease, you confuse Len. One at a time, if you please." He crossed his arms over his chest, looking very formidable in his white hat and white tunic-like uniform. Linnet, who could have been Mrs. Banning's twin, nodded.

Thomas put up his hand like a schoolboy. "Is mistress selling this house?" he asked, anxiously.

"No," she was able to tell him, and there were sighs of relief all around. "I believe she intends to lease it. She plans for Msr. Paul to come to the new establishment, but perhaps she will give the rest of you the choice of remaining or moving."

The rest of the questions were in a similar vein; she was not able to answer many of them, but enough that they had some notion of what the future might offer. The question that Linnet finally asked, with much trepidation, was, "Is the duke to preside over the new establishment?"

But rather than Elena answering that, it was Msr. Paul who shook his head. "*Non,*" he said decidedly. "It is not possible. Nor will his name be linked to it. For a member of the *ton* and of the nobility, it would be a double disgrace." He glanced at the housemaids, huddled together, and added, "I think that your days of fear are over. In the new establishment, he will have . . . other satisfactions. And here, you will be serving those who lease the house when it is occupied and the mistress at a distance when it is not."

Two of the girls burst into tears on hearing that, and the rest comforted each other. Those were clearly tears of relief, however. Before the duke, life for female servants had been tolerable. Afterward . . . they had lived with the same fears as Elena, with a greater burden of work.

Finally she had answered all the questions that she could (and as a reward, Msr. Paul had fed her), promised to let them know whatever else she learned, and ventured back upstairs. The duke and Serafina were still deeply involved in the dining room, now with a diagram of all of the floors and all of the rooms in the manor, and as far as Elena could tell, were discussing which rooms would serve what purpose.

For the first time in three years, she went to bed with more hope than fear. If this project engrossed them as much as she *thought* it might, Serafina would very likely send her all over the city on errands related to it. And that would mean wonders for her plan. At the very least, Serafina would have something to think about besides Elena. At the best, the mistress would forget about her for whole days at a time.

For once, Elena's hopes were realized.

After a few outings, she had to accompany the mistress, but as Serafina was impatient to have this renovation done, and there were only two or three servants she trusted to understand exactly what was wanted, she sent Elena out on any errands that involved fabric. Linens for the bedrooms, draperies for the entire manor, upholstery fabrics for re-covering the furnishings, it all fell under Elena's purview. The first task Elena was sent out on—to choose linens for the bedrooms—she accomplished well enough for Serafina to give her a rare accolade. The task had been complicated: there would be more servants than there had been in the manor before, and some of the guest rooms had been converted to other purposes, so new beds needed to be bought, and so did new linens for the new beds. There would be very *special* bedrooms, and so Elena had needed to choose and order three different qualities of linens, pillows, bolsters, and bed coverings, plus two featherbeds, because some customers would pay to remain overnight, and their aristocratic clients could not be expected to sleep on a woolen mattress. This, as Elena had suspected, had been her trial, and she had passed it. After that, the trips became more frequent. Since the drivers of the hired chaises she took were indifferent to her activities, she was able to further her plan with no one the wiser.

The driver knew Bath intimately and was able to take her to a small market where used clothing was bought and sold. There she found a small boy offering a woolen coat not terribly dirty and not terribly shabby, who was willing to trade it for her silk dress. The coat was almost certainly stolen, but that was better than something that had come off the body of someone murdered.

The driver knew all of the inns that the mail coach left from. The nearest one to the town house was within walking distance. She got several chances to peruse the schedules, and decided that Glastonbury was far enough that Serafina might find it difficult to find her. She reckoned that she could get a job as a stocking mender at a *modiste*, but if that proved impossible—or she could not get such a position immediately—she knew enough kitchen work and was now accustomed enough to hard work that involved a great deal of standing that she could manage as a scullery maid or a tweenie until a position turned up.

Working in her room when Serafina was out, she managed to cobble a decent dress together out of her old ones, and an apron and modest cap out of her brothers' shirts. Two of her petticoats became one. The outfit was scant, but decent, and the breast bindings of her boy's gear would do in place of stays. Better, actually; with a flat chest she would (hopefully) not attract unwanted attention. The bits and pieces of clothing fabric left over became a rucksack into which she could stuff all her belongings. A blanket discarded in the attic because of holes was easy to patch, and another trip gave her the opportunity to buy the few other things she needed: a cup, a fork, and a spoon (she already had Ben's pocketknife from his trunk), and a small pan, in case she needed to cook for herself. She reckoned that she could take food from the larder to keep her fed for two or three days until she could get a position, and if need be, she could find an outside staircase, or some other hidden nook where she could sleep.

Finally the day came when all of the work of cleaning, re-painting, and re-papering the manor was done. Serafina and the duke planned to spend the entire day there, with carpenters and an interior architect. They were going to go over the entire place room by room, decide on decorations, what needed replacing or mending. And that was the day Elena made her move.

Jane wasn't even awake yet; Elena hadn't slept at all. With her heart in her mouth, she stealthily slipped on her "common boy" clothing and pulled her rucksack and rolled-up blanket out from beneath the bed. With her shoes in hand (buckles pulled off; sadly, they had proved to be silvered brass and not silver) and in her stockings, she slipped down the servants' stair all the way to the bottom floor and the kitchen, feeling her way. It was dim, but still, thanks to the banked fires, she was able to see.

Or maybe it was her magic working; she seemed to be able to see in the dark far better than any of the other servants.

She had left a note on her bed.

I have thought and prayed over this, and I cannot bear being made into a whore. By the time you read this, I shall have thrown myself into the Avon.

Would they believe it? Maybe, but probably not. But doubt might give her a few precious hours of delay.

She felt her way into the pantry; by now she knew where Msr. Paul kept everything. She stole the older bread, broke a big piece off the common cheese, took stale cakes generally reserved for making posset, took carrots and radishes and a few raw potatoes. She stuffed all of those into her rucksack as well, tied the rolled-up blanket on top, and carefully lifted the latch on the door into the stableyard. She put on her shoes, wishing she had been able to trade them for the sturdier shoes most of the working servants wore, and, moving quickly, was off down the drive and then down the street. She walked with purpose, stopping only to pick up a loose cobblestone or two, and then only when she was certain no one was about to see her do so. Her path took her across a bridge over the River Avon; at the middle she stopped, knotted stones into the arms and legs of the garments, and threw her livery into it. Serafina had said that she had worked magic to delay her maturation; putting some sort of magic on the livery to track wherever Elena went would have been much easier. So if—probably *when*—Serafina invoked her magic to find Elena, she would find the livery in the river, and might give up, at least for another precious few hours. This probably would not deceive Serafina for long, because she could send her water creatures to make sure, but by the time she realized that Elena had lied, and all that was in the river were garments, Elena should be in Glastonbury.

And, hopefully, she would be some place where she could be alone, and she could call the sylphs for the first time in three years.

She walked as fast as she could, varying her pace with trotting until she was a little winded, then went back to walking. The combination of her constant fear and the new sensation of euphoria at having escaped gave her energy she had not had in three years. The few people on the street did not bother her; she looked too poor to have anything of value, and she also looked like she was in a hurry to get somewhere.

Well, I am. I don't want the coach to leave without me.

Even moving as fast as she could, munching on a stale cake to keep up her strength and calm the growling in her belly, she made it to the coaching inn *just* in time to pay the outside fare—seven shillings sixpence, which used the last of her savings—and scramble up to the top of the coach before the post-boy blew his horn, and with a tremendous lurch, they were away.

It was immediately obvious that this had been a bad idea; there were nine people at the top of the coach besides the luggage. She was crowded to the edge by three rowdy young men who smelled of beer and sausages, and it was harder to hang on up here than at her position as a tiger. The coach swayed more than any vehicle she had ever been in, even more than a high-perch phaeton. By now it was just light; and she was so terrified that she was white. She knew that she was white, because her hands clutching the baggage rails were white.

She regretted that cake. But there was no choice but to swallow to try to keep it down. Vomiting it up would anger her fellow passengers, possibly make the coachman force her off, and definitely leave her filthy and foul-smelling.

I can do this. It's only four or five hours. Failing right now means Serafina will use spells on me to take away my will, just as she took Father's.

As for the passing scenery, she had no idea what it was. She was too terrified to look anywhere but at her own hands to make sure they were not slipping. Swaying, bouncing, shuddering, the coach threatened to cast her off moment by moment! She was in a constant state of terror . . . but at least it was terror for a different reason.

It was relief so intense when they stopped to change horses she nearly fainted. But the coachman took one look at her, when he glanced back to see how his passengers were doing, and abruptly ordered the young man sitting on the box next to him, "Give o'er, and let the boy sit."

The young man objected immediately. "I was on the top first! I should—"

The coachman scowled; he looked a very tough man, one whose face reflected the scars of a hundred fisticuff battles.

"Ye can give o'er and let the boy sit, or ye get down and walk and he'll be sittin' anyway. It's all one to me," he growled.

The young man was tall and slender; the coachman was stocky and had arms like his horses' legs from all the controlling of the reins. The young man thought better of the situation, and clambered around the baggage to take Elena's place at the side, as Elena took his place on the driving box.

The position was better, if rather more terrifying, since it was a straight drop down to the tree and the rear ends of the first pair of horses. But there was a rail beside her to clutch, and a footboard to brace her legs against, and she was sitting on something meant to be sat on, not the roof of the coach. The bench was on a spring, too, and that might soften the worst of the motion. *I hope!*

First light would have awakened Jane. Would she even bother looking over at Elena's bed to see the letter? *Serafina's Elementals are water. We won't be near water until we get to Glastonbury. As long as she didn't enchant my shoes, I don't think she can find me.*

With a crack of the whip and a blast of the horn, they were on their way again.

The seat felt a lot safer, but the coach felt ready to upend at any moment. She planned the entire four hours of the journey how she would jump off if the coach tipped over.

The coach left her at another inn on High Street, and by this time of the morning it was crowded and bustling. Hunger, lightheadedness from the relief that she was finally down off that death-conveyance, and some confusion as to where she should go left her plastered against the wall of the inn for a moment. But a hint of greenery over the buildings drew her. She pointed her nose in that direction, dodging vehicles and pedestrians, and eventually she found herself in what looked like a lawn and garden full of ruined buildings, magnificent in their decay, with an intact building further on. Well, "lawn" was generous; it was full of sheep grazing on the long grass that looked as if it had not been mowed except by their busy teeth, and bushes and trees had run riot. She recognized the shapes of those buildings: this had been an abbey and cathedral, like the one in Bath that she had seen at a distance when on drives with Serafina.

She looked around, or rather, tried to look around without looking as if she was doing so. As busy as the High Street had been, there didn't seem to be anyone here in the ruined park. She moved quickly from the street to the shelter of the nearest bushes, then began looking for a place where she could hide. She felt her energy draining out, and sleep threatening to overtake her, but a curious thing had happened. The moment her foot touched the grass, she felt . . . safer.

She found a good place in the ruins, a spot where bushes ran riot; but near the wall, there was a little hollow place between the wall and the bushes. With another glance around, she got down on her hands and knees and crawled under the bushes, dragging her rucksack behind her so it would not catch on them, until she reached the void near the wall. Once there, she took off her rucksack, unrolled the blanket, and settled back, using the rucksack as a pillow between herself and the wall.

She sighed. She was hungry, but she was more tired than hungry, and muscles ached all over from bracing herself to keep from falling off the top of the coach. She wanted to sleep, badly, but muscle twitches and twinges were overpowering that need.

Finally she turned around and opened her rucksack for some food, because if she couldn't sleep, at least she could eat.

And that was when was suddenly swarmed by sylphs.

They didn't just flutter around her, they mobbed her, all of them jabbering in her head at once. They took it in turns to try to hug parts of her, or kiss her cheeks, until she was laughing silently at their antics. "Oh!" she exclaimed—but softly, in a whisper. "How I have missed you!" She paused, as they finally stopped mobbing her. "But I can't understand you when you are all speaking at once!"

That silenced them. After a moment during which she tried to gather her scattered wits, one of them, a completely naked thing with pearly white wings, came to hover just in front of her face.

We have been following you ever since SHE took you away, but we dared not approach for fear of HER. And we have told

NO ONE about you, not even our fellows, for fear SHE would come to hear of it and know you are more than you seem.

The poor little things seemed distressed, as if they thought *Elena* thought that they had disappeared for no reason. She managed to soothe their agitation, and she was *very* glad to see them, because they might know where her brothers were. But she was so tired that every time she let her eyes close for even a moment, she found herself starting to lean sideways and falling asleep.

One of them darted into her rucksack; she felt it rummaging around in there, behind her back, and suddenly it popped out again with a chunk of bread torn off roughly and a chunk of cheese that looked as if it had been hacked off with a jagged knife. These were almost as big as the sylph, but somehow she managed to get them as far as Elena's lap, where she dropped them.

You must eat! they insisted. So, wearily, she did. Each bite was an effort, but she was so hungry that it tasted like the best meal she had ever eaten.

"I," she began, when the same sylph interrupted her.

Stay! she insisted. *You must stay where you are and do not move! We are going to get help! Stay!*

She watched as all of them flew off, to only God knew where.

I don't have anywhere to go, she thought with confusion. She wasn't afraid; the sylphs had always been helpful in the past. But she couldn't imagine what sort of help they'd bring and how that would make any difference to her current needs for food, shelter, and a job.

Unless it's another Elemental mage. The thought managed to break through her fatigue-fogged mind. That jolted her awake. She managed to jerk awake several times, until she heard what sounded like wheels. She peered through a hole in the bushes, and first saw a cloud of sylphs, swarming around someone driving a donkey cart. In the next moment, the sylphs parted, revealing an old woman with completely white hair, in a white cap and brown round gown and immaculately white apron, sitting on the driving bench. She knew immediately that this must be the help that the sylphs had gone after. She didn't think twice about it—anyone the sylphs trusted would have to be a good person. She grabbed rucksack and blanket and crawled out to meet her.

The old woman jumped briskly from her cart, belying her apparent age. "My goodness, my dear, if you are in as much peril as my little friends think, we must get you into hiding as quickly as possible!" were the first words out her mouth. "Now you climb into the bed of my cart before anyone sees us."

She was too tired to argue. She did as she was told, lying down on what appeared to be a bed of hay, dragging her blanket and rucksack after her. The old woman took the blanket out of her unresisting hands and laid it over her, including her head.

She didn't quite fall asleep, but she wasn't quite awake either. The cart labored through the long grass, then rattled onto the cobbles, then stayed on the cobbles until the rhythm of the rattling turned to a different sort of rattling, which made Elena think it must have reached the roadway. For the first time in three years, a sensation of absolute safety settled around her. She could not keep her eyes open anymore. As the cart rumbled gently on, she fell deeply asleep.

Stephen Endicott had but one question when he walked through the front door of Halenthorpe Manor, home from Oxford. He had originally intended to go to Cambridge, but had learned that there was a College at Oxford that was already home to several Elemental students and proctors. It was the start of the long summer vacation, but he was not thinking about fetes or weekend parties or picnics or any of the other summer pleasures one would assume a young man of nineteen would have in mind.

No, as soon as he set foot over the threshold to greet his mother, the first words out of his mouth as he took both her hands in affectionate greeting were, "Have you any word about the girl?"

His mother sighed. Which was really all the answer he needed. He kissed her dutifully on the cheek, still holding her hands. She looked lovely today, but then, in his mind, she was still one of the most beautiful women he had ever seen. He didn't know much about women's fashions, but it was his opinion that she looked positively angelic in her lace-trimmed white muslin, with a matching, matronly cap on her ebony hair.

"I'm very sorry, my dear, but there is still nothing," she said, and linked her arm with his. "Come out to the terrace. You are just in time for tea."

"Well, I'm perishing," he admitted. "The food along the road is vastly inferior to Mrs. Waring's."

"I shall make certain to tell her that you said that," his mother said with a smile. It was a smile that said so much more than that. *I wonder why you are still so obsessed with this girl's welfare* and *Do you know something I do not?*

He did not, in fact, know anything more than his mother did about the girl, or, indeed, the mysterious Lady Whitstone. Except that her ladyship had made him very uneasy for no obvious reason when they had met her, and when he had learned—nearly *two months* after the incident—that Lord Whitstone had died, and the purported cause of his death was having all seven of his sons drown in a skating accident not more than two months after their ball—he had *immediately* become suspicious that Lady Whitstone was somehow involved. Really? *Seven* boys drowning at once? That was beyond belief—or rather it was beyond belief to think that such a thing was natural. Not even the information that they had been skating together on a frozen pond when the ice shattered and they all fell in made sense.

To that end, he had pestered his mother, because she had the contacts among the Elemental Masters and mages that he did not, to make inquiries immediately, and to attempt to make sure the girl Elena was safe.

Alas, by the time anyone took the time to do so, she and her stepmother had vanished utterly.

He did his very best, using all his powers as an Air Master, to find them. There was not a great deal he was able to discover. He had learned that the estate was entailed, and that they had been forced to vacate. They had left with everything his lordship had assigned to them in his will, and from there, the trail ended before it even began. It was as if they had been taken away by the fairies in some tale. He could not even find a record of their names anywhere, and surely a woman as vain as Lady Whitstone was would have made *some* attempt to regain her station. None of his sylphs had been able to find a trace of them.

He grimaced, but only mentally, and set the matter aside. For now.

He and his mother traveled through the house to the terrace at the back, just off the green drawing room, through the French doors, and out onto the marble terrace, where a small table had been set up with a spotless cloth, plates and implements, and a cold collation to which they were obviously meant to help themselves. He saw her settled into her chair, served her salad and ham, and filled his own plate before settling down in his own chair. The footman James Priest served them wine. After taking the edge off a ravenous hunger, he settled back in his chair and glanced at his mother. She sat serenely in her chair, giving no sign that she was worried about his state of mind.

Well, after three years, it was more resignation than urgent concern. He wasn't sure at all why the welfare of the girl Elena was so important to him. Was it guilt? But guilt for *what*? The only connection they had was that hour or two spent in the minstrel gallery at the Christmas ball. He was fairly certain it had not been a soulbond; at the time he had felt nothing at all toward her except that he was entertained and amused by a pretty child who was wise beyond her years. Perhaps it was only that she was so vulnerable, and that her stepmother set off feelings of unease, and her father was an ass.

Except that deep inside he knew it was far more than that. If he could have listed everything that he (at that time) could have wanted or asked for in a future bride, she would have ticked every item in the ledger. She was kind, thoughtful, clever, empathetic, used to making the best of a bad situation, and open hearted as well as open minded. *He* didn't care about the so-called "social graces" of dancing, singing or playing, or any of that other folderol that others seemed to think was so important. He wanted someone—like his father had found in his mother!—whom he could talk to, rely on, and hopefully love, who was also an Elemental mage or Master. That last, well, it was exceedingly important to him. He could not imagine having to hide that aspect of himself from a spouse—or worse, having to raise a gaggle of young mages without alerting a wife.

Oh, *some* in their circle had managed, either by gradually

introducing the spouse to their powers, or by wedding someone who was not, themselves, gifted with the powers, but who had been raised knowing about them. But he suspected that the ungifted partner would always harbor a sort of resentment toward the spouse who had been so blessed.

Or worse, feared for them constantly, since Elemental mages were often called into danger to rid the world of things that most of the world knew nothing of.

Or, worst of all, secretly feared their partner.

Horrid.

"A penny for your thoughts, my dear," said his mother, interrupting his musings.

He shrugged. "Nothing that is relevant. And it is very good to be home. I wish that Oxford was not so far from Glastonbury. Not that I did not enjoy the journey, for I did! I fear those of us of Air, like our Elementals, are always wishing to roam. But because of all the places I have been, *this* one is the most dear, and holds all that I love."

His mother laughed, and smiled at him. "You have learned a silver tongue at university," she teased. "You would never have made that speech nine months ago."

"Nine months ago, I would not have understood the sentiment," he replied, matching his smile to hers. "But Oxford is, in its way, glorious! I wish you would come make a visit in the fall, come with me when I go out again. They call it 'The City of the Dreaming Spires,' and for good reason. It has a beauty that is—unique. I could take you so many places, up Magdalene Tower, to the library—oh, you would love the library!—punting on the Cherwell! I think you would like it, ever so."

"Perhaps I shall," she mused, holding a bite of chicken that she had not eaten. "I do have acquaintances there I have never met in person, only by scrying. At least two will be among your teachers next year."

He feigned horror. "Lud, mother! You will be seeking to influence my teachers? The shame if anyone finds out!"

They both laughed together, knowing she would do no such thing. He was her only surviving child, and although she would do anything to protect him, fierce tigress that she was, she was also wise enough to let him go his way. They were closer than most mothers and sons, even among their own set, possibly because his father had died so suddenly, while Stephen was at an age when he was able to understand and share her inconsolable grief.

He decided to live in the moment for once, and simply give himself over to the pleasure of being home again, knowing that she would feel that and share it. It was a gift she deserved, after all.

So he finished his meal and sipped his wine, admiring how the soft afternoon light fell along the flawless expanse of lawn dotted with the sheep that kept it tidy, how the hill the manor was built on gradually slanted down toward the woods that his ancestors had protected and kept wild. How warm sunbeams filtered through the trees surrounding the hill, and made the very air golden. Off in the distance was Glastonbury, the tor rising above the ruins of the abbey, and the towers of the cathedral peeking over the trees surrounding it. Some day, no doubt, some up-and-coming fellow would manage to buy the property and build a manor on it, and perhaps pull the ruins down. And that would be a damned pity. They had their own haunting beauty that had pulled him to them again and again. There were legends surrounding that place, including some that were known only to Elemental magicians. Evil could not walk there, so it was said—although that did not stop King Henry's men, who looted the cathedral's riches and pulled it down.

Or worse than some newly rich merchant, Prinny will buy the property and put one of his ghastly gilded palaces on it. But at least he *will have the good taste to leave the ruins alone.*

Suddenly he was swarmed by sylphs, all chattering variations of "You're *home*" at full volume in his head. He fended them off with biscuits, laughing. They snatched the biscuits out of his hand, temporarily distracted, but there were more sylphs than biscuits, so they went to quarreling with each other, breaking the treats apart.

"I have been home for hours," he mock-scolded, while his mother laughed. "Where have you been?"

Suddenly they all stopped swarming him, and hovered in

place, tightly clutching biscuit fragments in their tiny hands. They glanced at each other, uncharacteristically silent.

Can't tell you, said his favorite, a pert little thing with wings that had the luster of mother-of-pearl. *Sworn to secrecy.*

That made both his and his mother's eyebrows rise. "Indeed," he said, after a moment. "And does this affect us?"

They all shook their heads, but said nothing more, leaving him with a baffling mystery. *Well, there's no point in trying to talk them around. I'll just have to wait until they forget that they were sworn to secrecy and extract it from them then.*

That was the thing about sylphs, they were very forgetful. Sometimes it was an annoyance, but sometimes you could use that to your advantage.

He glanced over at his mother. "I don't think any of the staff—"

She shook her head. "Not to my knowledge. The gifted among them would never do anything without asking me, and the ungifted would not be able to see the sylphs to swear them to secrecy."

"Are you certain of that?" Stephen kept his eyebrow raised. "As long as they were sure it wasn't going to harm us . . ."

His mother thought about that for a very long moment. "Then . . . possibly."

"We should not press them," he said firmly. "Our people are loyal and faithful, and this must be something of their own business. We should not pry."

"Whoever they are," agreed his mother. "Let us take a turn around the gardens together. It is just coming into bloom."

"Of course," he agreed, and rose, and offered her his hand. "It is so good to be home."

15

The sound of the wheels changed again, and woke Elena up. *This is softer earth, definitely softer earth.* From all of her time as Serafina's tiger, she knew every sound that wheels could make, and what sort of ground allowed them to make that sound. Cautiously she pulled the blanket off her head and looked over the side of the cart.

They were clearly deep into the countryside, with farm fields on one side of the road, looking so like the fields at Whitstone that she almost cried, and a gray stone wall on the left side that she could just see over. Dense trees at their immediate left, just beyond the wall, but in the far distance she saw a manor, larger than Whitstone, atop a low hill, with lawns falling gently off into the woods, dotted with sheep.

Surely we're not—

But to her relief, just as she thought that, the old woman turned the cart down a path lightly overgrown with grass, and pulled up at an iron gate in the wall. She jumped down, walked briskly to that gate, pushed it open, and came back to the cart. "You can come out of hiding, my dear," she said, smiling so that her eyes disappeared into her wrinkles. "We're safe enough here."

A sylph that had apparently been perched in the cart bed with Elena nodded her head vigorously. *Yes, yes. Very safe. Warded and safe!*

Well, Elena didn't know what *warded* meant, but as she sat

up, and the old woman drove the cart through the gate, she had the sensation that they had just pushed through a barrier. Like pushing one's hand through a jelly that had set up too firmly.

The donkey paused again so that the old woman could close the gate behind them. Ahead of them lay a green tunnel through the dense woods, and trees that looked as if they had been here since the dawn of time. Elena was enchanted; the woods at Whitstone were carefully managed, with regular harvests of timber and paths cut through them to enable the local hunt to make their gallops unimpeded. Though Father had no longer ridden to the hunt, he still allowed them free access to Whitstone property. In turn, the hunt had respected the manor farms, and did not trample their crops. That was not always the case outside of the walls, and there was many a tale of woe told down in the kitchen.

It would have been impossible to ride in pursuit of a fox here.

The sylphs flitted ahead, and the donkey plodded along with head and ears bobbing. The air was still and warm, and full of a sort of indescribable green scent that was ferny, leafy, and sweet, a scent of damp and leaf mold and sun-warmed grass all at the same time. Birdsong was all around them, more birds in one place than she had ever imagined existed. Sunlight lanced down through the canopy, shafts of gold, such as illuminated saints in the books in Father's library. But of course there were no saints here, and the golden glory illuminated only young vines, infant trees, a single flower, or sometimes, nothing at all.

There was light at the end of this tunnel of greenery, and as they neared it, Elena squinted to see what was there, but couldn't make out anything.

Then, at last, the donkey penetrated that light, and the cart and its passengers emerged onto a pleasant, grassy meadow, with a pond in the middle and a gray stone cottage, roofed with slate, tucked into the forest. The old lady directed the donkey toward the cottage, although it clearly wanted that sweet grass very badly.

"This is Lord Endicott's property," the old lady said, as she stopped beside the cottage, and the donkey immediately put his head down and began to graze. "No one ever comes here.

It was the gamekeeper's cottage, but he died just before the old lord, and the young lord never hired a new one. That was several years ago, but everything is still sweet and sound inside. You'll be safe here."

"How can you know that for certain?" Elena asked, clambering out of the cart bed, taking her rucksack, blanket, and half the grass with her. "Oh—I should have said thank you, first—thank you! Truly, thank you! But how can you be sure no one will come here?"

The old woman chuckled, and smiled, revealing a fine set of teeth. "Because I am the cook at the manor, and what the cook doesn't know about isn't worth knowing. Mrs. Waring, at your service, young miss."

Elena gaped at her. "How do you—"

"Know you are a girl? The sylphs told me, of course! I'm just a mage, and most of my knowledge is kitchen magic, but the sylphs bring me to those in need, or bring them to me. Usually it's wild things, but now and again, it's a person, one with at least a touch of the gift themselves." Mrs. Waring watched her as she assimilated all of that. Finally, Elena took a deep breath.

"I am deeply beholden to you, Mrs. Waring," she said, humbly. "And I do not know how I can repay you. I know enough to be a tweenie, or perhaps enough to be the lowest kitchen maid. I brought female clothing with me if—"

But Mrs. Waring would have none of that. "The cottage is not locked," she replied, which did not answer Elena's offer. "Go on in and have a look about. If I were you, I'd see if there was a scythe in there to cut some of this grass to make a bed, since I doubt the straw mattress has survived. I'll be back in a while once I've made her ladyship's tea, with things you'll be needing. The sylphs will be along with your brothers in the meantime."

And with that, she hopped back up on the seat of the donkey cart, interrupted the beastie's dinner, and sent him back down the path through the forest. The last sentence was so astonishing that she was gone before Elena had properly taken it in. And with that, her heart began to pound so alarmingly that she had to sit down.

Immediately, she began to doubt what she had heard. Because

surely this stranger could not know of her brothers! Unless—unless—

Wait, she said that sometimes the sylphs bring her wild things. Could this be where my brothers fled? Could the sylphs have brought them to her? She is a mage, so she can hear them—could the sylphs have told her their story?

It was the only thing that made sense! And anticipation and joy flooded through her, overwhelming her so profoundly that she felt faint and was glad she was sitting down. She hugged her legs to her chest, and put her head down on her knees and waited for the disorientation to pass.

When it had, she got to her feet and began to scan the sky, hand above her brows to shade her eyes.

No matter how long it took, she was determined to stand there, watching, waiting for the promised reunion, heart beating, hovering between disbelief and anticipation. But it could not have taken long, no more than an hour, when she heard the thunder of wings in the distance—and there, skimming over the treetops, they came, surrounded by sylphs whose wings beat so fast they were almost invisible. They made no other sound, but their necks moved slightly back and forth, as if they were looking for her. And when they spotted her, they arced their flight at once, and as the thunder of their wings pummeled her, they landed, one by one, in the pond.

The last was still landing as the first reached the shore, paddling frantically. They ran to her, encircled her, rubbing their heads against her and embracing her with their wings, as she went down on her knees among them, silent tears streaming down her face. Seven, yes, seven! All here, all safe, and they were all together again!

She lost herself in the painful joy of the meeting, lost track of time, never wanting the moment to end. "I thought I would never see you again!" she whispered over and over, as they caressed her with their cheeks, nibbled her hair, embraced her with a wing. "I thought—I thought—"

Then grief supplanted the joy, because, after all, they were still swans. "Oh! How can you bear it? How can *I* bear it? You are locked in this shape, and I don't know how to break you free!"

The tears came faster now, and her brothers crowded close, trying to comfort her.

She cried herself hoarse, fell into the pit of despair, climbed her way out of it, and finally hung her head and took a deep breath, closing her eyes. When she opened them, feeling warm weights in her lap, she saw that all seven swans had laid their heads there, lying down like petals around the heart of a flower, black eyes looking up at her. She stroked their heads and necks, their feathers soft and sleek under her hand, until her stomach rumbled again. All seven heads came up, all seven heads cocked to the side, all seven beaks opened, and a sort of wheezing sound came from them. For a moment she was alarmed, then she recognized what it was. They were *laughing* at her.

She shook her head, then began to laugh too, wiping the tears from her eyes and cheeks with her sleeve.

"I think I need to eat," she told them. "I don't have very much, but I can share—"

One of the swans gave a *huff*, got up, and began tearing at the grass like a goose. One by one the others did the same, leaving her free to fish in her rucksack for her slightly flattened bread, cheese that had started to sweat, and her radishes and Arthur's knife. She cut a bit of bread, a bit of cheese, a bit of radish, eating them in turn, going slowly to make them last. One of the swans padded over to her, and looked at the knife in her hand, and pecked at it. She held it up. "Arthur?" she asked. "Is that you?" But as the swan nodded, she sighed heavily. "I am never going to be able to tell you apart," she said tearfully, as the swan rubbed her cheek.

By this point the sun was somewhere down behind the trees, the entire clearing lay in soft blue shadow, and before she could break down in tears again, the donkey emerged from the forest, pulling the cart, and Mrs. Waring waved at her from the bench.

"Busy with your reunion, then?" she asked, with a kind smile. "Well, since your lads don't have arms to lift with, it will be just you and me unloading the cart, then."

Mrs. Waring got a bundle out of the back of the cart, leaving Elena to pick something for herself. She chose a couple of baskets with cloth laid over the top that were promisingly heavy.

The swans trailed along behind as Mrs. Waring opened up the cottage door, then went about opening up all the windows and shutters. Surprisingly, these windows were glazed; many of the windows in the cottages in Whitstone Village were not.

Between them they unloaded the cart of everything she needed to make the cottage into a home, from bedding for the bed (the straw mattress was, in fact, falling to pieces) to a broom, mop, and bucket, to food, wood, an ax to cut more wood (she didn't know how to use one, but that could be dealt with at a later date), to tallow candles. There were dishes and pots here already, though they needed a wash. She went down to the pond for a bucket of water while Mrs. Waring put things to rights, and the swans wandered all over inside, poking their beaks into everything. There was a water barrel inside, so she set to filling it, and by the time she was done, Mrs. Waring had a fire on the hearth, a bed made up on the floor next to it, everything swept, and a cold dinner set out for her.

At the sight of the bare cottage turned into a home, she was tempted to burst into tears again. But instead, she thanked Mrs. Waring so many times that the cook shook her head and told her to "Give o'er."

"I'll be staying for a bit," the old woman said, as sylphs drifted into the cottage and festooned themselves everywhere there was space. "I have a notion, and I want to see if it plays out."

They shared the dinner, and fortunately Mrs. Waring had packed plenty of biscuits, since most of them went to the sylphs. Elena ate far more than she had intended to; she was used to smaller portions, except when Msr. Paul fed her himself. The food was much like what Mrs. Banning used to feed all of the siblings: plain, but good. The main difference was that Mrs. Waring included boiled eggs with the ham. The swans all came in and arranged themselves in two rows, neatly packed together, on the floor, while she and Mrs. Waring ate like civilized creatures on the small table near one of the windows. Those windows had to be closed soon after dark, because it became quite cold, something that Elena remembered from Whitstone, but which had not been the case in the city. Perhaps all that stone took in and held the heat of the sun during the day.

Mrs. Waring lit a tallow dip at the fire and put it on the table between them. When they had finished, they wiped off the plates and the cutlery, but kept out their mugs for more tea. Mrs. Waring settled back into her chair, gave Elena a nod, and asked, "All right, lovey. What's your name? I already know you're not a lad, the sylphs told me as much." She paused, and pursed her lips. "Though, as God be my witness, I'd have taken you for one, you're that thin."

"Le—I mean, Elena," she said, stumbling over the name she had not used for three years. "Elena Whitstone."

"And how is it you come to be here, lovey?" the old cook persisted.

Oh, no, now what do I say? she thought in a panic. *Do I tell her everything? Should I? The sylphs trust her—*

As if sensing her indecision, one of the sylphs nearest them fluttered her wings to get Elena's attention, and looked her straight in the eye. *Tell her!* the sylph said insistently. *Tell her! She's known to Robin Goodfellow! She's our friend* and *your brothers' friend! Tell her everything!*

Well, Elena had no notion of who Robin Goodfellow was, but the rest all made sense. And besides . . . she realized in that moment just how unutterably weary she was of keeping secrets. She wanted to finally unburden herself of them, and Mrs. Waring seemed like the right person speak to.

"I'm not sure where to begin," she said, haltingly.

"When did things start to go wrong?" asked the cook, her brown eyes looking so kind that Elena felt the last of her resistance melt. "That's generally the best place to start."

It was a good question. She bit her lip as she thought about it for a while. Mrs. Waring did not press her, simply sat there in a silence punctuated only by the crackle of the fire in the fireplace, the little movements of the sylphs around the cottage, and the occasional rustle of feathers.

"I suppose that it all started to go wrong when Mama ran away." She rubbed her forehead. "But I should start with—we didn't—my brothers and I didn't—know about this. Not at the time, and not for a lot of years after. We only found out about it when we guessed part of it. The sylphs confirmed it, and the sylphs told us the parts we hadn't guessed. So, Mama was—is still, I suppose—a swan maiden...."

After a halting start, the words poured out of her, until she felt as if she could not stop. She told the old woman everything, from their relatively happy life, even if it had been lived under Father's domineering and disapproving gaze, to Stepmother's arrival. She left nothing out. Mrs. Waring listened, saying nothing, just nodding encouragingly, as she continued with the arrival of Father and their new stepmother, and the discovery that their stepmother had cast some sort of spell over him.

Now the cook interrupted her. "This spell—can you remember it?" she asked, putting her mug down on the table and looking so intently at Elena that Elena flinched a little. Mrs. Waring saw it and smiled thinly at her. "I don't doubt you, not at all, lovey. But if you can remember it, that'll tell me a good deal."

"It was in Latin," she said, haltingly, though of course she could remember it; it was branded into her memory as if written with a hot poker. "Aqua in sanguine tuo tantum me spectat. Aqua in sanguine tuo desiderat tantum mihi. Aqua in sanguine tuo tantum me amat. My brother translated it. 'The water in your blood looks only for me. The water in your blood longs only for me. The water in your blood loves only me.'"

"Ah," replied Mrs. Waring, sitting back again. "A Water mage. And a witch, too, I don't doubt. Dark, in both powers. Go on."

So she did, except, of course, when she got to the part where her brothers were almost murdered while skating, and she started to cry. Not hysterical sobbing, because at least now she and they were reunited and safe, but tears rolled silently down her cheeks as, one by one, the swans left their resting places, surrounded her chair, and put their heads in her lap until it was completely filled.

Mrs. Waring extracted a handkerchief from a pocket in her apron, and nodded encouragement.

She wiped her eyes and her nose, and described the rest, the expulsion from the manor, arrival in Bath, Stepmother's transformation into Serafina, the Cyprian, her own transformation into Len, Serafina's tiger, and, briefly, her life in Serafina's service. "I ... suppose I should be grateful," she said doubtfully. "Where else would I go?"

THE CYPRIAN

But all seven swans jerked their heads from her lap, hissing angrily. Mrs. Waring shushed them, and they subsided, but she nodded her agreement with their anger. "They're right, lovey. You've got no reason to be grateful to that miserable. . . ." She paused and pressed her lips together. "Hussy," she said, finally. "And . . . well, I will not go on, or I shall say some words I will not regret, but which polite people should not say. So . . . you ran away?"

Again, she hesitated. Her cheeks flamed, and she hung her head in shame. This part she really did *not* want her brothers to hear. Mrs. Waring saw all that, and said, "And finally her paramour suggested he should—" She paused, and her eyes narrowed. "No . . . wait . . . the new house they were planning. . . ." She reached across the table and took Elena's clenched hands in hers. "No need to go into it, lovey, I think I know what happened. And you ran away."

Grateful that she didn't have to confess anything aloud, Elena finished. "I waited until I had everything I needed, and I ran. I knotted rocks in my livery and threw it into the river, got a mail coach as far as it would take me, which was here. And then the sylphs said they would bring help, and they did."

"It's a blessing I was there already, lovey. The less time that you spent in the open, the less chance she'll track you down. Now you're beneath the Endicott ward and she'll not be able to find you. That was a clever trick, throwing your livery into the river, but it won't deceive her for long; her pukas and undines and mari-morgans will find the clothing and tell her you ain't in it." She reached over and patted Elena's clenched hands. "But I doubt the kitchen girl will do aught but get her clothes on and run downstairs to her duties. That Serafina will reckon you're taking the chance to sleep late. That Frenchy maid will either *get* another day off, or *take* it, and not even think of you. Come breakfast, that Frenchy cook might miss you, but I reckon he's going to think that Serafina took you with her. Which means come luncheon, still nobody's looking for you. Not till teatime or past. The note'll be found first, and there's more delay until *she* gets her nasty cre-a-tures looking for you, and that's long after I brought you *here*, and there is nothing she is going to see past the ward."

She seemed so sure—and the sylphs were all nodding in agreement—that Elena finally relaxed. She rubbed her hand over her forehead, suddenly aware of a terrible headache. "I *hate* her," she suddenly blurted. "I want to *hurt* her!"

Mrs. Waring nodded. "Perfectly right. But you already have. Right now, she's raging. You went from being the thing she cared least about to the thing she cares about most. You upset her plans. She reckoned she owned you, and you went and proved her wrong. That's the thing about people like her. They hate being proved wrong. Now, let's have another cup of tea."

Elena desperately wanted to ask Mrs. Waring about so many things that the thoughts tumbled over themselves and left her without anything to say. So she petted her brothers' heads, and listened as Mrs. Waring talked soothingly about nothing, just little bits about the household. Not gossip, but stories, like how the brownies had helped her find her missing favorite knife ("and right put out I was when I found Jemmy Groom had wanted it for ever so, and saw it laying on the counter and got the hob he'd been feeding to make off with it without a please or may I, and you may be sure I gave him the sharp end of my tongue"). Or that she'd discovered one of the kitchen maids was starting the morning fires with a salamander ("and didn't I tell her that you don't just *tell* the wee things to do somewhat and order them about like the Queen of Sheba, and how would she like it if I took that tone with *her*?"*)*. And at first it had all sounded like common kitchen gossip, but then she gradually realized that the hobs and the salamanders and the naiads weren't just the odd names of people serving Lord Endicott, they were spirits, like the sylphs, and that practically everyone on the estate had a touch—or a lot!—of magic.

She started listening more closely, and came to the conclusion that it was mostly a touch. But still! This might be somewhere they would fit in! And even if her brothers couldn't talk to her, everyone *here* would know they were not to be chased, or shot; everyone *here* would protect them. They'd all be *safe*. And—

But just as she came to that realization, the swans all suddenly backed away from her to the center of the room and began to—well—writhe.

She cried out in alarm, her heart beating in a state of panic, because it looked as if they were in terrible pain. Their heads pointed straight up at the ceiling, their wings spasmed against their bodies, their long necks swelling. . . .

Then all their feathers puffed up impossibly and—

Instead of swans there were seven very blond young men kneeling there, some with one or both hands on the floor, panting with exertion.

Naked young men.

But Elena could not have cared less about the fact that they were naked. All she cared about was that *they were her brothers!*

She leapt out of her chair so fast that she knocked it over and flung herself into their arms, babbling and crying.

Though they were doing a fair amount of babbling themselves. Mostly about how sorry they were that they hadn't been there to protect her, and how sorry they were that they had just *fled* and hadn't made some effort to watch her from a distance.

And she kept saying "It's all right!" and "I don't care!" and things of that nature, and they probably would have gone on forever in that vein if Mrs. Waring hadn't interrupted them with a sharp *"Hist."*

All eight heads—Elena's included—turned her way.

"You ain't going to stay this way long, I reckon," she said calmly, the fact that they were naked not bothering her in the least.

"No, madam," Ben said contritely. "About an hour, one hour at midnight."

"Then we had best make the most of it," she replied briskly, and proceeded to question them closely. Finally, she nodded. "I do believe that it wasn't that—*female*—that turned you. I believe that she set her mari-morgans to drown you, and that made your mother's blood in you save you by turning you."

The boys all nodded slowly, almost as one. "It was *horrid*!" Gus blurted, and looked about to cry.

"That I do not doubt," Mrs. Waring agreed. "It was because you don't have feathercloaks, I'll be bound. But at least you are all alive."

"So you don't think she turned us?" that was Arthur. "Huh."

"No, but I do think she bespelled you to keep you as swans," Mrs. Waring supplied, as the sylphs all looked on with wide eyes. "And because the cruelty is the point for her, she gives you all an hour at midnight to be lads again. So that forces you to look for someplace you can hide when that happens. And *that* means you spend half of your day eating, and half of your day trying to find that shelter and get into it. That gives you no time at all to try and figure out how to get help."

"Oh, how I hate her," Emil said bitterly.

"Well, now," Mrs. Waring said. "You're where you can get help *now*. This is more of a witchy thing than what a mage does . . . I reckon it will have to be me that studies it. Meanwhile, you can stay here, with your sister. You'll be safe. You can come in the cottage at night to sleep so when you change, you'll be fine."

"Mrs. Waring," said Ben, solemnly and with a hint of a tear in his eyes, "you are magnificent."

"Bosh," she replied, waving the compliment away. "Now make the most of your time, because there probably isn't much of it left."

Everyone was emotionally exhausted by the time that her brothers transformed back to swans. Elena was already physically exhausted, and all she could think about by that time was how much she wanted to sleep.

Mrs. Waring must have understood that, since she reassured Elena that she could get home easily enough, that the donkey knew his way in the dark, and that she would be fine. Before Elena could protest, she had already let herself out of the cottage, and her brothers had arranged themselves in a comforting circle around the bed on the floor.

So she joined them, and fell deeply and completely asleep, surrounded by peace, the warmth of their bodies, and the sound of their breathing.

"My lord, Mrs. Waring would like to speak to you," said the butler to Stephen as he sipped his morning tea on the terrace before getting to work with the estate manager. Being away at Oxford for so many months meant he was very behind on everything regarding the non-magical matters of the estate and it was going to take him several days to catch up. Of course, he could have left everything in the hands of his manager and his mother, but that felt far too much like shirking his duties. After all, his father had always said that a good caretaker served his people and their needs, and only after these things were addressed could he think of himself.

Still . . . Mrs. Waring seldom came up from the kitchen, and when she did, it was generally to talk to his mother. This must be something important.

"Have her come out, please, Harris," he said. "I'll be happy to see her."

Mrs. Waring ventured out of the door onto the stone terrace, and Stephen could tell in an instant that she was both contrite and a little worried. *Hmm. I wonder if this has anything to do with the sylphs saying they were sworn to secrecy about something. . . .*

"My lord," said the old woman, "I have a bit of some good news, and a bit of something to confess. And they're tangled up together."

Intriguing! he thought, and motioned to the chair across from him for her to sit down. She shook her head, but he was insistent. "Mrs. Waring, you are on your feet from sunup to sundown. Even the church permits sitting during confession!"

She blushed a little, but sat. "I'll get to the good news first. That little gel you've been fretting about. Would her name be Elena Whitstone?"

He felt as if he had been hit with a bucket of cold water. "Yes! Yes, it is!" he exclaimed. "How did you know?"

"Because I've put her up in the gamekeeper's cottage. Her and all her brothers. They're swans—I mean to say, her brothers are swans." She clasped her hands tightly in her lap, her voice and expression anxious. "I did it without asking, because I thought I might need to get her under the ward right quick. I swore the sylphs to secrecy until I could tell you myself."

Thunderstruck. This is what being thunderstruck feels like. "Start from the beginning, please, Mrs. Waring," he said, carefully. "And please, leave nothing out."

Mrs. Waring, schooled and trained in the art of doing everything in the right order, would have made an excellent storyteller. By the time she was done, Stephen was certain that he now knew all there was to know about the immediate situation. He had set his cup aside when she began, and by now it was cold.

"Well," he said when she had finished. "You did everything right, Mrs. Waring. Including swearing the sylphs to secrecy. If I had known, I probably would have blundered in there and frightened her into running again. Now the question is, what can we do? She's certainly safe where she is, under the Endicott ward, but this Serafina Valdestine, her stepmother—" He shook his head. "This is appalling. She must be brought to justice. I shall have to convene the White Lodge here, but the girl *must* be a witness, and we need to convince her to do so, rather than coercing her. She must do this of her own free will. And we must find a way to restore her brothers as well." He rubbed his temple, trying very hard to think as his father would have thought. His father had had decades of experience in handling such things. Stephen had only been a witness and an occasional participant in an occasional conclave and a Hunt or two.

It all seemed so—surreal. Below him stretched the peaceful lawn full of placid sheep, stretching down to the woods where birds sang, faint and far away. And there, in a cottage in his woods, was the victim of abuse both magical and physical, with her seven more victims of attempted murder and magical abuse—

And this Serafina has gone undetected for so long . . . we'll have to handle this with care or she will escape, and probably do something terrible to Elena and her brothers as she does.

"You have her confidence, Mrs. Waring," he said, finally, thinking out loud. "As you say, she and her brothers are safe in the cottage. What do you need?"

"Permission to keep bringing them what they need to live there," the old woman told him, her tension melted away. Why had she been so tense? *Oh, because she was afraid I'd go blundering out there and ruin everything.*

"You have it, of course," he said. "I'll give orders to the staff that you are to have full control over the situation. Mrs. Landrace may have ideas about supplies other than foodstuffs. What else do you need?"

She hesitated. "I've yet to suss out that spell that binds the swan boys, but I will say this, it was crafted by an expert. I'll need time. And I'm thinking maybe she needs some training in her Element."

"I can ask a zephyr. Actually, I can make a request for a willing one. Such things have generally been answered in the past," he promised. "Is there anything else?"

The old woman smiled, a smile of complete satisfaction. "No, my lord. Not at the moment."

"Well, if there is, you come to me. I *hate* the thought that such a terrible creature as this Serafina is still free to do her damage, but we cannot move until everything is ready or I fear . . . terrible consequences." He frowned, his headache getting worse. "She could fill the lungs of those come to take her with water. She could pull all the water *out* of our bodies. She could wait until we are coming for her and ambush us on a bridge."

"Don't dwell on it, my lord," she said kindly. "Take it one step at a time, like a recipe, and it'll all come right in the end."

He licked his lips, and nodded. "I am sure you are right, Mrs. Waring," he said, attempting to project a confidence he in no way felt. She made an abbreviated curtsy and left by the terrace door.

He went looking for Harris and found him in the butler's pantry. "Mrs. Waring has a visitor in need in the gamekeeper's cottage, with my approval," he said, and gave Harris the briefest explanation he could. "Make sure the staff know, and that Mrs. Waring has everything she needs. And alert the staff to watch for strangers, and Elementals that might be acting oddly—"

"Ah, your father's usual protocol, my lord?" the butler asked smoothly.

Stephen felt some of his tension leave him. "Yes, exactly," he agreed. *Of course Father had a protocol. And of course Harris knows it.* Harris was a very strong Fire mage, nearly a Master, and had been the old Lord Endicott's right hand man on Hunts for as long as Stephen could remember—actually, longer than that.

"If I may recommend, I shall remind the staff to be on the watch for strangers outside the ward, and to be on the alert for anything or anyone that seems out of place. We know that this *woman* is Water, but she may have nefarious allies in any of the Elements." Harris exuded the confidence that Stephen sorely lacked at this moment, and Stephen envied it—but was exceptionally grateful for it.

"You are a wonder, Harris," he said warmly.

Harris gave a slight smile. "One tries, my lord. One is flattered when that is appreciated. I shall go gather the staff for a meeting, my lord. You may leave this in my hands."

Stephan was entirely out of the mood to work with the estate manager now—and at any rate, that worthy would be in the meeting that Harris was calling. Instead he went to his working room, an austere place with a central plinth, the main diagrams most Air Masters needed embedded in the floor, and blank walls painted blue. He had a second workspace, out in the gardens, but right now he didn't want the distraction of breezes and birdsong.

He set up his personal wards and protections with a thought, reached high into the heavens, and gathered his power until he could not hold any more. With another thought, he released it into the Endicott ward, the protective dome that covered the entire estate. Some Masters preferred something more subtle, something that would spring up only at need and the Master's command, something that did not scream in a thousand esoteric voices, *"A Master lives here!"*

But that had never been the Endicott way.

When he had finished, he dispersed his personal protections and leaned against the plinth. *You didn't have to do that, you know,* he told himself.

Yes, but . . . it makes me feel effective.

He was cursed, after all, with a very good imagination. He could imagine all sorts of ways in which this woman could strike before any of them realized that she knew that *they* knew all about her. Poison the water. Dry it up. Flood the entire area. Probably a dozen things he couldn't even think of.

He felt the presence of his mother behind him.

"You are stronger, and wiser than you think," she said quietly, as he turned. "And you have something this terrible woman does not have."

"And what is that?" he asked, taking comfort in the confidence in him that she showed.

"You have an army of willing allies," she pointed out. "She has, at most, one, and they do not trust each other. She will not tolerate anyone stronger than she is, and she will abuse anyone weaker. Given the chance, they will turn on her or abandon her."

He let out the sigh he had not dared release before Harris and Mrs. Waring. "I hope you are right," he said.

She placed her hand on the side of his face, and looked deeply into his eyes. "I know I cannot stop you from trying to think and plan for any contingency, but let me give you a new thing to consider before you wear yourself out going over and over the same ground."

His headache receded a little. "What would that be?" he asked, intrigued.

"We know who she is and where she is, and she knows nothing of us," his mother pointed out. "We make that our weapon by disguising what we are, and even our powers. Ask Harris to lay a layer of Fire on the Endicott ward so that it looks as if the Master here is Fire and not Air. I am certain you can think of much more than that."

And in fact, his mind was abuzz already. He kissed her cheek. "You are as clever as you are beautiful," he told her. "I'll be in my study."

Her smile warmed him all the way there.

16

Elena and her brothers spent three not-unhappy days alone at the cottage. She contrived to make them each a sort of singlet out of the female clothing she'd brought so that when they changed to human, they weren't naked. During the day, when they were in swan form, her brothers floated on the pond, grazed on waterweed or grass, or watched from the door while she got rid of the remains of the straw mattress in the fireplace a handful at a time. At night they all came into the cottage and dozed, herself included, until midnight. Then she made proper cheese-on-toast for all of them, while they told her what had happened to them. The first night . . . well, the first night they relived their trauma, almost. They all huddled near the fire, the two eldest trying to be stoic, the others not even pretending that three years had meant nothing to how they felt.

Felix blurted out everything as soon as they all changed. "Elena, it was horrid! Horrid! I don't know about the others, but I . . . I felt hands pulling me under when the ice broke. Then I felt—well, I really cannot describe what it felt like to change, but suddenly the hands let me go and I thrashed my way out of the water onto the ice, and I wasn't cold, but nothing felt right, and my mind just stopped thinking." The others nodded almost as one, Ben and Arthur blank-faced, the rest visibly holding back fear or tears. "I remember Stepmother threatening to kill us, and all I could feel was the worst terror. It just took me over completely. And somehow I was in the air. I don't know how. It was as if my body knew how to do this thing, and I just let it. We just—flew. I think Arthur was in the lead, and we followed him?"

"Me," Ben corrected, expressionlessly. "We flew until we were exhausted and I finally landed us when I saw a flock of swans on the river. I hoped they would accept us, and they did, so for the first day we watched them and figured out how and what to eat, and the first night we all slept together with them. What else could we do? It was tolerable."

"But what happened when you changed at midnight?" she asked.

"We didn't," David told her. "We were all on the water. We thought—I thought, anyway—we'd all be swans forever. We did what the other swans did, and they slept on the river, so, so did we. We couldn't talk to each other, so that was all we could do. The closest thing to talking was a kind of squeal, and pointing with our heads. The first time we changed back, weeks later, we *weren't* on the water; the wild swans were all feeding in an empty grain field, picking out fallen grain, and we had followed them. There was a threshing barn nearby and I called to the others and led them in there, thinking there might be better scavenging in it. There was, and there were heaps of wheat-straw, which seemed to me warmer than sleeping on the river, so I stayed and so did the rest." He bit his lip. "And then the change happened. It felt like being turned inside out, at least to me. But that wasn't the worst, because obviously we were naked. It was frightening to find ourselves human and naked and freezing cold."

"I think Stepmother probably put that change into her spell so we'd drown, freeze to death, or get ourselves in trouble," added his twin. "I think Mama's blood kept us swans on the river, so at least we didn't drown."

"We huddled together under the straw until we changed back. After that we had to either find someplace we could keep from freezing at night, or spend the night on a lake or pond or near the hard bank where the water was still with the other swans. We had to make sure it was someplace where people wouldn't see us, too, and you might be surprised how many people are out at midnight." Ben picked up the thread. "That was our life for the next three years. We mostly slept on the water even in good weather. 'Tis *very* inconvenient to be naked! And of course the only time we could talk to each other was that single hour at midnight. That made it hard to plan anything. I don't know why we never saw the sylphs in all that time, but perhaps they did not want to draw attention to us."

"Then the sylphs came and obviously wanted us to follow them, so we did, and here we are," Arthur finished. "We didn't abandon you, Elena, but when we gathered our courage and went back to Whitstone Manor in August, there was a strange man living there, and no sign of you or Stepmother." He hung his head, and they all looked ashamed. "I am so very sorry we weren't brave enough to come back sooner. If we had, we could have lurked about, and followed your carriage to Bath, and perhaps lived on the river and maybe made ourselves known to you."

She didn't say anything at first, except "That's all right," because what else could she say? In their place, she would have been frightened to return; swans were rather obvious, not to be mistaken for any other bird, and too big to hide. Serafina might have told all the outdoor staff and the manor farmworkers to kill swans on sight as she had threatened. "I can't think what else you could have done, truly."

For the rest of that hour, they sat next to the fire until the change came, all of them unable to find words to express what to Elena were muddled and tumultuous feelings.

With that awkwardness out of the way, the next two nights were much better: sleeping until midnight, a wonderful hour together, then back to sleep until dawn. Mrs. Waring and her cart appeared on the fourth day, between breakfast and luncheon by manor hours, her cart loaded with more food, a few other things that Elena had missed, and long linen coat-smocks of the sort that farm laborers wore. The swans had gathered about the cart, curious to see what was in it, and made those squealing noises that Felix had described when they saw the coat-smocks.

Mrs. Waring handed those over to Elena with a smile. "Just throw the whole smock over each lad when you all go to bed, and they be decent when they turn," she said, and they both laughed.

The garments were huge, easy enough to drop over the top of a swan and envelop it. She took one and threw it over the nearest swan—there were a few moments of thrashing, as the bird sorted itself out inside all the fabric, and then the swan's head poked inquisitively out of the neck hole, which made them laugh harder. Her cheeks and mouth hurt from smiling, it had been so long since she had done so. She plucked the smock off the swan and helped Mrs. Waring carry her offerings into the cottage. Among other things were well-worn but well-cared-for boy's clothing and smallclothes that would certainly fit her, and Elena greeted these things with a sound of pleasure.

"Ah, good, I wasn't sure you'd want boy stuff, but there aren't any lady clothes to spare up at the manor," Mrs. Waring said with relief.

"Boy clothing is much more practical here than dragging skirts," Elena pointed out. "Even you would have trouble with this tall meadow grass."

"Well, a gel can always hike her skirts up, but point taken," Mrs. Waring agreed. "Oh, and I've told her ladyship and his lordship about you and your troubles, and I've been given leave to take whatever you need."

Elena's knees grew weak with relief at that. She had dreaded what might happen when Lord Endicott found out—as he inevitably would—that she and her brothers were living here without his permission.

"Here," the cook added, thrusting a stack of books tied up with twine into her hands. "Compliments of her ladyship. She says she has read these so many times she can recite them by heart, so you're to have them so you won't get bored."

I wouldn't be bored if I had my workbox, she thought, but books were certainly welcome!

"Now, I've got the kitchen set up to serve luncheon and tea without me," the old lady continued. "That's a good several hours for me to study the spell that holds your brothers as swans, and discover what's what."

At that, the swan that had been with them ran to the pond (which nearly convulsed Elena all over again; swans were the most awkward things she had ever seen, running) and herded up his brothers, bringing them all to Mrs. Waring's feet to stare alternately at her and Elena.

"This will take time," Mrs. Waring warned them. "You might as well groom yourselves or nap. I ain't going to be putting on a show. This is as much witchy magic as Elemental magic, but I suspect *she* is as much witch as mage."

"Can the spell be broken?" Elena asked anxiously.

"Every spell can be broken, or un-cast, it's just a matter of *how*. If you've got a spell like this one, a harmful spell that's cast on the unwilling, it can't be something that can't be broken." The old woman paced around the huddle of swans as their heads followed her path. "That would be like putting a sealed pot with water in it on the hearth. Sooner or later, the lid will go flying and the pot might bust. No, just let me poke and prod and mutter. Likely, it'll be something that hussy thinks is impossible, and would cause pain—"

"I don't care!" Elena cried. "Whatever it is, I'll do it!"

Mrs. Waring *tsk*ed and looked as if she might say something about impetuous words. But she didn't. She just walked around and around the drift of swans, muttering, making odd gestures, or drawing things in the air. Sylphs appeared and gathered around her, and from their intent faces, Elena thought they might be helping the old woman. After an hour or so of this, Elena retired to the cottage to change her clothing. The garb she had been living in for almost a week was certainly in need of a wash, and so was she. She gave herself an all-over scrub and a bit of a rinse, and put on the new stuff. It was big on her, but that made it comfortable.

Mrs. Waring was still at it at luncheon time, though she had backed up enough that the swans could eat grass. The sylphs still hovered around her. The cook did not even stop for luncheon; she accepted a mug of tea and a couple of cakes from Elena, but somehow incorporated eating and drinking into her ritual, and carried on. As she had promised, there really wasn't a great deal to see; even when Elena squinted and concentrated, the most she saw were shifting drifts and threads of color, and occasional sparks. Whatever Mrs. Waring was doing, it had meaning only to her.

Feeling useless now, she went inside, put her dirty clothing into the stone sink, poured cold water from the barrel and hot water from the kettle over it, and scrubbed it against the stone sides with some of the brown soap Mrs. Waring had brought until she thought it was reasonably clean. She took the clothing outside and spread it on a bush to dry, and when she turned around, Mrs. Waring had stopped pacing and muttering, and instead was staring off into the distance with her arms crossed over her chest. Before Elena could say anything, the cook had turned and spotted her.

"Well, gather up," she said, in a voice that carried off to where the drift of swans had wandered. "I know what needs to be done, and it's cursed difficult."

Elena and the swans surrounded her. Mrs. Waring's brows were creased in a way that made Elena nervous. *What is this going to take? What if I have to . . . sacrifice one of them to save the rest? That would be just the sort of thing Serafina would think of!*

"I confess that I am buffle-headed as to *why* this she-napper created this . . . maze. Nor where she got her ideas. But—well, I'll just get to it." She looked straight at Elena. "In order to break the spell, the person must make shirts of nettle, and throw them on the swans the way I threw that smock on one. And they must do it at almost the same time—they can't just make a shirt and throw it on a swan, then make another, and throw it on the next one when it's finished. And from the time you start until the time you finish, you cannot speak a single word."

Elena stared at her. "Shirts of *nettle*? How do you make shirts of nettle?" In her mind she envisioned leafy nettle stalks clumsily woven together into a shirt shape. She shook her head, despair creeping over her. How was this even possible?

"Nettle's got a core, like flax. You treat it like flax. You dry it and beat it, then crush it and scutch it to get the fiber out, then you hackle the fiber until it's smooth, and then you spin the hackled fiber. You could weave it, I suppose," she said, eyeing the cottage dubiously, as if measuring it for a loom. "But it would be faster to crochet or knit or net the string you spin into the right shape. I reckon the lads won't care what it looks like as long as they're human again."

The despair left her. "I can spin," she offered.

"Then I can bring up a drop spindle, a scutcher and a hackle." Mrs. Waring's expression eased. "But these are stinging nettles, lovey. You'll have to harvest them, and beat them and all, spin all the string and make up the shirts *by yourself.* You can't wear gloves. We can't save you from the burning and the pain, that's clear in the spell; it's the *point*, really."

"Pain is always the point where Serafina is concerned," she replied, bitterly. But she squared her shoulders and looked Mrs. Waring straight in the eye. "It won't kill me; I can bear it. I can bear not speaking, too. If this is what is needed to save my brothers, I will do it."

Mrs. Waring let out her breath as if she had been holding it in. "Then it's just a matter of finding a big patch of nettles—"

The sylphs shot off in all directions as if they had been frightened by something, and came flying back almost as quickly. *This clearing is ringed with nettles!* one of them announced. *There are nettles everywhere but the cottage!*

"Well, that settles that." Mrs. Waring gave Elena a measuring look. "You're sure?"

"I am *certain*," she said firmly.

"Begin tonight?" Mrs. Waring asked. "Or tomorrow? Remember, once you start, you won't be able to speak."

She thought about that, as the seven swans looked at her intently. She fancied there was longing, pleading in their eyes. *What does it matter I won't be able to speak?* she decided. "Now," she said firmly. "There is time to cut quite a lot of nettles and stook them. Like flax?" She had seen flax being stooked at the manor, and she thought she knew how to do it.

"I've never seen anyone spin nettle, so . . . I suppose so." Mrs. Waring shrugged, and before she could change her mind, Elena ran into the little stone cottage; she remembered that she had hung the hand scythe Mrs. Waring had found and sharpened up on a peg in the wall, out of the way. She took a deep breath, steadied herself, and reached for it.

It felt as if she had been struck by lightning! Light and energy crackled all around her. She was fixed in place, unable to move. It didn't *hurt*, yet it felt terrible, as if she was in the grip of something huge, uncaring, implacable.

Then whatever had seized her released her, and she found herself standing in the middle of the room, scythe in her hand, mind completely blank for a moment. *What was that?* she wondered. Was it a kind of linked spell that had settled over her as soon as she made the first concrete step toward freeing her brothers?

If so... she felt shaken to her core. This was *much* more powerful than she could have imagined! Somewhere in the back of her mind she must have thought that Serafina had been bluffing when she said that she had command of creatures much more powerful than Elena could imagine. Now... now she was not so sure.

Her knees felt weak, her hands shook, and her stomach flipped. It took several long moments before she felt capable of turning around and walking out the door. *The sylphs said that there were nettles all around the clearing, so if I start behind the cottage, I should find some.* The only time she had been behind the cottage had been to use the stone privy, and the undergrowth had been tangled and daunting back then. But this time, it seemed, she would have some help. The sylphs danced and swirled above the undergrowth, and it flattened under them in little swirls. *Wait—I thought I wasn't supposed to get any help—*

But as she thought about it, Mrs. Waring had only said that she couldn't have help with the process of making the shirts. She had said nothing about getting help with everything else. The sylphs had understood this before she had, and were clearing the way for her.

And sooner than she would have thought, they had cleared the way to the nettles.

She gaped at them, for they were at least six feet tall, reaching all the way to the lower branches of the trees they were growing beneath. They looked so innocuous, almost like mint, except that their main stems were completely straight, and the branches much more delicate. She stared at them, remembering the first time she had encountered nettles, when she had been running about down by the woods past the garden with her brother Gus, and had fallen into a patch of them. And instantly it had felt like her skin was on fire. She had tried to roll out of the patch, crying, and that had only made it worse. Nanny had come running, plucked her out, and rubbed dock leaves on the patches of skin on her arms and face, and that hadn't helped at all. Mint *had*, a little, but she had spent quite a miserable time of it.

This was going to be so much worse.

She shut her eyes, reminded herself of the lines in Aesop's fable about grasping nettles firmly, and did just that, seizing the stalk of the one nearest her. And just as Aesop had said . . . it wasn't as bad. But there were hundreds of leaves on the thing, and every time one of them brushed up against her, it would burn . . .

She thought of poor Gus last night, how his eyes had pleaded with her just as he turned into a swan again. How all of them had thrashed and writhed in ways that looked as if they must end in broken bones. *That must hurt so much more.*

She cut the stalk and backed up carefully, with the whole thing dragging behind her, until she was a good way into the flattened grass and vegetation. She laid it out on the ground, and went for the next.

And the next. And the next.

Before long, despite her best efforts, her arms and hands were on fire, there were burning trails across her cheeks and forehead, and she had to keep blinking to keep her eyes free of tears. Nettle after nettle she added to the stack, reminding herself with every new brush of pain that there was no other way but *through* this. *It will be better. It is only the cutting that will be this bad. This will be better.*

Eventually it all blurred together under the burning. Cut. Drag. Stack. Return. She only stopped when she felt a tugging at her sleeve, and looked through watery eyes at a sylph, who was pointing at her stack of stems. It was . . . quite formidable. For a moment, she couldn't imagine what the sylph wanted, because the sun was still high in the sky, and beneath the pain, she was stubbornly aware that she could go on for quite a bit longer. But then the sylph pointed at a pole out in the sunlight, a pole that the sylphs must have planted for her, and her pain-fogged mind worked its way around to what the sylph wanted.

Oh. Stooking. I have enough to stook.

One by one, she dragged the cut stalks out into the sun. One by one, she leaned them up against the pole. It was easier now;

the leaves had already begun to wilt, and no longer sent their miniature lances of pain into her red and welted skin. When the last of the cut stalks had been piled into a cone around the pole, she went back to cutting.

I guess as long as they don't touch the nettles themselves, the sylphs can help. I hope they can help with the burning when I'm done for the day.

It seemed to take forever, but as she piled the last of her stalks against the sixth stook, she realized that it had almost become too dark to see. She stumbled toward two spots of warm light—the windows of the cottage, each with a lit tallow dip in them.

Bright white shapes—the swans—lined up on either side of her and guided her safely to the cottage door. Once on the threshold she leaned against the frame and cried, silently. That was when she noticed two things: gentle dabbing sensations on her face, hands, and arms, and the sting of vinegar in her nose. She sneezed and opened her eyes. A half-dozen sylphs were dabbing her hands and face with tiny wet cloths, and there was an old glass wine bottle in the sink. *Vinegar,* she slowly realized. *Mrs. Waring must have left some vinegar.* And indeed, with every dab, the burning pain lessened. It wasn't completely *gone*, but it was a lot less, enough that she could make her way to the table, put down the scythe, cork the vinegar bottle so that none of the precious liquid would spill, and turn her attention to food.

She scarcely knew what she was eating, only that her stomach stopped complaining, and she put the rest away in the cupboard and lay down, fully clothed, on the bed on the floor. She had scarcely closed her eyes when she felt her brothers snuggle up beside her, and a cooling breeze over her. She opened her eyes just long enough to see the sylphs fanning her with their wings.

When the clearing was ringed with stooks, the first was ready to be broken, and the morning that she woke knowing it was time to work with the dried stalks she could have wept all over again to think that the cutting had come to an end. But there was no time for weeping; she would need a second and possibly a third growth to make enough yarn for seven crocheted shirts, and there was not a second to lose. The swans, Mrs. Waring, even the sylphs had fallen into the background; there was only the nettles and the task in front of her, for when October came, the nettles would die. And if she did not have enough yarn by then, she would not be able to create more until late spring at the very earliest.

Mrs. Waring must have seen that she had cut and stooked the last of the nettles, because that very morning she arrived with two more people in the cart, both wearing cheerful expressions, straw bonnets over their brown hair, plain linen dresses with aprons over them, sturdy shoes, and peculiar knitted "sleeves" that reached from their knuckles to their upper arms. These two worthies were a Mrs. Layton and her daughter, Violet, and they were flax workers. "You work nettles like you work flax," Mrs. Waring explained, as the two unloaded several unfamiliar objects from the bed of the cart. "They're here to show you how."

And so they did, strictly obeying the stricture that only she was to touch the nettles. The only thing they did besides teaching her each step was that the daughter took pity on her blistered arms and stripped off her own "sleeves," presenting them to Elena. Elena was so grateful she fell on the girl's neck with kisses. Poor Violet blushed as scarlet as a poppy.

First, she was instructed to chop the seven-foot-long stalks in half, or even thirds. "Otherwise, 'tis too awkward to work with 'er," said Mrs. Layton, as her daughter nodded. Elena had thought that the last third or so might be too small and not hold enough fiber to be worth the processing, so this was welcome to hear. Evidently Mrs. Waring had advised these helpers that every single fiber was needed.

The first two steps in turning the nettles into yarn were straightforward: break the fibers that were at the center of the stalks out, and free them, then "scutch" the broken stalks with a "scutching knife," a blade made of wood. With the broken stems held against the edge of a C-shaped board—shaped that way to prevent her from pounding her own fingers accidentally—she scraped along the surface of the stems to free the fibers from the stems. That created a *lot* of dust, and she ended up coughing a great deal, and blowing a lot of thick brown stuff out of her nose, until she tied a bit of cloth over her face.

Then came the hackling, slapping the fibers down on a series of boards with nails spaced closer and closer together, until the fibers were clean, straight, and glossy.

She had been afraid of the dried stings, thinking they would be freed to work more mischief on her body when the breaking, scutching, and hackling began, but evidently the stings became too fragile to survive once dried, so all she had to contend with was the dust.

When she had completed all of these tasks to the ladies' satisfaction with a double-handful of dried stalks, they pronounced her able to proceed on her own, and went back to what Mrs. Waring promised would be a truly sumptuous and toothsome tea.

All this was more work than she had ever done in her entire life. Arms, legs, back, and shoulders were dreadfully sore until she got used to the work; at night her brothers would lament that they couldn't help, but really, what could they have done? She discovered muscles she had never used before as they protested the work in a nightly chorus of aches and pains, but not even that could keep her awake once her head touched a pillow. Exhaustion trumped pain, every time.

Finally the last batch of the last stook had been reduced to hanks of fibers. The hanks waited for spinning in neat piles, each hank neatly twisted and secured with a bit of the "tow," fibers too short and coarse to be of any use to her. She sat down to a hot cooked dinner that Mrs. Waring had stayed to make for her. Her brothers clustered around her and begged for peas while Mrs. Waring sat down across from her to join her at the feast. "Are we ready to cut again?" Mrs. Waring asked.

She shook her head, partly in regret, and partly in relief.

"I'll bring a drop spindle tomorrow, then, and Al Ketchum. He's an Earth mage. Reckon he can speed up the growing." Mrs. Waring reached across the table with a damp towel and wiped Elena's forehead for her. The towel came away gray with the dust from the hackling. "I'm thinking you should have a bath in the pond."

She nodded. She took off her clothing every night and shook and beat all the bits of stalk and dust out, and she had a sink bath every night and again every morning, but she was feeling distinctly itchy. And she didn't want to think about another round of cutting and stooking.

"What would you say to his lordship coming out with me tomorrow?" Mrs. Waring asked, unexpectedly. Elena looked up at her, startled, and—truth to tell, a little panicked. "He wants to make sure you're protected magically from that she-devil. He wants to see your brothers for himself. There might be more that he wants, but if there is, he's keeping it to himself."

Well, what could she possibly say? This was *his* land. He could have turned her and the swans away. He didn't have to keep sending Mrs. Waring and supplies over. She nodded cautiously, and Mrs. Waring made a little sound of approval. "Finish your dinner, go get that bath before the sun goes down, and we'll all come over tomorrow. Al will be in my cart; his lordship will probably ride. Have a good rest, Elena. Tomorrow you'll start on the yarn, and we'll have some notion how far one round of the pond will go."

As soon as Elena was done eating and had cleaned her dinner things, she took the soap and a set of clean clothing down to the pond. The sun-warmed water felt wonderful on skin that seemed coated with dust, but she was so busy scrubbing herself so hard that she scarcely noticed. She even washed her hair, which felt glorious once clean. As dusk moved over the clearing, she pulled on the smallclothes, loose shirt, and trousers and pushed her way back through the tall grass to the cottage. By the time she got there, she was yawning, and she never even woke at midnight when her brothers changed.

Hoofbeats thudding on turf woke her in the morning; Mrs. Waring had come over very early, right after sunrise, and Elena was very glad that she had gone to bed dressed. But she was just a little disappointed to see that only the donkey cart had arrived. A sunburnt, middle-aged man in a smock, trousers, and straw hat jumped down out of the cart bed. He spotted her at once and came striding toward her, hand already held out. She offered him hers, and he shook it vigorously. "Al Ketchum, at your service, lovey," he said, in a booming voice that filled the clearing. "Earth mage. Show me your nettles, and I'll be seeing if there's aught I can do with 'em."

The patch right behind the cottage was nearest, so that was where she took him. He squatted down before the cut-off stalks, dug his fingers into the earth, and stayed there for what seemed like ages, humming under his breath, with his eyes closed. The scent of freshly turned earth rose up around him, even though the ground was undisturbed.

She had better luck "seeing" what he was doing that she had with Mrs. Waring. Tendrils of golden light, like roots, emerged from his fingers and probed into the ground among the nettles. At length, he opened his eyes and stood up. "That's right good land here," he pronounced, and smiled. "I can force two more rounds of growth from this soil before the first frost."

She was so happy to hear that, she actually jumped up and down and clapped her hands with glee, and Al grinned broadly, showing a set of teeth that would have made a horse proud. "I'll just be starting, then," he told her. "Mrs. Waring knows what I'll be needing, so you get to spinning and don't you be a-worriting about me."

He was as good as his word, squatting back down on his haunches, digging his fingers into the ground, closing his eyes, and humming tunelessly. She went back to the front of the cottage, where Mrs. Waring was waiting for her.

"Can he force a harvest?" she asked immediately. Elena nodded, and held up two fingers. "Two rounds?" the cook exclaimed with pleasure. "Well, I'll be seeing to him, don't you fret. You go start the spinning."

There was a fine heavy drop spindle with soapstone whorls and brass hooks on the whorl end, a niddy-noddy and a ball winder waiting on the table, a bowl of water beside them. With a feeling of familiarity and even a kind of happiness, she was about to sit down, when the sound of hoofbeats heralded what *must* be Lord Endicott. So instead of starting, it was with a sense of vague disappointment and irritation that she went out to greet him.

He was just dismounting from a fine bay mare. She was something of an expert in what men of the *ton* looked like by now—and he was something of an unexpected mix. No one could have faulted his boots. His buckskin breeches, however were not as form-fitting as the peak of fashion would have dictated. Like the breeches, his blue clawhammer coat was not as fitted as a nonpareil would have chosen, although it was, without a doubt, made of the finest of materials, as were his plain blue waistcoat and shirt. But his stock was tied carelessly, and he was hatless, his brown hair looking as if it had been arranged by the wind rather than by a valet. She had the advantage of seeing him before he saw her, and some of her irritation left her—and left her feeling a little ashamed at being irritated for no cause. He was not a beautiful man, with unexceptional features, but he had the strong advantage of looking as if he was exceptionally amiable. And when he spotted her, his eyes lit up, and he smiled—not too broadly, but as if he was happy to see her and intended to welcome her with a full heart.

"Ah! Elena! At last!" he said—and it had to be said he had a wonderful voice, on the low side of tenor. He advanced toward her, extending his gloved hand just enough that she had the option of taking it or not. She took it, and he clasped it just tightly enough, and just long enough, to be comfortable. "What? You do not remember me?"

She blinked in surprise, because indeed, she did *not* remember him.

"The minstrel's gallery," he prompted her. "The night of your wretched stepmother's ball. You gifted my mother with the design of a gown, which she was exceedingly pleased with. In fact, so pleased that she had it made up immediately, and wears it still."

It all came rushing back, and both of her hands flew of their own accord to her mouth, as she blushed so hotly her cheeks might well have been stung by nettles again.

"Oh, my friend—may I call you my friend?—you need not feel any guilt on this matter," he said swiftly. "You have endured far too much for me to fault you for forgetting such a thing. And I am *dreadfully* sorry that I did not hear of the beginning of your trials until it was too late to trace you and find you."

Her blush faded, she furrowed her brows, and tilted her

head to the side, while her brothers came down from the pond and clustered about him. "Why should I have done that? Two reasons. I knew when I met you that you must be an Air mage at the least, for you had a sylph with you, and you were clearly aware of it. We Elemental mages take it as a duty to find and educate those people outside our ranks who also have been gifted with magic, and see that they are protected and trained in the use of their abilities. And for the second reason—that I liked you at first meeting, and that does not happen very often."

Now sylphs had joined her brothers in clustering around the two of them, and at least three of them giggled. He looked at them and made a fierce face at them. That only made them giggle harder. He sighed, and shrugged his shoulders. For her part, she felt her cheeks growing warm again.

"I cannot tell you how astonished I was when dear Mrs. Waring came to me and confessed that she had taken you under her wing and brought you to my gamekeeper's cottage. And how astonished and *enraged* I was when she told me your full story, and that of your brothers." He looked down at the swans around him, as they looked inquisitively up at him. "And I beg your pardon, gentlemen, I was not ignoring you by any means. Welcome to my home. It will be your home for as long as is needful."

The swans bowed as one, dipping their heads gracefully, and tilting their bodies down.

"Our first order of business *must* be to restore your brothers to their proper forms, Elena," he continued. "That is of paramount importance."

The swans hung their heads, and Elena petted the two nearest her to comfort them.

"In the meantime, I've come to . . . well, I hope that this doesn't sound as if I am speaking down to you, but I have come to assist you in learning how to use the magic with which you have been gifted," he continued. "I see that *someone* has taught you how to prevent another mage from discovering what you are. So I think we can build from that, if you are willing?"

She nodded.

"But there is some further instruction I can give you," he continued, "that will be of immediate interest." His face hardened. "And this is so we can invest a great deal of power into that yarn you are about to spin. And protective intention. When your brothers are human once more, *no one* will be able to harm them magically again."

In her elation, she had not failed to notice he had said a thing that made her heart sing. *We.*

First Mrs. Waring, then Al and Violet and her mother—and now it was official, Stephen Endicott had accepted her presence here. She was not alone.

17

The summer months passed. When Elena looked at the shrinking amount of time she had before the frost, it seemed as if those months passed far too quickly. But when she was trying to work every single minute she could stay awake, time seemed to drag, or vanish altogether. While waiting for the nettles to grow tall enough for the second cutting, she spun until she ran out of fiber, then she crocheted shirts that looked more like netting. She had thought about doing actual netting, which would have been faster, but she was not sure of her yarn; left to itself, it tended to roll up into little four-ply fingers, making the shirt a knotted mess.

She made the shirts all in one piece, all the while doing as Lord Endicott—Stephen—had taught her. Pulling power out of the air itself, and sending it into the yarn, wrapping love and protection around every inch, until to her eyes, the yarn and shirt in her hands shimmered a vivid blue.

By the time she spun and used up all the yarn, the nettles were ready for their second cutting, and she had two shirts completed. It seemed absurd that all that work had gone into the making of a mere pair of shirts . . . and it was not a good sign that she had only gotten two of the seven she needed out of the first cutting. Two shirts per cutting meant she would be one short before late spring came, the earliest she could expect to do a fourth cutting.

She had designed the shirts after measuring Arthur and

Ben, because it was easier to make shirts all the same size, and really, they did not vary much except in height. Her brothers had developed remarkable physiques, with incredible chests and arms, very likely from all that flying. Their legs, however . . . did not match their upper parts.

The night she had measured them was one of the nights that Stephen had stayed to speak to them, and he teased them. "By Jove, from the waist up, you'd make a tailor proud, but from the waist down, you'll make a poor showing in buckskin breeches! You'll never win a maiden's heart with those skinny calves!" They all blushed, and looked very awkward, as they did not know how to respond. And that was when she realized that if—*when!*—they were turned back . . . their troubles were just beginning, in a different way. *They've been swans for three years. Arthur and Ben are twenty! Carl and David are nineteen, Emil and Felix are eighteen—and of age! And of course Gus is seventeen, like me. They have never had anything to do with people in all that time. They don't know anything, really, about being in polite society. They wouldn't begin to know how to address a lady, or how to make polite conversation, or . . .*

Her dismay must have shown on her face, because Stephen quickly patted Arthur on the back reassuringly. "Don't worry, I'll have you riding my hunters and walking the grounds, and we'll have you up to snuff in no time!"

"That's very kind of you, Stephen," Ben said quickly, looking very chagrined, with a blush to match. "But we're a lot of unlicked cubs, and not fit for female company, I'm afraid."

To his credit, Stephen was not at all at a loss for answers. "My mother can have you sorted out on *that* in no time. After all, she civilized me, and I was a young barbarian."

It was a kind answer, but not really fit for the purpose. There was *so much* that they had missed by being swans all this time . . .

I won't worry about it, she told herself, though of course that was easier said than done. Still, there were two more harvests of nettles to be done with first, and she would have to adjust her pattern if she was to get seven shirts out of them.

There was plenty of time for worrying about almost everything while she was spinning and crocheting, but when it was time for the second round of cutting and stooking, she had no energy for worrying about anything at all. The first round had been difficult. The second was brutal.

Al had been . . . quite successful at making the nettles grow. They were thicker than the first round, and tougher, and even though the sleeves that Violet had given her helped, the nettle stings were everywhere, and her face, neck, and hands burned from sunup to sundown. Add to that, she was cutting and stooking for more hours, for the days were longer and she made use of every bit of daylight. She bathed herself in vinegar every night, and still went to sleep with skin as well as muscles burning. Stephen did what he could without helping her directly, but she almost wished he wouldn't—his distress on her account made her unhappier. She tried to concentrate on the goal, and that there actually *was* a goal at the end of this, and her brothers would be human again.

But more and thicker nettles meant more fiber, and more fiber meant more yarn. Now she knew how much yarn went into a shirt. And when the second cutting was done and she began processing the dried stalks, she started spinning in the evenings after the processing was done and it was too dark outside to see. That was when Stephen picked up one of the untouched novels that he had brought her, and began reading it aloud to her. And *that* was worth far more than he probably realized, because it kept her mind from spinning like the spindle whorl over all the unsolved problems they would face when this was over. He could not have given her a greater gift. She would fall into an exhausted slumber with her mind occupied with the trials of the novel's heroes and heroines, and not her own.

He had taken to arriving around noon, removing his horse's bit and staking the mare out on a line in the meadow, close enough to the pond that she could drink. That took care of her needs, and Mrs. Waring always turned up just past teatime with tea and supper for both of them, and breakfast for her for the next day. Then he'd stay past midnight, although she rarely managed to stay awake that long. Sometimes she would half rouse, and listen for a moment to the sound of male voices talking together, and it would be so reassuring she would fall right back to sleep.

The third cutting was easier, not because the stems were smaller and the number of stems had decreased, but because she was getting used to the work. The rash didn't last as long, either. Perhaps her skin was getting used to the abuse, or perhaps it had gotten tougher. It did cross her mind how ironic it was that although Serafina was perfectly willing to commit unspeakable crimes, the fact that Elena was ruining her complexion would have horrified her. And though the days were getting shorter, she got the cutting done faster. There had been rain, but not enough to interfere with the stems drying.

She knew now that Stephen had been staying every day until midnight specifically to talk to her brothers, and she had been concerned about him riding home in the dark, until he assured her that the sylphs could light his way. And sure enough, one night when she actually managed to stay awake past the minute that her brothers reverted to swans again, and Stephen went out to his patient horse to put the bridle back on and ride home, she watched from the door and saw the sylphs glowing like torches for him, giving plenty of light for his horse to see by.

When she had processed the last of the third cutting, and had laid the last of the hanks of fiber ready for spinning, she straightened up as if she had just awakened from a stupor. The days as well as nights were getting colder now, and with a start, she realized it was well into September. There was no chance for a fourth cutting; a hard frost was due at any time now, and any nettles started now would not have enough fiber to be worth the harvesting.

It was done . . . at least for now . . . it was done. The only work left was the spinning and crocheting. And for just a moment, before her anxieties reawakened, she indulged in a moment of relief.

A spatter of rain and rumble of thunder made Stephen sprint outside to get his mare under cover. She watched him, feeling truly awake for the first time in months.

Stephen managed to get inside the cottage just before the rain really started, and the two of them stared out the door at the downpour for a long time.

Stephen looked at the neat stack of four shirts, carefully

folded, on the slats of the unused bed, at the skeins of spun yarn, then at the hanks of fiber waiting to be spun. Then he touched her shoulder to get her attention, and she looked up into his eyes.

"You'll never get a fourth cutting in," he said, echoing her own thoughts.

She nodded.

"Mother wanted me to ask you if you would come stay in the manor to finish your work," he continued, watching her steadily. "She doesn't like it that you are all alone out here. Not that you're not safe!" he added quickly. "But she has a great many concerns. And, of course, it is inconvenient for Mrs. Waring to come trundling over here every day. . . ." He paused, as if waiting for her to say something, then recollected that she could not, and continued, a bit awkwardly. "I do not think she could come at all if it happened to be raining like this, or snowing, or the roads became unsafe in any way, and we would not want you to go hungry that day, or have to stop working. And there are your brothers, of course. We have a lovely swannery on the lake at the front of the manor, with a shed full of straw and regular feedings of grain. It is quite a good shelter, for it is meant to look like a cottage like this one, and it is all of stone. Of course, they could fly back and forth from here when there is no grass or waterweed to eat, and no one would harm them, but you might be anxious about them." He licked his lips and continued into the sound of the heavy rain. "And . . . I would feel better if you were at the manor. It would be much more comfortable for you there—"

She thought about it, then went to the cupboard where the kitchen things were and picked up the pan and spoon she used to summon the lads from the pond if she needed them. She went to the door and banged on the pan a few times, and the swans came running up from the pond through the rain, looking ridiculous, as they always did when they ran. From the front, they swayed from side to side with every step, and if they opened their wings for more stability, that only made them look funnier. They paused at the doorway to shake themselves free of water and quickly ducked inside, then stood around her and Stephen, looking up at them expectantly. She gestured to Stephen, who cleared his throat. Seven sets of bead-like, glittering jet eyes focused on him intently.

"Mother would like to invite you all to come stay at the man—" he began, and didn't get any further than that, as all seven of them squealed and flapped their wings in excitement, heads bobbing vigorously.

He looked back at Elena, who smiled and shrugged.

"Well," Stephen said, a smile starting at the corners of his mouth and broadening into a grin. "I suppose that settles it. I'll ride home as soon as this rain ends and tell Mother and Mrs. Waring. Someone will come with a cart for you and all your work tomorrow, and your brothers can either ride in the cart or fly over."

After he had left, while her brothers were still milling about in the cottage, restless and—she supposed—happy about the move, she wondered if she had done the right thing. For all of them.

When they transformed that night, she stopped spinning and made everyone proper cheese toast. Her brothers were very excited, and she couldn't blame them.

"Do you think they'll let us in the house at night?" Gus asked, with his mouth full of toasted cheese. "Surely they'll let us in the house at night!"

"Well, I don't think Stephen would condemn us to transform in the cold and dark of the swannery, much less out in the open!" Arthur laughed—and it was the first time she remembered him *laughing* since they all found each other again. "Besides, *everyone* in that household is either a mage themselves or knows all about magic. They'll probably be very curious about us."

"I hope they have strong stomachs," Ben replied. "Our transformations are not an easy thing to watch."

She nodded. It was *still* hard to watch them, and she generally looked away, even though she was somewhat used to it by now.

Gus opened his mouth, probably to state the obvious, that the transformations were even harder on the ones being transformed, but thought better of it and put some toasted cheese in his mouth instead of talking. *My twin has finally learned not to blurt out whatever is in his head!*

"There may be a garden entrance with a room used for muddy boots, dogs going in and out, and the like, where we can doze until midnight," Emil put in, thoughtfully. "There was one at home. Then we can just wait there until morning, and whoever happens to want to use that room can let us out again. These feathers are surprisingly warm; just being in an unheated room will be fine shelter overnight."

As they talked, she didn't fail to notice that they were concentrating on the *right now*, and avoiding talking about what would happen once they were all permanently human again. Perhaps they didn't want to think about that, because in some ways, that was exceedingly intimidating. *Where do we go? What do we do? We cannot take advantage of Stephen's good nature forever!*

She *supposed* that Arthur could try to regain the title and manor, but how? And how to explain their miraculous return from the "dead" and three-year disappearance? The cousin that had gotten both would certainly object vehemently to being displaced.

All their old plans for independence were certainly not viable. None of her brothers were likely to find a position where they could support more than themselves. She could find a position as a stocking mender, but that would be meager pay indeed. Her brothers had a very limited education—Ben and Arthur could probably set up as teachers in a boys' school or as tutors, but the rest had . . . well . . . nothing. They *could* enlist, take the king's shilling, but what would come at the end of that? For that matter, what would become of them if they were severely hurt and mustered out? She had seen plenty of former soldiers lacking arms, legs, and eyes left to beg in Bath.

If she had not been so tired, all these worries would have kept her awake, but as soon as the boys transformed back, and settled into their usual nighttime positions around her pallet on the floor, she started nodding and nearly dropped her spindle. She picked her way through them, and curled up among them, unable to sustain another thought.

The next day, quite early, the promised cart arrived. Three of the swans lumbered into the bed of it; the rest opted to fly. She still could not tell which swan was which brother, since in swan form they were all alike (and indistinguishable from real swans), but she suspected at least one of the three was Gus, since he had always preferred to sleep as late as he could, and all three of them immediately tucked their heads under their wings and went back to sleep. Other than her brothers and the magic shirts, spindle, scutching knife, scutching board, hackles, yarn, and hanks of nettle fiber, there really wasn't much to load into the cart—her brothers' clothing for when they transformed, and her own clothing, and that was just about all there was.

She got up on the box beside the driver, who tugged at his hat and smiled at her, but said nothing. It was a fine, if cold, morning, bright and fresh after last night's rain. There had not yet been a frost, so the leaves on the branches arching over the path to the road, and the road itself, were as green as summer, and created a kind of emerald tunnel through which golden beams of light shone from above through gaps in the branches. The cart rumbled along, thankfully without getting stuck anywhere, until it turned in at the great iron gate, which stood hospitably open, and onto the drive. At the end of the drive was a huge manor house, much older and larger than Whitstone Manor, though she could not have told what era it was from. On the left of the drive was the promised lake, with several dozen swans floating serenely on it or feeding at the verges, and the swannery, a stone "cottage" nearly identical to the gamekeeper's cottage, but with an open front, that stood at the back of the lake. To the right of the drive was an expanse of lawn dotted with trees that gradually turned into a forest that curved around to the back of the manor.

She poked at the three swans in the cart, as four more circled overhead and landed on the lake. They woke up, looked up, and dropped off the back of the cart to make a leisurely walk to the lake itself.

She had expected that the cart would go along to the back of the manor and a servants' entrance, but no. It pulled right up to the front, where Stephen and a middle-aged woman, still lovely, gowned in a beautiful shade of blue, waited.

"Welcome, my dear!" cried the lady, who came forward with both hands extended. "I cannot tell you how relieved I am that you were willing to accept our hospitality! Let me take you and your things to your room, so that you can resume your task!"

In short order, she was shown to a room that had a good view of the lake, a room that was worlds away finer than her room at Whitstone Manor. Lady Endicott showed her a wardrobe of everything a girl could wish for, and promised that her boy's clothing would be returned to her cleaned and ready for use should she need or desire to wear it. Then she was taken down to the dining room (*not* the one in servants' hall) and encouraged to eat her fill of things she had regarded as luxuries only Serafina could have. After that, she was shown exactly what her brothers had hoped for: a side entrance within a short flight of the lake that led into a spacious room—with a fireplace!—where muddy boots stood under pegs with clean smocks and working aprons hung on them. Seven sets of good linen shirts, trousers, smallclothes, stockings, and slippers awaited on a bench along the right-hand side. And the door had a string-pull latch on the outside, so that the swans could let themselves in!

That tipped her over the edge; she burst into tears of gratitude. Lady Endicott seemed to understand; she simply folded Elena into her arms, pulled Elena's head against her shoulder, and let her weep herself out, producing a handkerchief for her midway through her outburst. "Tonight you can go down to the lake at about sunset, and lead your brothers here. They are welcome to come and go as they please, and if the swannery is too cold, they can certainly stay here," her ladyship said, as Elena finally got herself under control and pulled away, dabbing at her eyes. "In the meantime, well, Stephen and I want you comfortable! By now someone will have drawn a nice hot bath for you in your room, so you can have a clean self in clean clothing—" Lady Endicott hesitated. "I hope you are not offended that I supplied you with female—"

Elena's vigorous headshake made the lady smile. "Well, then, shall we go back to your room so that you can make yourself completely at home?"

The manor was laid out in the old style, with each room leading into each other, so that daylight illuminated every room and there were no dark corridors that needed lighting a great deal of the time. It was actually easier to find her way about, as all she needed to do was remember what each room in the sequence was. As they passed from the work rooms into the more public rooms of the manor, she spotted servants cleaning and tidying, often accompanied by strange creatures, usually smaller than waist high. Some of them were even helping: sylphs keeping ashes where they belonged with gentle puffs of air as the servant cleaned a fireplace; miniature people in colorful, antique garments tidying alongside the humans; even a fiery lizard leaping into a newly laid set of logs and setting them ablaze. Her expression must have been something to behold, since Lady Endicott burst into cheerful laughter.

"We encourage everyone here who can get Elemental help with their duties to do so," she explained, as they went up a staircase that both servants and masters used. To Elena's mute surprise, given how servants were supposed to efface themselves both back at home and at Serafina's establishment, mistress and servants just exchanged friendly nods on the stair as they passed each other. "Duties are discharged so much faster, and that leaves our servants with time to spend on what they choose. Everyone is the happier for it. And for those who are learning or improving their magical abilities, there is plenty of time to hone their skills." She glanced where Elena was looking, and added, "That is a brownie. Especially skilled at household chores and cookery. The kitchen is full of them. Without them, I daresay, we would have frequent kitchen accidents and injuries. As it is, I cannot recall the last time someone was hurt in the kitchen. Perhaps a minor cut from a slip of a knife, but no burns, no blood."

Elena shuddered, remembering a time when she was about nine years old and one of the tweenies' skirts caught afire, and the agony the poor girl endured after. And the terrible scars she probably bore to this day. Her screams had echoed all the way up to the nursery, and Nanny had covered Elena's ears until they subsided.

Returned to the room that was now hers, there was, indeed, a tin bath just on the hearth. And that was when she got an idea of just how useful the Elementals were, for the bath seemed to be filling on its own, as two young girls stood beside it, one with a pitcher in her hand. She smiled at Elena, just as the water reached a good level, and held out the pitcher. Something small, green, and human-shaped launched itself out of the bath and into the pitcher. The second girl frowned with concentration, and a flaming lizard jumped from the fire to the side of the bath, and breathed on the water, which promptly began to steam.

Elena could remember how arduous it had been for servants to haul hot water in cans all the way up to the nursery; how dangerous it had been as well, because in order to provide a warm bath, the water had to be scalding hot when it left the kitchen. There were *so* many questions she wanted to ask, but of course, she could not. So she just tried to convey with gestures that she was grateful for the bath, as the two servant girls (as alike as two peas, so they must, like her, be twins) passed her on their way to other duties.

"I will leave you to your bath," said Lady Endicott. "And to your vital task. No one will come here except a servant if you ring for one—" she gestured at a bell-pull "—or you invite them here. If you would rather have company while you work, please feel free to join me in the solar. Your sylphs will know where it is. Otherwise, please join us in the dining room when you hear the bell."

Without waiting to be thanked, Lady Endicott turned and left, and Elena lost no time in stripping off clothing that felt . . . rather too "lived in" . . . and getting into that bath.

When she was clean and dry, with a sylph happily fanning her curls so that they dried faster, she got into a very nice blue linen gown and all the proper underpinnings for the first time in three years and sat down to spin. She discovered to her own amusement that she had to learn a different way to spin the spindle, since she could not spin it up on her thigh! But her mind started to spin along with her spindle before too long. Anxiety built in the silence of her room, until she just could not sit still anymore. She picked up a hank of nettle, and took that and her spindle with her. She looked around and spotted a sylph at the window—a window made of many palm-sized panes of glass, gazing out at the swans as if the pretty thing was just waiting for Elena to need her. She didn't recognize her as one of the ones she was familiar with, but the little thing seemed to have sensed her attention, spun, smiled, and flew to her. This one had blue-beetle wings, which was new to her. *Hello, mistress. Would you like me to take you to Mistress Marianne?*

She nodded, and the sylph flew very slowly just in front of her, looking back at her to be sure she was keeping up. Elena kept careful track of the rooms, then the direction the sylph went once they got down the staircase, then . . . more rooms. Then she heard Stephen's voice, and followed it to a room that somehow managed to be flooded with sunlight despite the windows being smaller than the ones at Whitstone Manor. Both Stephen and his mother looked up as she entered, and Stephen looked . . . well, very surprised at her appearance.

She made a face at him, and he laughed. "I'm sorry, I just am so used to seeing you in breeches, I was rather startled. Where did your legs go?"

She clapped both hands over her mouth to prevent a laugh from escaping. She was taking no chance that any sound would compromise the magic. He grinned at her, and his mother chortled.

"Stephen was reading the London paper to me," her ladyship said, both hands occupied with—knitting? "I am making stockings for some of our male servants who have been pensioned out to our cottages, for winter is coming. The poor fellows have difficulty knitting for themselves and have no one to do it for them."

Serafina had continued to keep her supplied with ladies' magazines in order to design new gowns in the most current mode, and nothing Elena had read in them had inclined her to think that ladies of Lady Endicott's rank would knit servants' stockings. The few patterns within those pages had inevitably been for delicate lace shawls and long scarves for draping gracefully about one's neck.

Lady Endicott glanced at the work in her hands and smiled. "Yes, Elena, we do things very differently. Granted, *most* Elemental Masters do, for it is much easier if one is surrounded by people who share the gifts, or who are at least happy in their work. We are, perhaps, a bit more liberal than many, but only a bit. Happenstance placed us in a privileged position, and my late husband's ancestors and mine deemed it our duty to see that those beneath us in rank were accorded dignity, support, and freedom."

These were the most astonishing words Elena had ever heard anyone speak. Certain *her* father could not have cared a whit about the welfare of his servants! As long as his needs were met, promptly and with the closest of attention, they could all have been hanging in closet until summoned for all he knew—or cared.

"If you've no objection to the material, come and sit, and Stephen will continue," her ladyship said, suggesting with a wave of her hand that Elena take any of the chairs or small, two-person sofas in the very comfortable, pleasant room. She picked a chair at random, laid the hank of fiber in her lap, and began spinning.

Stephen had a pleasant voice, as she knew from his novel reading, and even if she didn't understand more than half of what he was saying—particularly when he got to reading about politics—she found it soothing. And she found Lady Endicott's quiet—or irritated!—observations extremely educational. It certainly kept her from fretting about what their future might be. She had changed to her second spindle when Stephen put the paper down.

"Mother and I had an idea," he said, slowly. "But you may not like it."

She stopped the spindle and looked from him to Lady Endicott.

"When—not 'if'—your brothers are themselves again, we thought you would certainly want to reclaim your title and estate," he said, keeping his expression neutral. "We have thought of a way. But it involves lying."

She made a "go on" gesture.

"You will have to explain how they have *returned from the dead*, and where they have been for three years." He took a deep breath. "We will tell the authorities that your stepmother arranged for them to be kidnapped and sent to Canada as indentured servants."

She dropped the spindle in surprise. This was not something she would have thought of! And certainly Serafina's rage and very public tantrums when she discovered that the estate was entailed would reinforce the claim with a clear motive. But how to *prove* that?

Apparently they had thought of that. "I speak regularly with another Air Master in Canada. He would certainly send letters confirming that he had bought their contracts if I asked him to," Lady Endicott said. "Those letters would take a few months to arrive, and with a good solicitor—"

"—of which we know many," Stephen interjected.

"—the case would likely resolve to a satisfactory conclusion. And in the meantime, *we* will convene a hearing of the White Lodge against Serafina herself, if you are willing to testify against her."

Elena pointed to her mouth. Lady Endicott gave her an encouraging look. "Of course we would wait until you have finished the shirts, and the first act of testimony will be that you break the spell upon your brothers in front of the conclave."

Her mouth made a silent "O," and she stopped to think about this. Because she was certain that this would place her in very real danger. Serafina *always* seemed to be ready for trouble. She *always* seemed to have an attack of some kind up her sleeve. She had the duke, who presumably would not be facing the conclave yet, to act on her behalf, and Elena did not know precisely what he could do . . . but Serafina could think of something that Stephen and his mother might not have.

The duke could hire enough blackguards to physically overpower the people in this conclave long enough for Serafina to escape, and having done so, Serafina would be doubly dangerous. And the first person she would unleash her wrath upon was Elena.

In the course of that escape, people would be hurt. Some might be killed. Men who already had prices on their head for murder would not care about more blood on their hands.

She had no idea how to convey this danger to her hosts. She was fairly certain that *not talking* also meant *not writing*. Serafina would surely have thought of that.

All she could do was to hope that the two people before her

had thought of that. Hope that they *were* prepared for a purely physical confrontation.

They must have taken her hesitancy for concern about the lying. "It is generally not recommended for an Elemental magician to lie," Stephen admitted. "But in this case . . . Serafina has lied so much, and so often, that we are willing to take the chance that the lies will balance out—"

She shook her head, hoping they would understand. After a moment of thought, it was Lady Endicott who grasped the least of her concerns. "She is not a member of the White Lodge of Bath, and I cannot conceive of how she would know a conclave was being called against her."

Elena sighed unhappily. They had no idea . . .

"In any event, with or without you, I *must* call a conclave against her and her paramour, because as you told Mrs. Waring when you first arrived, they have been using their magic to cheat at cards. She has been using her magic to fleece her protectors, and she used her magic to control and coerce your father," Stephen said, his face growing hard. "She is a potential danger to the government and ultimately the Crown. Who knows what she would be moved to do if she got a member of the House of Lords into her power? She could become a spy for Napoleon!"

It was clear that there was no stopping him at this point. Elena sighed, shuddered, and nodded her head. Stephen was all smiles again. "Well done, Elena! And you are exceedingly brave! If we can punish her purely on the basis of what she *has done*, without a shadow of doubt, to you and your brothers, we will not have to go hunting for evidence of her other crimes, nor speculate on future ones."

Her hands were shaking too hard to spin now, and Stephen crossed the room to take them in his. "I pledge that I will protect you," he said solemnly. "You will not lose by this."

All she could do was hope he was right. Because if he was not, they would all be paying Serafina's price.

She worked in a kind of fever dream for the next month, spinning and crocheting every waking moment that she was not eating or sleeping. As she embarked on the seventh shirt, Stephen and his mother began contacting other mages of what they called the White Lodge. Elena assumed it was some kind of parliament of Elemental magicians. And as she neared completion of the shirt, people began arriving to Endicott Manor; she had expected that they would all be nobles, or at least, very wealthy individuals, but to her surprise, they were from all walks of life. Mrs. Waring, it seemed, was included among them, as were many others of the staff. The highest rank was an extremely elderly viscount; the lowest was one of Stephen's shepherds. They had two things in common: they were all of legal age, or older (some much older, like the viscount), and all were practiced in using their magic offensively. These people (mostly men, with a bare scattering of women) were experienced and practiced in using their power, and at need, their Elementals, in real battles. All of them had participated in at least one Hunt, as Stephen called it, an occasion where it was necessary to seize, and possibly even slay, some creature, spirit, or human, who had used their powers to kill.

She felt rather better about the conclave when she learned that. Surely they would be prepared for anything! Even cold-blooded mercenaries or murderous highwaymen.

And it was the very evening before the conclave itself—which would be held in the Endicott chapel, as being the only part of the manor capable of holding as many people as had assembled—when she was one sleeve from finishing the seventh shirt. The plan was that in the morning Lady Endicott would announce why the conclave had been called, and against whom; they had not announced it beforehand, to prevent Serafina from finding out. Elena would bring the swans in after the announcement and throw the shirts over their heads. They would transform before the eyes of everyone there, proving that they had been bound into those shapes. Elena would tell her story, and Ben would tell theirs, leaving nothing out, including the salient item that they were all half-blooded swan-folk, and that Serafina had intended to use her water Elementals to drown them, and if that failed, had come prepared to bind them into their swan forms so that they could not claim their inheritance.

It seemed a good plan. And what was more, *all* of the men of the estate would be stationed around the walls, armed, to prevent Duke Alberton from bringing in outsiders.

So far as Elena could see, every possible problem had been planned for.

But she could not shake the feeling that they had overlooked something.

She had scarcely been able to eat, and had left dinner early. She went to her room, prepared to work all night to finish the shirt. She went straight to where she had laid out her work.

And that was when she discovered the unthinkable.

Someone had taken the last skein of yarn.

There were three sylphs following her that night, and they stared at the disaster too. She wanted to ask them if they had seen anything—but of course they had not. And there was no use asking any other Elemental; they kept out of her room unless invited.

She stared at her work, her heart racing, and fear gripping her. She *knew* she had exactly enough! She had laid it out with the shirt to start as soon as dinner was over. Who could have done this? There was no doubt in her mind *why* someone had—to prevent Stephen from revealing Serafina's treachery. Without Elena to perform the transformation on her brothers, he had nothing, and the best he could do would be to tell the conclave about Serafina using her magic to cheat at cards and to catch and hold paramours. He was very young—would anyone believe him? And if they did, there would be no urgency in discovering if what he claimed was true. The idea that Serafina would use her powers to control a member of the House of Lords was . . . a house of cards, based purely on speculation.

The sleeve was half finished, and as she stared at it, her mind raced for solutions. Finally it landed on one.

Instead of crocheting yarn, she could net fiber. That took spinning out of the picture. All she needed were some dry nettles.

There are nettles in the churchyard, in the part with the oldest tombs. They are dead and dry. I have the scutching knife and board here, and the hackling boards too. I can have the fiber done by midnight and the netting done by morning . . .

Three sylphs—who must have been following her thoughts—all lit up in glowing light. She cried a sudden burst of tears of gratitude, but forced herself to stop. There was no time for anything except to get to the churchyard, get those nettles, and get back here to process them into something she could use to claw back a victory.

She didn't even stop to think, or tell anyone where she was going. She threw on a shawl, ran down the stairs and into the dark, led by the sylphs, who were better than torches. A wicked wind whipped around her, tangling her skirts around her legs, as she planned what she would do when she found the nettles. *I can't pull them out of the ground, but they must be dry and brittle enough to break off near the roots. I'll break them in pieces long enough to knot the rest of the sleeve right there, and bring them back to my room. And—*

The sylph-light vanished, leaving her in the dark, with light-dazzled eyes. She stumbled twice. Felt powerful arms seizing her.

Then, before she could even feel fear, a blow to the back of her head, and she fell into darkness deeper than the moonless night.

Oh, my head . . .

She had never felt pain like this before. It squeezed out all thought. She tried to open her eyes, and closed them immediately, when the light just brought more pain. She knew she *had* to think, but it was so hard, trying to get through the pain.

I'm . . . all in a heap. On the ground?

Someone above her was speaking. She fought through the pain to listen, and *that voice* cut right through the pain to bring terror.

Serafina!

". . . this august convocation," Serafina said, confidence in every word. "Of course, I do not belong to your White Lodge, so technically I should not be speaking to you, but I could not in good conscience refrain from coming here to warn you about this girl."

What . . . she means me!

"She is a treacherous creature; she has already drowned her own brothers, seven of them! It is because of her that Lord Whitstone died of grief. Who knows how many she has deceived—perhaps even murdered!—in the three years since. *I* only discovered her perfidy when she attempted to murder *me*, and only the presence of my dear maid Fleurette prevented that very thing. Three years she stayed with me—three years I cared for her, nurtured her, spent *my own income* on her, only to have her turn on me once she was of age! When I recovered, I made it my business to track her down—and now I find her, here, working her wiles on poor Lord Endicott!"

Elena forced her eyes open; she was lying at Serafina's feet. The shirts were there as well. The musky scent of the nettle yarn almost made her throw up. She faced the altar of the chapel; that must mean that all the people of the convocation were behind her.

What did she do to my brothers? Horror as well as terror filled her when the first thing that sprang into her mind was that Serafina and the duke, and who knew how many minions they had brought, must have killed them.

The horror broke the hold that the terror had on her, and she forced herself to move. But all she could manage was one hand. She grasped one of the shirts.

"Look at this!" Serafina said. "Look at this *thing* she has made. The least of you can see how she has suffused it with *terrible*, powerful magic! Who knows what she intended to do with it? Enchant Lord Endicott? Lady Endicott? That is only two of the seven shirts—who else among you did she plan on controlling?"

Why are they all silent?

Because Serafina was exerting some of her own power . . . that was the only explanation. *She might have planted spell parchments all over the chapel. No one would suspect anything, not inside the Endicott ward. No one would guess what she had done, until she came in here with me and the shirts, and started speaking. And now they are all under her control.*

Even Stephen.

She managed to push herself up, a little. Serafina did not

notice. She was too enraptured by her own words and the intoxication of controlling so *many* Elemental magicians at once. *I have to stop her. I have to do something.* No matter what it cost her, she couldn't allow Serafina to corrupt all these people and turn them to her service. Stephen had been right in his speculation; Serafina must have more ambitious plans than running an expensive brothel. Or at least, now that she had tasted this power, she had realized what she could do with it.

"My fellows in magic, there is only one thing you can do with a *creature*, a *beast* like this perfidious girl. You must end her life, before—"

Elena lurched to her feet—

And with a deafening crash, seven swans exploded through the rose window above the altar. Glass fragments showered down over Serafina and Elena; swans tumbled down out of the air to land, in barely controlled flight, all around them. As Serafina covered her eyes instinctively with her arms, Elena snatched the nettle shirt out of her hands and flung it over the nearest swan's neck and shoulders.

Serafina staggered away, bleeding from a hundred cuts. So was Elena, but she was so used to the pain of the nettles she could ignore it. She snatched up another shirt and enrobed a second swan, and the first writhed and spasmed in the first stages of transformation. She got a third; now the swans had recovered from their suicidal entrance and clustered around her, necks extended, waiting for their shirts. Four and five, and the first swan stretched up: Ben, the shirt *barely* giving him modesty. Six—the sixth swan was Emil, more covered. Seven, and she felt the power she had placed in those shirts singing, expanding, creating a growing bubble of strength and love and protection that filled the area in front of the altar, filled the chapel to the first pews, where Stephen and his mother shook their heads as if shaking off a nightmare and looked at them all with widened eyes. Despite her pounding head and the stinging of hundreds of cuts, she pulled more power from the air as she had been taught, called silently for help, and expanded the bubble of protection until it filled the entire chapel.

Sylphs, zephyrs, and great, transparent, dragon-like creatures she did not recognize poured into the chapel, singing, a song that was half love and half wrath. The dragons cornered Serafina behind the altar, snapping at her when she tried to move. The Elemental mages assembled in the pews snapped out of the web Serafina had woven with snarls and shouts of rage.

But Elena had no time and no eyes for them. She fell to her knees beside her twin, Gus, who had gotten the one-armed shirt. He looked up at her with a stricken expression, eyes full of tears—for where his arm should have been was a swan wing.

"Gus!" she cried in anguish. *Oh, dear God! I did this to him! How will he ever forgive me? How will I ever forgive myself?*

"Elena!" A hand shoved the missing skein of yarn in her hands. The same hand pulled a length off the ball, and cut it off with a pocketknife. "Hold the spell! You *must* hold the spell! Her magic is almost broken, and if you can hold your spell against it, we shall be able to help!"

It was Stephen, pulling length after length of yarn off the ball, passing them to his mother, who skillfully knotted them into the armscye and began making a crude knotted net where the sleeve would have been. She was joined by three more people, taking lengths from Stephen and filling in the entire armscye, fingers flashing, knot after knot.

Elena held that original spell, ignoring blood running down her face, ignoring the lightning in her head, grief turning to joy as beneath those flashing fingers, feathers melted away, feathers became flesh—upper arm—elbow—lower arm—and at last with an explosive rush, feathers became hand, and Gus was whole again.

Then—

It felt as if something *snapped*.

Serafina uttered a terrible scream, a scream that turned to choking, to gurgles—

Elena turned away from Gus to see Serafina staggering backward, the dragon-like creatures recoiling, water pouring from her mouth as if she was a figure on a fountain.

She fell to the ground.

Water erupted from her open mouth, then slowed, dropped, became a trickle.

Ended.

But there was no doubt. She was dead.

"The spell breaking broke her power," Lady Endicott said, in what sounded like surprise. "And when her power broke . . . her Elementals rose against her."

But Elena had no time, or care, to think about that. Not when the warm, loving, *human* bodies of her brothers surrounded her, arms around her and each other. *That* was all that she needed or wanted.

EPILOGUE

Duke Alberton and his minions were caught on the grounds; they had managed to slaughter three swans by the time Stephen's people seized them. They did not fare well. The minions were all discovered to have prices, and death sentences, on their heads. The members of the White Lodge dealt with the duke themselves. After he was taken away, he was found later, wandering witless near his own properties. His wife brought him home and cared for him. She was once heard to remark, when tendered sympathy for having to care for a man in such a state, that she liked him better this way.

It took more than a year, and much legal wrangling, but the absurd story of being kidnapped and sent to Canada was accepted. Arthur, of age now, became Lord Whitstone; he married one of the Endicott cousins, a middle-aged spinster, after they met at the manor and fell in ridiculously in love. Ben belatedly went to Oxford, and became a parish priest, taking over the Whitstone living, and wedding a modest heiress, the Whitstone village doctor's daughter. Carl and David went to Cambridge; Carl became a respected historian and never married, David a professor of mathematics who married an amateur lady mathematician. Emil and Felix went into politics; neither of them had any stomach for the military or the navy after their experiences. Both married well; neither married magicians. Gus's experience awakened Air magic that had been slumbering deep inside him, and he retained the ability to transform into a swan and back again. He went looking for their mother. He never found her, but he did find a swan bride, and remained in Wales with her.

And, as only befits a fairy tale, Elena and Stephen married, and raised seven little Air mages of their own. Life at Endicott Manor was never boring.

For more fantastic fiction, author events,
exclusive excerpts, competitions, limited editions and more

VISIT OUR WEBSITE
titanbooks.com

LIKE US ON FACEBOOK
facebook.com/titanbooks

FOLLOW US ON TWITTER AND INSTAGRAM
@TitanBooks

EMAIL US
readerfeedback@titanemail.com